Praise for *The Work Wife*

"[A] knockout debut.... Vengefully delicious."

—*People*, Book of the Week

"Written with great verve and flair, *The Work Wife* is deeply satisfying from start to finish."

—Jami Attenberg, *New York Times* bestselling author of *All This Could Be Yours*

"This timely, wry debut tackles major subjects...with intimacy and heart. Witty, clever, and propulsively plotted."

—Courtney Maum, author of *Touch* and *Costalegre*

"There's never a moment's slip in authenticity or momentum.... One hell of a debut."

—*Kirkus Reviews* (starred review)

"A novel with nerve, this is the work of an empathetic mind, deeply curious about what women are asked to sacrifice to make it to the top."

—Kaitlyn Greenidge, author of *Libertie*

"Hart has created an engrossing, piercing look at the compromises and choices women make to succeed and thrive."

—*Booklist*

"Feminist and furious and sometimes very funny, *The Work Wife* is bursting with love for these wounded characters."

—Marcy Dermansky, author of *Very Nice*

"A beautifully written, feminist page-turner. Filled with biting commentary and insights, *The Work Wife* is a dazzling debut. I couldn't put it down."

—Angie Kim, *New York Times* bestselling author of *Happiness Falls*

"*The Work Wife* is a bold and wholly satisfying novel about power, ambition, and the price women must often pay for their dreams."

—Emma Straub, *New York Times* bestselling author of *All Adults Here*

Also by Alison B. Hart

The Work Wife

APRIL
MAY
JUNE
JULY

A NOVEL

ALISON B. HART

GRAYDON
HOUSE

GRAYDON
HOUSE®

ISBN-13: 978-1-525-80427-4

April May June July

Graydon House
22 Adelaide St. West, 41st Floor
Toronto, Ontario M5H 4E3, Canada
www.GraydonHouseBooks.com
www.BookClubbish.com

Printed in U.S.A.

Recycling programs
for this product may
not exist in your area.

For my family, wherever we go

April 2014

1

April

April looked through the glass walls of the third-floor conference room, where her colleagues had been camped out all week
negotiating deal terms, and tried—and failed—to refrain from
picturing opposing counsel naked.

She hadn't been this horny on a daily basis since she was sixteen, and Bobby Coffey's heavy lidded stares during precalc
foretold another lunchtime rendezvous in the park across from
Taco Bell, his tongue urgent and slick with enchilada sauce, his
hands daring to go ever farther under her clothes as her breath
caught in her throat. She'd nearly gotten a C in math that semester, until her teacher's call home prompted a stinging lecture
from Nancy about college and the importance of maintaining
her GPA and using her goddamn brain. Her teenaged brain,
while miraculous and expansive, could not compartmentalize
as neatly as her thirty-six-year-old brain could, and so she'd had
to give Bobby up before they went all the way.

Now that she was a responsible adult, though, a partner at Sullivan, Hawthorne, and Pollard and a married mother of two, she knew how to walk and chew gum at the same time. She could do her job at the Baltimore law firm where she'd worked her whole career, and she could navigate the unexpected pulses of heat and want that shot through her at the sight of her ex-lover just a few feet away. The past two weeks, with him so close by, had tested her focus, but she wouldn't let him derail her.

She went down the hall to her office to get some distance. On the corner of her desk was a square envelope that she'd brought from home this morning. It was cream-colored with hand lettering, and April knew without checking the return address what it was: the invitation to her little sister's wedding. The engagement dinner was tonight in Philadelphia.

She steeled herself, then slid her fingertip along the envelope's seam and tugged out the card.

Ahmed and Maryam Monsour
request the honor of your presence at the marriage of their daughter
Hana and Juniper
daughter of Francis and Nancy Barber
Saturday, June 14, at 3 o'clock in the afternoon
Prospect House, Princeton University
Reception to follow

Juniper. So she was sticking with it, then. The name. A juniper was a tree or a berry, not a sister; an affectation she'd picked up at college the way April had picked up clove cigarettes. She was June on her birth certificate, Junie to her family, third in a line of four Barber siblings whose names tripped off the tongue like a song. April, May, June, July.

But it was their father's name on the next line that made April's heart capsize. The lovely, proper Christian name that called to mind a knobby-kneed British schoolboy in short pants and tall socks, not the stocky kid on the Chesapeake Bay. The curly swoosh capping the *F* like the beret on a Papal Swiss Guard. So much pomp and circumstance hoping and failing to obscure one man's absence.

He'd been gone nearly ten years, but no one had ever called their father Francis. He'd only ever been Frank—at work, at home and with his friends, in the headlines.

Every time the Barbers gathered without Frank felt wrong—each Christmas or birthday somehow off-key and out of tempo, until they'd just stopped insisting on them, letting holidays pass unremarked upon or finding new constellations of people to celebrate with—but a wedding? How? Maybe if Frank were dead, they could've found a way to honor him through it. Holding a thought for lost loved ones during the ceremony, maybe, or dancing to his favorite song at the reception. Or if he'd abandoned them all, they could've forgotten him, cut him out of their rituals without guilt or fear. But he wasn't dead or a deadbeat, he was just...gone. Missing, leaving a hole in their lives. And the anniversary of his disappearance was the week after the wedding.

Like it or not, the ceremony was barreling toward them. She'd have to get new dress shoes for her son, April thought, shoving her messy grief in the junk drawer, turning to the safety and momentum of a to-do list. And pants that were long enough. A new dress for her daughter.

April recalled the struggle to outfit her siblings for her own wedding, fourteen years ago. May, a legitimately terrible maid of honor, who'd shown up late and with no speech prepared, wearing Doc Martens under her dress; Junie, the awkward flower girl who hated the ruffly Gunne Sax dress their mom had picked out for her; July, fidgety in his first suit.

April had gotten married so young, the summer before her last year of law school, Ross the newest associate at Thurman Architects. At twenty-four, she'd become a mother. It had all felt like progress at the time, but now she saw how much she'd rushed through, the liminal spaces where anything and every-thing was possible. Soon after giving birth, she became regret-fully aware of all the other things in life she could not, now, do. Skydiving. Vows of silence. Hiking the Appalachian Trail or weeks-long business trips to Hong Kong or Mumbai. Sure, kids were portable, but there were limits. The second time she got pregnant, she was experienced enough to know that there was no way to prepare for the chaos. It didn't matter if you had a summer baby or a winter baby, if you breastfed or not, if the older one potty-trained early or late. There was a long dark tun-nel and you were going in it. You might have marginally more confidence, but even so, inside the tunnel mistakes would be made. The beautiful plan you'd dreamed up in your head was going to be torn to shreds. If you were lucky, you'd all come out the other end, mostly happy and alive.

If you were lucky, and April hadn't felt lucky in a long time.

Oh, enough already, she chided herself. Self-pity didn't pay the bills. She turned her attention to the mounds of paper on her desk, the never-ending work that was expected of her. She had an hour before she had to leave for the engagement party.

Right on cue, April's cell phone lit up. It was Maddie, her oldest, whose magical powers for detecting when her mother needed to concentrate were as sharp at age twelve as they'd been as a baby.

"What's up, Pup?" April asked, thumbing through the settle-ment terms for another acquisition.

"I can't believe you're not coming to see me play. I mean, I'm only in sixth grade once."

"Nice try." April was used to deflecting her preteen's guilt trips, as if she wielded Wonder Woman's bracelets, but today she felt all too mortal. She was sorry to miss Maddie's concert tonight, but there would be others, and one engagement din-ner for Junie. "Daddy and Coop will be front row center, and I'll come to the next one."

"But everyone else's mom will be there!"

"Hey," April heard Ross bark from across the room. Then suddenly he was on the line instead. "She was just supposed to call to say hi. Don't worry about her. In ten minutes she'll be relieved you're not coming and mortified that I am."

"I know."

Her daughter's adolescence and everything that came with it—moodiness, hormones, hair in new places and breasts she alternately wanted to smother under a sweatshirt or show off in her sports bra, crushes that were written all over her face alongside the murderous looks she'd give you if you had the temerity to ask about them—it was the weather their household lived under. And it didn't matter how devoted and present a father Ross was, April was still the mother. She was the parent Maddie raged against in her quest for individuation. The brain science talk the guidance counselors had given the parents at the start of the year was no help, like holding up a shitty little five-dollar umbrella in the storm of feelings that were roiling in middle school. The conversation with her daughter about how the girl's body and mind were changing was oceanic and ongoing and, nine times out of ten, April had to badger Maddie into having it. Maybe she wasn't quite the mother she'd thought she would be, patient and endlessly available, but she had so many other roles: loving wife, dutiful daughter, big sister, the youngest woman to make partner at the firm, number two in billable hours. And now she had this engagement dinner looming, where she'd need to be chatty and effervescent when she felt anything but.

"Just go and have fun tonight," Ross said as Craig popped his head in April's office, one eyebrow raised in that way of his that only ever meant one thing. "Tell Junie I said hi."

"You know it's still cheating even if we do it in a car?" Craig said when she should have been sitting down with her family in Philly but was sitting on him instead. "We don't get bonus points for not using a bed."

"Shut up," she said, her head ramming into the roof of his BMW in the parking lot behind the Walgreens. She sank into him with her hips and closed her eyes, unwilling to lose hold of this thread she'd caught, leading into the sweet, aching center of herself. She came extravagantly. In the stillness that followed was that grateful moment, all too brief, in which she forgot everything and everyone, even herself. The push-pull of their fucking was the engine of her desire. April craved this stolen pleasure, the only thing that cut through the noise of her life, *and* she loathed herself for chasing it again so soon.

She had to stop this. She'd known it the first time she tried to end things with Craig. Two months ago she'd broken it off— because it was wrong and greedy, because her husband was a good man and didn't deserve to have only pieces of her, because her firm did too much business with Craig's flagship client and it was only a matter of time before they had a direct conflict of interest. Now here she was again, her promises to herself broken and that big speech—about how he couldn't expect her to just drop everything whenever he called (though if she were honest, it was her doing most of the calling) and if he really wanted to turn her on, then he'd let her go, delete her number, focus on his own marriage and let her live her life—all for nothing.

She had to do something. She had to rewrite the pathways in her mind, the ones that sent her, again and again, racing away from her responsibilities into her lover's arms. She'd never imagined, when she was the one sending out wedding invitations, that one day she'd find herself here, lying to her family, breaking her vows. But after she'd crossed the line once, it was so simple to step over it again.

She couldn't lie to herself anymore. Quitting Craig cold turkey hadn't worked. He was just too easy to find. True change wouldn't take root without reinforcements. She needed to get far, far away—an ocean and a plane ride away. She needed to escape the escape.

The next morning, she called her mom. She chalked up the missed engagement dinner to a work emergency and bemoaned the way her hectic life interfered with her priorities. Then she said, "Let's take a trip. Just you and me."

2

May

"Go ahead," Keith radioed back to May. Her supervisor had served as a medic in Afghanistan before heading up the large mammals section of the Chesapeake Zoo, and he still brought an army captain's zeal to comms. May pictured him at the drive-through ordering *large fries, over,* or on the phone with his doctor's office, spelling out his name *KILO-ECHO-INDIA-TANGO-HOTEL.*

"Scout's hurt," May said over the airwaves. "His right front foot."

The elephant calf was limping. Her best guess: he'd developed a crack in his toenail or the sole of his foot, common enough among animals in captivity, though no signs had been present when they'd examined him three days ago. To be certain, the keepers would need to take him inside the elephant barn and get him to raise his foot for inspection, and that meant separating him, briefly, from his mother, against whom he was leaning for support.

"Roger that."

"I'll grab Randy and Kristen and we can get started on the footwork." May waited a bit, hated herself, and then added: "Over."

"Negative. Do not examine him without me present. I repeat, do not examine the elephant without me. Do you copy?"

"Yeah, I got it."

"What's your 20?"

"I'm at the puzzle feeders." The puzzle feeders were holes in the enclosure wall, into which she'd stuffed alfalfa, sweet potatoes, and zucchini. She'd accessed the feeders by climbing a ladder, and from there, she had a clear line of sight into the enclosure.

"Roger. Rendezvous at the barn in fifteen minutes. Out."

May put the radio away. "Prick."

Last month Keith had caught her rubbing a lion's mane during enrichment time, a violation of protected-contact regulations, so she'd been moved off large cats, where she'd spent the bulk of the last three years, over to elephants. The reassignment should've been punishment enough—both for her and for the cats, who probably didn't understand why they no longer saw her every day—but she was still on Keith's shit list.

For weeks May had been working at a painfully respectful distance from the giant beasts—refilling the feeders; dragging browse into the enclosure while the elephants were in the barn; acting as the third set of hands during footwork—but mostly she'd been falling in love. On trips to this zoo as a child, she'd whisked past Sabrina, the matriarch, sparing a few quick gawks and then dashing off to see the monkeys. But spending every day with the small herd, she was in thrall. Not to anthropomorphize, but look how gently Sabrina tended to her son with her massive foot. See how eager her daughters were, particularly the adolescent, to babysit the baby, fighting for the chance to nuzzle him when Sabrina was indisposed.

May gathered the empty buckets and watched Sabrina clock

her departure from her perch above the wall. Some of the cutest animals were dumb fucks—koalas whose baseline was high as a kite, dachshunds who fawned over you after mere moments apart, like you were the prodigal son returned as a salt lick—but May felt positively indicted by the elephants. *Where do you think you're going with that shitty attitude? Must be nice, coming and going freely.*

"Jesus, okay, I'll try harder," May said to the elephant, loud enough for a family on the observation deck to raise their heads in her direction.

May had had an unconventional path here to this zoo, an hour north of Baltimore. Two back-to-back engineering degrees she'd hardly used and night school for the two-year degree in veterinary assistance. Ten years in a series of improvised jobs—dog walking, pet grooming, a brief stint at the local vet's office—proving to her that she would be okay, one-foot-in-front-of-the-other okay, as long as she worked with animals. She sometimes thought about continuing on to get her DVM, but she was already thirty-three. When she'd heard about the keeper opening, she'd jumped at the chance. Setting aside the question of whether it was right to hold animals in an environment where they couldn't run at a sprint (it clearly wasn't), zookeeper jobs were highly coveted. Once you got in, it was almost impossible to be fired and, in time, she'd have enough saved to finally move out of her mother's house in Aberdeen.

No one, not her mom or her ultra-successful siblings or even May's younger self had ever pictured her winding up here. The mental vision board she'd created for herself in college had looked like this: a backpack and a passport with all the pages stamped, her passable French and Spanish and Rosetta Stone for everything else, flings that lasted as long as it took to bring water to the village, changing the world. When the stupidity of that vision became cringingly clear, she'd had no clue how to make another plan for herself that she could trust. How did other people do it? Could anyone explain it to her, anyone she wasn't related to, that is, anyone who wasn't still marching toward their destiny (the law, soccer, good teeth) like it would save them? Sometimes the irony of her situation—that ten years later, she was still in her hometown, boxed in like her dad was before he accepted the job in Iraq—was too fucking much.

It took an hour, all told, to get to the bottom of what was ailing Scout, and May was permitted to help hold the calf's foot while Kristen razored down the pits on the sole and filed the cracked and infected distal toenail. Afterward, she went into the park to sneak a cigarette under the umbrella of a fig tree that mostly hid the staff door from the public restrooms. How was it possible, she wondered, for an elephant's foot to smell so very bad and a lion's mane to smell so very good? There was a small breeze and she turned her back to it to get a light, praying the nicotine would chase away the stench she still carried on her fingertips.

"May?" someone behind her called.

Fuck, she thought. If that was Keith, it'd be weeks before he'd let her near the animals again. *Regulations*, he'd say. *A question of judgment.* It was always one step forward, two steps back with him.

But it wasn't Keith. It was… "Will?"

May dropped her smoke and stepped on it. Will fucking Mackenzie. He was laughing, after all these years and the way she'd left things between them. Their basic dispositions hadn't changed: Will still tended toward delight, and she still hated surprises. She was down to just one precious smoke a day—and now it was smushed under her shoe.

"I said to myself, there's no way that's Mayhem, wearing a uniform. But smoking by the bathroom? That's on brand."

May blushed, not because nobody called her that anymore, but because the May Barber Will had known would have had to be dragged here by the tattered edges of her oversized army jacket. She would've looked around, her eyes ringed in black and hidden behind hair she'd mussed to gritty perfection with dry shampoo, and she would've seen a prison. She wouldn't have believed she could ever be this wholesome, cosplaying as a big-game hunter in a goddamn pith helmet.

"Who's this?" she asked to put the attention back on Will. After all, he had more to explain than she did, specifically the little girl holding his hand. She couldn't have been more than three years old, his spitting image.

"This is my daughter, Zoe."

Of course Will was a dad. Not a shock, only an eventuality.

"Hi, Zoe," May said.

"Can you say hi?" Will asked, but Zoe wrapped herself around her father's leg. "We practiced this but it looks like we're a little shy today."

Practiced?

"Were you waiting for me?" she asked, and she knew by the way Will avoided her eyes (like father, like daughter) that he had been.

Will cleared his throat (more proof) and said, "Were you talking to the elephants? We thought we heard you."

So they were the family that had been standing on the observation deck. Now it was May's turn to be embarrassed.

"Did you come to see Scout?" she said to Zoe in a way she hoped would be charming to the toddler, but obviously she was doing it all wrong because Zoe only pressed her face harder into Will's knee. May was terrible with kids, scary clown when she meant to be fun auntie. She'd never had that tenderness Scout's sisters had. Her own sisters had always been happy to dote on their little brother, the oops-baby who came along when most people assumed that either Nancy had had her tubes tied or Frank had had the snip. Teenaged May would watch April cooing at baby July or Junie hoisting him up on her own small hips, and she'd wonder what was wrong with her that she didn't want to do those things, too. She'd look at her little brother, cheeks red from crying or eyes wet with joy, and she'd think, *Nah*. It had always been that way for her and still was, mostly. Except for her dad, people were tough to love. Animals were easy.

"We did," Will said, "but he was too far away to get a good look."

"He's a little shy today, too," May said. There, finally. A glimmer of a smile on Zoe's face.

"We should get going. It's nearly nap time and if we miss it, I'm…" Will mouthed the word *fucked*. "It's a little harder sticking to routine at daddy's house than mama's house isn't it?"

Zoe nodded, as if she'd understood him perfectly. And now May understood that he was single.

"Are you at the same number?" he asked. "We should get coffee sometime. Really catch up."

Was Will Mackenzie asking her out? Did she want him to be? Her palms were sweating, a sure sign if memory served, if she could think that far back to a time when she used to feel things.

"Yeah," she said. "Same number."

"Great," Will said, clearing his throat again but unable to hide the grin spread wide across his face. "I mean, it's really great seeing you."

The rest of that afternoon, May felt effervescent one minute, then annoyed with herself the next. It wasn't as if she'd had a meet-cute with Jane Goodall. It was only Will, but then he'd always made her feel this way, bubbling with a kind of potency. Even before they'd started dating her last year at UM, spending time with him was like charging up. Maybe at the rave-like hours their study group had kept, anything would've been persuasive, but Will made deeply nerdy things seem like great ideas. Dropping an egg and a watermelon off the roof of the engineering quad at the same time, running a 5K chained together like pistons in a V6 engine, doing an extra year to get their master's. He made it cool to focus, something May had never been able to do in a classroom before. Despite her mechanical aptitude, her grades in high school had been middling and her near-perfect score on the math SAT had come as a shock. No one, least of all May, had expected her to actually like college, let alone excel there.

The summer between undergrad and grad school, he finally worked up the nerve to ask her out. She'd just broken up with a poet who was so gloomy, and there was Will, who'd always made her laugh, offering himself as an alternative. *Let me be your boy toy*, he'd said, and she'd thought, *Why not? It's one date.* He wasn't really her type—too clean-cut, not enough scars or tattoos—but sexually, he understood better than any guy she'd been with what she liked and how to get her off. One date turned into several turned into the first real serious relationship she'd ever had. People in the department started to talk about them as if they were one brain. Willandmay. Their pairing started to feel inevitable. For May, a little too inevitable. Maybe everyone else had forgotten about her plans to see the world, but she hadn't. She was counting down the days until they had their master's and she'd leave for the Peace Corps. Then Frank was taken, and her life cratered.

She'd always wondered when or even if she'd see Will again, but she'd never imagined surging with crush potential for her ex.

When she got home that evening, she went to her room, the one she'd once shared with April and now had all to herself. It looked like a sick room, dark, soft, and built for sleep. She cracked open the window to let in some light and fresh air. There were piles everywhere—of clothes, paperwork, empty food wrappers. Even the dog had given up. Jack Nicholson slept at the foot of Nancy's bed now instead of in here with his person.

Nancy's crisp footsteps plinked down the hall. When she appeared in the door, the usual ribbed turtleneck and clogs in which she hunched over mouths in the over-air-conditioned dental office had been swapped out for a diaphanous blouse and kitten heels.

"What have you done with my mother?"

"Do you like?" Nancy asked, posing.

"You look like one of the Golden Girls. What are you, going on a cruise?"

"Yes! With April! It's a last-minute thing. She got some time off at work and wanted to go, and I told Tom he can do without me for a week or so."

You couldn't pay me, May thought. Not that she had any leg to stand on, still living at home, but vacationing with your mother? Voluntarily?

Jack sashayed in to say hello, too old to trot at anyone's heels anymore but too dignified to betray the effort it had required to heave himself up from the patch of sunlight by the back door. May took his face in her hands and kissed his gray snout, then reached down and rubbed his belly.

"Maybe we can do some honeymoon research for Junie and Hana. Speaking of, where were you last night?" Nancy asked, bearing a stack of bills and catalogs that would surely bury May.

"At work." She'd come home at the usual time to a gloriously empty house and fallen asleep in front of *Orange Is the New Black*. "Why?"

"You missed your sister's engagement dinner. Did you at least call her to tell her you wouldn't be there?"

"We texted last week. She didn't care."

"How do you know?"

"Because it's Junie. Not caring what I'm doing is kind of her thing, and hey, more power to her. She's always liked hanging out with her friends more than with me."

"Maybe if you were nicer to her. You and April always left her out of your little games."

May burst out laughing. "What games? She was a brat!"

"Well I was the only family on her side who came last night."

"What? Not even angelic April?"

"She had a conflict. I felt bad for Junie. Here she is, trying to bring the families together, and none of hers can be bothered to show?"

"Whose fault is that? I haven't seen her in, what, three years? Four?"

Jack Nicholson slumped at her feet, May's own personal mic drop.

"Oh, May, I don't want to fight about it. Anyway, look."

Nancy handed her an envelope that was slightly larger and nicer than the rest. May's name was printed in calligraphy on the front, Junie's address on the back. The wedding invitation.

"A June wedding for a June bride!" Nancy sing-songed for the umpteenth time, as if she'd been waiting twenty-eight years to milk this pun for all it was worth. Relocating to Philadelphia had put Junie at a safe distance from their mother's enthusiasms, but May was stuck with them.

"Mom, stop. That's not even her name anymore. She upgraded." May had to marvel at how quickly her sister had accelerated into a different life, without the contrails of tragedy that followed her own.

"Don't be such a grouch," Nancy said, jabbing the invitation at her until she had no choice but to accept it. "She's in love, you can't blame her for that. Just because you don't want to get married, doesn't mean you can't be happy for her."

Was it an absolute truth that May didn't want to get married? Nancy seemed to think so, and it wasn't worth arguing the point or, worse, telling her that she'd seen Will today— handsome, divorced, weekend-dad Will, catnip-to-nagging-mothers-everywhere Will.

"I'm happy for Junie," May said. She tossed the wedding invitation on the bed with the rest of the mail, unopened.

3

Juniper

All of Lancaster had turned out for Juniper and Hana's second engagement party in the Monsours' backyard. The first engagement party, a week ago, had been intimate, just family (mostly Hana's) and a few close friends; tonight the depth of the Monsours' roots in America became clear. Everyone who'd ever meant something to them was here: family and chosen family; the Syrians whom Hana's parents had raised their children alongside; neighbors and friends; teachers and coaches; Ahmed's colleagues from the hospital and Maryam's from the library; people from the city council and the mayor's office and even some of the donors Hana's brother was courting for his campaign; along with the Islamic Community Center's most prominent families, who'd come not because Ahmed was a regular at Friday prayers (he wasn't and hadn't been since his children were small) or because they suddenly supported gay marriage (some did, most didn't) but because the possibility that Mo might one

day be their man in Washington made this an elegant oppor-
tunity to show their allegiance. The list of honorary cohosts
was as long as a fundraiser's and Juniper knew this night wasn't
really about her any more than it was about Hana. It was a tes-
tament to and a celebration of the Monsour family, which in
two months would officially include her but had already em-
braced her years ago.

Tonight Juniper would do her best to perform several roles
seamlessly: happy bride, charming daughter-in-law, proud Penn-
sylvanian, Linden College's winningest soccer coach, molder
of young women. Playing the part of fashionable femme she'd
leave to her fiancée, who'd selected a stylish black leather dress
and pumps while Juniper wore what she always did when she
had to dress up a bit, a cotton button-down with a tank top underneath, slacks, a nice belt, Sambas swapped out for oxfords.

She'd been nervous, but Hana had promised her she wouldn't
need to give a speech, so the long drive from Philly had felt like a
date—a much-needed one-night hiatus from wedding planning,
nothing actually required of them but to share road snacks and
vibe to Janet Jackson and remember how much they still cracked
each other up before the party guests claimed each of them for
separate interrogations about their future, like this whole thing
was a game show and they'd be quizzed on their answers later.

Currently one of Hana's uncles was trying to bait Juniper
into agreeing that the World Cup should be projected on a big
screen at the wedding—this June, on the lawn outside Prospect
House on the Princeton campus.

"Not during the ceremony, obviously," Hassan said. "Only
at the reception."

"I love your initiative, but I'm not willing to end my life for
England–Italy. Maryam would kill me and you know it."

"Suck-up," he said.

Juniper laughed. "Saboteur."

"Hana's trained you well."

Juniper spotted Hana under the maple tree, leaning down to listen to the mayor's pint-size wife. That sexy slouch had sent a jolt right through Juniper the first time she was the beneficiary of it, during her first preseason at Princeton. The corners of Hana's mouth turned up now, and Juniper knew her fiancée sensed her watching, had been watching her, too.

A trill chirruped through the air as Ahmed and Maryam arranged themselves on the stairs to the deck, clinking their glasses for attention. It was a beautiful spring night, mild enough for everyone to be outdoors, though not even a downpour would've spoiled the gathering; Juniper had seen at least this many people crowded inside the split-level ranch for Eid. String lights wrapped around a maple tree and reached from its branches to the pergola over the deck.

She stepped toward a waiter to fetch a glass of champagne.

"No, no," Hassan said conspiratorially. "That's cider. Over here."

She followed him toward another waiter—if she'd had a tray in her hand, she could've passed as one herself—and he lifted two flutes off a round tray, handing her one and keeping the other.

"Hello, everyone!" Ahmed boomed. "Thank you so much for coming tonight. You honor us, the Monsours and the Barbers, with your presence."

Juniper lifted the glass to her lips for a sip to calm her nerves, but in the nick of time she caught herself. She had to wait for the toasts, of which there were sure to be several.

"I promised Maryam I would keep my remarks brief and save my embarrassing stories about ya Hana until the main event this summer. With so many hosts waiting to speak, our dear family and friends—" and he waved his arm at the couples lined up beside him "—no one wants to hear a proud father prattle on."

Juniper felt Hana hook her pinky through her fingers, joining her where she stood. They'd been together ten years, too long to recapture that initial jolt, but a current sped through Juniper's body nonetheless. She leaned back against Hana's shoulder, grateful for the ballast. The first time their bodies had made contact—as new teammates scrimmaging against each other, a goalie and a striker waiting for a corner kick, both scrambling to be the first to the ball—it had been erotic. Every time they pressed against each other like this, their bodies remembered, even if the moment itself couldn't always hold space for the charge.

"But please permit me to tell you all how proud I am, anyway," Ahmed continued. "My wise and beautiful daughter—the youngest product director at Essex Pharmaceuticals!—has the great fortune of having found the love of her life. Now, when my colleague and friend Dr. Srinivasan placed little Hana in my arms thirty years ago—a helpless, angry-faced thing; even then, the resemblance to her mother was quite strong—" (Dr. Srinivasan chuckled now, and Maryam play-swatted her husband) "—was this the love story I imagined for her? I confess, it was not. I pictured the usual things a father wants for his daughter: someone intelligent and kind, someone talented in their own way who would not be intimidated by Hana's prodigious gifts, someone with more luck growing a beard than me," he said, stroking his clean-shaven face while the crowd laughed. "Someone who might share Hana's interests, perhaps even a talented striker who would lead their team to the NCAA playoffs!"

"Go Tigers!" Hassan hooted, giving Juniper a thumbs-up.

"I was dreaming, you see, and—except for the beard—in a most unexpected and beautiful way, that dream has come true. Juniper, you've given us our daughter back, and now we have another daughter in you."

How had she given them back Hana? It's true that Hana had needed space from her family to explore her sexuality, but it couldn't have been that great a rift or else they wouldn't have overcome it so soon. She'd never been truly lost, but it was sweet of him to say, anyway.

Ahmed looked at Hana and put his hand to his heart. Then he winked at Juniper and warmth surged through her while her chest tightened. A one-two punch of comfort chased by pain.

"Please join me in extending our best wishes to the happy couple, Hana and Juniper."

Juniper took a drink amid a chorus of *hear hear*'s, the fizziness of the champagne hinting at the buzzy lift sure to follow. The drink, the speeches, the love, why was none of it ever quite enough to conquer the unsteadiness she always felt?

"Let's get out of here," Juniper said into Hana's ear, pretending to launch a seduction.

Hana glanced down and purred, her long eyelashes brushing against soft cheeks.

"And here's to the new head coach of Princeton University, inshallah," Ahmed added with excitement.

"Baba!" Hana said, raising her head with a start, like he was a bad dog with her slipper in his teeth, and Juniper's heart began to race. Maryam grabbed Ahmed's elbow and put her hand on his chest, as if she were holding him back from further familial embarrassment.

"We're not making news here," Maryam said over Ahmed's protests, locking eyes with Juniper. "It's only an interview. But we have every faith in you, ya habibti."

It was only the truth, at least as the Monsours saw it, so why did Juniper feel like such a fraud, like she was playacting at this adulthood thing? Wedding, honeymoon, promotion, baby—that was the plan. She was twenty-eight, Hana was thirty. It was time. They'd put their names on the wait list for the Faculty Club even before they were engaged, as soon as the New Jersey judge ruled in favor of the Freedom to Marry bill last September. *On principle*, Juniper had said then. And now their alma mater was looking for a new head coach for the women's soccer team. It would be a leap for Juniper, who'd had a good run in Division 2 with three consecutive titles at Linden but was still on the young side to head up a Division 1 team.

"If I may also be so bold, and then I promise I'll yield the floor, another toast," Ahmed said. "To our son, Mohammed, the next representative of Pennsylvania's eleventh congressional district!"

"I'll drink to that," Juniper said to no one, grateful to have the focus taken off her and directed toward the Monsours' oldest child and only son. No one called him Mohammed except for his parents and his opponent, who surely hoped to underscore his supposed foreignness. To everyone else, he was Mo. Charismatic and sunny-faced, never met a stranger, a natural politician you'd peg for the White House were it not for the fact of his birth in Damascus. The Monsours had immigrated to America when he was two. Hana was the first of the children to be born here, and seven years later Fariha came along.

Both in their late fifties, Hana's parents had lived in America longer than they'd lived in Syria, and they wore the blend of cultures differently: Ahmed in a dark brown suit and his favorite bolo tie, Maryam effortless in a long navy belted dress with bell-shaped sleeves; Ahmed slower to speak of the fact that his two daughters were both lesbians, but opening up over the years, while Maryam had known the truth since they were small but fretted initially over what people would say, all the ways her girls might struggle. A miracle, really, what a happy couple they still were given all the changes they'd lived through, the home they'd lost, the new one they'd built in a country that didn't always welcome them, the selves they'd shed and reclaimed a dozen times over.

Juniper's phone vibrated in her pocket and she fished it out.

"Your mom," Hana said, seeing the word appear at the top of the screen.

Juniper hadn't told her family about the party tonight. No

need to feel disappointed when they didn't come or anxious when they did. She declined the call and put the phone away.

"I'll call her later."

"More With Mo!" Hassan called out, echoing the slogan on the newly printed lawn signs lined up by the front door like goody bags at a toddler's birthday party.

"If you need to take it—" Hana whispered, nodding toward her brother who was rising up the stairs to join his parents, as if they were presenting him with an Oscar. "Looks like you've got a minute."

"No, I'm sure it's nothing," Juniper said. She didn't want to ruin the evening's happy spell with Barber sadness, but Ahmed wrapped his arms around his son and held him fiercely, as if they'd been separated for years, not minutes, and she realized it was too late for that. She felt like a skipping stone, dancing on the surface of the water one minute, sinking fast the next, the neat trick of the toss belying the stone's true weight.

It had been a kindness for Ahmed to mention Juniper's family when none of them were present. The first engagement party— a sit-down dinner the Monsours had hosted at a restaurant near Juniper and Hana's row house in Philadelphia, intended as a bringing together of the families—had been a bust. Maryam had asked Juniper for her list, and Juniper had puzzled over whom to invite. Her mother, obviously, her sisters and brother, and then who else? None of the grands were left, Nancy was an only child, her dad's sister had died of breast cancer when Juniper was little, two cousins lived all the way out in Oregon. It gave off bad signals, didn't it, to have so few relations, even fewer you could be sure would attend? All her siblings had sent their regrets—July had a midterm, May didn't give a reason when Juniper chased her down by text, April had dropped out at the eleventh hour to go to her daughter's orchestra concert. Maryam had been surprised (though she'd tried to hide it), but Juniper wasn't. The Barbers just weren't a family that put each other first like the Monsours did. They weren't a sprawling clan of blood and affinity who showed up in numbers whenever it was time to celebrate or mourn, not anymore at least. Nancy had come alone, even though her invitation included a plus-one, and Juniper had been relieved. She still thought of Tom as her dentist, not as her mother's companion. Certainly not a father replacement.

The wedding invitations had gone out this week, and she felt the same thing all over again, that fear of not measuring up. Two hundred and fifty guests, most of whom were on the Monsour side or Princeton friends. Half the people on Nancy's list Juniper didn't even recognize.

If it had been up to her, the ceremony would've been much smaller, but Syrian weddings were big and celebratory, with live music, performers, and an arsenal of sweets (she was excited about that part). There was a circularity to the logic behind an epic bash that caught Juniper in a knot. When you invited this many people, you had to entertain them; and with this much fun on offer, it was cruel to hoard it for yourselves. The weeks leading up to the wedding would be action packed: a trip to the hammam and, after the rehearsal, a henna party. Ahmed had his heart set on a sword dance at the reception (the troop he'd hired were very talented and the scimitars they used very dull, he assured), Maryam was a champion ululator, and Hana couldn't guarantee they wouldn't at some point be hoisted up on Mo's and his friend's shoulders.

"Why Princeton?" Nancy had asked, when Juniper called to tell her she was engaged to be married at her alma mater.

Why not get married here in Maryland, your home? she'd meant, and Juniper had told her mother it was because Princeton was special to her and Hana. It's where they'd met and fallen in love; Coach Mac would even be officiating. All of this was true, but so was this simple math: the closer to home she went, the more she missed her dad. She wished she could have his steady arm to hold as she walked down the aisle. But even worse, the part Juniper couldn't say out loud, not even to Hana: the closer she got to Aberdeen and her family, the stronger that tug of guilt, like stones in her pockets pulling her under, telling her it was her fault Frank was gone.

4

July

July was late to the Oxbridge Mingle at Johns Hopkins. He was often late to events that had some bearing on his future, which he had yet to fully conceive of beyond the decision to study abroad his junior year. He didn't like to have the shape and reach of his dreams intruded upon by collective opinion. He also found it difficult to imagine *mingling*—that word! So old-fashioned and slight, it sounded like what it probably would be: an enormous waste of time—with a bunch of straight people in striped button-down shirts and Dockers, who'd probably gone to boarding school and rowed crew and had a family tree that went back to the Magna Carta. On the other hand, a bunch of straight guys who rowed crew! It was like a walking-and-talking Abercrombie & Fitch catalog. What to wear? What to say? He was always late when he was nervous.

July remembered to tuck his shirt in just in time. He took a peek at his reflection in the walls of the Glass Pavilion—the same cowlick he always had, the same unremarkable face, the short-sleeved Ben Sherman he'd thrifted. He picked up his name badge from the check-in desk inside the event space.

The crowd—Oxford- and Cambridge-bound students from Baltimore-area colleges—was less handsome than he'd expected. The usual mix of achievers were in the room: the socially awkward brainiacs, the well-rounded joiners who networked with the blunt force of a sledgehammer, the lucky ones who already knew everyone they needed to know and clustered in hilariously bored circles. April and Juniper, the type As of the family, would have fit right in. May, the antihero, never would have come. July, the watcher, felt safest on the margins.

July went to the bar to get a soda and avoid socializing for a couple more minutes.

"Is that really your name?" the server asked, her nose scrunched up like he was playing a bad joke on her. But no, the joke was on him.

"Yeah, it really is," he said. He looked around for an inconspicuous spot to set up camp, but the damn room was made of windows, and he felt he'd be on display if he parked himself in front of one. He found a plant to stand next to instead. He wished his roommate were here to keep him company, but Lucas wasn't going abroad and kept up a frantic academic pace being pre-med.

"Is this plant taken?" a girl asked, sidling up to July. Her name tag said *Hello my name is Hazel*. She looked like an avatar of herself, in boots and a flouncy skirt, two side buns, and glasses with chunky black frames. According to their name tags, they were both going to Oxford.

"Nope," July said. "Pull up a frond."

"These things are always so torturous, aren't they, with all the questions. What's your major? Where are you studying? What's your five-year plan?"

"International relations. Oxford. And, uh, to relate internationally?"

"Sorry, I was kidding. But A+ to you on those answers. July. Is that Southern?"

"I don't think so."

"Sounds like something out of Faulkner."

"Let's go with that," July said. "And how about you, Hazel? What would you like everyone here to know about yourself?"

"I'm not sure about everyone knowing this, but I might have a blunt in my purse for later."

"Good to know." July nodded, duly impressed. "Oh, shit."

"What?" Hazel followed his gaze over to Nathan Guillory at the check-in desk and beamed. "You know Nate?"

July hadn't seen him since high school. They'd never been friends. In fact, they'd carefully avoided each other throughout most of their lives, two of a kind repelling each other like the positive ends of magnets.

"Hey!" she said as Nate approached.

"Hey!" Nate called back. Hazel pulled him into a hug. "What's up?" he asked July after the clinch.

"Heyyyyy," July said in a wilted mimicry of their greeting that he'd meant to sound wry but just felt bitchy. Nate was also going to Oxford. *Fuck me.*

"Uh-oh. What's the deal with you two?" Hazel asked. "You hate each other or something? Who dumped who?"

Nate shrugged like he had no idea what Hazel was talking about, as if he were above having beef with anyone. July had always hated this about him, how effortlessly he projected effortlessness.

"We went to high school together," July said. "Nate was the only other out gay and, therefore, my nemesis."

"Ah, I see. And all the fag hags fought over you while you two fought over who got to take the quarterback to prom?" Hazel asked.

"I wish," July said. "It wasn't the most accepting place."

"Yeah. But I was too busy being the only Black kid to worry about being gay," Nate said.

Great, July thought. *Now I'm an asshole.* He was ready to find someone else to talk to, anyone, an axe murderer, a mime. But then Hazel excused herself to go pee, and he was trapped with Nathan Guillory, the golden boy of Aberdeen who was too discerning to be co-opted, well-liked without belonging to a single clique, the one person July had always taken pains not to be stuck next to because he was sure he would suffer by the comparison.

"How do you and Hazel know each other?" July asked him.

"Mutual friends."

"Ah."

A lull descended. Last July knew, Nate was studying at MICA and had moved to Baltimore year-round, unlike July, who still spent summers in Aberdeen.

"You still doing your art thing?" July asked.

Nate threw away a smile. "Yeah. My art thing."

"Sorry, I didn't mean it like… I'm not… Anyway, that's cool."

Nate blew on his hands, like he was warming them up, a gesture that briefly filled the silence and excused either of them from talking for about ten seconds. July stretched; looked forlornly at the door to the women's restroom, still closed; prayed for a rapturing.

"So, uh, any news in your dad's case?" Nate asked.

In his mind July's jaw plummeted to the floor, but in reality he just froze. His standard dissociating response, playing dead when the *Real Housewives* version of July would've tossed a drink in Nate's face.

Everyone in Aberdeen knew about Frank Barber. They'd tied black ribbons around their tree for him in those first months, and still, years later, when even Nancy's ribbon had been folded away, the town carried a flag for him in their Memorial Day parade. Nate knew good and damn well how long July's dad had been gone and that the length of his absence was its own sort of answer to the question *any news?* So no. There was no news in his dad's case. There never was, and it was cruel to ask, especially after the effort July had made not to drag the shadow of his father here with him to Hopkins.

But now, thank the goddess, July saw Hazel returning. "*Anyway*," he said.

"Great," Hazel said. "Nobody killed anyone. What are we talking about?"

"Nothing," July and Nate said at the same time.

Hazel looked from one to the other.

"Got it," she said. "Desperate measures. Okay, follow me."

And so they ended up back at sophomore housing in Charles Commons. If July and Lucas's suite on the fifth floor was a monument to bro-hood—soulless, musty, one freebie lacrosse poster tacked up with pushpins, basically just a backdrop for study or Xbox—Hazel's suite on the eighth floor occupied a separate universe entirely. There were tapestries hanging on the wall, rugs and throw pillows scattered across the floor in fetching vignettes, a vanilla candle mellowing out the piney musk of the weed. Joni Mitchell playing, obviously.

"And you're sure," Hazel said from atop a cushion where she perched like a cat, "you guys never went out."

"Positive," July said.

"Definitely not," Nate said, a little too emphatically, July thought.

Nate took the joint from Hazel. He was also on the floor, stretched out like Burt Lancaster in *From Here to Eternity*. July had settled awkwardly into the couch.

Nate offered him a turn. July didn't like pot all that much, but he accepted. He realized now that he'd never seen Lucas high and wondered what that would be like. Come to think of it, he wondered what Lucas would think of this room, whether he'd take inspiration from any of it, the decor, the relaxed vibe, the feeling that anything or nothing might happen next.

"Mind if I text my roommate, invite him up?" July asked.

"Proceed," Hazel said.

July sent the text. Then it occurred to him that he'd made a mistake. Nate knew all about Frank Barber, the local father who'd been kidnapped in Iraq, but July had kept things pretty basic whenever he talked about his family with Lucas. His dad was "out of the picture." Being vague about his childhood had made it easier to be himself, without the truth sensationalizing things. But what if Nate let it slip?

By the time they heard the knock at the door, July felt well and truly strange. He was trapped in his head—this always happened when he smoked. When he saw Lucas standing in the open doorway, he forgot for a moment that he'd invited him.

"Ah," Nate said, looking Lucas over as Hazel held open the door. "Now I'm getting it."

Lucas had a six-pack of Bud Light. "Is it too late to catch up?"

"No," July said, scrambling to his feet. Every time he saw Lucas, he felt an actual pang in his heart. He'd often wondered whether he shouldn't have it checked out.

Woozy, he fell back into his seat. Lucas lifted a bottle in his direction, but July shook his head no.

"I'm Lucas," Lucas said to the room.

"Sorry," July said. "Hazel, Nate—this is Lucas."

"Where you'd all come from?" Lucas took the other end of the couch. "Must have been some party."

"The Oxbridge Mingle," July said. "Am I the only person who thinks that sounds like a molestation cult?"

"Hey, what's that old guy doing in the bushes?" Hazel said. "Oh, nothing, just giving her the ol' Oxbridge Mingle."

"Giving *him*," Nate said. "The Oxbridge Mingle would definitely be man-on-boy."

Lucas smiled uncomfortably.

"Sorry," Hazel said. "Inappropriate conversational fodder. Next topic: summer plans, everyone?"

"I'm moving off campus for next year," Lucas said, "but I don't know where yet."

"You should try my friend Kiara's building. I'm staying with her for the summer. They have a pool, where I plan to spend a considerable amount of time. And it's down the street from Nate!" she said, as if that would be a selling point for him.

Would it? July wondered. Most people liked Nate right off the bat. Why not Lucas, too? If anyone could turn Lucas gay, it would be Nate, wouldn't it? With his self-possession and artist's hands and off-campus apartment, the seduction practically wrote itself. Meanwhile, July was stalled in the friend zone, although there were times he wasn't so sure. What about when Lucas leaned against him while they were playing *Grand Theft Auto*, or when he fell asleep in the middle of *The Godfather* with his head on July's shoulder? What about the look he gave when July ranted about the midterm elections or dark money, the look that said *you're the only one here who gets it*?

See, July thought, catching himself longing again. *This is why you've got to get out of here.* College was supposed to have been a fresh start, but it seemed he already needed another one.

"I'm getting the fuck outta here, that's for sure," Nate said, and July's head whipped up in disbelief. Had he been doing his thinking out loud (and if so, for how long?!), or was this some sort of déjà vu? Or telepathy? Pot made him too paranoid. Never again. "I'm giving up my lease soon. Gonna leave early and travel some before the fall semester starts."

That sounded like the right idea to July. "I should do that."

"Idea's free," Nate said.

"But I've got an internship. Plus, my sister's getting married in June. I should probably stick around for that."

"That's a choice," Nate said.

"What does *that* mean?" July asked.

Nate shrugged. "Marriage is regressive. I seriously don't understand why a woman would enter into that kind of social contract."

"Oh, jeez, here you go again," Hazel said.

"What?" Lucas asked.

"He thinks monogamy is a trap."

"Unless you actively choose it," Nate said. "But for most people, monogamy's an unexamined reflex, just another way of conforming. For gay men especially, there are other frameworks that often make more sense."

"Like polyamory," Lucas said.

"Sure."

"Throuples," Lucas said, letting the word loll there on his tongue as if it were a newly discovered berry and he the explorer sent to taste it. Was he drunk after one beer? Did he want to be in a throuple? July briefly considered the potential triangles in this room and whether it was possible to have a starring role in any of them.

"What about jealousy?" Hazel asked, as if she were reading his mind.

"That's part of it," Nate said. "People are human."

"Well, my sister's gay," July said.

"Okay." Confusion wriggled across Nate's forehead.

"So it's not regressive when you're marrying your girlfriend."

Nate shrugged again. "Best wishes to the brides, then."

"Damn right." July nodded with conviction, even though he had no real idea if he'd won the argument or if they'd even been in one, or why he was sticking up for a sister he hardly knew anymore. The Barbers were like that line in *Anna Karenina*: "All happy families are alike; each unhappy family is unhappy in its own way." No shit. Trouble was, July didn't understand the way his unhappy family worked. He understood only its sadness, not its glue.

"Hey, you're pre-med, too, right?" Lucas asked Hazel. "I think I've seen you in bio."

"Mm-hmm. Test tomorrow, which I am *not* ready for. What I really need is a disco nap so I can study."

They all stood to go. Soon, July was in the elevator with Lucas and Nate. As Lucas reached for the five button and Nate for the *L* button, their hands brushed and little apologies tumbled forth like pennies, and the butterflies in July's stomach turned to ashes. He prayed that at Oxford he'd find an end to this pining for Lucas. When he got back to the room, he stretched out on his bed and folded his arms around himself like a blanket.

5

April

The mother-daughter cruise went off course entirely when she
saw him.

Six days after setting out from Venice, April and her mother
spent the morning overlooking Dubrovnik from Mount Srđ,
Nancy documenting each twist of the Dalmatian coastline with
her camera as if she were planning to map it herself when she got
home. They rode the cable car back down to the Old Town and
sat at a café by the harbor, where Nancy held forth on her personal disappointments and psychoanalyzed April's siblings for the
umpteenth time. July was too young to be going so far away from
home this fall. Would he be safe? Would he drift away like Junie
had? The engagement party had made it plain: at this point Junie
was closer to Hana's mother than she was to her own. But why?
Nancy had only ever wanted her children's happiness. And May!
So moody and lost, with no friends and no love life to speak of.
You were only as happy as your unhappiest child, and May had
never given Nancy a moment's peace. Then there was April, her

perfect, dependable oldest who knew not to say anything about her own troubles, which she hardly understood herself.

Dubrovnik was the final port of call, and when April had booked the trip a week ago, it had seemed like a terrific idea to stay an extra few days to sightsee before flying back to the States. But she couldn't take another minute of her mother's monologizing, so she invented a work call.

"Have another coffee," she told Nancy after lunch. "Write your postcards. I'll be back in a jiff."

When they'd passed the Hotel Renaissance earlier, a pricey modern joint on a side street off the main square, April had felt the familiar urge to duck in and get a room. She went there now, the sun following her like a drone. She wanted to get lost. What had she been thinking, coming to Europe with her mother? The woman was so petite you could forget the way she dominated discussions. Nancy approached other humans much like she approached a set of teeth, ready to turn on the bright lights and fix them.

At the lobby bar April ordered an espresso and drummed her fingertips on the counter. She allowed her thoughts to clear, like clouds leaving a sky. Ross and the kids, her mom's preoccupation with her siblings, the man who'd gouged a hole into her life when he disappeared from it ten years ago, the burden to be *fine*, *absolutely fine*, for everyone's sake—she pinched her upper lip and banished them all.

Judging by the ground floor decor, she assumed the rooms upstairs would be small but spare. White bedding, black carpet, a splash of emerald on a pillow. A view of red-tiled rooftops and the Adriatic—but who would have time to look? The nauseating anticipation when you were the first to arrive; the breathless leap when you arrived second…

This was the gift of an anonymous hotel: it allowed you to pretend you were filling a hole when you were really just making it bigger. Only today, thousands of miles away from her life in Baltimore, there was no one to get in trouble with. She'd dragged her mother all this way to serve as a reminder that bad habits could be corrected, but it wasn't working. All April could do was sit, getting tipsy on spiked coffee, and imagine how she might wreck her life in the guise of a moment's pleasure.

A moment's pleasure. That was what April was thinking about when she saw him outside the hotel's glass doors. Walking down the street like it was nothing: her father, who'd disappeared in Mosul, Iraq, a decade before.

April pulled a couple of colored bills out of her pocket and threw them on the counter for the bartender. "Enough? It's okay? Sorry!" she said and darted out of the hotel.

Her father! His feet gracing these paving stones, his lungs inhaling this air, both of them touched by this same dome of sunshine. It made no sense! Why would he be here in Dubrovnik, thousands of miles from Iraq and half a world away from home?

April watched him turn into the main square, headed in the direction of the Church of St. Blaise. He wore a black baseball cap with a tiger-striped *P* on the front—the same hat he'd bought when Junie got into Princeton. There was another man walking in step with him, wearing a light jacket and a backpack.

April had to catch them. She would tackle him and sit on his chest if necessary, the way she and her sisters used to pin him in their wrestling matches.

She started across the square. They were less than a minute ahead of her, almost to the Sponza Palace. As they rounded the corner, her view shrunk to a bobbing black cap shielding a sliver of hair.

April sped up. How many times had she dreamed of this moment, in the ragged terrain of sleep? Running to her dad and pressing her cheek to his chest. In the dreams sometimes his mood was playful, like in a game of hide-and-seek; sometimes he was frustratingly mercurial, seeking solitude in a room with a trick door April couldn't unlock; sometimes there was the thick uneasy feeling she'd had during her parents' fights, when he'd seemed to disappear. But it never mattered, because she'd found him.

And now here he was! In real life!

Past the palace he turned left onto the Stradun, the limestone boulevard with its tent-covered stalls where April and Nancy planned to shop for keepsakes later. It was crowded at this hour. She could lose him. April sprinted to close the distance and turned onto the Stradun, too. The space between them filled with other tourists, amblers, wide-hipped grandmothers shuffling toward tchotchkes, young parents and their stroller-clutching toddlers stretched across the promenade like a clothesline, whole families stumbling with dripping ice-cream cones.

"Frank!" she yelled.

The people in April's way ignored her.

"Dad!" she screamed.

An old woman raised an eyebrow. A little boy dropped his cone and cried.

The man turned another corner.

"Wait for me!" April's voice broke, and it was this, the sound of her own desperation and childish terror at being left behind, that convinced her it was not a dream. Tears ran down her cheeks. *Please let me catch him. Please let me catch him. Please let me catch him.*

She rounded the corner, but he was nowhere to be seen.

April's heart sped up and emptied simultaneously. She wouldn't have known a heart could feel this way if it weren't how she felt every time she woke from one of those dreams, with a fist full of nothing in her chest.

The first time April lost her father, it was like he was the ball in a terrible Rube Goldberg machine that misfired, one misfortune triggering another and then another and then suddenly he'd vanished. First, the layoff from Snaxco at the start of 2003. Then the interviews that went nowhere, the frozen smile on the hiring manager's face telling him each time he was too old by half. Savings blown on the mortgage, payments on the Tahoe, car insurance for five and college tuition for two. Next, Nancy T-boned on the way to ShopRite, the Acura totaled, her wrist fractured in three places, and six months of rehab before she could return to her dental hygienist practice. No wonder, then, that by Christmas Frank had signed on at CCA, the largest employer in Aberdeen and the anchor tenant of the industrial park that bordered the nearby military base. His work was classified, but it wasn't a stretch to conclude that a chemical engineer at an army proving ground was probably tinkering with chemical weapons. The starting salary for a civilian contractor was just okay, but there was bonus pay for overseas assignments and hazard pay for working near the front. Frank shipped out to Mosul in March 2004. Three months later, he and three Iraqi associates were kidnapped.

April wasn't willing to lose him a second time. She pushed a bulky man out of the way and sprinted down the side street, glancing in windows and doorways, all the way to Onofrio's Fountain, a huge brick-domed cistern that blocked her way. Tourists ringed the fountain, catching sips of water with their hands, taking pictures, resting lazily on its steps.

On the other side of the fountain, she saw it was hopeless. Food stall after food stall, and not a sign of her dad. She followed the trail all the way to the city's main gate and outside the ancient walls.

He was gone.

It took half an hour—all of it spent in a daze—for April to get back to the waterfront, back to her mother.

"You're lucky I'm still here," Nancy said in a huff. "Three different men tried to join me, all old enough to be my father. Absolute scoundrels."

April sank into the chair, her arms hanging limp at her sides. Nancy lifted April's bra strap back onto her shoulder.

"Maybe they were just tired and wanted to sit, Mom."

Nancy tutted at this.

April tried again. "Maybe they thought you were pretty."

Nancy smiled and shook her head, flattered in spite of herself. "Did you get your business handled?"

"What?" April asked. "Oh. The phone call. All handled."

Nancy frowned. "You okay, honey?"

April had that familiar far-away feeling. Too distant to look for Ross's face when she came in the door at night, too snowed under to ask Maddie why she wasn't speaking to her best friend anymore, too distracted to get to the bottom of Cooper's obsession with *Minecraft*.

"Just a headache," she told her mom now.

Nancy patted her hand. "Let's go back to the hotel."

As they walked to the seaport and the chain hotel where they'd dropped their bags earlier, the possibilities pulled April out of her stupor. Her father, alive. Seemingly healthy. Safer than she'd pictured him in her nightmares. Taking a brisk stroll on a spring afternoon. And the timing—was it a sign? Junie's wedding was less than two months away. What if April could bring him home in time to walk her sister down the aisle?

The Suits—those cautious, tight-lipped, painfully unhelpful government men who'd been with the family in the first days of his disappearance—wouldn't have sanctioned this kind of magical thinking. But so what? What was it May had said when, after four months without contact from the kidnappers, the Suits told the family to prepare themselves?

Fuck you, she'd said, jabbing her finger at the first Suit, then rounding on the others like she was in a shooting gallery. *Fuck you and fuck you and fuck you, too.*

April couldn't tell her mother. This was as obvious as July being Nancy's favorite or Frank seeing himself in May and forgiving everything she'd ever done wrong. Her mother had once been strong, but she wasn't anymore. It didn't matter that she was moving on, in her way—her boss, Tom, now her boyfriend, no matter how difficult Nancy found it to use that word. What else could you call a man who bought you a new car every three years, who took you on a cruise every New Year's and ballroom dancing in the park each Monday in June? Despite this new life she was building, April knew Frank's disappearance had shattered Nancy. And she was older now, almost sixty. It wasn't fair to put her through another round of Find Frank. No, April wouldn't tell her mother until she found him again.

They had separate rooms at the hotel, which Nancy thought was extravagant, but April had insisted, justifying the splurge by using points. It was her penance to be in a romantic European city with her mom, but for god's sake, it was still a vacation.

"When we get home," Nancy said at her door, "I'm going to build a nap into my daily schedule."

"Sure you will."

"Take an aspirin for that headache. Come get me in an hour?"

April nodded. A wave of fear slithered through her, just as it had the day he disappeared. There was so much to do to try to bring him back, and she didn't know how, and he wasn't here to show her the way.

Alone at last in her room, April collapsed into tears. Her father! After all this time.

She sat on the bed, her head slumped forward. It was too much to keep this secret, too hard to believe her own eyes. If only she could have looked him in the face. April rubbed her nose with the back of her arm. She had to talk to someone, and here, again, was the problem at the center of her life.

She didn't know who to call.

Of everyone, Ross knew best the toll the last ten years had taken on April, because he'd paid the price, too. Frank's sudden disappearance had marked the beginning of April's withdrawal from their marriage. It had happened in fits and starts. They went weeks without talking about anything but the kids and work. Then Ross would get a sitter and she'd force herself to think of the little things—smile at him over tapas, tell him the funny joke she'd heard at the nail salon. But these were surface things. She didn't know how to tell him that inside she felt like helium, heady, inert, drifting away. When they made love, he pierced her surface briefly, making her flesh again, rough and real and weighted. But when they plunged into sleep—Ross into rest and April into nightmares—she lost herself again.

It was easier to *just be* around Craig because he hadn't known her before everything that happened with her dad. They'd been two faces of a hundred in the lecture halls at Georgetown Law, but hadn't ever spoken until later, at an acquisitions symposium in Crystal City. It had taken Craig several hookups to realize she was *that* former classmate of his, the one whose father had been kidnapped.

"Oh, shit, April," he'd said, lying half-naked on top of her, still inside her when she told him.

She'd blurted it out—*my dad was kidnapped*—because she felt close to him right then and it suddenly seemed unbearable that he didn't know. But as soon as Craig rolled off her, tugging the condom off with one hand, the other flopping helplessly by her shoulder, she knew she shouldn't have told him. She wasn't ready to have this conversation.

"It's okay," she said.

"It's okay that your dad was kidnapped?" he asked.

"It's okay that you don't know what to say. I don't, either."

And that set the pattern. She'd stood up and run a shower. The blast of water had drawn a curtain of sound between them, and from then on, she made sure to keep a scrim between her time with Craig and her actual life.

No. Neither her husband nor her lover was the person April needed to talk to in this moment. She went to the desk, picked up the handset, and dialed out.

"Hello?" May answered.

"It's me."

"Can I call you later? I'm late for work."

"Wait, don't go."

April pictured her sister in the yellow kitchen in Aberdeen, packing a brown-bag lunch, hurrying out the door every morning to a job April could no more imagine performing herself (did it involve shoveling tiger shit?) than she could imagine voluntarily cleaning another human's teeth. Was May becoming their mother? How the fuck had that happened? Since the kidnapping, her life had become so small, so ordinary. April sometimes thought of her as a clipped bird.

"May, I have to tell you something. Right now. It's important."

"Okay, fine. I'm listening."

"It's the most incredible thing. I saw Dad today. Here in Dubrovnik."

April could hear her sister breathing, the TV mumbling in the background.

"May? Are you there? Did you hear what I said?"

"Yeah. You said you saw Dad."

A quiet hung between them, like cobwebs in a boarded-up house. April waited.

"Alive?" May finally asked.

"Completely. I chased after him, but he got away."

This was why she'd called May. Despite everything, she trusted her sister's instincts more than her own. May would know what to do. Across the line she heard a sharp breath.

"May?"

"Go to hell."

6

May

For as long as she could remember, May's dad had been her best friend. It didn't matter that she had a big sister who was just dying to dress her up and order her around. May wasn't interested in sisters or dresses or elaborate scenarios involving dolls and diapers. She only wanted Frank. Everybody always said how alike they were, both bowlegged and hotheaded, both quick at math and good with their hands. Their happy place was the hardware store, with row after row of useful treasures tucked into drawers, sorted by fractional increments. The way he looked at her when she'd take a screwdriver to one of her busted toys instead of asking for help, she knew she was special. Not special the way each child is special—like Nancy would say so they'd think she didn't play favorites—but *actually* special. Her dad would smile, the dimple in his chin winking at her, and she'd know. Together, they were magic.

On Saturday mornings when she was little, she had him all to herself—Nancy home with baby June, Goody Two-shoes April staying behind to play mother's helper. Frank would let May ride on his lap, and on the way there she'd concentrate as hard as she could on the parts of the journey she was responsible for, steering the truck around the road's gentle curves, telling her dad when to press his foot on the clutch (you could go by the RPMs but you could also hear it in the engine's moan, feel it in your chest), shifting into third when it was time. At the store he'd ask her for advice about whatever thing they were fixing that week. Should they use lag bolts or carriage bolts? Sheet metal or wood screws? (*Never* wood screws; they were soft and too easy to strip.) Afterward they'd stop at Burger King, because the Whopper was clearly a better burger than the Big Mac and who needed the ball pit at PlayPlace anyway when you had your best friend? *Don't tell your mom*, he'd say, and May knew that she was pledging secrecy about more than just the chocolate shake and the driving. No one needed to know how much fun they had when it was just the two of them.

Fun—what did that word even mean anymore? For ten years she'd been without her partner in crime. Where was her best friend, the one who sang "I Am the Walrus" as he stuck fries up his nose, who made her laugh so hard that milk shot out of hers? That man would've come home if he could. That man would not be walking around goddamned Europe as if she'd never existed.

May stood in the kitchen, gripping the counter for support because her legs were gummy worms. Something was burning, too. The toaster groaned and up shuddered a piece of toast. July appeared out of nowhere and grabbed it.

"Holy fuck. What are you doing here?"

"Good morning to you, too," he said.

He poured himself a cup of coffee and sat at the round table by the window, Jack Nicholson curled up in the sunny spot behind his chair.

"When did you get in?" May asked. With her mom gone the past week, she'd gotten used to having the house to herself. July

still had a key, but he rarely used it. He'd only been home from
school once since Christmas.

"Late last night. I need my birth certificate to get a passport."

"Did you hear all that? On the phone?" May asked.

July's blank face told her no.

"Have you heard from April?" May asked.

"No. What's going on?"

"Great." Of course, it fell to her to tell him.

July rolled his eyes. Growing up with sisters and their drama,
he had as many different eye rolls as Benjamin Moore had shades
of gray. This one meant *I'm on your side, provisionally.*

"April called just now with a crazy story. About Dad." She
joined him at the table.

"Okay." July wiped his hands off over his plate. He'd been
ten years old when Frank was taken.

"She said she saw him."

"What? Where? In Venice?" he asked, sitting up straight.

"Dubrovnik."

"Why would Dad be in Dubrovnik?"

"He wouldn't."

"What happened? What did he say?"

"She saw him and she followed him. She didn't talk to him."

"Why not?"

"Because she couldn't catch up to him. Because it couldn't
have been him."

"Why couldn't it?"

"Oh, honey."

"*Oh, honey* what?" he said. "Why couldn't he be in Dubrovnik? Why couldn't it have been him?"

"July, listen to yourself. If Dad were alive, he would've come
home. To us. It's terrible to think about, but we knew it was a
possibility—no, a probability—that he's dead. That he's been
dead for a long time."

But she could see something forming in her brother. Not

that again, dammit. Not hope. It was as if all the intervening years that had toughened him up, given him edge, had just been erased. Classic April, dropping a bombshell with no thought to how it would feel inside the blast radius.

"I don't know. Anything's possible, isn't it?" he asked.

"It isn't." She got up. She wouldn't indulge this collective fantasy.

"But what if…what if it's really him?"

May found her purse on the kitchen counter and shook it until she heard the keys jingle inside. Jack Nicholson stirred, his ears tented, trying to determine whether this outing of hers would include him, whether he should drag himself up to standing. The vet was rounding on the elephants today and she wanted to be there when he examined Scout. She was going to be late.

"You didn't know him, July. Not like I did. He wouldn't have left like that. Okay? He wouldn't do that to me."

May headed for the door, but on the periphery she saw July roll his eyes again. This time it meant *harsh*. Underneath she saw the flicker of real pain.

She hadn't meant to hurt him. On the drive to the zoo she considered that a different person would've apologized or corrected herself. *I meant "he wouldn't do that to us."* But that wasn't what she'd meant. She was sure their dad loved her best. It was something you either felt, or you didn't, and she'd felt it all the time.

She spent the day zigzagging, like a ball in a pinball machine, between grief and confusion, furious with April and sorry about July. Just a glimpse of Scout rolling in the mud or whipping his trunk around like a baton would've helped lift her out of the muck of her emotions, but his infection hadn't healed the way they'd all hoped it would. Sabrina's ears were pinned back with worry as Scout moaned through the vet's examination and his sister Stella blasted her displeasure. The keepers would have to increase his footwork, abrading his feet and nails daily until he was better. When May volunteered to take it on, Keith demurred, saying she wasn't ready for that responsibility, and when she complained, he threatened to send her to the children's farm.

"The children's farm?" Will mumbled that night at dinner, raising a finger to beg for May's patience while he swallowed a bite of his cheeseburger. When he was done, he dragged a napkin over his face. "That sounds bad. Cute, but bad."

"I'm not ready yet?" May barked into her fries. "Motherfucker knows I'm a good keeper."

She'd agreed to meet Will in Baltimore's Inner Harbor, the midway point between College Park, where he lived and worked, and Aberdeen. They were here to *really catch up*, and here she was ruining it, rattling off every work grievance—partly to avoid the topic of her dad—like Will was her therapist. Yesterday she'd been dizzy with anticipation, casually prowling the aisles of the drugstore for a leave-in conditioner and a hydrating mask—just general upkeep, she told herself—as if she were on hidden camera and at any moment a suspicious TV host might stick a microphone in her face and ask, *What's next? Makeup? Shaving your legs? Condoms?!* But she couldn't kid herself. She'd wanted Will to light up when he saw her today, not because of his natural optimism, but because she was back.

She was, wasn't she? Or, at least, it had felt like it until that call from April. The girl Will had jockeyed to be in the same study group with; Mayhem, who'd dated musicians and photographers and painters, not nerds in her major; the sexy tornado (his words) he'd waited out until one day she stopped spinning and there he was. May thought she'd lost that part of herself along with her dad, but it was just buried under layers of grief, trampled by disillusionment.

She'd planned on changing out of her stiff work shirt tonight into a V-neck T-shirt that hung just right on her. She'd planned on being funny and alluring with shiny hair, dewy cheeks, and great tits. But this morning she'd stormed out of the house in a rage, all her plans and wardrobe changes forgotten. Now her breasts were stuck in the same work shirt (it wasn't even clean!), and she was stuck inside the wrong May. She heard herself ranting about Keith and chain-of-command management styles and the importance of keeping an elephant on its feet.

"They're walking animals," she said to a bewildered Will, his eyebrows wrinkling while the rest of his face held politely still. "Once they go down, it's murder to get them up again. They gain weight; they get depressed. It's only a matter of time before your only options are to move them to another zoo or euthanize. And they're not candidates for an adaptive device, or believe me, I'd try. It's such a precarious balance. Did you know that elephants already walk on tiptoe?"

"Was this covered in *Dumbo*?" Will asked. "Because the sum of my personal understanding about elephants comes from a movie I can't watch without dissolving into a puddle of tears."

"It's the most amazing thing. If you look at an X-ray, you see that the bones in the leg and foot are all nearly vertical, and they're just resting on top of this big fatty cushion."

"Like a high heel shoe."

"A platform wedge. Exactly. So in a way, elephants already have these natural prosthetics that are distributing their weight through the padding of their feet to the ground. It's an incredible design."

"When did you become such an animal lover? You didn't even have a pet growing up."

May flinched, unused to being known in such a specific way. She hadn't gotten this close to anyone since Will. The mere thought of explaining herself and all that she'd lost to someone new had been its own kind of fatigue. She'd had some hookups with guys she met in bars, but nothing you'd call a date, nobody who'd sparked her curiosity. As far as these things went, the fact that she hadn't had a childhood pet was a pretty harmless piece of trivia, but it hinted at other deeper forms of knowledge that Will had also retained about her, carnal and otherwise. Ready or not, it was time to *really catch up.*

She pushed her plate away and sat back. Will did the same and smiled at her, waiting.

"After I got back from Iraq and dropped out of the Peace Corps, I didn't know what to do next. I temped, I tended bar. I did some house sitting, but I killed so many plants. One of those gigs was kind of a house-sitting/dog-sitting combo, and that was more my speed. My dad was allergic to dogs, so I never knew how good it felt to sleep with a wet nose tucked into your armpit. I offered to walk their dog every weekday, and I picked up some other clients and did that for a while. Then I..."

She paused here, looking for the just-right words to express how difficult it was to get out of bed sometimes, the sinking realization that she couldn't work just anywhere, that she needed bosses who understood about needing sick days sometimes. It hadn't worked out becoming a tech for the super-strict local vet, but she'd found a job at a grooming salon, a place with so much turnover that she provided much-needed stability even if she only made it in 80 percent of the time. Will wouldn't have recognized her the other 20 percent, tired, withdrawn, unable to grapple with the future and cast a vision of herself into it. The anguish over losing her dad had never quite lifted. She'd learned she had to handle it gingerly, respectfully, or it could drag her under, for who knew how long. Even if she believed her, she couldn't afford to play April's game of *What If Dad's Still Alive?*

"I wanted a little more structure," she went on, saying the words quickly so she wouldn't trip on their inadequacy, "so I trained to work with animals—vet's offices, grooming salons, stuff like that. That's when I started helping out animals with special needs. I don't know, it just felt wrong to put a bow on a dog who was gonna collapse in his own shit as soon as he got home. So I'd show people how to make a sling or a ramp, whatever would help. Sometimes, when the owners weren't handy enough to do it themselves, I'd do it for them. One day a greyhound rescue asked me to come in and help. I volunteered there for a while, and I guess word started to get around about the adaptive devices I was making. A bird sanctuary asked me to do a consult next."

Will sat forward, a gleam in his eye that meant his wheels were turning. "A cockatoo consult?" he asked hopefully.

"Not exactly."

"A toucan touchpoint? A sparrow summit."

"An eagle missing half its beak. I made him a prosthesis."

"No shit? Are you sure you aren't Doctor Dolittle?"

"And then a wild cat refuge called."

"No. Not a…"

She nodded. "Tiger."

"Fuuuuuuuuck."

"Yeah, that one was a little scary. But so cool, to help this creature who was powerful enough to kill me get some mobility back. That led to the large carnivore job at the zoo."

"Totally normal," Will said, nodding. "Not intimidating at all."

May felt her mood shifting, as if Will had led her away from the meager fire she'd been hovering over, trying to warm herself on its dying embers, and now she could see that there was no need, that it was a beautiful day out and the warm sun could reach her anywhere.

"Have you thought about helping…I don't know…people? Walter Reed's not far from here. All those soldiers who come home from the war missing a part of themselves."

"I don't know," May said, taking a sip of her beer.

"Wouldn't that be the ultimate challenge?"

"But animals are so blameless."

"Soldiers aren't?"

"Humans. We're so fucking greedy and stupid and cruel. I worry that I wouldn't bring the same compassion to it."

"Oof."

"Yeah. Greedy, stupid, cruel human right here." She pointed at herself, exhibit A. "Anyway, what about you? What's been keeping you busy the last ten years? Besides Zoe, or maybe there's no such thing."

"Yeah. She's pretty all-consuming, but in a great way. I didn't always like who I was before, but then you have a kid and you realize that none of that shit matters at all. All you care about is that she's safe and happy and laughs at your jokes."

May couldn't get her head around it. Will had always seemed so sure of himself, so untroubled. When they TA'ed together, she used to watch the way the undergrads clamored for his attention. Stumped for an answer, he'd run his fingers through his dark hair, from forehead to crown, a gesture that said *I'm taming the thoughts crowding my gigantic mind* and bought him time to respond, a stalling tactic that had the side benefit of showing off his strong brow bone and his aquamarine eyes. Mostly he gave the impression of being a guy who already had all the answers.

"You didn't like yourself? Where's the evidence?" May asked now, questioning him the way they'd been taught to challenge their students.

"I don't know. I could get pretty sorry for myself. Feeling like the world somehow owed me something better. The divorce was not my finest moment. But then Zoe came along and—"

"She was born *after* your divorce?"

"Yeah. We found out Kelly was pregnant when we were separated, but in the end we decided—or she decided, really—that it didn't change anything. So we stopped being spouses and became co-parents instead, which works a whole lot better. And I got tenure last year—"

"Congratulations."

"Thanks. Trust me, in this job market, I know how lucky I am. So yeah, no complaints."

Will took a drink of his beer and set it down without looking at her. He was working up to something.

"What?" she asked.

"All this time—I didn't picture you living at home, an hour away from me," he said. "I figured you were in Timbuktu, off on your adventures."

May was momentarily speechless. He was accusing her of something, but what exactly? Not leaving him for a more extraordinary life? Spoiling his memories of their time together? She wasn't such a conquest if Mayhem wasn't a real person, just an ideal she hadn't managed to live up to.

But what was there to say? He was right. She lived at home. She wanted to move out, but so far she hadn't been able to get it together. Explaining why would involve explaining so much more that she didn't want to get into tonight. Couldn't they keep things light? For now?

"And I didn't think you'd be such a sap," she said. "Is it just the Disney classics that make you cry, or Pixar, too?"

"Well *Up*, obviously."

"Sure."

"And *Wall-E* was just bleak."

"What about *Toy Story*? To be forgotten like that. By a child!"

"But the sequels were so much sadder, don't you think?"

"Dude, I'm childless. I'm not, like, obligated to see every kid movie ever made."

"You're missing out."

"Nah. That's just something parents tell themselves while the rest of us are watching *Magic Mike*."

"Oh, Zoe loves *Magic Mike*. That's the one where the kids time travel, right?"

"Does it feel good to finally be a repository of legitimate dad jokes?"

"The best."

Later Will walked her to her car, and May realized that nothing—not going for a run or rubbing Jack's velvety belly while watching *Breaking Bad* or even sleep—had made time skip a beat like talking to Will tonight had.

"This is me," she said when they got to her Honda.

Will nodded, stuffing his hands in his jean pockets. They'd come to that point in the night, the awkward good-night dance, though she'd always thought of it differently. It was the edge of the cliff you'd either back away from or go over. She could live forever in the exquisite tension contained in that moment of uncertainty, when there was still space between you, enough for a spark to jump across.

As the one who'd done the breaking up, the next move had to come from her. May leaned in, aiming for Will's lips but ready to swerve for his cheek if his mouth didn't meet hers. He closed his eyes, so she closed hers, too. She shuddered with the frisson of wanting, his shallow breath against her skin. Then they were kissing, but not like they used to. He was more confident, had more time. She leaned into him more, and his hands landed on her hips, pulling her in with a grunt. Through his sweater, she felt his abs. He'd always been thin, but since when did he work out? He still smelled like sharpened pencils and vanilla. Oh, God, the odors that must be coming off her, embedded in her uniform. No, no, this would not do.

"Dinner again?" she asked, wriggling free and crashing into the driver-side door. "Next time I promise to change first."

But what if Will didn't want to see her again? Fuck her maybe, but dinner? What if tonight had only been a lark, just a curiosity to satisfy, an itch to scratch, and now that he had, he was disappointed that she wasn't the girl he remembered?

He smiled, and there was that weird zing charging through her skin, as if she'd licked the terminals of a nine-volt battery.

"Don't change a thing," he said.

7

Juniper

In her office in the Linden College gym, Juniper laced up her turf shoes. Today, with Fariha's help, she'd conduct a demo practice under the watchful eyes of Doug Tuttle, the Princeton hiring manager who'd determine whether Juniper Barber had what it took to coach D1 soccer. She already understood her players' strengths and weaknesses; she'd been building the field module for three years, not to impress Princeton but to develop her team and win games for Linden. *Do the work and show up,* she told herself, repeating the mantra Coach Mac drilled into all her players and that Juniper still lived by. She wished she could flash forward to a moment slightly in the future, when Doug would be on I-95 heading home and she would be free and clear. Well, almost free and clear. There was still the matter of her wedding, a month and a half away. She glanced at the bottom drawer of her desk, knowing what waited inside, tucked behind the hanging files—liquid courage. There was so much to accomplish between now and her wedding day. And she wasn't ready.

"What are you talking about?" Fariha asked, stretching her quads in the open doorway. Hana's kid sister had been in middle school when they first met. After attending Princeton, too, Fariha followed Juniper to Linden, where she became her assistant coach and best friend. Soon they'd be sisters, too. "What about that insane spreadsheet with all the rows ticked off? Venue, photographer, band, caterers. You've got it all covered."

"I don't have anyone to stand up for me, since you'll be on the other side of the aisle. Traitor."

"What about your sisters?"

Juniper shrugged. She knew she should ask them—if she closed her eyes, it was always April and May she pictured beside her at the altar, and July, of course—but she'd been dragging her heels, afraid they'd refuse.

Long before she'd wanted to be Mia Hamm, Juniper had wanted to be her sisters. Her dad used to say that was where her athleticism came from. Walking early, running fast, brushing off scrapes and picking herself up again—all of it so she could catch up to them, only to be sloughed off most of the time. Junie the Pest, they called her. When they left for college, she promised herself she'd be a better big sister to July, that she'd call home regularly when she left, that she'd know all his secret crushes and most embarrassing moments. She'd even chosen Princeton because it was closer to home than the other schools that recruited her.

But she'd turned out to be just as distant as her sisters, if not worse. It'd been easier after her dad disappeared for Juniper to disappear herself. May moved back home to Aberdeen. April stayed close to Nancy because of the grandkids. But Juniper had stopped making the effort to be connected.

"So that's one thing you haven't covered yet. Just ask them. What else?" Fariha asked.

"The stuff you can't put on a spreadsheet."

"Like?"

Juniper held up her thumb to enumerate them one by one. "Learn how to dance like no one is watching. Devise a plan for the inevitable awkwardness of my family. Create talking points for my mom so she doesn't steamroll anyone with her verbal diarrhea. And for April so she remembers to keep it light. And for May so she doesn't go full-misanthrope. Actually, talking points for everyone, full stop."

Fariha shoved Juniper.

"You don't get it," Juniper said. "You guys actually like each other."

"What's so bad about the Barbers?"

How to put it into words? "I don't know. We just don't make sense. Your family are like puzzle pieces that fit together snugly. My family's one of those cheapo puzzles where the pieces are cut wrong and the picture's peeling away from the cardboard and no matter how hard you try, you can't finish it because there's always one piece missing."

Fariha's teasing expression softened with pity. "Hey. Focus on Princeton. You got this."

Good advice since the hiring manager was due to arrive any minute.

"If I get it, this job will be up for grabs," Juniper said. "Could be yours."

"Me? I'm too young!"

"That's what I thought when I started out. Don't discount your experience."

Fariha made a face that said *who me?* and *why not?* all at once. "See you out there?" she said. Then she bounded out of the gym with the graceful ease of an impala.

She'd wanted to go pro—all their Princeton teammates had—but only Juniper had gotten close. She still wondered sometimes what would've happened if she'd stayed in Kansas City after the club there cut her. The head coach had said Juniper could keep training with the squad if she wanted. No promises, but maybe if she slid back to defense she'd have a better chance the next year. But being just a contributor when she was used to being a star? Maybe if Hana had been with her she could've managed, but Juniper had been all alone, in a depressing condo that fronted the highway, with long stretches of free time for doubt to run wild. She'd never done well with idleness or uncertainty. So she came home to Philly, to Hana and to Linden.

Her players streamed past her office to the gym's heavy double doors that led outside. In the fall she saw them every day; in the spring just once a week, unless they enrolled in her exercise science class. Over the summer she'd miss their messy exuberance, their chimera-like insistence on being everything: girls, women, student-athletes, sharp-tongued and soft-hearted, kinetic and full of potential. She would never understand how anyone could expect that in a few years, or ten, each of them would settle for being (or even know how to be) just one thing for the rest of their lives.

As Juniper locked the door behind her, her phone rang. Her sister. Whatever April wanted, she'd keep calling until she got it. Better to just answer.

"Hi, April."

"Can you pick me and Mom up from the airport tomorrow?" April said. No *hello*, no *how are you*. None of the buildup or explanation Juniper would've felt necessary if she'd been the one reaching out. Just her oldest sister in drill-sergeant mode, barking orders like she always did.

"Where are you?" Juniper asked.

"Dubrovnik. We're flying into Philadelphia. American. Eight o'clock."

"Dubrovnik? Since when do you and Mom go overseas together?" She unlocked the door and went back into her office.

"Juniper?" April said. "Eight o'clock, okay? I'll text if we're delayed."

"Can't you just take a cab?" Juniper said, reaching for any option that would get her off the hook for a long car ride with her sister and mother. On the other hand, April would owe her a bridesmaid-sized favor in return.

"Junie, please," April said. "It's important. American Airlines, okay? Flight number 443."

"Okay." Juniper wrote it down. "Okay. I'll be there."

What the hell was that about? she wondered, unsettled by the call. Something bad, probably. The older Juniper got, the harder it was to tap her reserves of optimism and spirit. The contents of the desk drawer taunted her, promising a lift. *Bad idea*, a quiet voice inside her quavered, begging to be heard. The field module required her full focus. On the pitch was where she needed to be. When nothing else made sense, soccer always did.

"You pretend you don't, but I know you miss them," Hana said that night when Juniper told her about the airport run. She'd been saying it since the beginning, gently encouraging Juniper to reach out to her family more, like she had—and look how well that had turned out. "The wedding's in six weeks. It's the perfect moment to reconnect. There's still time to enjoy this *with* them, not in spite of them."

"Wasn't the engagement party supposed to be that moment?" Juniper closed her eyes, the only way she could endure Hana's painfully therapeutic foot rubs.

"It was. And now you get another one. Fate is smiling on you. Don't let her down."

"The Queen of Second Chances," Juniper said, shaking her head.

It was just like Hana to extend the Barber family this grace. She'd forgiven a lot of false starts and missteps over the years, including Juniper's first few days at Princeton. That's how their relationship had started.

Juniper had felt a hundred years old compared to the other freshman recruits, who'd followed up their high school graduations with lifeguarding and soccer clinics, road trips and summer flings. Meanwhile Juniper had been holed up at home with the front curtains drawn, hiding from the news vans and the sympathetic wackos, waiting for someone knowledgeable to tell her who had taken her dad and why. When she got to preseason training, she was a space cadet, unable to keep track of who was who on the squad apart from the hot giantess in goal. Each collision with her felt like coming up for air. It was a relief to have one tangible force to hurl herself against.

That first weekend she woke up one morning with no clue how she'd made it home. She remembered having her first taste of a wine cooler in the dorms the night before, then serving herself from the keg on the eating club lawn; after that, things were foggy. Her head felt like a bag of rocks; her teeth tasted like Kleenex. Her roommate told her she'd tried to climb a tree.

She'd missed breakfast, so she went to the vegetarian co-op to find something to settle her stomach and instead she found the giantess in the open kitchen, kneading bread. *She bakes*, Juniper thought. She watched Hana's fingers, pushing and pulling at the dough, and imagined her lacing them together to give her a boost up into the tree. But no, oh, God, she remembered now that she'd asked for one and Hana had refused.

"You look rough," Hana said, and Juniper wished for invisibility. "Hungry?"

"Yeah," Juniper admitted, soaking in shame. She sat on a stool at the island where Hana worked at the glutens in the dough, and considered her afresh. She already knew intimately her dimensions on the pitch, in relation to the crossbar, which Hana could reach easily, but now she studied her in relation to the stove, which came up to her crotch. Juniper could smell the appley shampoo Hana had used that morning. Her hair was so silky when it wasn't sweaty, and she wore a silver watch (her mother's, Juniper learned later), which caught the light as she moved the dough around. Juniper was a soccer player through and through, but Hana was other things, too, an adult among them.

"So I've been trying to figure you out. And I think I know why you've been such a bitch," Hana said, sliding a cutting board with a loaf of sourdough, already baked and sliced, toward her. Juniper took small wary, grateful bites. "I googled you."

Her stomach clenched. She thought she might be sick. Right here. Right now.

"I'm sorry about your dad," Hana said. Juniper's thoughts swung out wide, far away from this school, this kitchen, the bread between her fingertips. Tires screeching, glass breaking, a gunshot piercing the air. The detritus of a crime scene. She blinked a few times. It didn't help. "I can't believe you're even here."

Here, away from the men in suits who'd sat across from her on the living room sofa with nothing to say, away from her sisters fighting in the kitchen while her brother tried to get their mother to stop crying. She'd felt useless at home. Anyone could open up a can of soup and heat it. Anyone could sort the mail and do the laundry. What they needed was someone who could speak Arabic and a Black Hawk helicopter and a team of Navy SEALs. At first she'd been glad to have the chores to do, but that was all she had; there was no information and no plan to get her dad back, just a lot of vague talk about inquiries and intelligence and word on the street, which was nothing to hold on to at all.

"It's only been two months," Hana said. "Right?"

"I know. I'll go," Juniper said, and she pushed herself up from her stool. It was wrong for her to be here instead of back at home with her family. But it'd been nice getting to be just a soccer player again, even if it couldn't last.

"No, wait," Hana said, lunging across the island to grab her shirt, the same way she'd caught her pinny in the six-yard box. "I'm glad you're here. You're so strong, to be able to focus like this. I can't imagine what your life is like right now, but we need you. You can really shoot."

The next weekend, on the lawn at Tiger Inn, Hana showed up without the field hockey player she'd been canoodling with the Saturday before and tracked down Juniper at the keg. "Come on, let's go before you get sloppy."

They walked across campus together, Hana making easy conversation about her parents, who lived close enough to come to some of the home games, and her cocky brother and her brainy little sister, both of whom she was sure would rule the world one day, as if she herself weren't already ruling her little corner of it. Juniper felt an enormous weight settling on her chest, crushing her lungs. It had been hard enough adjusting to the idea that her dad would miss her first season at Princeton, but now it seemed he might miss the rest of her life?

"Hey," Hana said, squeezing her arm, forcing the life back into her. "Favorite bands. We keep going until one of us runs out. I'll start. Soap Kills."

"Who?" Juniper asked. If this was a test of her coolness, she'd already failed.

"Don't think. Just blurt!"

"Tegan and Sara!" Juniper shouted.

"The Breeders!"

"Um, Brandi Carlile!"

"One Direction." Juniper raised her eyebrows in surprise. Hana shrugged. "I contain multitudes."

Who else did Juniper love? Well, obviously there were the patron saints of her heart: "The Indigo Girls."

Hana laughed. "I'm sensing a theme."

"Don't laugh," Juniper said. She felt like a raw, throbbing nerve.

"Why not? I'm happy."

"Don't laugh," Juniper said again, and Hana let the mirth drain from her face.

"I'm not. I'm listening to every word."

They weren't walking anymore. The moon was low and full and huge, making a corona of Hana's messy curls. She had a reputation for going through women so quickly she'd needed a rule against dating teammates, but Juniper, for some reason, wasn't afraid. She reached up and touched Hana's cheek—so soft! She'd only meant to tuck a loose lock of hair behind her ear, but now she couldn't let go. Now she was up on her toes, pulling Hana to her, now they were kissing, now their hands were everywhere all at once.

Hana had always known what was good for her, even and especially when Juniper stood in her own way. She'd found her a therapist years ago, when the insomnia first got really bad, someone off campus Juniper could see without Mac or the team catching wind of it. And she hadn't nagged when Juniper stopped going. She'd summoned Juniper home from Kansas City after her failed bid at turning pro, when Juniper was too proud to admit defeat and too close to unraveling as a human. And now—after years of reminding Juniper to call her mom, asking about her childhood and being politely shut down, bringing her home to Lancaster where family was everything—she thought it was a fine idea to play chauffeur to a sister she hardly ever spoke to anymore. She was in full support of Juniper doing April's bidding, whatever that was.

The next night, Juniper made it to the terminal just as her mother and sister arrived at the curb with their luggage. She still wasn't used to the unnaturally red hair her mother had sported since she'd started seeing Tom. She looked like a Romanian gymnast, between the crimson hair and being five feet nothing and apparently also owning a warm-up suit—ironic since she was the least athletic person Juniper knew.

"Finally!" Nancy said, gripping Juniper in a rushed embrace when she made it to the curb.

Juniper felt the way she always did around her mother, precious but unsatisfactory.

Nancy got in the front seat and gave the slideshow version of their cruise on the drive to Aberdeen. "Venice was magical, but ugh, so polluted. And Split is too popular. The tourists, my God! But Dubrovnik. That was my favorite. So lovely, and peculiar, don't you think, Ape? Of course, you didn't see as much of it as I did."

April, who'd gone from brunette to blond at some point, was quiet in the back. It wasn't like her not to have anything to say.

"You should go for your honeymoon, June," Nancy said. "There's so much to see, and you can't beat the weather. Right, April? I think they'd love it there, don't you?"

"Mm-hmm," April said.

"How's the wedding planning coming along?" Nancy asked. "Didn't you say New Jersey isn't the best state to get married in? I had the lawn re-turfed last year, and it's never looked better. There's still time to switch the venue."

There she went again, still making the case for Aberdeen. The situation in New Jersey *was* complicated. The courts had ruled in favor of same-sex marriage, but the governor was against it, first threatening to veto it, then tabling the idea for now. It was too soon to know how it would all net out, which rights were solid and which could be contested after the fact. The smart thing to do—or the cynical thing, depending on how you looked at it— was to make it official now, while they still could. But thinking this much about the whims of a bunch of old white men—it sucked the romance right out of everything.

"The invitations already went out, Mom. Didn't you get yours?" she asked.

"Yes," Nancy said, knowing she'd lost the argument. "Yes, I did."

"Besides, we're making a statement. If enough of us marry in New Jersey, with institutional backing, it'll be that much harder for the governor to claim he has the people's support to strike it down."

"Mmmm," April purred. "Sounds dreamy."

"Well, anyway, won't that be special?" Nancy clapped. "Did you find a dress?"

"Not yet."

"Junie! You only have—" she counted on her fingers "—six weeks! Why don't we all go shopping together?"

"No, that's okay—"

"It'll be fun, we'll all help. April, you'll come, right? And we'll tell May. And July, too, if he's into that sort of thing."

"*I'm* not into that sort of thing, Mom," Juniper said.

"I insist. I'm invoking my parental privileges."

The truth was she could use the help. Juniper hadn't worn a dress—big, white, or otherwise—since her high school graduation, when she'd worn a simple sundress under her robe to try to fit in. And wasn't this what weddings were supposed to be about, Quality Family Time? She knew what Hana would tell her to do.

"Okay," she said. "We can try."

"Do you girls want to come in for a few minutes?" Nancy asked while Juniper unloaded her bags in the driveway in Aberdeen. "Stay the night."

Juniper still didn't understand why she'd been drafted to drive, and not Ross or May. Were she and her sister staying here for the night? She reached for her bags, but April pushed her back and shut the trunk, then headed for the front passenger seat, suddenly alert.

"Can't, Mom," she said. "Gotta get home to the kids. It's late."

April nodded at Juniper: *Get in.*

What the fuck? Juniper was starting to feel like Thelma to her sister's Louise.

"Well, all right," Nancy said. She hugged Juniper. "This was nice, Junie. Call me about the dress-shopping. Or I'll call you!"

Back in the car, Juniper's stomach was in knots. Hana was right that she missed her family, but she didn't miss this feeling. Ever since the kidnapping, the few times she saw them she had a gnawing sense of unease, as if a crisis was brewing.

"Junie, I have to tell you something," April said once they were on the highway.

Juniper knew by the look on her sister's face—both wild and laser-focused—that it was bigger than divorce, more sweeping than layoffs. That the unease was warranted.

April didn't break eye contact as she said it. "I saw Dad."

It was after eleven o'clock when they got to April's house in Baltimore. Ross was on the couch watching the Orioles game. It had been years since Juniper had seen him. He was one of those guys who seemed to age in reverse, turkey-leg calves sculpted from exercise, his blond-gray hair cropped so short that his ears stuck out.

"Long time no see," Ross said to Juniper, standing to give her a hug. "And, hey, you're getting married! Congratulations."

"Thanks."

"Sorry to miss your engagement dinner. April told me it was really nice. Trust me, she got the better end of the stick. Listening to a children's orchestra… Well, it's an act of love. But we'll all be at the wedding—with bells on!"

"Oh, uh…" What was he talking about?

"You're so sweet to wait up," April said, "but I'm sure you're ready to turn in. We're gonna catch up a little bit down here, okay?"

"Sure. You guys have a lot to talk about." He shut off the TV. "Night, guys," he said and headed upstairs.

They went to the kitchen, where April cracked open two beers, and sat at the table.

Juniper inhaled the puff of air that had been trapped in the bottle's neck and drank. She was tired. "What was that about?" she asked. "You didn't come to our dinner."

"No, I wanted to, obviously, but I ended up having to work late. He's just got his nights mixed up. Mom did tell me how nice Hana's family is, though."

"Oh, my god, Mom. What are we going to tell her?" Juniper asked.

"Nothing. Not until we're sure there's something to tell."

"I don't know how you managed to keep it from her this long," Juniper said.

On the ride to Baltimore from Aberdeen, April had given a rundown of everything that had happened *after* she saw their father four days ago. The next morning, she'd faked a stomach ailment, and to keep Nancy from hovering, she'd tipped the hotel concierge handsomely to sign their mother up for two days of guided tours of the city's museums and historical sites. With Nancy occupied, April was free to sit on hard chairs in the cold hallways of the local police and the consulate, waiting to be seen by men who listened blankly and then copied down her phone number. When it became clear she was getting nowhere, April pronounced her gut biome healed, and she and Nancy flew home.

Juniper took a long pull from her beer, but it did little to make sense of her sister's story. Their father might be alive and well in Dubrovnik? Before this night she'd given so little thought to Dubrovnik, it was astonishing.

Worse, even with her father's kidnapping, even with ten years' worth of perspective, she still couldn't follow the narrative in Iraq and Afghanistan. She couldn't articulate what the US was doing in the Middle East or to whom, or what was at stake for anyone beyond her own family. The puppet regimes and warring factions toppling each other, where America put its thumb on the global political scale and why—it was always shifting and too confusing to track. She tried to understand. She failed. At parties, the most informed of her friends, the ones who read *The New York Times* cover to cover, would say, *It's all about the oil*, with dripping cynicism. That would be the last word, and someone always changed the subject.

"Are you going to wear a wedding dress?" April asked.

"Huh?" The cogs in Juniper's brain jammed with this detour. "I don't know."

"I don't see you in one."

"Me, either."

"A suit?"

"Those appear to be the two major categories," Juniper said listlessly.

Her childhood imagination hadn't prepared her for this fashion predicament. She'd been drawn to adventure stories and sci-fi, not marriage plots. But when the Supreme Court struck down DOMA last summer, her imagination began to rebuild itself around the institution of marriage. Why shouldn't she marry? Hana was the love of her life, the Thea to her Edie, the person she planned to grow old alongside. One night, over a roast chicken and a bottle of wine, she confessed her softening views on marriage to Hana, who proposed on the spot.

"How about a bridal shower?" April asked.

Juniper shook her head.

"We should do that," April said, unable to disguise her absolute fatigue.

"No, it's fine. I don't need one."

"Mom will kill me if I don't. We'll keep it simple. No cheesy games, just lunch. We gotta eat, right?"

"Does this make you my bridesmaid?" Juniper asked, before she lost her nerve. *Don't think, just blurt!*

"Duh. I'm your sister, aren't I?" April asked.

Juniper couldn't believe it was that easy. She got up and threw away the empty bottle.

"Do you have anything else?" she asked.

"Some soda. Or juice."

"Hang on," Juniper said.

She went out to the driveway and grabbed her duffel bag from the car.

Back in the kitchen, she unzipped the bag and fished around inside. "Ta-da!" she said, producing a small bottle of Absolut. She didn't want to think about April's story anymore, where it would lead. Another wild goose chase, grieving all over again. She didn't want to think about the Princeton ball cap April saw on the man's head.

"The fuck, June? You keep vodka in the same bag as your cleats?"

"It was a gift," Juniper lied.

"What kind of gift?"

"An engagement present."

"It's not even a nice bottle."

Juniper had to laugh. What did April think teachers could afford? It wasn't Popov at least, cheap and tasteless, or Gordon's or Smirnoff, mildly better, smooth and clean but you'd still get change back from a twenty.

Juniper found a glass in the cabinet. She reached for a second one, and when April nodded, Juniper took down that one, too, put ice in both, and poured a couple fingers of vodka in one and a little more in the other. Then she topped them up with a bottle of cranberry juice from the fridge. She handed the weaker drink to her sister.

They didn't clink glasses. You couldn't clink glasses over something like this.

"You're probably wondering how it's possible," April said. "Where he's been all this time."

Juniper had not been wondering these things. She'd been trying to ignore that buzzing in her brain, a small but persistent dread gathering. What if he was coming home? Would he be able to look at her, knowing he never would've gone to Iraq if it hadn't been for her?

"It's a lot of money," she'd said at the register that day, at the Princeton bookstore during her recruiting visit.

"It's twenty bucks," her dad had answered, slipping a bill from his wallet and handing it to the clerk.

"Not the hat," she'd laughed. "College."

"We'll get you where you need to go. Don't worry."

Had she embarrassed him, bringing up money in front of a stranger? There were other schools offering scholarships, but she'd wanted to play D1 for Princeton. She'd wanted to go to an Ivy. Not even April, the grade-skipper, had done that.

He'd ripped the tag off the hat and tugged it down on his head, leaving her at the counter without a look back.

It was her fault he took the job in Iraq, ergo her fault he was kidnapped.

"I'm too tired to think anymore," Juniper said. "It's been a long day."

April put her glass in the sink and made a bed on the couch for Juniper. "You gonna be okay down here?" she asked from the bottom of the stairs.

"Yeah, sure."

Juniper listened to her sister moving around directly overhead. When she heard April crawl into bed and the noise stopped, Juniper went back to the kitchen for the rest of the bottle.

8

July

The idea of July's father out there somewhere, walking among the Croats, was a notion that seemed to belong in the Marvel Cinematic Universe, not in his actual life. He'd called April twice to get all the details, so he could see it the way she had, but she'd texted back to say she'd explain it all when she got home. In the meantime May's words had lingered with him, like a haunting. *You didn't know him like I did.* She was right. July didn't know his father. He could look at pictures of him and he had a handful of vivid memories of him to search for clues, but only up to a point. He'd been ten years old when his dad went to Iraq. He was twenty now. Memories, especially ones from childhood, faded and became distorted.

Would he finally get the chance to know his father? His sisters had all had more time with him. He'd raised his daughters, but hadn't finished the job with July, who had a theory that he was only half formed as a result, the other half being a plan his dad had neglected to share with anyone before he was taken.

Who had Frank expected him to become? Someone more like him? And who was that, exactly?

July had so many questions, pivoting toward lunch with Hazel and her friend Kiara, including this one: Was the owner of Papermoon in cahoots with John Waters? Because the diner he arrived at, not far from campus, was as kitschy as *Hairspray*, as chaotic as Divine. Hazel fit right in, waving to July from among the statuary, on one side of her a tower of severed doll heads and on the other a red mannequin clutching the thin trunks of a crepe myrtle.

"I'm so glad you called!" she said as he walked up to her.

"Me, too, me, too!"

He'd needed to get out of his head, and Lucas was so hard to pin down these days between chem lab and study group, so he'd reached out to Hazel, who'd invited him along to her weekly lunch with her best friend. She'd switched out the Princess Leia knots for braids today, and was wearing another dress with platform boots. July was starting to get a hang of her aesthetic: space hostess meets Prince. She was a good hugger, too. He already felt like he'd known her forever.

"There's Kiara. And she brought...Naaaate," Hazel said, sliding into the name like an ambulance into a crash scene, its siren dying, as she pointed at their car pulling up. "Sorry, I guess she was thinking the same thing I was. Mystery guest!"

"Whatever. We're not, like, sworn enemies or anything."

"What's the actual story with you two?" Hazel asked while they watched Kiara parallel park across the street.

"Like I said, we've just never been close."

"Mm-hmm," Hazel said, the tone in her voice implying that was a fine place to start but nowhere near the full story.

"He just always seemed so, I don't know, wary of me. And I didn't know why." July knew it had something to do with their both being gay—neither of them closeted as teens but not old enough yet to be out in the world, either, where they could meet other gays and measure their currency in the marketplace of men. No one in Aberdeen was buying what they were selling, unless they wanted to buy from each other.

"And that made you wary of him, too?"

"Do I seem wary?"

"No, not at all. Nuh-uh."

July laughed. There wasn't enough time or privacy to go into the rest of it. Maybe one day he'd tell her about the homecoming dance freshman year when their respective besties had tried to force a spark between them. It had all been so embarrassingly formal, two straight girls shuttling back and forth across the gym like ambassadors to warring countries, but even so, July had been willing, his body humming with the current of possibility. Where would the moment lead—a dance? A kiss? Even friendship would've been nice. But then Nate left the dance early, the gym door yawning shut behind him, Alice shaking her head at Aubrey to call the deal off, both of them looking at July like he was a pound dog on his last legs.

July hoped it was just a coincidence that he and Nate were both here now. He couldn't handle another failed fix-up.

Kiara and Nate crossed the street to meet them, Kiara in overalls, Nate in carpenter pants that slouched nicely on his hips. They lucked out and were seated at the table underneath the restaurant's most gonzo mannequin installation, a mass of flesh-colored body parts that bloomed like a coral reef. After a few minutes the server came to take their orders.

"I'll have the French toast," Hazel started.

"Breakfast for lunch," Nate said, flipping his menu over to consider the other options. "I respect that."

The server looked at Kiara next. "Yeah, the breakfast here is too good. Can I have the eggs Benedict and a peanut butter milkshake?"

And then Nate: "The egg sandwich and black coffee, thanks."

The server jotted all this down and then turned to July. "I'll have the burger, with salad instead of fries, please."

"Oh, it's like that," Kiara said.

"What?" July asked.

Next to him, Nate glowered at July over the tops of his non-existent reading glasses like a disappointed librarian. "The rest of us are out here trying to keep it morning and now you're trying to fast-forward to the afternoon?"

"Oh. Okay. Um, let's do the tofu scramble and iced tea."

Kiara jumped back in her seat. "Now you're shaming us with your healthy choices?"

"Fine! Sausage gravy and a bacon milkshake!"

"All righty, then," the server said, collecting all the menus and disappearing before anyone changed their minds again.

"No joke, that sounds disgusting," Kiara said.

Hazel nodded.

"Et tu, Brute?" July asked her. Where was the solidarity?

Her shoulders crumpled in guilty apology.

"Bacon in a milkshake," Nate said, shaking his head. But then he squeezed July's bicep and laughed, and one after another they all joined in, even July, until they were all sharing that laugh like a dance crew passing around the worm.

"Bacon!" Hazel squealed, holding her stomach to keep her guts from spilling.

"Whose terrible idea was that?" July said, his chest burning with joy.

For one entire hour July forgot about Dubrovnik and his dad. But when Hazel and Kiara got up to check out the Pez collection by the door, July caught his breath, and it all came flooding back. He grimaced, an actual pain stabbing at his right temple.

"Hey," Nate said. "You okay?"

Maybe it was the real note of concern July heard or maybe it was the way the bric-a-brac all over the diner's walls and ceiling seemed to welcome pandemonium—a butt and a pair of breasts swanned over Nate's head—but next thing he knew, he was letting it all out.

"Remember you asked about my dad's case? Well, out of the blue, my sister says she saw my dad."

"Oh, my god. What? Where?"

"In Croatia."

"Croatia!"

"And then she lost him," July said. He stared at a tangle of doll parts and scrap metal dangling from the ceiling. Was that... a baby in a hang glider? The odd art on display only added to the surreal-ness of his situation. "But if it were me over there, would I have recognized him in the first place? I was so young when he was taken. Would I have walked right past my own father, like he was a stranger?"

"No way."

"I don't know..."

The girls came back and July cleared his throat and Nate smiled so lightly at them that even July couldn't tell what they'd missed, that he'd just dipped into some deep trauma and needed a moment to collect himself. Really all he could do was admire the way Nate floated them both along to the next moment and the splitting of the bill.

On the way out he saw that he'd missed a text from April. Family meeting. Tomorrow. 9 AM. My house.

Finally some answers.

Hazel and Kiara drifted ahead, but Nate hung back and, without breaking a step, said softly, "One thing. Why Croatia?"

It would have been easier to admit his ignorance to Lucas, who knew nothing about his dad. It was much harder to say it to someone who was also from Aberdeen, where people thought Frank Barber was either a patriot, a wounded warrior, or a saint.

July was supposed to be the expert on him, the keeper of the flame, but he was as confused as Nate was.

"I wish I knew."

When July got to April's house the next morning, there was Juniper pouring herself a cup of coffee. She was just out of the shower, wet spots on her T-shirt from her long hair, so she must have spent the night, which threw him. His sisters were doing sleepovers now? Since when were April and Juniper this chummy? Maybe it shouldn't have surprised him that Junie was here—this was a family meeting, and she *was* family—but after so many holidays without her, he'd stopped looking for her in group photos, stopped thinking of her as part of the group. He could hardly remember being her little sidekick, once upon a time. When he'd RSVP'd no to her engagement dinner, the only person who seemed to mind was their mom. He would go to the actual wedding, of course, but then he was off to Oxford and who knew how long it would be before he and his sister saw each other again?

"Hey," he said.

"Hey," she said, and an uncomfortable pause followed while they decided whether they should hug. She leaned in, and he patted his sister's back.

April walked into the kitchen, looking scattered, and he let go.

"What happened over there?" he asked. "Did you find him? What did he say? Why didn't he come back with you?"

"July, *please*," April said, as if he were a child, not a grown man every bit as invested in this story as she was. She was sixteen years older than him, so yeah, he got it, but why couldn't she talk to him like an adult? He had a mom; he didn't need another. "Let's wait until May gets here so we can all go through it together," she added.

Ross rounded up the kids for school and July wandered into

the living room, picking up his nephew's abandoned game of *Minecraft*. He traveled to a new plot of land and began to dig a pit and lay a foundation for something new.

In the kitchen two of his sisters were bitching about the third. May was late, according to April. Not according to the clock, he might have pointed out, but he'd learned that it was best not to involve himself in every one of his sisters' disagreements. Besides, May had no use for a lapdog.

When she arrived, the volume in the kitchen pitched higher.

"Finally," April said.

"Who calls a meeting at nine a.m.?" May boomed. "*So* glad I got to enjoy the rush-hour traffic. Really. Thanks for that."

"Coffee?" Juniper asked.

"Yeah, hook me up."

He heard Juniper's chair scrape across the floor and the sound of the coffee pot being lifted from its berth. July could picture May extending her arm, as if to be connected to a caffeine IV.

"What are you doing here?" May asked Juniper. "I thought stuff like this just rolled off your back."

"Of course it doesn't," Juniper said.

"I don't know. You seemed to move on pretty quickly. Went to school, got a girlfriend, won a giant trophy."

"We lost the championship actually."

"Enough," April said. "Let's talk about where things stand. I'd like to talk to my contacts at the State Department, and it would be helpful to review what we already know first."

"Which is nothing," Juniper said.

"*Your* contacts?" May said.

"*Our* contacts. Whatever."

Of course, they got started without July. Here he was again, gaming in one room while his sisters caballed in another. Ten years ago they'd sent him to the den when the men in suits came. They'd whispered about the volume of blood left behind in the SUV, type B+ like their dad. Meanwhile July was behind the barrel of a gun on the surface of a Halo ring, saving humanity from the Covenant. *Rip their skulls from their spines and toss them away laughing!* his sergeant had ordered, and he'd reloaded, unleashing on the bastards until their alien blood bled blue.

"*Contacts,*" May said with disdain. "They weren't networking with you, April. They were avoiding you, if you recall."

"Someone had to stay on good terms with them. They were our only source of information. We couldn't all tell them to go fuck themselves."

"Even though we wanted to," Juniper admitted.

Without meaning to, July's design had transformed into *Halo*: the observation deck on board the Autumn spacecraft.

"I swear I'm not trying to be a jerk," Juniper went on, "but April, are you *sure* it was him?"

July was still wondering the same thing.

"I couldn't catch him to be sure. But a guy who looks just like him wearing a Princeton baseball cap? I mean, maybe it's a coincidence, but…what if it was him, and I didn't follow up just because I was afraid of what people would think?"

"People? Like me, you mean," May said.

"I just don't get it. Why would Dad be in Croatia of all places?" Juniper asked.

July had added a series of air-lock doors and corridors that branched off the cryobay and ran to the bridge. He was better off here with the Xbox than in there with his sisters, trying to unearth their father's motives for…anything, actually. How did a man who'd flavored snack foods for a living suddenly turn all that knowledge toward the development of chemical weapons? How did he justify it to himself, knowing what governments did with them? Look at what was happening in Syria now. Forget about that, how did he justify voting for Bush? Or leaving four children behind to go to Iraq—voluntarily? How Frank Barber might have ended up in Dubrovnik was the least of their mysteries, as far as July was concerned.

But then it came to him. Something he'd studied last semester, in a class on US foreign policy.

July shut off the Xbox and joined his sisters in the kitchen.

"I know why Dad went to Dubrovnik," he said.

His sisters seemed surprised to see him. He was sick of the way they overlooked and underestimated him.

"Croatia doesn't have an extradition treaty with the US. None of the Balkans do. If you want to hide, Croatia's a good place to go."

For once his sisters were perfectly silent.

"A lot of countries don't like that we have the death penalty," he said, "and they don't want their citizens being prosecuted here. After their civil war, the Balkans had that much more reason to be guarded."

"How do you know that?" April asked.

He threw his eyes upward, and then opened the refrigerator and addressed his affront to the vegetables. He emerged with a can of soda to find her still staring at him. "I *read*." He hopped up on the countertop, cracked open the can, and took a sip. He shook his head at the ceiling.

"So what?" May said, pacing. "I don't give a shit about Croatia's foreign policy stance. If Dad were alive, he would've come home, end of story."

"But what if he couldn't?" Juniper asked. "What if he's still being coerced?"

"By who?"

"There was another man with him," April said. "Maybe it was whoever took him. Maybe he had a gun, underneath his jacket."

"And now Dad's stuck in Croatia having his morning coffee by the sea? Bullshit," May said.

"You have a better idea?"

"Yeah. Your mind is playing tricks on you. You miss Dad— we all do—and when you saw a guy who looked like him, your brain filled in the rest."

"No. If you'd been there, May. If you saw the way he walked. Bowlegged, just like Dad."

"Just like you," Juniper said to May.

May let out a great sigh.

"I'll admit, I can't be one hundred percent sure what I saw. Who I saw. But the bigger point, in my mind, is that we can't disprove it. Presumed dead isn't the same as dead. I can't keep living like this. Never knowing what happened, how badly he was hurt, if he's okay now or…"

"Not," July said.

April nodded.

He felt a shiver coming, but he saw Juniper close her eyes and shudder first.

"When's the last time we had contact with the kidnappers?" he asked.

"Not since that summer," May said. "I still say the FBI scared them off."

"Yeah but any cards we had, we played them once we paid the ransom," April said. "We had to go to the authorities after that."

"We paid a ransom?" July jumped down from his perch on the counter. No one told him there'd been a ransom demand, or that they'd paid it. What good was a family meeting if the people you trusted to tell you your history kept it hidden from you?

"Yeah. We did." May went and stood beside him.

"Of course, we did," April said, shrugging it off.

"How much?" July asked.

"Fifty-thousand," May said.

"What? Where did we come up with that kind of money?" He remembered how tight money had been before his dad left, the way his mom used to talk him out of anything he had his eye on. *I just bought you a pair of shoes; they need to last you until the fall.* Later, after she and Tom became a thing, the spigot started flowing again. The new *Halo.* A jean jacket with a sheepskin collar. But fifty-thousand dollars at a time when there'd been nothing extra? How the hell had they managed it? He'd had no idea. What else didn't he know?

"Ross and I had some savings," April said. "Mom drew against the house. Tom loaned us the rest."

"When were you gonna tell me?"

Juniper put her hand on April's arm. "We didn't want to scare him, remember?"

"That's a pretty big fucking detail to keep from me."

"You were just a little kid, July," April said.

And he was what, now, a big kid? "What's your excuse now? I asked about this. I went to Mom a few years ago and I asked her to tell me everything. She swore up and down there was nothing else to tell. And you were all in on it?"

"She was just trying to protect you. We all were."

"Do me a favor. Don't." He headed for the door.

"Hey. Where are you going?" April asked.

"I've got class."

"You want to be treated like an adult?" April asked. "Stick around and act like one. The four of us have work to do."

May 2014

9

April

April arrived early to the Pentagon City mall. She wanted to find a good table: in view of Au Bon Pain, where they'd agreed to meet, but sheltered from the cacophony of the food court.

She'd tracked down Leyla Halabi, the only Suit left, after trying the other names with whom she'd once been in daily contact. Matthew Ruminski was doing corporate security in the private sector. Todd Zucker had transferred to Beijing to work on trade issues. Victor Garcia was a chef! Working on kidnapping cases took its own toll. Only Leyla was still at State, still in DC.

April had a list of questions written down in her day planner, but more urgent were all the questions that kept her up at night. How certain could she be that the man she'd seen was her father? Would Leyla believe her enough to get involved? Had April upset her brother and sisters for nothing?

It had made her hot and nauseated when July said there was no extradition treaty between Croatia and the US. Suddenly he had thrown a dark cloud over everything, forcing her to imagine the ways in which Frank was still being coerced, still in danger. Was the man walking in lockstep alongside him concealing weapons? Quite frankly she'd forgotten July was even there. The beeps and clicks coming from the Xbox in the living room had been just background noise, like the score of a movie she'd been trapped inside the last ten years. Somehow her little brother had grown into a person who knew about extradition treaties, and now at least they understood why their father was in Croatia of all places, one question answered but many more to go.

April almost didn't recognize Leyla Halabi walking toward her from the mall's Metro entrance. Leyla had been the youngest person on the case. She'd shown up for a task-force meeting at April's parents' house in a suit that looked borrowed, too big for her petite frame. She was there to provide "context," which was code, April gathered, for being Iraqi-born, American-bred. But the others—men representing a hodgepodge of abbreviated government entities—barely acknowledged the new kid hovering on the living room's perimeter. Leyla wasn't a kid anymore. She'd acquired a layer of polish. April recognized the cream-colored silk blouse and black pencil skirt from Brooks Brothers. Gone was the messy bun, replaced with a glossy blowout. There was a giant ring on her finger that hadn't been there before.

"Thank you so much for coming," April said. She had tracked Leyla down at the Office of Islamic Cooperation, where she was the Deputy to the Special Envoy. She didn't work kidnappings anymore, she'd said, but April had begged. "Coffee," Leyla had agreed.

April could have hugged her now, except they didn't know each other in that way. Shaking hands felt too formal, and April was determined to push past the bureaucratic bullshit. She settled on a warm smile and sat down. She'd gotten them two coffees and a couple croissants. "Here," she said, gesturing to the treats and the empty chair. "You still drink it black?"

Leyla sat. "As I said, I don't know how much help I can provide. But I'll try. It's good to see you. You're looking well."

April hated the idea that Leyla might think her grooming, her
vanities, were more important to her than her father. But she'd
had to go on. She had children, a career. And she couldn't very
well show up for meetings wearing a cloak of mourning. Five
years ago, when her first gray hair came in, she started high-
lighting her brown hair. Now she was completely blond.

Leyla seemed to read her embarrassment. "I've thought about
your family a lot over the years. How are your children?"

"Good. Maddie's twelve and Cooper's almost ten." She'd been
pregnant with Coop when Frank was kidnapped.

Leyla smiled. "And your mother?"

"Doing okay." She didn't mention Tom, worried it would
count as a strike against them if people knew Nancy was dating again. Not even dating, really, which sounded playful and
suggested a rotation of suitors. There was just Tom, her old
friend and yes, technically, her boss, but who could ever boss
Nancy around?

Leyla smiled patiently.

"And my sister June is getting married this summer. She's part
of the reason I called you. My mom and I took a vacation together last week. A cruise. We started in Venice and then sailed
down the coast of Croatia. Our last stop was Dubrovnik, and
something strange happened there." April stopped. She took
a big sip of coffee to work up her courage, but the smell just
made her queasy.

"What happened?"

"There was a man. He walked by, and I followed him, I almost caught him, but then I lost him."

Leyla waited. "Yes?"

"I think it was my father."

Leyla looked confused, sympathetic.

"I know it sounds crazy. I promise you I don't go around all day thinking *are you my father? are you my father?* like that bird in that children's book. The resemblance was eerie. Remarkable."

"Hmmm," Leyla said.

Concrete questions. April needed to make a specific request before Leyla ran out of there like a nun who'd stumbled onto an orgy. She flipped to the page in her planner with her questions. "I know there probably isn't anyone actively on the case anymore, but I wondered if someone could check with the consulate in Dubrovnik or the local police. I tried, but they wouldn't speak to me. We have photos, and the FBI has his prints. Maybe he's turned up in the system under a different name."

Leyla made a face with her lips, the face you made when you were about to give exactly two seconds of thought to a problem before politely, regrettably, declaring it unsolvable.

April went on: "The people who took my father and Mr. Yassin and Tariq—I know the official theory was that they were politically motivated. Death to the American Tyrant, and all that. But shouldn't we have found the bodies? Desecrated, like those men in Fallujah."

Just weeks after Frank arrived at Camp Freedom, four civilian contractors in Fallujah had been bombed in their SUV, their charred corpses hung from a bridge.

"What if the kidnappers were after something else?" April went on. "Maybe they needed my father alive."

"I don't know. You've always been practical, April. What happened to your family was everyone's worst nightmare. Your clear thinking pulled them through."

She was practical. She was also strategic. Leyla mentioned her family; now it was time to use them to her advantage. It was time for an emotional appeal.

"That's why it kills me not to be able to give them closure. Good or bad, whatever actually happened, there would be comfort in finally knowing for certain. We haven't had a wedding in the family since he was taken. It's too hard celebrating the big things, or even the little things, when he might be in harm's way. Junie's getting married, and we're all trying to put on a good face for her. But if we could bring my dad home to walk her down the aisle? Can you imagine?"

"It would be incredible." Leyla's eyes softened and she absent-mindedly patted her own wedding ring.

April saw her chance. "To say nothing of what it would mean to the rest of us. July's in college now, and he's so smart. But there's something about him. A vulnerability. I look at my son and wonder how his heart could survive something like that at his age. July had to grow up without the one person—" April's voice broke. The emotional strategy was backfiring. She had to get a grip, keep hold of the narrative, but July...

"The one person—" Why only one person? Why hadn't she been there for him more? She should have stepped up, but she'd been so overwhelmed. When Coop was born, she could hardly look at her son. It took all she had just to learn the language of his cries and not tune out, to come when he called, to offer him her body for comfort. There was nothing left over after that for July.

Since the family meeting, he had been dodging her calls. He was going through this all alone. She thought about what her dad would say if he knew how scattered his family had become in his absence, if he saw how weak their bonds had become and how little she'd done to fix it. *You're the big sister, April. You have to do more*, he always said. It was her responsibility to make things right. July missed his father, too.

"July had to get through this without the one person who could make things right for him," she said.

Leyla reached across the table. "I'm sorry," she said and laid her hand on April's wrist.

"No, I'm sorry. I didn't ask you here to listen to me fall apart."

"It's okay."

"I know you're not a magician. You can't fix everything. No one can. But do you think you could talk to someone in Croatia? Just ask a few questions?"

Leyla took her hand back and tucked her hair behind her ear. "I only worked on one kidnapping case, you know. This one. It was very...upsetting." She rested two fingertips on her lower lip.

April held her breath.

Leyla nodded.

"Yes. Okay."

"Oh, thank you! Thank you so much."

"I can't promise you answers. But if it were my family, I'd want to know that we'd searched under every stone."

"I won't forget this," April said.

What April *had* forgotten, and what came rushing back as she clicked her seat belt across her chest, was the way hope felt indistinguishable from despair. These last several years of stasis had spared her that. She thought she'd outgrown optimism, but here she was again, waiting for the clues to add up. As if she hadn't already learned: to have a lead was to see it lead nowhere. To want something was to watch it be taken from you. To hope was to be disappointed all over again, only worse each time.

It was better to be numb.

She was due back at the office, but she felt too restless to work. She texted Craig, Where are you?

She'd promised herself she wouldn't meet him again. She'd focus on Ross and the kids, maybe even find a therapist. And now here she was, two weeks from their last time, starting it all back up again. Her weakness disgusted her.

She pulled out of the mall's parking lot, turned onto the parkway, and headed north toward the beltway. Seeing Leyla again had taken her back in time, returning her to a bodily state she loathed. Jittery, exhausted. She smelled herself now, the familiar earthy tang under her arms. That was fear. But there was something else now, too. A close milky scent. She was wet. This was different. This was new.

Craig texted back, **Bethesda**.

April tried to keep one eye on the road while she typed out a message with her thumb as quickly as she could. **Let's meet**.

What was wrong with her, that she wanted this right now? Not Craig, not him exactly, but what he could do to her. Hope was a fever burning under her skin. She wanted him to fuck it out of her.

She'd always been restless in a certain kind of way. Well past the point when she and Ross had become exclusive, she was still wondering what it would be like to be with other men. In her fantasies, she had sex with strangers, or friends of his. She had sex in front of windows or open doors while someone watched. Would she be less herself with someone less nurturing than Ross, someone who didn't know her entire backstory? Or would she be more herself with a stranger? This last possibility, that there were parts of herself she hadn't explored and might never reach, haunted her and drove her imagination further into the wild places.

They were visions she cultivated in secret. In a perfect world she would have explored these fantasies with Ross. On their honeymoon in Costa Rica she'd floated a few trial balloons. On a day trip she'd tugged Ross behind a waterfall and made love to him while their guide and a couple college kids swam a few feet away in the lagoon. In a nightclub in Playa Jaco she'd danced for him with another man, then led Ross to the beach for a tumble. When they returned, they found the man and his date at the bar, and April ordered a round of drinks. They were beautiful, the man and the woman, and happy to talk to them. But when April nudged Ross to ask the woman to dance, he'd said he was sorry, it was time for him to turn in.

Back in their room Ross said, "Enough. Enough with the sex Olympics."

"I thought we were having fun," April said.

"You were."

"She was beautiful, and so graceful. I thought you'd like to dance with her."

"You wanted me to do more than that, though, didn't you?"

April stalled. It felt like a trap to agree. She shrugged and smiled, like she didn't know what she wanted.

"But I only want to be with you, babe," Ross said. He pulled her in close and buried his face in her hair. "You're more than enough for me."

She'd thought, then, with an innocence that would seem foolish after her father's disappearance, that they'd have forever to find their way to sexual fulfillment.

Craig had texted her the address for a nondescript high-rise hotel a couple blocks from the beltway. No showy entrance, just a driveway down to the parking garage. She followed the signs to the P3 level where the promised vacant spots awaited her. She got out, then locked her car door and hitched her leather tote bag over her shoulder by habit. It was heavy with case files from work and the files about her dad she'd packed for the meeting with Leyla.

She wouldn't need them upstairs. April beeped the unlock button on her key fob and opened the back-seat door to put the bag away. She heard the shuffle of footsteps first, too close, and her heart leaped into her throat. She yelped but a hand went over her mouth and she was pushed, hard, face down over the seat. She struck out with her arms but couldn't reach behind her. Her legs were pinned, knees apart. She heard a zipper. She smelled the unmistakable combination of wintergreen gum laid over coffee, and it clicked. A hand reached up her skirt and forced her panties down. She took him into her.

"Did you really get a room?" she asked, after. They were sitting together in the back seat, clothes yanked back up and smoothed into place.

"Didn't have time," Craig said. "But I can."

"No, don't bother."

"You okay?"

She nodded. He meant the role-play. He'd been rough with her before. Surprised her, too. But they'd never taken it this far. She wasn't sure if she'd enjoyed it, but it was what she'd wanted. Fertile ground for a therapist, she assumed—if she could ever bring herself to talk about it; that since the kidnapping, scenes like this, snatching and scuffling and stuffing into cars, lurked in the wild places, too.

"My dad," she said, fingering a tender spot on her knee.

"Mm-hmm." Craig was staring at himself in the window, rubbing his jaw where she had scratched him.

"There's been a development in his case," she said. "But this happens. It's probably nothing."

Craig turned toward her.

"I just wish I had better sources," she said. "The government only tells you what they want you to know. But he's *my* father. I deserve to know everything."

"I've got a buddy at work who's in risk management," Craig revealed. "He did a K&R tabletop for one of my clients recently."

K&R meant kidnap and ransom. April wasn't sure what a tabletop was. She squinted at him.

"You get a company's key people together—this would be a company with reasons to feel vulnerable, given the kind of business they're in or where they operate—and run through some scenarios. Figure out whether they've got the right policies in place to protect their assets."

"Protect their assets," she mused. It was the kind of thing CCA would have been concerned with, if they'd considered her dad an asset, which they hadn't. They'd talked about him like he was a lone wolf, as if he'd arrived in Mosul completely independent of them, reckless and hyped to see some action.

"You should talk to him," Craig said.

She remembered how frustrating this was, reaching out to strangers for the knowledge that, by rights, *you* should have, as the one who was living through it. Still, it was another angle to try. She smiled at Craig.

"Thanks."

He opened the door. "I'll get you his number. See you around, kid."

She put up a hand—a weak wave—and let it fall.

10

May

The morning after the woman from State told April she'd look into things, May called in sick and went back to bed. But she couldn't sleep. She thought of this period—after a new lead turned up, before it inevitably petered out—as the spin cycle, when she had to chew on her father's disappearance all over again and everything inside her got dredged up and shaken around. The spin cycle seemed to last about six months, give or take. Leads usually dried up fast. It took longer for the feelings that were stirred up to die down, except they never really did, not completely.

Her phone rang and she reached for it, thinking it might be Will calling about their date tonight. After all this time, their connection was still there. Hard to believe; a gift, really. She wouldn't have blamed him if he'd kept walking when he saw her outside the elephant exhibit, refusing to waste another minute on that girl who'd dropped him without so much as a goodbye. They both knew where this thing between them was headed:

another date, making love, their bodies finding each other again; already little doors inside her had opened to the possibilities. But today May felt herself grinding down again, like a motor running on molasses. She didn't want to hear the anticipation in Will's voice, fearing that she couldn't match it.

But it wasn't him. It was Juniper. Partly out of curiosity, partly to build some karma with the Gods of Getting Back to People, May answered.

"Hey, did I catch you at a bad time?" her sister asked.

"Nope. Just on a break," she lied, unwilling for her sister to know just how much she was dragging. "What's up?"

"Oh, okay. I'll keep this quick, then. I wanted to ask you a favor. Well, two favors, really."

"Shoot."

"So I wanted to know if you'd stand up for me, at the wedding. I asked April, too."

May was surprised, but she wasn't sure why. Sisters as bridesmaids? It was such a conventional move, and yet Junie wasn't nostalgic. She hadn't even kept her name. Wasn't there someone else by now she'd rather have with her on the big day—a friend, a teammate, a soul sister? May's track record as a bridesmaid was less than stellar, as April could attest.

"Do I have to wear one of those dresses?" she asked.

"God no. Wear whatever you want. But about that…"

"Yeah?"

"Mom wants us all to go shopping together for me. Tomorrow. I'm driving down to Baltimore. I know it's last minute."

"Dude. That's not really my area. And I'm working tomorrow." She wasn't, but the last place she wanted to be was at a bridal salon with her family when they were keeping a huge secret from their pit bull of a mother. Not now, but honestly, not ever.

"Right. Of course," Juniper said quickly. "But you'll stand up for me?"

"I said I would," May said. It was only later that she realized she actually hadn't.

★ ★ ★

Despite her best judgment, May opened up her laptop and dove down the internet rabbit hole, searching for an explanation for what April had seen. She studied street view Google maps of Dubrovnik, half expecting to find her dad sitting at a sidewalk café, an arrow pointed straight at him, half knowing she'd never see him again. She pored over regional maps and UN reports, trying to understand what calculus of migration could lead, over land or water, from the Middle East to the Balkans. For every fact she learned, she had to extrapolate backward into a decade's worth of chaos—before the surge of troops and the New Way Forward in Iraq; before Baghdad became the Green Zone and the old way forward meant hanging a mission-accomplished banner from the bridge of an aircraft carrier; before she drove her father to the airport for the flight to Kuwait City, the first leg in his journey to Iraq. She'd made a special trip home from school that spring so she could be the one to take him. The man she'd kissed goodbye at curbside check-in was dressed in jeans, a golf shirt, and that Princeton baseball cap, chuffed that Junie was Ivy-bound in the fall. There was a sudoku book in the outside pocket of his carry-on. "Change your oil," he'd told her. "Yeah, yeah, Grandpa," she'd said back, and he'd chuckled and pulled her in close. If she'd known what was coming, she never would've let go.

She'd been sure he was dead. She still was, mostly. Ten years without word from him, ten years without answers. Who took him? Why? And the hardest question to answer: how could she go on without him?

She hadn't, really. She hadn't traveled or acquired another language, hadn't learned to throw pots or axes or herself out of airplanes. Each day had followed the one before it, May safe in her cocoon. Once upon a time she'd had a list of places she knew she would visit: the rock-cut tombs of Petra, Angkor Wat, Machu Picchu, Havana, the medina in Tangier.

She'd talked herself out of every great destination after her disastrous trip to Iraq.

Will was the only one she'd told she was going—her family would've freaked if they knew. Insurgents had entered Mosul over the summer, bombing a church, a bank, the police academy, and the university, and targeting Kurds, too. But what choice did she have? The Suits knew more than they were saying, and the investigation wasn't getting anywhere. In November 2004, her Iranian visa came through, so she bought a ticket to Tehran, where she showed the customs agent the offer letter for a job teaching English at the language institute, then hired the first in a series of drivers to take her the rest of the way. One delivered her to the border crossing at Bashmaq, where she got out and walked into Iraq. The next picked her up on the other side and dropped her at a hotel in Sulaymaniyah, where she got a few hours of sleep. From there she emailed Will the name of Adar, the last driver who'd take her the rest of the way to Mosul. She'd go to Camp Freedom, of course, but first she wanted to look around the city herself and investigate the bus station, where Frank was supposed to have been released.

The first two drivers had spoken only minimal English, but Adar was fluent, which was good because May spoke only the little Arabic she'd learned in the last few months, no Kurdish, no Farsi. In high school the choice to learn either French or Spanish had seemed character-defining; now she saw the decision for the false dichotomy it was. Adar was going to Mosul to visit his brother's widow and her children. May was headed there for "work," in case anyone asked, a contractor job with an IT provider. They drove through a countryside of rolling hills and grazing sheep, mountains in the distance. It was nothing like the scenes on the news: the faded opulence and ransacked bureaucracy of sunbaked Baghdad; dusty, bombed-out Fallujah. Her dad had been missing five months and she still hadn't cried yet.

Farmland gave way to flat desert, traffic grew thick, and they stopped for lunch in Erbil, the capital of Iraqi Kurdistan. Outside the café's door was the brisk commerce of the bazaar, a steady stream of pedestrians, and the ancient citadel, layers of history rising over the rest of the city. Some women wore hijab, some didn't. May kept her hair covered.

"It's hard to tell there's a war going on here," May said, still innocent of what was to come.

Adar smiled ruefully. "We are still in Kurdistan. It will be different when we leave."

When it all went to shit in Mosul a day later, April was the only person May called, her sister so furious with her they didn't talk for months. May went home to Aberdeen and stayed. Her plan to join the Peace Corps—abandoned. And Will—what was the point in stringing him along? They were so young, there's no way they could last now.

Her world had blown apart.

In the afternoon May went to the kitchen to find something to eat. She wasn't hungry, but she'd learned that if she didn't make herself eat something, she'd drag even more the next day and a vicious cycle would ensue. There wasn't a team of keepers to get her back up when she went down.

Nancy was home on a break. She stood at the counter with an army of amber bottles arranged before her, filling pill strips. May envied Nancy's ability to concentrate. If her mom knew what April had been up to in Dubrovnik, if she thought there was a chance her husband was still alive while she doted on another man, she'd be a wreck. There was no sense stirring up the woman's survivor's guilt over nothing. May and April didn't agree on much, but on that, at least, they did.

"You didn't go to work today?" Nancy asked.

"Tom can't fill his own pill strips?" May asked.

It was silly, Nancy and Tom maintaining separate houses when in every practical respect they were a couple, but Nancy didn't want her personal business out on the street. People in Aberdeen knew her as Frank's wife, and as long as he was missing, it was important to her that she be thought of as steadfast.

"You're not feeling sick are you?" Nancy asked. "We've got to help Junie find a dress tomorrow."

"Oh, I'm not coming."

"You absolutely are."

"I already told Junie. I have to work."

"And yet you didn't go in today? No, you just tell your boss your sister needs you. Or call in sick again, if you have to."

"Mom—"

"You're coming. End of story."

May poured herself a bowl of cereal and shuffled back to her lair.

Some hours later (who could say?) the doorbell rang and May jumped. She was long past the point in the LED-illuminated darkness when she'd stopped learning anything useful on her laptop and was just retracing the same paranoid circles in her brain.

Will. *Shit*, their date. He'd offered to pick her up, ever the gentleman, and here she was still in boxers and a sweatshirt with holes in the wrists. May quickly changed into a pair of jeans and a T-shirt and brushed her teeth lightning-fast (her mother would not approve).

"Hey," she said at the door, trying not to sound out of breath. Too late she realized she'd forgotten a bra.

"Hey." Will was dressed casually, too, jeans and a white T-shirt, his hair just the right length for his wavy curls. Next week he'd look like a frizzy mop, but not today. He looked down, knocked one heel against the other like he was shaking mud off his shoes. He ran his hand through his hair. Then he looked up. "Can you go for a drive?" he asked.

And in a heartbeat it was ten years ago. They were standing in this same spot, a couple weeks after Frank was taken, and Will, who'd driven up from school to check on her, was asking her to go for a walk or a drive. *Whatever you need*, he said, and she said, *I need to be here.* It was months before she left for Iraq. The FBI had just come on the case, and it was still early enough in the nightmare for the family to believe, foolishly, falsely, that this would help. Only Junie, lingering behind May in the foyer, thought to offer Will a glass of water. May realized how dark it was inside the house. Nancy appeared from her bedroom. Dear God, she'd gotten thin, she was wasting away. *Go*, Nancy said. *We'll come find you if there's any news.* May and Will walked to the elementary school and he pushed her on the swings. She hated him seeing her like that, a shell of herself.

"May?" Will asked now, summoning her back to herself.

"There's somewhere I want to take you," she said, hoping to replace that memory with better ones.

Just south of Aberdeen, on the Bird River, was the little blue house where May's father had grown up. It was the first in a row of cottages that fronted a natural area, on the other side of which was an inlet of the Chesapeake Bay. Her grandmother had lived here until she had her stroke. It was the kind of place you kept in the family, if you could, but when Frank lost his job, it was the first thing they sold, for not very much money. It wouldn't have even covered the ransom.

"I used to spend my summers here, with my sisters and our grandmother," May said as they pulled up outside.

"Chasing fireflies or boys?" Will asked.

"Both."

He smiled, and he didn't have to say it, she knew what he was thinking: *Mayhem.* She *was* pure chaos back then. She and April left the house each morning, barefoot, unbathed except for dunks in the river, with a couple of PB&Js each that were wrapped in wax paper. They ate them down at the put-in, May shoving both sandwiches in her face right away, April responsibly saving one for later and then giving it away anyway, as soon as the Harveys showed, those curfew-less twins who rode dirt bikes and broke bones and shoplifted candy bars and kissed girls. Summer was when May learned everything her dad couldn't teach her. It was the only time she and April got along.

May got out of the car now and stared up the block at the Harvey house. It was nearly unrecognizable in its present incarnation, new shutters and a fresh coat of paint, the grass mown, a rental sign out front. Her grandmother's house had gone in the other direction. Weedy and cobwebby, it looked uninhabited. May walked up the porch steps and peeked in the front door. The furniture was draped in cloth.

She sat at the top of the steps. Will joined her.

"You okay?" he asked.

"It's my dad."

She gave him the highlights. It was like describing an apocalyptic blockbuster. None of it felt real.

"I thought I knew him better than anyone did. Maybe I didn't know the first thing."

"I wish I'd really gotten to know him. I thought there'd be time," he said.

Time, because they all thought Frank would come home when his contract was up, or time, because Will hadn't seen their breakup coming? There was no denying the cloud hanging over them. May had never given Will closure. She simply hadn't been able to when she returned from Iraq, her dreams of finding her father dashed. Maybe that had been the simplest part of her excitement at reconnecting with Will, the fantasy that they could pick up right where they'd left off, that she'd never have to explain to him why her feelings had shut off so quickly then. But they would have to have that talk. Eventually.

"He liked you. You're the only guy I dated he couldn't find any fault with."

She'd introduced Will to her parents at her college graduation. They were still just friends then, or she would've been more nervous, probably would've avoided the meeting altogether. They'd stood around in a clump after the ceremony, Nancy cornering Will's parents, Frank cornering Will, their sisters and brothers yawning and wondering how much longer until they could go to the Olive Garden.

"I think I snuck by on a technicality," Will said. "But, I mean, I get it. Nobody's good enough for your little girl."

Normally May hated that saying—how was a woman supposed to feel, hearing that, except like chattel or a chaste appendage to the patriarch?—but instead she felt swooped up by everything Will felt for Zoe. He was invested, attentive, a hands-on dad, just like Frank had been. Zoe was lucky to have him.

"This road goes all the way down to the put-in. We used to have picnics there. Do you want to flop for a while?" she asked.

"I'm all yours," he said.

Something inside May loosened, like a corset coming undone. *Oh, right*, she remembered. *Breathe, you jerk.* One of the more humiliating truths of the last ten years was that she could go for days, weeks even, in hold-your-breath mode, wait-for-the-other-shoe-to-drop mode, never-know-for-sure-if-your-dad-is-okay mode, and have no idea she was doing it. Her poor fucking diaphragm.

"One sec," Will said as they reached the street. He took a blanket out of his trunk, the kind that folded up neatly with a Velcro tie, that some families brought to the beach or a summer concert or to watch fireworks on the Mall.

"You're such a dad," May said, and he didn't blush, just shrugged. She understood then that she could only tease him so far on this point, that it made her foolish, not him. Will *was* a dad. It wasn't an extraordinary act of foresight that he had a stain-proof blanket in the trunk of his car, it was just who he was now.

They walked along a lane that led away from the street, over a rise, and down to the river. The water lapped against a small floating dock, and the seagrass crawling up the bank was every shade of spring—harlequin, mantis, celadon, chartreuse, mint, jade green.

Will spread the blanket amid the tall grass, tamping it down heroically, then gestured to it. *After you.* She sat cross-legged and he flopped beside her, stretching out on his back. He put one arm out and patted his shoulder.

She lay back and curled up against him. "Do you want to be my date for my sister's wedding next month?"

"Yes," he said. With his free hand, he combed her hair off her face, her ear, her neck.

She could hear his heart beat through his shirt, a little fast at first, then slowing with the tides. She closed her eyes, all the times she'd drowsed on his chest before tugging her, finally, toward sleep.

When she woke, the building twilight told her that some amount of time had passed. She'd drooled a bit on his shirt.

Will didn't seem to mind. His eyes were closed, but he was smiling. He opened them and looked down at her. "There's no one around," he said. "I mean, not a soul."

She sat up on her elbow and stared down at him now. "Are you gonna murder me?" she asked.

"Are *you*?" he said, looking up at her with certainty, as if whatever she offered now—a little kiss, a little death—was exactly what he'd always expected.

She straddled him. "Just a little bit," she said, lifting off her shirt, the evening air bringing out her nipples. "But I promise it won't hurt."

11

Juniper

It wasn't Juniper's fault she was late to the bridal shop; it was Mac's. At last the call had come with good news, red meat to throw to Nancy when Juniper finally arrived: the field module had been a success and she'd been invited to join the Princeton Athletic Director and the rest of the hiring committee next month for a formal discussion of the women's soccer head coaching position. Afterward Mac would take her to lunch at the Faculty Club, the same room where she'd dine with her guests at her wedding reception a week later.

"It's a lot of responsibility, Barber. You ready?" Mac asked over the phone.

"*Coach.*"

Hadn't she always been a loyal alum, putting on her orange-striped shirt and making the pilgrimage back every June for Reunions? Hadn't she been the program's most vocal ambassador, crediting Mac's coaching philosophy for turning her into the coach she was today? Look at her record, championships three years running.

"No one's going to hand this to you, you're gonna have to earn it. Just be yourself. Do the work—"

"And show up," Juniper said.

Mac laughed. "Took the words right out of my mouth."

Given her fear of public speaking, Juniper would need to prep for the interview carefully, but first, alas, she needed to find something to wear for the wedding.

Hana was the only person who understood, in the universe of apparel Juniper would feel comfortable in, what would also look good on her. She had already chosen her own ensemble, without Juniper's help, and it hung safe from prying eyes in the guest room at her parents' house. But she wasn't coming today because *tradition*.

This left Nancy and April to advise. Juniper wasn't optimistic. They were always so put together, Nancy in her sweater sets, April in her corporate power suits; meanwhile everything Juniper owned came from Adidas and Old Navy. Fariha was just as clueless; on special occasions she wore whatever Maryam instructed, but at least she'd be there for emotional support.

Juniper wasn't just daunted; she was exhausted, too. The nightmares were back with a vengeance, a recurring one she'd had since college. In the dream her family was gathering—usually in Aberdeen, sometimes on campus, sometimes at the airport. They'd finally gotten the call: Frank was alive and on his way home! Nancy laughed the way she used to, with her entire body. April and May hugged each other like they never had. July was a pogo stick in boy form. Juniper was quiet, but she couldn't wait to see her father.

They converged in the driveway, or at the door, or on the tarmac. At first Frank was just an outline, and they all crowded in to get a better look. Then the outline began to fill in, and for reasons she couldn't articulate, Juniper felt afraid. She stepped back, away from her family, away from her father. Disappointment was written across her siblings' foreheads. "How could you?" Nancy asked. The family tribunal parted to reveal her father, walking toward her. Technically he was smiling, but his face was a rictus of teeth. Panic gripped Juniper by the throat. She had to get away, get out of there before he grabbed her and—

She'd woken up sobbing after the first one. Freshman year.

"What?" Hana had asked. "Baby, what happened?"

But how could Juniper tell her that for a moment, even a false one, she'd been afraid of her own father? Or that she couldn't remember his real smile anymore, only the clown grimace?

She'd unpacked it a little with the shrink Hana found, but talking about herself with a stranger wasn't for her. She knew that dreams were just symbols, that recurring nightmares were part and parcel of grief, that they happened whether you were stressed in your day-to-day life or basically doing fine, so you couldn't use them as any kind of indicator of emotional growth. They came and they went. But it still felt like a personal failing.

Now the dream was back. She'd had it every night since she'd picked April up from the airport. Sometimes she couldn't get away in time. Her dad, or the form of him, grabbed her by the arm and she could see that he wasn't smiling after all, he was screaming.

When she arrived at the bridal salon, Juniper was expecting their mom to be in one of her moods—as a woman whose professional life was booked in fifteen-minute blocks, Nancy detested lateness—but she'd gone into army-general mode instead. She'd commandeered a salesperson who'd set them up with a large fitting room and flutes of champagne. She'd toured the racks and sent the salesperson to the back of the store for a selection of dresses, which now hung in a row in huge plastic bags along the fitting room wall. April and Fariha—and hold up, May, too?— had been waiting for Juniper in the fitting room.

"Whoa," she said, hugging May first. "I thought you had to work?"

"Boss lady thought otherwise," May said.

"Har-har. Junie, I told Serena here you're not into anything fussy," Nancy said. "These are all classic looks—mermaid, A-line, tea-length, trumpet, column; I knew you wouldn't want a ball gown—and we'll just see what you like and what you don't."

Mermaid? Juniper thought. *Does it come with fins?*

"Chin-chin," Fariha said, offering Juniper some bubbly.

They all put their glasses in, April clinking hers without glancing up from her Blackberry. May took a quick sip and then set her glass on the floor, a distracted expression on her face.

"Shall we get started?" Serena asked, sliding the curtain across the opening between the fitting room and the salon.

Too late Juniper remembered she was wearing her period underwear. A sports bra wasn't the best choice, either; she'd have to take it off. "Um, yeah. These look great. Beautiful, I mean. But do you have anything less...big?"

Serena scrunched up her lips on one side of her face.

"Let's just start with these, Junie," her mom cooed. "And then we'll see where we are." It was the same soft voice she'd once used when Juniper had had a fever or gotten into a fight with one of her friends.

"I just started working here. You're my first official client," Serena said as she reached for Juniper's champagne flute.

Juniper downed it and handed it over.

"Yay, fun!" Serena said. "Okay, let's do this!"

What Juniper learned about mermaid dresses is that they were all wrong for her.

"You've got the body for it, actually," Fariha said, and then she took a picture with her phone.

"Don't post that," Juniper ordered. What was even the point of hips this big? She looked like Jessica Rabbit.

April shook her head once, rejecting the dress with brutal efficiency. May seemed uncomfortable, like she'd rather be anywhere but here.

"I agree," their mom said to Fariha, failing to read the room. "You look beautiful. I wish I'd had your figure at your age."

All Nancy wanted was to have fun with her daughters, and Juniper wanted to give her that, but it was hard when they were all lying to her. Who cared about wedding dresses when their dad could be alive?

April thumbed at her Blackberry. May bounced her knee and frowned. Juniper felt six years old all over again, begging for their attention. Except this time she wasn't going to.

"You guys can go if you want. This is clearly not working." She pointed to her hips (surely they would knock drinks off tables) and her tits, which were spilling out the top of the dress.

"Nonsense!" Nancy said. "We just haven't found the right one yet. Remember when we went shopping for your dress, April? Plenty of nice gowns, but when we found The One, we all just knew. Oh, you were so gorgeous. And you will, too, Junie. Can't give up!"

Juniper remembered that day. She'd been fourteen at the time, sitting in a chair out in the salon, reading one of the *Earthsea* books. She couldn't tell what all the fuss over weddings was about. So many racks of dresses, and you couldn't even go anywhere if you pushed through them, no Mr. Tumnus waiting for you on the other side.

Nancy pawed through the upcoming dresses in the queue while Serena liberated Juniper from the current one.

Also all wrong for her: anything strapless (too naked) or plunging (same); anything with lace (too virginal); satin (too Hollywood); tulle (too much).

She finished the champagne.

"I think we have some jumpsuits. Let me go check," Serena said, her expression somehow both desperate and optimistic.

"Can we get another bottle, too?" Juniper asked.

"None for me," May said.

"Maybe something with a bolero jacket," Nancy said, following Serena out of the fitting room.

"Oh, sweet Jesus," Juniper said.

"What if you have something made?" Fariha said.

"It's too late for that," April said. "Quick, while Mom's gone. I heard from Leyla."

Juniper could tell by the pinch of her sister's eyebrows that Leyla was one of the Suits. "Which one was she again?"

May jerked her head in surprise, like she couldn't believe this had to be explained. "The woman?"

"Oh, right," April said, "she came on the case after you left for school. Anyway, she talked to the consulate in Dubrovnik."

Juniper took May's abandoned glass and finished it.

"I was ready for her to tell me this was all just stray voltage," April said, pulling the curtain back to check on their mom.

Fariha's face went slack in confusion. But why would she understand any of this? *We must sound like Martians*, Juniper thought.

"Stray voltage are leads that will probably turn out to be nothing," Juniper said. She'd told Fariha about the family meeting, but not in great detail. "That's what the Suits used to call them. Huh. You'd think I'd remember a girl in a suit. What kind of lesbian am I?"

"This is a waste of time," May said. Juniper didn't know if she meant the meeting with Leyla, the trip to the bridal salon, or both.

"That's just it. It wasn't. They looked again at the dates Mom and I were in Dubrovnik and they got a hit. Someone who was traveling on Tariq Ibrahim's passport entered Kosovo and Croatia last month."

"Oh, shit," Juniper said. Tariq had been her father's interpreter.

April coughed. Nancy and Serena were on their way back.

"We found more options!" Nancy called out from behind

Serena, who entered with yet another armload of outfits. "I'm sure one of these will work."

Her mom was being so nice. It made her feel like shit.

"You got a tutu in there? Let's stuff me into one of those."

Nancy had also scored a second bottle of champagne.

"Oh, good," Juniper said. She took the bottle and unwrapped the wire cage over the cork while Serena muscled the hangers onto hooks.

"You think you should slow down a bit?" May asked.

Fariha pointed at the doorway. "Away from the dresses."

"Right." Juniper let the cork fly. The bubbly came up out of the bottle's neck. She opened her mouth to catch as much as she could.

"Shit," said Serena, protecting the gowns with her body.

"No problem, no problem, I got it," Juniper said, wiping her chin.

"You need a belt with this one," Serena said.

They were well into the double digits of dresses at this point and still Juniper couldn't tell an A-line from a bias-cut sheath. She was never getting a divorce and she was never getting re-married and she was never shopping for another fucking wedding dress. But she liked belts. Belts she understood. She wore a brown belt with her cargo pants.

She wiggled into the accompanying jumpsuit, which gave her camel toe. From the garment bag, Serena withdrew some sort of bedazzled, befeathered choke chain. If that was a belt, then Juniper was fucked. Serena nudged Juniper's elbows up and reached both ends of the "belt" around her waist, cinching it closed via magic. Juniper stepped into the sample heels they'd given her. She felt ridiculous and tall, like an ostrich at a gathering of swallows. Light-headed, too. She felt like a tall, light-headed liar. She needed to sit, but all the seats—white, tufted, poofy things—were taken.

She plopped down on the floor.

"Oh. Okay," Serena said. "You need a little break?"

"Junie, what's wrong?" Nancy asked. "Are you tired? Do you need to eat?"

"It's not that. It's this fucking situation."

"The wedding planning's getting to her," April said, shooting Juniper a warning look. *Keep your mouth shut* is what that look meant.

"I'll give you a few minutes," Serena said and went out to the salon.

Nancy left her poof and crouched in front of June. She tucked the strays from her daughter's ponytail behind her ears. "Hang in there, honey. We'll find you the right dress. Or maybe a suit? This just isn't the right store. We'll find a better one next time."

The duality of the word *suit* made Juniper laugh. A formal ensemble or a government official—either one made her want to run. Her face fell. It wasn't funny. It wasn't funny at all.

"It's not the clothes. It's…just… I can't stand watching everyone get their hopes up for nothing."

"Getting their hopes up about what?" Nancy asked. "What are you talking about?"

"June—" April said.

"About Dad."

Nancy looked to April, then May. "What's she talking about?"

"Fucking great, June," April said.

May put her head in her hands. Fariha disappeared into the curtain in an attempt to grant the family some privacy.

Nancy grabbed Juniper's knees to stop them bouncing. She'd never been able to keep a secret from her mother. Only the physical distance between them had made that possible and now there was none.

Juniper's voice was small. "April saw a man who looked like Dad. In Croatia, on your trip."

Nancy let go and pushed herself up. Then she sank onto her ottoman. "When? Why didn't you say anything?"

"In Dubrovnik," April answered. "I didn't want to upset you."

"What did he look like?" Nancy was staring at a spot on the wall, as if she were standing on one leg and needed a focal point to keep upright.

"Like Dad," April said softly.

"Like Dad how?"

"Tall. About his build. Bowlegged. And he really hustled, too, the way Dad would when he was running late?"

Nancy blinked a few times. "Could be anyone," she said at last.

"The hat," Juniper said.

"What?" Her mom's gaze lurched up.

Juniper felt her tongue go thick. Her cheeks began to sting. "Tell her about the hat," she mumbled.

"Goddammit, will you girls just tell me everything? All of it."

"He was wearing a Princeton baseball cap," April said.

"I don't understand. Croatia? Your father's never been there. Why would he go to Croatia?" She was getting shrill now, and why not?

"We don't know. But the Croatian consulate has Dad's interpreter passing through customs in Dubrovnik at the same time."

"Oh," Nancy said quietly.

Watching her mother absorb this, Juniper finally let it sink in, too. Now that there was proof one of the hostages was in Dubrovnik, it was harder to write off what April had seen as a hallucination, no matter what May might say.

Nancy took in a gulp of air and then another. She was doing that thing Juniper sometimes did, when she forgot that inhaling and exhaling were coupled and that to catch her breath she had to release it first.

"You're awfully quiet," Nancy said to May on the ottoman beside her. "What do you think about all this?"

May lifted up her hands to show they were empty, that she was grasping at nothing.

"I need some air," Nancy said, leaving the changing room. They heard the bells on the shop door jingle.

April poked her head out of the fitting room, bumping into Fariha, who said, "Sorry, sorry."

"She's on the sidewalk," April said. "She's pacing. Fucking A, Juniper. Fucking A."

Juniper was relieved the secret was out, but felt weak for revealing it. She hadn't done it on principle. The pressure of holding it in had simply been too great.

"You're drunk," May said, and Juniper couldn't deny it.

"Hey, Juniper?" Fariha asked, stepping out from her hiding place in the curtains. "You remember that speech Mo gave on Monday? The one the Islamic Community Center hosted?"

Juniper couldn't keep all of Mo's events straight anymore, but she remembered Fariha had left practice early for it.

"There was a reception beforehand, and the guy I talked to was a diplomat. Iraqi. Kurdish."

"He works at the embassy?" April asked, turning around.

"I guess so. In Dupont Circle?"

"That's it."

"Do you want me to find out if he'll talk to you guys? I'm happy to ask. Nura seemed pretty friendly with his wife. But maybe it would just be more...stray voltage." Nura was Mo's wife, and though she was naturally more introverted than he was, she did a good job of connecting with the women at his campaign stops.

"No, no. That'd be awesome," April said. "I'm gonna go check on Mom."

April left the changing room, and May stood up. "We're done

here, right? They're not coming back. Nice to meet you," she said to Fariha and left.

"See you around," Juniper said from the floor. What a stupid thing to say. *See you at my wedding!* Juniper felt like adding, or maybe *see you never!*

Fariha smiled at her. It was just the two of them and a rack of dresses and jumpsuits.

Juniper fingered the feathered belt dangling in her lap. "Who am I, Cher?" She felt sick on adrenaline, the way she did at the state fair when the operator pushed the button to start the ride, and it was too late to back out, and all she could do was let herself be lifted up higher than she wanted to go, faster than she wanted to circle, around and around, closing her eyes, trying not to puke. Maybe now Fariha could understand why the Barbers were nothing like the Monsours. She hated it when her worlds mixed like this, which was why she made sure they rarely did.

Fariha put out her hand, and Juniper grabbed it. "All right, Barber. Up. Let's get this jumpsuit off and get the fuck out of here."

Hana found Juniper in the living room that night at three a.m., tapping golf balls across the carpet into a plastic cup.

"Another bad dream?" she asked, standing in a T-shirt and panties.

Juniper nodded. The nightmares weren't just archetypes anymore, imagined family encounters ruined by her betrayal. Now they were destroying her lived memories. Tonight her father came for her at an Orioles game, a month after the planes hit the towers, when they'd watched Cal Ripken Jr. play for the last time.

"How long've you been up?" Hana asked.

"A couple hours?"

Hana spotted the glass of Baileys on the coffee table and stared a beat too long. It was warm and milky, good for insomnia, or that had been Juniper's reasoning. The first few nights after the nightmares returned, Hana had mixed the drinks herself, but lately she'd been urging Juniper to try more holistic methods. Yoga. A warm bath. Cherry juice with valerian root extract.

Juniper handed over the club. Hana lined up the putt and sank it.

"I told my mom about Dad."

"Good," Hana said. "She should know."

Juniper shrugged. "Maybe ignorance is bliss."

"It's ten years next month, right?" Hana asked. "Since he was taken?"

"Yeah. Happy anniversary."

"What was the actual date? Oh, God—"

"No, it was the twentieth."

The wedding would be on the fourteenth. Not the exact date of the kidnapping, but close enough. Every June was hard, but this one would be totally bizarre. She should've thought about it when they were choosing the date, but they'd been lucky to book the Faculty Club at all. And she'd assumed everything would work out for the best instead of preparing for the worst, like she should have.

Juniper rolled the cupful of balls to Hana, who plinked them one by one back into the cup. Anything Hana could do with her hands—blocking shots with her fists, cracking eggs with one hand, wrapping presents, putting up shelves, giving foot rubs—she aced.

"You think he would've liked me?" Hana asked.

"He would've loved you."

"Yeah?"

"Yeah."

Juniper pictured how it would've been if he'd never gone away: him driving the two of them to dinner after their games, Hana riding shotgun, Juniper in the back seat, shutting her eyes and half listening to their conversations. He and Hana would have had so much in common, like soccer, and chemistry, which they both studied, and Juniper, of course. Who knows what else?

"How much?" Hana asked. "Like, favorite son-in-law status? More than Ross?"

"More than me, even."

Hana's smile transformed into a yawn. When she was sleepy, she looked like a bunny, squinty and soft-cheeked.

There was something lovely, but also stingy and lopsided and desperately sad, about the place they saved for Juniper's ghost dad, when Hana's dad's was so hearty and real. Ahmed was going to be the best father-in-law, but Frank would've been, too. He never would've let an estrangement take root in his family, and it was hard to believe that Ahmed ever had.

"What did your dad mean, at the engagement party, when he said I'd given him his daughter back?" Juniper asked.

"Oh. Well, it's probably true that I'm closer with my family since I met you."

"What are you talking about? They already came to all your games."

"Not *all* of them."

Juniper frowned, hand on her hip, calling bullshit. "A lot."

"Okay fine. But my love life, I always kept that stuff secret— well, not secret, but separate from them." Juniper knew Fariha did this, too, saying little to her family about the dates she went on, categorizing them as *nothing serious*, as if it were a requirement that she be serious about someone in order to confide in her parents about her feelings for a woman. It couldn't have been easy for her to skirt the subject as elegantly as she did, although she didn't date as much as Hana had in her heyday. She didn't seem to need the wholly double life. "I never brought a girl home before you. Never wanted to. You already know all of this."

Yeah, but why? Juniper wondered. Because she was such a special person? She knew that wasn't it. She wasn't Mother Teresa. She was a regular person with the same needs and petty contraditions as anyone else, just with a tragic backstory. She was sure the tragedy was part of it.

"When it changed for you, was it because of my dad?"

Hana squinted like a bunny in trouble. "Kinda?"

Juniper didn't know whether to be shocked or upset, vindicated or seen.

"I realized how lucky I was to even have a choice about whether to let my parents know that side of me. And I'd been making the wrong one. I wanted them to get to know the woman I was falling for. They love you so much, babe."

"I know. I love them, too. All of them—even Mo."

Hana laughed.

"You called him Dad," she said. "The man in Dubrovnik— you called him Dad."

"I did?"

"You really think it's him?"

Juniper felt her eyes fill with tears. "I want it to be."

Hana dropped the club and put her arms around her. "I do, too."

"Look at me. The smallest whiff of what might be good news, and I'm a mess. I'm not normal."

"There's no normal for this."

"I wish he'd never gone to Iraq. But if he hadn't, I never would've met you."

"I hate that stupid war. I wish politicians had to think about all the families who were gonna get hurt, here and over there, before they let the military industrial complex paint all these best-case scenarios and hang people out to dry. Not to mention—"

"What?"

"Forget it." Hana took her hand and tried to lead Juniper toward the stairs. "Come back to bed. Let's try that meditation app again."

But Juniper needed her to finish that sentence. She wouldn't get back to sleep now, anyway. "What were you going to say?"

Hana exhaled and sat on the edge of the sofa. She was still holding Juniper's hand.

"If it is your dad, and he comes home…"

"Yeah?"

"I mean, it'll be so incredible. It'll be amazing. But I can't help thinking that somehow, it's going to blow back on us. My family."

Juniper hadn't thought about that. "Mo's campaign." The other side was already running ugly political ads against him.

"Maybe if we were Christians, it would be easier. It's already a small enough needle he has to thread: brown but not *too* brown; believes in a higher power but not Sharia law; hates Islamic fundamentalists as much as every other red-blooded American, maybe more. But you know how jingoistic this country can be."

"Yeah." Hana never let Frank's participation in the war effort be a wedge between them, but Juniper sometimes felt sheepish about it, culpable. If they hadn't met when and how they did—with soccer as their common purpose and the aphrodisiac that drew them together—she wondered whether Hana could've looked past it.

"If your dad is released, he'll be a hero, but the Muslims in his life will be suspect. Did we know his kidnappers? Are we back-channeling with terrorists? How dare we get so close to Frank Barber. How dare we corrupt him with our hateful ideology. Once the other side gets a hold of the story…it's just so easy to imagine the spin they'll put on it. And we'll be targets."

Juniper could hear the ratcheted-up rhetoric now. *Born in the Middle East. A friend to terrorists. Mohammed Monsour is too dangerous for Pennsylvania.* They would blanket the airwaves. Mo would lose the election in a landslide—running as a Democrat in a conservative district, he might anyway, but Hana and her family and so many of their friends would be frightened or worse. And for what? Because an American came home from the war?

"I'm so sorry. I'm sure it won't come to that," Juniper said, not because Hana was wrong about America but because, until they had something more solid to go on, she had to keep telling herself this was all just stray voltage.

12

July

July tried not to bring the stress of the news about his dad back with him to campus. For two weeks he'd been keeping his head down, going on long runs in the morning, staying late at the library to study for finals, all of it with his headphones in, trying to keep it flawless the way Beyoncé would've wanted him to. *I woke up like this*, he wanted to say with unfettered swagger, but he just couldn't. He was miserable. The dad-sighting was too much to carry himself, and he had no one to talk to. He was still too pissed at his mom and his sisters. Why had no one said anything to him about the ransom? Did they think he couldn't handle it? That he didn't deserve to know? What he needed was a friend to confide in, preferably one he hadn't been in love with for two years, whose pity he feared more than his indifference.

July had first spotted Lucas in the dining hall the second morning of freshman orientation, sitting at a table by the window with his *Washington Post* and his coffee. *He's a news junkie, too*, he'd thought. That afternoon they were assigned to the same scavenger hunt team, and it had felt so natural, lagging behind the search to talk about the election. Neither of them really thought the bump in Romney's polling numbers would survive the Democratic convention in a few weeks, but July admitted it was nerve-racking, waiting and seeing.

"Sure it is," Lucas said. "Especially for someone like you."

"What, neurotic?"

"No, gay."

So there it was, no need for July to put it out on the table because Lucas had already worked it all out. Was it that obvious? Apparently it was. One of them was gay, and the other was not. Still, July felt like he'd been pushed from a plane and was scrambling to find the rip cord.

"You are, right? Oh, shit, should I have waited to let you tell me?" Lucas asked.

"No," July said, willing himself to chill. "It's fine. You're right. I'm gay."

"Cool," Lucas said, nodding several times, and July wondered whether he might go on forever like that, like a bobblehead doll on a dashboard. "I've got Xbox?"

There'd been a handful of confusing moments over the last two years that had given him hope this friendship might tip over into something physical—a hesitation, a brush of skin, a lingering gaze that could have been dismissed with a laugh but wasn't. But he'd also had to ask himself many times if he was fooling himself, if he'd read more than there was into that confusion, projected feelings onto Lucas that were his alone.

Hence Oxford. He would have gone abroad a semester sooner if he could have, but he was missing some prereqs, so junior year it would have to be.

Right now he didn't need an unrequited crush, he needed someone to listen. But what if he told Lucas about his dad and it changed everything? He couldn't bear it if Lucas got that panicked look in his eyes that people usually got, the one that meant they had no clue how to address the issue emotionally or even politically and only felt put on the spot. The school year was almost over, and there'd be no time to normalize again before they moved out of the dorms, Lucas into his new apartment, July back home for the summer and then off to England in the fall. Their friendship would calcify in Strangeland, in Awkward-ville, in Nice-Knowing-You Town.

Would it be chickening out or would it be practicing if he told Hazel first? He took the elevator up to the eighth floor and tried her door.

"Duuuuuude," she said, after July told her everything. Then she climbed across the couch and hugged him. "Can I ask you a question?"

She pulled away and sat back on her heels.

"Sure."

"What's the story you've been telling yourself all this time? About your dad? I mean, when you were ten, were you old enough to understand or did you still believe in, you know, magic?"

Something that was knotted up inside untangled itself, just as it had with Nate at lunch the day before the family meeting. Keeping all of this at bay, being the guy without the tragic past—it had seemed like a good idea, but it wasn't.

"The hard part was figuring out what they did with him. He was a big guy, or at least he always seemed that way to me, so—wow, I haven't told anyone this. I guess I always figured he did get away, but the reason he hadn't come home was he was stuck in another world—this, like, lawless dimension. And probably he had to earn his way out, like Odysseus, and by the time he got home, we would all be older, maybe some of us would be dead, some of us wouldn't recognize him, and he'd be…just… himself. Worn out and hardened and super taciturn from not having had any close relationships in so long, like Tom Hanks in *Cast Away*, but basically, still him on the inside. Still my dad."

"Oh, sweetie."

"Yeah."

They were quiet for a minute.

"But I knew, obviously, that I couldn't tell anyone that. You get a room with that many adults in it, all whispering, and you know it's bad. Then my mom started dating my dentist."

"Were you mad at her?"

"I guess? But it didn't feel like I could be. I mean, she's not heartless. It's more like, her dating again told me what's what. Like, oh, shit, he's really not coming back. I wish they'd just given it to me straight: Hey, we gave those fuckers fifty-thousand dollars and they still didn't give him back. So now it's gone and so is he."

"Unless he isn't."

July shook his head.

"You can't go there?" Hazel asked.

"It's just a lot to process."

There was a knock on the door then. Hazel scrambled up.

"I'll get rid of them."

But when she opened the door, Lucas was there.

"Hey," she said.

"Hey."

"You looking for July?" she asked and Lucas, seeing July inside, said again, "Hey."

"Come on in," Hazel said. "We'll tell you all about it."

"All about what?" Lucas asked. He came in and shut the door. July wondered how Lucas had known where to find him.

"July's dad. Or his doppelganger. Or whoever this dude is, marching around Croatia and causing a lot of people a lot of grief."

Lucas furrowed his forehead and the warm and open expression on Hazel's face dissolved in confusion. She glanced from Lucas to July, her mouth frozen in an O, unable to put words to what she now understood.

"He doesn't know," July said. "Ironic, right? That I'm the biggest secret keeper of all?"

"Tell him," Hazel said.

Lucas cocked his head. "Tell me."

For five minutes afterward Lucas seemed like a deer in head-lights, and July feared the worst. Hazel took that moment to make them cinnamon tea, which somehow added to the feel-ing that something traumatic had transpired.

When she placed the warm mug in his hands, Lucas spoke. "#FreeFrankBarber is your *dad*? Man. That's fucking crazy."

"Right?" Hazel said. She held up her pinch hitter in an of-fering.

Lucas raised his eyebrows at July as if to say, *Need some? Go right ahead.* But July shook his head. He didn't want to be stoned for this.

Lucas waved off the joint, too. "Nah, I can't think when I smoke," he said. "Okay. Given: the simplest line of reasoning is that the kidnappers killed everyone right away, and they just took the ransom and ran. Right? We can all agree to that."

"Lucas," Hazel said, her tone shocked and protective, but July just said, "Agreed."

"All right, but let's assume, for a moment, that the guy your sister saw in Croatia really was your dad. Then the question be-comes, what happened to the ransom? It's not blood money any-more, it's operating expenses. So: what's the operation? That's question one. Question two is: what do they do with your dad? Do they keep him or trade him away? If they keep him, he's ex-pensive and he puts them at greater risk, so he needs to be worth their while. There were no more ransom demands after that?"

"Not that I know of."

"So that means he's useful to them in other ways, not just fundraising. You said he was a chemical engineer?"

"Yeah."

"Chemical agents, then. Weapons. If I lived in a war zone and I took someone who knew about that stuff, I'd probably think twice about giving him back. Unless, of course, they traded him to someone else."

"Wait. Like who?" Hazel asked.

"Another radical group with deeper pockets. The Mahdi Army, Ansar al-Islam, the Islamic Army, al-Qaeda in Iraq…"

"Fuuuuuck," she said.

It was dizzying the way Lucas's mind worked. July found it equal parts thrilling and nauseating.

Later they went downstairs and played *FIFA*, just to chill out their brains. Eventually Lucas shut off the game. The glow of the screen illuminated the cheekbones that had emerged like icebergs in the last year.

"Dude. I'm so fucking sorry. Why didn't you tell me sooner?"

July sighed. "I don't know."

"Is it because you didn't want to talk about it? Or did you want to talk about it and not think you could? With me?"

"Maybe both?"

It occurred to July that he'd been drawn to Lucas in part because of his emotional reserve, so they wouldn't have to be the kind of friends who told each other everything. July didn't have to tell Lucas anything he didn't want to—not this, and not how he really felt about him, either. Because he was pretty sure his feelings weren't reciprocated.

Except right then, Lucas dipped his shoulder into July's and nudged him.

"Hey," he said.

Lucas put his hand on July's leg and squeezed. Then he left it there.

"You can tell me anything. Okay? I want you to."

July couldn't think straight. He could only feel the hand on his thigh and wonder whether that was Lucas's pulse, throbbing through his fingertips, or his own rising up to meet it.

"Okay?" Lucas said again.

"Yeah. Okay."

He held his breath until Lucas lifted his hand, stood up, and left to brush his teeth.

When July woke the next morning, Lucas was standing at the wardrobe, having just tugged a pair of basketball shorts over the boxers he slept in. July sucked in his breath. Of course, it wasn't the first time he'd seen Lucas shirtless, but he usually tried not to stare, to act like a regular roommate who definitely was not attracted to him. There was a sort of star-shaped mole on Lucas's lower back, just above the waistband of his shorts, and July wanted desperately to kiss it.

Lucas took the towel off the hook on the door and turned around. July sat up and fumbled for his running shoes.

"What's your day like?" Lucas asked.

"I've got class, then work. Lunch in between?"

"I've got my study group, and I'll probably get dinner with them, too. Meet back here after?"

"Cool."

At the library that afternoon, July reshelved books for a while and then hid out in a corner to work on the final paper for his Nationalism seminar, but he couldn't make any headway. He'd decided over a month ago to write about the Balkans; now the timing seemed like a sick joke. The siege of Dubrovnik merited no more than a paragraph in the paper, which tracked events in Sarajevo more closely, but all he wanted to do was look at maps of the Old Town, with its 650 artillery hits, and photos showing the Stradun littered with rubble, the destroyed Inter-University Centre library, and the Hotel Libertas in flames. And though it had happened over twenty years ago and in the intervening years the Old Town had been rebuilt, the cityscape now pockmarked with bright new red-tiled roofs, some blurring of history and conflict was taking place in July's mind. He pictured his father walking seamlessly out of one war zone and into another, Princeton ball cap pulled down tight over his eyebrows, a survivor.

Maybe Hazel had said it best when she asked if July believed in magic. Because if he were honest with himself, he did believe April had seen their father.

At the end of his shift, his supervisor stopped him.

"Your sister's at the front desk."

"Which one?" July asked.

His supervisor stared back blankly.

"Never mind. Thanks."

It was April, dressed too casually for the office in a cotton sundress with spaghetti straps.

"Did you play hooky today?" he asked.

"Took the day off. I figured if the mountain won't come to Mohammed... Anyway, let's eat, mountain. I'm hungry."

He gave directions and she drove them to a nice restaurant in Hampden. He'd hoped to annoy her with such an expensive choice, but she seemed pleased, eager to feed him. As they walked inside, he remembered being guided across parking lots or down grocery store aisles when he was a little boy, one of his sisters steering him with her hand on his neck. He was too old and too tall for that now, but he felt the same watchful attention.

The host sat them at a table by the window. It was obvious April wanted to talk. He wondered whether she'd let him eat first and then lecture him or whether she'd pounce while his mouth was full. The waiter came and he ordered the steak frites. April said she'd have the same.

"I'm sorry," she said after the waiter had gone.

July didn't know what to say. The last thing he'd expected was an apology.

"The meeting at my house—I could have handled a lot of things better. I told you to buck up, but you were in shock. It wasn't fair of me. No wonder you stopped returning my calls."

"You think that's what I'm mad about?" July asked. "Your tone? I mean, sure, that, too. But I'm mostly sick of being lied to."

"I never lied to you..."

"What?"

"I left things out. Okay, big things."

"Essential things. And now we're keeping things from Mom."

"She knows. We told her at the bridal store."

"Oh." Their mom must have lost it. He could imagine it all—the flush of red breaking out across her neck, her voice jumping an octave in alarm. Juniper had texted him the address of the bridal shop and Nancy had left him a voice mail asking him to come—*pretty please, it'll be so much fun if we're all there*—but he'd still been too pissed to reply to either of them.

April caught him up on the latest development: Tariq Ibrahim's passport showing up in Dubrovnik.

"So it *was* Dad you saw, then."

"Looks like it."

"Wow," July said, too stunned to process. Did this mean he might get his dad back? That his belief in his father's survival hadn't just been magical thinking—Santa was real and all dogs go to heaven and his dad might actually come home one day?

"I'm sorry I didn't tell you about the ransom before. I didn't think you needed to know."

"Why would I? All it means is that we did everything the kidnappers asked. That there was a plan for Dad to be returned to us and it failed. Why would I need to know something like that?"

"I was trying to protect you. It was all so ambiguous. *Unbear-*

ably ambiguous. It was hard for me to live with, and I was an adult. You were just a kid. I didn't want to get your hopes up for nothing."

"So instead you left me confused. I had no idea how bad things actually were."

She closed her eyes and nodded. He watched her travel back to that time, the pain so near the surface of her memories, easily recovered and experienced again. It was a terrible skill, this capacity for emotional time travel, and they all had it now.

"I just want to know what happened," he said.

April opened her eyes. She put down her fork and sat up straighter. "It was June. Nobody knew he was gone yet, and then Mom got an email. They said they had Dad and not to tell anyone, so we didn't at first. They asked for a hundred-thousand dollars, which—there was no way. We didn't have it. We didn't have even half that. The next day CCA called Mom to notify her there'd been *an incident*. That's when we found out he'd been taken with his interpreter, Tariq, and two other men. But they wouldn't tell us anything more. We told them about the ransom demand. We figured they would help, since Dad was their employee, but they got really cagey. They reminded us that he was a contract worker, told us their hands were tied. We thought about going to the FBI right then, but CCA said it would do more harm than good, since it was against the policy of the US government to pay ransoms. They said they'd be in touch and to keep the communication channels open."

She shook her head. "Such bullshit."

July pushed his plate away. He couldn't eat through this.

"The thing about the ransom," April went on, "is it meant whoever took him was at least partially motivated by economic factors, not just hate or politics or religion. And I figured a bird in the hand was worth two in the bush. If we couldn't get them all of the money, they'd probably settle for less."

"So you negotiated them down?"

"Yeah."

"You did? Or Mom did?"

"I did."

"How'd you know it would be okay to do that?"

She pinched the bridge of her nose and wiped her hand down her jaw. "I didn't. But we had to do something. The clock was ticking and I was more afraid of what they might do if we didn't at least try to comply. So I emailed them back and told them we'd send them fifty-thousand. They agreed. That's when Mom went to Tom."

"And this was how long into things?"

"Day five. We'd wire the money, and they'd deliver Dad to the bus station in Mosul at seven a.m, where he'd call us. By eight a.m., Dad hadn't called, so we told CCA what we'd done. They sent some guys to the bus station to look for him. They were supposed to keep a low profile and maybe they didn't, maybe the kidnappers were late and CCA scared them off. Or maybe CCA handled it perfectly. We'll never know. But Dad never showed.

"Mosul is eight hours ahead, so it was midnight for us here. I'd had a bad feeling the whole time, but at eleven o'clock, I still honestly thought Dad was gonna show. I just believed it would all be okay because the alternative was so awful, so painful, that I don't think my brain would let me feel anything else. By three a.m., CCA had checked the bus station and come up empty. It was the worst night of my life."

She stopped talking. July waited.

"There've been other setbacks since then, times when we thought we had reason to hope but we were disappointed all over again—like when Obama picked Hillary for State and her people told us they were going to take another look at Dad's case, they were going to put their best people on it, and it didn't change anything. There have been plenty of sleepless nights. But they were all just, like, aftershocks of that first night, when we didn't get Dad back.

"When CCA called us back, we learned there'd been a ransom demand for Mahmoud Yassin, too. That was the first time we heard his name and learned that the fourth man was his driver, Omar al-Jabouri, the only one the kidnappers let go. Apparently, Mr. Yassin and Dad were on their way to do some business in Duhok—that's a town just north of Mosul—and they were grabbed together. Mr. Yassin's family paid his ransom, and we paid Dad's, and both men were supposed to be returned. But neither one showed."

"And then you called the FBI?"

"Then we called the FBI."

April put her hands in her lap. Her story was finished.

July felt ill. He closed his eyes now, hoping the sunlight streaming through the window would soothe the tightness he felt all over, tease it out, draw it away from him. But the room began to spin. He made himself breathe the way he did when he ran, in through his nose, out through his mouth.

"You were only a little older than Coop is now," April said. "Can you honestly imagine leveling with a boy that age?"

He had to admit he couldn't. "No."

"You're right. Eventually, we should have told you. I should have. I didn't mean to wait this long, honestly. I didn't realize back then how much things would change between us."

"What do you mean?"

"Well." She paused, weighing her words. "We've grown apart, haven't we? All of us. It's painful being together. You can't help but think about what you've lost. As we all got older, we built our own lives."

"Not me."

"Sure you have. Or you're about to. You're on the precipice."

"You make it sound so dangerous."

"No. It's good. You should have your own life. But when you

do, will I be in it? Will May and Junie? Will Mom be more than just a phone call you feel obliged to make?"

July considered this. He'd been accepted to the University of Chicago and could have gone there, but he hadn't. He'd stayed in Maryland, close to home. But it's true, in none of his fantasies about going to Oxford did he imagine his family coming to visit.

"Let's look at the bright side," she said.

"Which is?"

"I haven't seen you since Christmas. If we didn't have this to talk about, would we have seen each other before the wedding?"

She waited for an answer.

"I don't know?"

She narrowed her eyelids.

"Probably not," he said.

She hugged him. "I *miss* you."

"Oh, brother."

"Oh, brother is right."

July needed to finish that paper on the Balkans, but seeing his sister had drained him. Back in his dorm room he kicked off his sneakers and lay down. The sky outside darkened with twilight. Just a few minutes, that's all he needed. He rolled over onto his stomach and hugged the pillow, burying his face. Soon he was walking down a dark corridor, checking behind doors, searching for the man with the *P* on his forehead. In one room he saw only faceless figures standing in a cold rain. In the next he got a better look at the men inside: their hard naked bodies, a tattooed bicep, a star-shaped mole. He wanted to stay. This was where he belonged, but his dad wasn't here and wouldn't want him here, either. He shut the door. In another room the sun blinded him. It wasn't safe for him to stand in the open like that, unprotected. He moved on uneasily. The next door wouldn't budge. July started to wonder if these weren't the circles of hell reordered. Behind the next door, a surprise: the Eiffel Tower. The next door revealed the circus-striped onion domes of the Kremlin. The rules had changed; each door led to a city, and he only needed to keep looking until he found Dubrovnik. But there were so many other cities to be endured: Athens with its Acropolis, the Forbidden City in Beijing, St. Louis and the arch. Behind the next door: an intense yellow sun, and he wondered if he'd gone backward to the start of the game, to the room he'd been in before. But his eyes adjusted and he saw a river. He knew it was the Tigris and this was Mosul, the city where, until recently, his father had last been seen. July shut the door, certain Dubrovnik would be at the next threshold, but then he panicked. He should have stayed in Mosul and poked around first. There was no telling which direction time moved here, forward or backward. Maybe he'd left Mosul Just Before the Kidnapping or Mosul Right After. His dad might still be there, waiting for the search party to rescue him. July went back and shook the doorknob but it wouldn't turn, it was dead in his hands. He put his shoulder into it, but the door wouldn't give.

"July!"

He opened his eyes. Lucas had his hand on his shoulder, shaking him awake.

"You all right?"

July rubbed his eyes. The desk lamp was on; outside that circle of light everything was dark. What time was it? He scooted over and Lucas sat down next to him.

"I had the weirdest dream."

"About your dad?"

"Yeah—" Lucas's T-shirt was riding up at his waist; July remembered the mole he'd seen this morning, and in the dream as well "—and other things."

Lucas nudged him over some more and lay back on the bed.

Their hips touched. July's stomach did a little flip. They'd never been fully horizontal together.

"You were mumbling."

Heat and panic flashed over July like a burner catching alight. "What did I say?"

"It's hard to make it out. You usually just sound scared."

"Usually?"

"Yeah."

July closed his eyes. He was mortified. "I'm sorry."

"Don't be. It makes sense now."

"God, I'm such a freak."

"No, you're not. July, you're amazing."

Lucas's fingers found July's and folded around them.

"All this time, you kept it all to yourself. You could've used this tragedy to get ahead or make friends, but you're not doing any of that. If anything, you're too private. I care about you so much, you know? I want to be here for you."

"I know," July said, but he hadn't known. Lucas had a way of existing in the world that was so goal-oriented, so contained. Probably it was just shyness, but it often struck July as churlish, as if Lucas couldn't be bothered to care. In those moments July had told himself they weren't meant to be more than friends.

"You never have to hide from me," Lucas said.

July breathed in, his chest filling with a fizzy kind of hope and courage. Everything was okay. He had not scared Lucas off. In fact he'd done the opposite. He'd been his true, messy self and the boy he loved had come closer.

Lucas faced him, a halo of light behind him warming his skin, catching the tips of his eyelashes. July's heart pounded so hard that he was sure it shook the bed. The boy he loved was looking at him. The boy he had loved for so long, and so completely, smiled at him and July knew that if he didn't act now he never would.

July leaned in. He pressed his lips into Lucas's delicately, as if he were dabbing a spot of wine on a piece of mulberry silk. Maybe now they could be everything to each other. Now they could begin.

And Lucas, with a look of pity as sharp as glass, pulled back.

13

April

April woke up the day before Mother's Day, determined to make a fresh start. No more disappointing the people she loved. Her dad was alive and she was hot on his trail. It had to have been him in Dubrovnik—Tariq's passport hit all but confirmed it. Her initial moment of vindication had been cut short when Junie spilled the beans like that, the news coming out in such a jumble that Nancy felt sucker punched when she should've been thrilled. But days had passed and with it April's frustration. She'd trusted her gut and followed the clues and for once they were actually leading somewhere.

Now her gut was telling her something else. She'd been checked out from her real life for far too long. Maybe it was having had her kids so young, or having had them so close together, or the concurrence of the kidnapping with a time that was supposed to have been zany and improvisational, but along the way *something* had made her brisk, brittle, all-business. *Just have fun with them*, Ross would always say, as if it were a gear she could slide into as easily as she could a dress or a bath.

Well, today she would try.

And Ross. Since the kidnapping, she'd been running away from him, desperately seeking release wherever she could find it. In the beginning she'd limited herself to flirting with men when she was out of town on business. The first time it had felt so freeing to ignore the fact that it was two years since her dad was taken, that in the last 730 days she'd stopped counting forward, only backward, not *how many months until* but *how many months since*. Laughing with a stranger in the hotel's gym or sharing dinner at the restaurant downstairs—it was harmless mostly, unless they were bold enough to kiss her. Then she was abashed, and they were either apologetic or peeved, but either way the jig was up.

When she met Craig in the hotel bar at that symposium, she knew her confusion wouldn't deter him. Honestly, that was his appeal.

But every time she tested her boundaries, Ross was waiting at home for her. She wished she could unwind time, back to the days when they were in this together, before the business trips, before Craig, before she crossed over that bright line.

She could come back to him now, though. He was right here in bed with her, his foot hooked over her ankle. His eyes were still closed.

"Are you awake?" she asked.

"Are you?" he whispered back.

"Faker."

"One of us needs to get in the shower," he said.

She grunted and rolled over, tugging the sheet over her shoulder. He scooted up behind her and put his arm over her stomach, brushed her hair up onto the pillow and pressed his lips to her neck.

With his touch she felt herself beginning to drift, like a satellite launching and sending back an aerial view of her marriage: a husband and wife tangled in the sheets, their moves grown clumsy with lack of practice. They hadn't had sex since she'd returned from the cruise. Sure, they'd been tired, and drawn back into the saga of the kidnapping—but none of that had kept her from the parking garage in Bethesda, had it?

Come back, she told herself, and she rolled back over and climbed on top. They kissed and when, a moment later, he got hard, she understood how much he needed this, too. She guided him into her, giving him a view of her breasts, her neck, her lips.

He sucked on her breasts. She wanted him to bite her, but instead he lay back and squeezed her nipples gently.

April brought his hand to her neck. He gripped her shoulder instead, getting the leverage he needed. She put his hand back on her neck, and took his other one, too, placed it around her throat. She squeezed her thighs and pulsed her hips faster. She wanted to feel the tendons straining, the thumbs that could bruise her, but when she pushed against him, he let go.

"I'm sorry," Ross said quickly, the way he would have if he'd stepped on her toe.

"It's okay." She moved his hands back around her throat, pressing them into her skin.

But the force in his grip was gone. "Er—oh, shit," he said, slipping out of her.

She rolled off him and turned to face the wall. It wasn't working. But if they stopped, they would have to talk about it—about why her fantasies were so fucked up and his weren't—or more likely they wouldn't talk about it, because what was there to say? That they were failing each other?

She hovered above herself, the two of them lying there together, two spoons not spooning. This isn't what she wanted. She longed to charge into the wild places but she didn't know how to get there with him. She didn't know how to be anything

other than the wife he wanted—efficient, punctual, vanilla—
and the effort of being only that was breaking her.

Just have fun, she told herself. She had to try.

April reached behind her, pulled her husband to her, and
guided his hand down between her legs.

"Okay," he said, spreading her open with his fingers, and she
groaned and leaned back into him, hoping the choreography
would anchor her here in this moment.

This used to be their favorite position, perfect for furtive
dorm-room sex, back when they couldn't keep their hands off
each other and didn't care if Ross's roommate might wake to
their muffled cries. April began to whimper quietly in that
pleading way that always turned Ross on. He slid inside her
again and thrust, his hips against her ass, middle finger bearing
down on her. She moaned louder, and Ross put his hand over
her mouth to stifle her—the children. She bit down as they
convulsed together.

Afterward they lay completely still, half drugged, half straining for evidence of discovery by their kids. The TV droned on
downstairs.

Ross flopped onto his back and laughed, and April did, too.
She was relieved they could still give this to each other.

"Damn," he said. "Where did that come from?"

She turned toward him and smiled into her shoulder. He
touched her cheek and she promised herself that she was done
with Craig. Done. Forever.

After a shower and coffee Ross drove them all to the mall. The
kids needed outfits for the wedding, and she needed a bridesmaid
dress. Ross wanted new shoes. The bridal shower she'd promised to throw was next weekend in Aberdeen, so she had to get
a hers-and-hers gift for that, too, plus decorations. They might
not be able to tackle it all today, but they could make a dent.

In the car April listened to the symphony of her family—Ross punching the dials on the radio, Maddie groaning if he let it linger too long on NPR's monotones or the wailing guitars of classic rock, the bloop of texts coming and going from their phones, Coop hosting his own quiz show, asking with an eager persistence if they knew that the concrete in the Burj Khalifa in Dubai weighs as much as a hundred-thousand elephants?

"Says who?" Ross asked.

"The internet," Coop said.

They started at Macy's. After a few minutes of tense negotiations they found a dress for Maddie and then she split, reluctantly agreeing to meet them at the food court in an hour. April headed to housewares next, while Ross and Coop hit the shoes. By the time she caught up with them, Coop was sorted, but Ross had tried on six pairs of perfectly good brown shoes and deemed each of them lacking.

"Too pointy," he said about the seventh pair, leather lace-ups the color of a broken-in saddle.

"You knew before you put them on they were pointy," April said.

"But I didn't know if they'd look pointy relative to me." He sat to unlace them.

"Can I go to Game Zone?" Coop asked, holding his box of shoes out to her. She put the bag she was already carrying (with two fluffy white bathrobes for the brides; she'd get some bath salts to go with them) in her other hand and took it.

"No! Yes!" she and Ross answered in tandem.

"Stay close, we're almost done," she said.

"But it's right over there." Coop pointed through the open doors to a storefront with bright red lettering across the top.

"Yeah, go ahead," Ross said.

Coop took off, head up, chest out, his right hip deftly skirting a display of men's sandals. Careful, purposeful, just like his dad.

"So much for a united front," April said. She sat next to Ross, who was swaddling the pointy shoes in their box.

"Ten minutes, Coop!" Ross called after him, and the boy raised his hand in receipt of the message.

"Ten minutes, my ass."

"What about your ass?" Ross reached around to squeeze April's butt and she flinched—not because she minded; she was just surprised.

"In ten minutes you'll have to go in after him. And in twenty minutes I'll have to go in to get you both, and in thirty our daughter will be out in the parking lot with the football team getting pregnant."

Ross winced.

"Too soon?"

He shook his head. "Do we have to do this again?"

"Come on. I was only kidding."

"Sometimes I can't tell the difference between your dark humor and…just…darkness."

So much for her fresh start. It wasn't even lunchtime yet and she was back to disappointing people. She was too task-oriented, too stiff, too cynical. She never got it right.

"I'm fine. It's no big deal."

"Obviously it is. Seeing that guy over there spooked you. And that makes sense. But I can feel the whole machinery gearing back up. And you going to that bleak place again, and for how long this time?"

"I have to look into it, for my family's sake."

"What about our family?"

"It was a joke!"

"She's going to be a teenager soon, Ape. But she's still a sweet girl, she's still ours. She'll be jaded and messed up soon enough, and you won't be able to get this time back with her. And when she's gone, you won't congratulate yourself on letting go of her first. You'll be kicking yourself."

Ross took Coop's box of shoes from her and left to go pay.

She didn't know why she'd made that crack about the football team. As far as she knew, Maddie hadn't even kissed a boy yet.

April reached into her purse and her hand came out with her phone. It was a reflexive habit; she wasn't looking for anything in particular but there was a message from Craig. I'm bored. As an opening line it lacked wit, but it was mutually agreed upon. Me too, she sometimes answered, or Let's play. When she ignored him, he might up the stakes, but just as often he took the hint and left her alone. She darkened the screen and put the phone away.

April went downstairs to wander the racks for a bridesmaid dress. Yesterday she'd asked her sister what her colors were and Juniper had texted back ?????. April had said she'd figure something out. She didn't like anything she saw at Macy's, so she went out into the mall to check the smaller stores.

In White House Black Market, she perused the LBDs. Black would be unifying—July in a black suit, she and May in dresses with the same fabric but different necklines—and at this price point, May ought to be able to find something she could afford and wear again. April tried on a pleated halter dress that showed off her shoulders. Functional, classic, big-sister vibes. Vanilla. She bought it.

At the food court she pushed two smaller tables together and commandeered four chairs. While she waited for her family, she considered her options: a quesadilla from the lackluster Mexican place, warmed-over Chinese food, or a greasy slice. She texted May a few of the other dress options from the store, in order of preference: the V-neck midi, the sheath with studded shoulders, the one with the asymmetrical neck.

Maddie came from the direction of the makeup store, her

cheeks rosy, eyelids awash in green glitter, the combined effect casting a festive pallor over her young face.

"Where is everyone else?" she asked.

"They'll be here soon. Hungry?"

"Not really. A bunch of us got smoothies."

April scanned the atrium for Ross's face.

"Let me guess. Olivia and Rosie. Who else?" Parenting pre-teens often made April feel like a groupie, deeply uncool and pathetic. But if she didn't pry, she'd never know a thing about her children's lives.

"Charlotte, Sam, and Hudson."

Charlotte was a new friend this year. April didn't know whether Sam was a girl or a boy, but she'd heard Hudson's name before, and from the blasé way Maddie said it now, tacked on at the end of the sequence like an afterthought, it was obvious he was important.

"Who's Hudson?"

"Charlotte's brother."

"And Sam?"

"His girlfriend."

"Ah." April felt a jerk of concern—so serious, at this age?—as well as an ebb of relief—if Hudson was taken, then he was no threat.

"For now," Maddie added. "He'll probably break up with her. She's not really his speed."

"What speed is she?"

"You know. Fast."

"That's an old-fashioned word. Does it still mean what it used to?"

"Did it used to mean slutty?"

"Hey. Is this how you talk about your friends?"

"What? She's kissed a lot of guys, okay? If she doesn't want people to talk about her, she shouldn't do that."

"Listen, Maddie. Girls need to stick together. One day they're talking about Sam like that, the next day it could be you. It's nobody's business what Sam does with her body but Sam's. And her mom's," she added.

"Okay, *fine.*"

Still, April thought, they were so young. Twelve years old. She was used to Maddie's crushes on the guys from One Direction, fantasy figures, but now those stirrings were shifting to real live boys from the same zip code. She'd truly been kidding when she joked about Maddie's sexual awakening earlier, but maybe her daughter was inching closer to it than she'd realized.

"Sam's just kissing boys, or more than that?"

"Probably more. I don't know. She's fourteen," Maddie said gravely, as if everyone knew the burdens and expectations that came with being fourteen.

"How old's Hudson?"

"Sixteen."

"Sixteen! And he's dumping a fourteen-year-old for being fast?"

"That's what Charlotte thinks."

April could see she was at the unreliable tip of a mountain of gossip, the puritanical rigidity of preteen girls forming a cloud of uncertainty above her. She felt her phone buzz in her purse, but she ignored it.

"How many girlfriends has Hudson had?"

Maddie shrugged.

"More than one?" Her daughter nodded. "More than two?" Another assent. "Lots?"

"Yes, duh. He's, like, ridiculously beautiful."

"Does he like you?"

Maddie's face flushed velvet red.

"Oh, honey. Okay. And you like him back."

"I like him, but he probably doesn't even know I exist. I'm just his little sister's annoying friend."

"Don't do that. You're way more than that. You can tell he notices you, and it feels good. Right?"

Maddie bit her lip. Everyone said the girl was the spitting image of her mother, and April always felt humbled by the comparison, even if she couldn't see the resemblance herself. Her daughter was the caterpillar who'd morphed into a beautiful butterfly, and then another, and then another, and then again.

"I know. It feels good to be noticed, and also funny and confusing. It's all totally normal—" The phone buzzed once more, probably announcing that a voice mail message had been left. "Hang on, somebody was calling me. Let me see if it's Dad."

There was a text message from Ross—he and Coop were on their way—and a voice mail from an unprogrammed but familiar number. She pressed play.

As the message unspooled and Leyla Halabi's voice sent its tendrils through her, April felt herself dropping through a series of trap doors, down, down, down.

"Mom?"

Down she went into the dark and scared place, her vision narrowing like the shutter on a camera.

"Mom? Mommy?"

She could hear the panic in her daughter's voice, but she needed her to be quiet.

"Shhh!"

April needed to listen. Leyla went on until finally she said, "I'm sorry. I know this is a lot. You have my number if you want to talk." Then the message ended.

April shivered. She stared at the phone, as if it could answer all the questions she now had.

"April? What happened?"

She saw Ross bent down beside their daughter, who was crying into his shoulder, and he was checking her arms, her cheek, her neck, for a reason.

"Mom?" Coop said. He stood a few feet away, his arms hanging at his side. He looked at her like she'd sprouted horns, a be-loved but alien creature, just barely recognizable.

April cleared her throat to speak but she didn't know what to say.

"Honey?" Ross asked.

"Something happened to Mommy," Maddie said, sounding every bit like the child she still was, and April wondered if they'd really been talking about boys only a minute ago.

Ross noticed the phone in her hand. "Who was that?"

She cleared her throat again. "Leyla. From the State Department."

Ross took the phone from her and laid it on the table. He had one arm around Maddie and held April's hand. He nodded to Coop to sit down, next to his mother.

The boy's body gave off the faint scent of fear mixed with sweat, and it woke April up. She felt heavy with shock, but she moved to put her arm around her son.

"Leyla Halabi is someone I used to know a long time ago. When Grandpa went missing, she was one of the people who helped us look for him. Even though they never found Grandpa, they keep going over the old clues and looking for new ones, just in case."

"Did they find a new clue?" Cooper asked.

"Yes."

Ross squeezed her hand.

"What is it?" Cooper asked. His scared but hopeful face.

Just breathe, she told herself. She thought again of those first few months after the kidnapping. Maddie whisked away to the playground by Ross. Newborn Coop dozing in her arms, the only one in the house not set on edge by the Suits. When things had gotten too tense, she'd looked at his gentle face and told herself to breathe. Just breathe. She hadn't wanted to frighten her children, nor did she want to now.

"When somebody is kidnapped, the police hope to get a phone

call or a video, something that shows the person who's missing is okay. It's called proof of life."

"Okay," Coop said, unfazed. "Did we get a proof of life for Grandpa?"

"No," April said. "And after a while, we lost all contact with the people who took him."

"That's bad, right?"

"We thought so, yes. But what we didn't know at the time, and Leyla just told me, is that there *was* a video."

"What?" Ross said.

"The CIA received a video, but they neglected to tell the FBI."

"Jesus," he said, plainly disgusted, and she could have kissed him right then for being so pissed off.

"It was really grainy and the faces were hard to make out. They basically didn't know what they had, so they filed it away. But when Leyla asked around again this week, and Grandpa's interpreter, Tariq, turned up in Croatia, they ran his passport photo through facial recognition software. I guess the technology has improved a lot, and this time they got a match."

Her phone vibrated on the table, and Ross checked to see who'd texted her.

"Is it Leyla?"

He frowned at the phone.

"Juniper?" she asked.

"No, just the phone company. They got our monthly payment." He put the phone in his pocket. "So. They have Tariq on video."

"Not just Tariq. Grandpa, too."

"Oh, my God," Maddie said, her baseline tone of hyperbole finally justified.

"Are they okay in it?" Cooper asked. "Are they, you know… tied up?"

Just breathe, she told herself again.

"Leyla said that, in the video, they look like they're in a camp of some kind. They appear unharmed."

"When was this?" Ross asked.

"In 2006. *Two years* after they went missing."

14

May

May woke to the sound of hammering. Someone was outside her window, nailing something into the garden gate. Her phone said ten o'clock; the sun said morning.

"Mom, let's put the cupcakes back inside," she heard April say. "I don't want the bugs to eat them before we do."

May groaned. She needed a shower and at least two cups of coffee before she'd have a tenth of the energy her older sister had as a baseline. Juniper and Hana's bridal shower wasn't for another hour, but April had arrived bright-eyed and bushy-tailed to set up.

May crawled out of bed and headed for the backyard.

"Good morning, Your Grace," Nancy said as May pulled open the sliding glass door. "We're nearly finished, but your sister can tell you what else needs doing."

Nancy passed by with the tray of cupcakes, all iced different colors. May's stomach growled its displeasure with her for not eating sooner.

While she'd been sleeping, the garden had been transformed from an unexceptional suburban backyard into some kind of gay *Alice in Wonderland* tea party tableau. May couldn't tell where her mother's ideas left off and her sister's began. The tables were covered in rainbow-striped tablecloths and there were rainbow bunches of balloons tied to the grill and the planters and weighted down here and there with satchels of pebbles. A garland of gold letters tied to the back fence spelled out the words 2 BRIDES ARE BETTER THAN 1. Tom had even mowed the lawn.

Rainbows or soccer balls? she imagined her mother or sister asking herself in the party supply store, trying to settle on a theme.

May went around to the side yard, where April had just finished hanging on the gate to the driveway another banner/balloon combo that said HERE COME THE BRIDES.

"Did you bring it?" May asked.

"What, May? I brought everything—the cupcakes, the table linens, the balloons, the booze and extra pitchers, and my card table. You've gotta be more specific. Nice hair, by the way."

"The laptop," May said, letting the bedhead crack roll off her like every other insult her sister had ever hurled at her appearance. May didn't give a shit, never had, and April could never quite believe it.

What May wanted was to watch the proof-of-life video. Leyla had sent it by secure link to April, and it could only be viewed by her. April had described the scene to her siblings in an email, but it wasn't enough to read about it secondhand. April had promised to bring her laptop so May could watch for herself.

May withdrew a half-empty pack of cigarettes and a lighter from her sweatpants pocket, tamped the pack against her palm, then plucked one out.

"Seriously? You're still smoking?" April asked.

"Just go get the laptop. Please?"

April stuck out her tongue, disgusted, and left.

May lit the cigarette and took a long drag. Technically she was always in the process of quitting, except for this week: she'd been chain-smoking ever since she got her sister's email. She'd read it so carefully she'd almost convinced herself she knew every frame of that video. It had been filmed from above by a surveillance drone and later a video engineer had zoomed in and cleaned up the resolution. A shadow from a nearby cinder block structure made it impossible for the earlier software to recognize his face, but in 2014, April wrote, it was plain as day. Frank stood talking with Tariq and an unidentified man— neither Mahmoud Yassin, who remained missing, nor Omar al-Jabouri, the Sunni Arab who'd been Yassin's driver for many years and was, until a week ago, the sole known survivor of the attack. Jabouri, April reminded her family, had been questioned by every agency from the Coalition Provisional Authority to the Peshmerga, the CIA to the DoD. He'd given up nothing. In the video Frank and Tariq speak to the unidentified man for thirty-seven seconds before they all go inside.

The existence of the video was proof: Frank was alive in 2006. Put that together with Tariq being in Dubrovnik last month, and even May—the skeptic, the holdout—had to admit: April probably had seen their father. These facts should have given May hope, but instead they crushed her. What was her dad doing in Croatia when he could have come home instead? April thought he was still being coerced—she'd mentioned a traveling companion with a presumed gun—but it didn't add up for May. All this time—a chance like that—and he hadn't been able to escape?

April returned with the laptop and May followed her through the gate and across the driveway to the front porch, where they sat on the concrete slab, their feet dipping into the sparsely planted flower bed.

What would May discover by watching the video? A look, a glance, a clue to whatever had happened to Frank? She would know it when she saw it.

April pulled up Leyla's email and clicked on the link. At a prompt she typed in a password. A black square appeared on the screen. Then the video began.

"There's no sound?" May asked.

April shook her head.

May couldn't tell what she was looking at, at first. The camera panned across an open yard.

"There," April said, pointing to the trio of men who came into the picture.

May thought her heart would be in her throat by now, but she didn't recognize a thing. Where was her father? Her sister turned her finger sideways, indicating the outline of one of the figures.

"*That's* Dad?"

This was no help. May had expected a smoking gun—even a literal one slung over Frank's shoulder, two bullet magazines crisscrossing his chest like he was Che Guevara—but there was nothing like that. Still, the longer she stared at him, the more he began to seem familiar. He had his arms folded the way he often did when he wanted to convey respect and attention, with his hands tucked high in his armpits. There was no longer a beer belly to rest his arms across. He was leaner than she'd ever known him to be.

"What was that?" May asked. "That thing he did with his hand?"

The three men were walking now, as May knew they would, into the cinder block building they'd been standing outside, first the unknown man, then Tariq, then Frank.

"Can you back it up?"

"No, but I can play it again."

The video ended and April returned to the prompt and re-typed the password. Watching it again, it was like May's eyes had adjusted to a darkened bedroom. The open yard, she could see now, was a garden with raised beds. There was a goat nibbling at the ground, a rope collar at its neck. Her father had a limp. He wore loose jeans and an oversized T-shirt. They weren't clothes she recognized; perhaps he'd been given them. Tariq and the other man wore long tunics over pants.

"Who's she?" May asked.

"Who?" April asked. "Wait, there's a woman?"

"Yeah. Look. A ponytail. And she's smaller."

April leaned in. "I didn't see her before," she said.

Their father listened to Tariq, arms folded across his chest at first, and then he unfolded them and held out his hand.

"There," May said. "He's gesturing at the building."

"So?"

"He's leading them. He walks in last, but it's his idea to go inside. He's letting them go first. *After you*. He's being polite. A gentleman."

"He's not their hostage," April concluded.

"Not anyone's," May said.

The video ended again. May reached over and shut the laptop. They sat in silence.

She stubbed out her cigarette on the concrete and got up.

"Wait. Let's talk about next steps." April was gassed up. She'd always fed off the spin cycle. Today she was particularly triumphant, like a cat who'd left its murdered prey on the doorstep for all to admire. "I was thinking tomorrow—"

"I gotta get ready."

In the shower May tried to send her feelings down the drain, but there wasn't enough water in the world. What a fool she'd been.

"You finally get to see the world, Dad," she'd said on the ride to the airport. As if he were going to visit the pyramids or to Italy to make pasta, not into a war zone. How could she have been so cavalier, letting him leave, trusting that he would be safe in Iraq? He worked on weapons systems, for Christ's sake.

Back in her room she got dressed, then collapsed on the floor next to Jack's bed. She nuzzled his snout and scratched behind his ears.

"Thank God for you," she told him.

There was a knock at her door, but Jack couldn't hear it.

"Yeah?" May said.

July poked his head in, and Jack deigned to lift his slightly. "Mom said to come get you. People are starting to arrive."

"Hey," she said.

"Hey," her brother said, hesitant.

"Are we speaking? I thought you were pissed at all of us."

"Oh. Yeah. I was, but I've decided to move on." He stepped all the way in and offered her a hand. "Come on."

Juniper and Hana's guests came by the carload from Pennsylvania, the aunties from Lancaster, the lesbians from Philly, a couple of scientists from Hana's work (one of whom was a guy, which meant July wasn't the only XY in attendance). A few of Nancy's colleagues were here, and some of the neighbors now streamed through the garden gate. On her best day May wasn't up for this much socializing, and today she was far from her best.

"Kill me now," May said under her breath, loud enough for only July to hear.

He took her hand, then led her straight into the maw of the party, where Junie was standing with Hana, Fariha, Hana's mother (the resemblance to her daughters was obvious), and Nancy.

Junie had that deer-in-headlights look she used to get whenever their parents threw a party—New Year's Eve or Frank's fortieth or when Nancy finished the dental hygienist program—and trotted out the offspring to make an appearance, and they all had to pretend they were happy and harmonious like the Family Von Trapp. May used to pinch her little sister in the waist to make her laugh and loosen up.

"Maryam, this is my brother, July," Junie said while they all shook hands, "and my sister May."

"How lucky you are, Juniper, to have so much family around you," Maryam said. "I have five sisters. We fought like cats when we were young, but now they're my best friends. I feel as if I stinted my children, not giving them more siblings."

Junie pointed out three of Maryam's sisters who were in attendance; a fourth, she explained, lived in Toronto and the fifth in Liverpool.

"I always tell my four, the longest relationships you'll ever have are the ones you have with each other," Nancy said. "I was an only child, and I was lonely. I'm so glad they have each other."

"Six girls, wow!" July said to Maryam. The little shit was so good at chitchat. May had never had that sweetness, but college had honed his charm, his lightness.

"Your mother must have been a saint," Nancy said.

"She was," Fariha said, nodding.

"She had a lot of…gravitas," Hana said, less sure.

"She was a witch!" Maryam said with a bawdy laugh, and Nancy almost sprayed her lemon drop all over her.

"Okay, everyone," April interrupted. "It's time to put Junie and Hana on the hot seats. Come here, you two."

She patted the tops of a couple of stools like they were bongo drums. Behind them was a piece of foam core propped up on an easel. It had a circle with a spinner in the middle, and the segments of the circle were colored like the rainbow. Despite herself, May was in awe. When had April had the time to pull this craft project out of her ass?

"I promised my sister there would be no cheesy games today, but what's a bridal shower without one? Sorry, Junie. So without further ado, it's time to play—say it with me now—" she pointed to the words above the spinning wheel and the group called out in unison "—That's What She Said!"

Junie took her seat last, having stopped at the card table to fix herself another drink. It must have been a nightmare for her, May thought, having this much attention for anything besides soccer. Inside she was probably shaking, but she pushed her sleeves up and gave everyone a smile.

Some of the guests sat at the tables, but May and July parked themselves on the cinder block retaining wall behind everyone.

"As you can see, the wheel has six categories," April went on, "Frenemies, Appetites, Celebrity Crushes, Ancient History, The *L* Word, and The Future. You'll each take turns spinning the dial, and I'll ask you a question from that category. I interviewed each bride separately, and I have your answers here. So let's see how well you two really know each other. Who wants to start?"

Hana shrugged, relaxed and ready. "I'll go." She spun the wheel and it landed on Ancient History.

"Okay, Hana." April was drawing this out like she was the host of *Family Feud*. "Between soccer and some epic vacations, you're a couple that's traveled far and wide together. Which place did my sister say was the most meaningful?"

"Pittsburgh," Hana said without missing a beat.

"Whoa, that was fast. No shade to Pittsburgh, but why?"

Hana looked down and smiled. Junie blushed. "No comment."

"Okay. Well, doesn't matter, because you're right! That's what she said!"

May couldn't focus on this inane game. Her thoughts kept spinning on her dad. He'd survived the kidnapping, but she couldn't make it make sense. The Iraqi police had found the SUV. The broken glass, the bullet casings, all that blood. How had he made it out of that wreck alive? What was he doing buddying up to those people in the video two years later? What had he gotten himself into? And why go to Dubrovnik now? For weeks they'd been assuming the absence of an extradition treaty between Croatia and the US provided protection for the kidnappers, but maybe they had it all wrong. Maybe it protected Frank, too.

"Salted caramel," Junie said.

"That's what she said!"

Last night, May had gone down another internet rabbit hole. This time it took her to the American Security Institute. Kidnapping school. If she could figure out how her father had survived his abduction, then maybe she could understand why he'd stayed away from her.

"Two kids, right?" Hana said.

"That's what she said!" By now the crowd was joining in with enthusiasm.

ASI boasted of students in Newark, Mexico City, and Medellín. The instructor was a former officer in the French Foreign Legion who'd served in Afghanistan after 9/11 and looked a little like Jean-Claude Van Damme in battle fatigues and a green beret, craggy mountains in the distance. The website touted military-grade training in survival, evasion, resistance, and escape. For an extra fee you could learn about enhanced interrogation techniques. May knew what that meant: stress positions, waterboarding. She couldn't afford it. She'd bookmarked the page, anyway.

"I mean, I wanna say Shane," Juniper said, "but honestly, I'm probably more of a Dana. Before the diagnosis, obviously."

"That's what she said!" July yelled beside May. He cupped his hands around his mouth as he let out a couple whoops.

He'd been so young when Frank was taken. They couldn't tell him everything then. It was up to him to decide how he'd handle the whole truth now. He could put his nose to the grindstone, racking up achievements, like April had; he could become invisible, like she had; he could run away, like Juniper. There were as many ways to hide or hurt yourself as there were people in the world.

Finally the game was over and everyone lined up at the buffet for finger sandwiches, kale Caesar salad, deviled eggs that had been pickled ROYGBIV, and cupcakes. The Barbers went through the line last, following Family Hold Back rules, standing in reverse birth order behind their mother.

"This is so fun, isn't it?" Nancy put her arm around July. "It's so nice to be together. Isn't it, Junie?"

"Yeah," Junie said. "Thanks for doing this, you guys. I know there's a lot going on right now."

"Nope, we're not thinking about that today. No worried faces. May, I'm talking to you," Nancy said.

"I'm sorry, I can't help it."

"Come on, now," Nancy said, the warning tone edging into her voice, but May didn't care.

"Is anyone else as confused as I am? How does he end up in Croatia?" she asked.

"I don't know." April rubbed her hand in circles on May's back.

"Get off," May said, shaking her loose.

"May—" April said, feigning wounded-ness the way she always did when she came on too strong.

"Where the fuck has he been all this time? Consorting with terrorists?"

"Of course not," Nancy said in a whisper that screamed *lower your voice*. "What is wrong with you?"

"Watch the video. Dad looks awfully chummy with those men. I don't know what else to call it but *collaborating*."

"Your father would never get mixed up in something like that. Tell them, Junie."

But Junie seemed frozen.

"What are you asking her for?" May snorted.

"Someone needs to speak some sense about your father."

"And you think *she* can? The one who moved on like fathers were optional?"

"Hey," Hana said sharply, stepping back from the line ahead to put her body between Juniper and May.

But May's beef wasn't with Junie, not really. She turned to face April. "How could you let him get away?"

"What? I... I..."

"You had one job. Grab him and bring him home."

"I tried."

"Useless."

"What did you say?"

"You heard me." Now May dragged out her words. "Use. Less."

"Girls, we're not doing this. Not here."

Nancy took a quick look around the yard to confirm that, yes, all of their guests were watching this family squabble, or pretending hard not to. Maryam smiled at May and tilted her head in sympathy.

"You're jealous," April said with a slight hint of a smile, the satisfaction that comes with knowing what button to push. "You're jealous that I'm the one who saw him and not you."

The insult landed where she'd meant it to this time, right in the gut. You had to admire the accuracy. May thought she might be sick, but she had to say something. You couldn't let a blow like that go unanswered.

"You're right. You saw him, not me. You had it so easy. You just walked off a fucking cruise ship and stumbled into him. He was gift-wrapped for you, April, and you still blew it. If it'd been me over there, he'd be home now."

May stepped out of the buffet line. She was getting the hell out of here. *Go ahead and waterboard me*, she thought, if that's what it took to get away from her sister's self-righteous certainty.

"Perfect. So you go AWOL and I'm left holding the bag again?" April said.

"That's not what happened."

"The hell it isn't. You take off like some kind of keystone cop, and next thing I know I've got two messes to clean up instead of one? No. You're an adult. You don't get to pull this stupid shit anymore."

"What?" Nancy said. She and July went after May, but only Nancy followed her inside. As May grabbed her keys and patted her thigh for Jack to come, her mother continued, "What's April talking about? Keystone cop? May, please. I know how difficult this is. Don't you think my hopes are up, too? Don't you think I'm terrified of being disappointed again? Just sit down and talk to me."

"I can't." May pulled the front door behind her hard. *Don't follow me*, the slam said.

In her car she put the key in the ignition and her head on the steering wheel. She knew kidnapping school wouldn't help, but she couldn't stay here, either. She couldn't tell her mom or anyone else in her family how she was really feeling. Because it wasn't that her hopes were up. It's that she was furious with Frank. Fuck him if he was still alive. Fuck him if a bunch of terrorists meant more to him than she did, or if he was one himself. May had never teamed up with anyone against her dad, not ever, and she didn't know how to do it now.

15

Juniper

Juniper woke in the dark of the morning, sick with fear and self-loathing. The dream again, playing on a loop. She'd need her wits about her for the meeting today in DC, and it was impossible to get any rest like this. She dozed off just in time for the dawn to yank her awake.

The sunlight made a prism of the glass of water on her nightstand, throwing triangles of light and shadow over Hana's sleeping face. In a little over three weeks they'd be making promises to each other under an arch in the Prospect House garden, but yesterday a district court judge had struck down Pennsylvania's ban on gay marriage. They could get married today if they wanted to. Maybe they should.

The clock said 6:32 a.m. After the trip to the bridal salon Juniper had decided not to self-medicate, to clean out her system. She and Hana had made pacts together before to cut back: only on the weekends, only a glass of wine with dinner, only at restaurants, Dryuary. This time Juniper was doing it alone, no big announcement. So far the results were spotty at best. She'd manage not to drink one day, and then the next morning she'd be at the fancy grocery store, the one that opened at seven a.m., had a small overpriced selection of booze, and was on the way to school. She'd given herself a free pass for the day of the bridal shower, and thank God. She'd been a nervous wreck going in. Would she feel torn between her two families? (Yes.) Would she be put on the spot? (Two words: hot seat.) Would she rise to the challenge? (Sort of.) She'd needed plenty of lubrication to be a good sport during the game. At least everyone seemed to be having a good time, pleased with how perfectly the brides completed each other's sentences. But then May exploded, and the celebratory mood cratered. The party never recovered.

Juniper had yet to string two dry days together. How would she get through another day without thinking of all the mistakes she'd made? How did April do it? How did May? They were stronger than her. Everyone else thought Juniper had it so together, but even as kids her sisters had been able to see right through her. They'd known when she was lying about having done her homework, could read it on her contorted face when she had to take a shit. There was a time when she was afraid to shower and she used to pretend she had, leaving the water running for the right amount of time while she sat on the edge of the tub and waited. Nancy never caught on, but April and May did. "Here, Junie," April would say, guiding her in and watching until she got soaked. May was more blunt. "Gross," she'd say, pointing at the shower. "Get in." If they could see her now, they'd know how weak she really was. It would be obvious to them that she was only hanging on by the barest of threads.

Hana's beautiful, peaceful face was pressed against the pillow. Any strength Juniper had left came from her. She would do anything to wake up to this face forever.

Juniper kissed her eyelids, and Hana stirred.

"Let's get married," Juniper whispered in her ear.

She felt Hana's cheeks lift into a smile. "Mmm. Okay."

"No, really." Juniper scrambled atop her and laced their fingers together. "Let's get married *today*."

Hana blinked awake. "Are you going to propose to me every day until the wedding?"

"Look at what's happening down at the courthouse! Old ladies lining up in their wheelchairs and their walkers. They've been together since before Apple meant computers, and they're getting married. Here, in Philadelphia! No more running off to Canada or New Jersey or Maryland or whatever place will have us. What's more romantic than that?"

"Nothing."

Hana took Juniper's face in her hands and pulled her in for a long kiss. Her hands slid down to her butt, but Juniper wiggled free and jumped out of bed.

"Let's do it, then!"

"Wait, are you serious?"

"As a heart attack."

Hana got up and walked to the bathroom. Juniper followed.

"What?"

"The wedding's less than a month away. We've planned a week of celebrations. Or I should say *I've* planned it, so *you* could focus on getting the Princeton job. All of my parents' friends are showing up for what, for most of them, is going to be their first gay wedding. And they're actually happy for us. Do you know what a big deal that is?"

"Well, I mean, even Dick Cheney came around eventually."

Hana's face fell.

"I'm kidding! Oh, come on. Why are you taking this so seriously? I'm sorry."

Hana turned on the shower, the blast of water speaking for her as well as any tirade could.

"Babe," Juniper said.

Hana climbed in and tugged the curtain closed between them. "Can't hear you," she yelled from the other side.

At lunchtime Juniper drove herself to the Philadelphia North station to catch the train to DC, where she'd link up with April. They had an appointment with a man at the Kurdish embassy, the one Fariha had told them about who was a political connection of Mo's. It was just the two of them going. At one point April had mused about whether all four Barber siblings should attend, but the day after the fight with May she said her gut told her a smaller, more intimate conversation would be better. The plan was to appeal to the Kurdish government for assistance in locating their dad. Two of the four men in the SUV were Kurds, which meant their fate and Frank's were linked.

From her window seat in the quiet car Juniper explored the website for the Kurdistan Regional Government. The man she was on her way to meet was Mustafa Karim, cousin of the prime minister of the KRG. The Kurds were a sizeable voting bloc in Iraq and had done well in the parliamentary elections in 2005, claiming the presidency and leadership of several ministries. But since then, Iraq's prime minister, a compromise candidate from the Shia majority, supported by the US and Iran, had moved to centralize control within his own party. As a result the Kurds had created a de facto independent state in the northeast, stretching from Duhok province, north of Mosul and on the border with Turkey, southeast to Sulaymaniyah and the lands bordering Iran. In the middle lay Erbil, the capital, five hours north of Baghdad.

Officially Karim was the KRG Representative to the US, but he was more powerful than the Iraqi ambassador, according to the political blogs Juniper now read. He had been in Washington for the better part of a decade and knew how the game was played.

They'd never have gotten a meeting this quickly without Mo's help, and Juniper had been counting on his deft people skills to make up for her total lack of them in nonathletic settings, but at the last minute he'd begged off attending. He said he'd been summoned to Harrisburg to talk to the senator about an endorsement—and, of course, he had to go—but she wondered if that was the whole truth or if Mo needed distance from her father's case. Now the work of charming Mustafa Karim would fall entirely to Juniper and April, and she hoped they could do it. She hoped they didn't make things worse. If Frank truly had been at that camp of his own volition, as May believed, and if that camp had given harbor to terrorists (still a question mark), then bringing any political attention to his activities could be dangerous. Juniper still didn't know what to believe. The idea that her father could be working with terrorists, or even be one himself? She just couldn't go there. If she had to think about it for too long, she was pretty sure she'd fall all the way apart.

She'd put on a short-sleeve blouse and a dark wool skirt, borrowed a pair of flats from Fariha (Hana's feet were too big), and taken her long hair out of its ponytail. Today she wasn't a soccer coach; she was a grieving daughter. The back of her knee was sweating in the sun and she uncrossed her legs, exposing a red disc on the opposite knee that she tried to rub away. She felt like a fraud.

As the train pulled into Union Station, she got a text message from April. Running late. Be there in 10.

Juniper followed the stream of passengers from the platform to the Main Hall. The great arched ceiling only echoed the significance of her mission. Her hands were shaking. She hadn't eaten anything but a banana this morning. The center café was too expensive, so she wandered over to a directory to check out the offerings downstairs in the food court. Pretzels, sandwiches, pizza, but then another vendor caught her eye. Union Wine and Liquor. She checked the time. She could do it. She could get down there and back before April got here.

No. One day sober could become two days, and two could stretch to three, and if she strung enough of these days together, maybe she could sleep again. She bought an overpriced yogurt instead and walked out onto the wide driveway facing Massachusetts Avenue to wait for her sister.

At last April arrived in her car. A black SUV. If the word *suits* had taken on a double meaning in the last ten years, then the words *black SUV* had coalesced to only one. *Danger.*

Nevertheless Juniper got in. "It doesn't seem morbid to you? Driving a car like this?"

"Like what?" April glanced in her rearview mirror, then quickly at Juniper, before returning her gaze ahead. She drove forward. "Oh. No. I had two car seats to deal with. I had to get over it." April brought the car to a stop at the edge of the station's driveway. "How many times have we got ahead of ourselves, only to be disappointed? But still. This guy's pretty connected. Are you ready?"

Juniper swallowed, the back of her throat aching with hope and fear.

"Let's go," she said, and April slipped into traffic.

They found the office of the KRG on the wrong side of Dupont Circle, far from the mansions on Embassy Row. The building was deceptively modest, a slender confused piece of architecture, part stone, part shingles, jammed next to a tall apartment complex like a barnacle clinging to a whale. Two flags—the tricolor of Iraq and the Kurdish banner with a sunburst in the middle—hung from the second-floor balcony, the only hint of the levers of power within.

They were asked to wait in a small parlor off the foyer for the representative, on a couch upholstered in faded silk. April shot her a stern look, then dropped her glance to Juniper's knees, which were bouncing nervously. Juniper sat on her hands and shot her a stern look back.

A Suit arrived—not the representative, who wore a goatee in

every photograph Juniper had seen of him—but someone with a mustache, heavier, a little older. *Old-school*, Juniper thought.

"Hello," he said, extending his hand to April. "I am Samir Sardar, Director of Diplomatic Affairs."

The sisters stood and he shook Juniper's hand next.

"Let's go upstairs, please."

He took them to a small conference room largely occupied by a round mahogany table on a pedestal base. In the center was a speakerphone and around the table were cheap desk chairs on casters. The room had the same patched together air of formality as the building itself. The director gestured to them to sit and Juniper let April take the seat closest to him. She sat on the other side of April.

A woman entered carrying a tea service. She set down on the table a teapot and three delicate glasses edged with gold. The director poured. He passed them each a cup.

"Thank you," April said.

"Yes, thank you," Juniper said.

They sipped theirs while the director finished his in two large gulps. Then he slid his empty cup to the other side of him.

"The representative regrets that his busy schedule doesn't permit him to greet you today, but I am briefed on this matter," he said, and Juniper's heart sank. She noticed April's shoulders drop, too. "How can this office assist you?"

April pushed her cup forward and turned to look at the director head on.

"On June twentieth, 2004, our father, Francis Barber, was kidnapped near Mosul along with three other men," she began. "One of them, Mahmoud Yassin, was a prominent Kurdish businessman. Our father's translator, Tariq Ibrahim, was also Kurdish. Given their involvement, our two governments cooperated in the recovery of the car's driver, Omar al-Jabouri, whom the kidnappers released. He was detained and later questioned by several parties, including the Peshmerga."

"Yes."

"We've recently come across new information that proves that our father, who was presumed missing, possibly dead, did in fact survive the assault and was still alive in 2006 if not later."

"You are encouraged by this, naturally."

"Yes, of course."

"And you have come here seeking answers."

April nodded.

"I'm afraid I don't have any. We don't know where your father is. If we did, we would certainly have communicated this to your government."

"I didn't ask if you knew where our father is, though I appreciate your being so forthcoming."

Juniper pressed her knee against her sister's. April shook her off, reaching into her purse for a photograph and placing it on the table. It was a picture of Frank and Tariq together at Camp Freedom. They had their arms around each other and they were smiling into the sun. One of Frank's colleagues had mailed it to Nancy right after the kidnapping. Juniper hadn't seen it in years. She gazed at it, trying to soak in the details of his face, his scrunched-up cheeks, the twinkle in his eye. *This* was her dad's real smile.

"It's my understanding," April said, "that the State Department has shared with you a video, recently discovered, that shows our father and Tariq Ibrahim attending a meeting at a training camp of some kind. Mr. Yassin was not present. I'm wondering whether your intelligence officers have viewed this footage and run it against your own database of known militants."

"The Istikhbarat is an Iraqi entity, not Kurdish. What they view or do not view, I don't know."

This is how these interviews always worked. The family shared what they knew, and the government—any government, US, Iraqi, or Kurdish, it didn't matter—stonewalled. The information only ever went one way.

"I'm not asking about the Istikhbarat," April went on, unfazed. "I'm asking about *your* intelligence, within Kurdistan. The Asayish."

The director's eyes narrowed. "*If* the State Department has shared intelligence, I'm sure our officers are treating it with the utmost care and importance."

April bit her lower lip, half smiling, half holding herself back. "I'm sorry, sir, but our meeting was to be with Mr. Karim. The representative. Can we speak with him, please?"

The director smiled wanly at them both. This was going all wrong, Juniper thought. He wasn't inclined to be open and April's badgering wasn't going to change his mind.

"Okay," April said, leaning forward, about to rise.

Juniper put her hand out to stop her. "Mr. Sardar, my name is June. I was eighteen years old when my father was kidnapped. It was the summer before I started college, and I was so excited about the next chapter of my life. Then we got the call, and it was like time stopped. Our hearts stopped. He was a good man, a family man. All my life, he'd been there to help and guide us. The only reason he took that job, so far away, was to pay for our schooling. After he was taken, we used to climb into our mother's bed at night, all of us together, but we couldn't sleep. We waited for word, some clue to where he was, a rescue plan. We waited for word and it never came."

The air-conditioning abruptly switched off and the room went silent. She could hear the blood pumping in her ears.

"My father named me June, but that was the month he was taken and I can't bear to be called that anymore. I want my father back. I'm getting married next month, and he should be there. He should walk his daughter down the aisle. If that's not possible, I want to know what happened to him. My mother and my siblings and I, we need to know so we can move on and find peace.

"My fiancée's brother, Mohammed Monsour, was kind

enough to ask for this meeting with Mr. Karim. I realize what a busy and important man he is. But if there's any way he could speak to us, just for a moment, it would mean the world to my sister and me."

The director's face softened. Just as quickly as it had turned off, the air conditioner came back on again, sending a shushing sound through the hiatus in the conversation. Juniper waited for him to say something. He also seemed to be waiting, but for what? What was supposed to happen now? She was afraid to lose whatever this connection was.

Just then, the door opened. The director turned and stood. It was the representative.

Karim patted his colleague's shoulder, effectively excusing him. The director paused at the door. "Good luck, miss," he said to Juniper and closed the door behind him.

Karim sat in the director's chair. The skin on the back of Juniper's neck was prickly. How had he arrived at just this moment? He must have been monitoring the meeting. One of the buttons on the phone glowed green.

"Thank you for coming," April said, a trace of vindication in her voice.

"Of course. I'm happy to meet with you both, face-to-face. Face-to-face is better, don't you think?"

"Yes," Juniper agreed.

"I understand that Mr. Sardar had to be cautious," April said. "But I'm hoping that we can be more open with each other."

Karim laughed. If she had to guess, she'd say he was a good fifteen years younger than the other man. His short hair was fashionably tousled and his accent slight.

"Openness. Yes. Openness is important."

April folded her hands on the table. Juniper hoped her sister would temper herself now. April was an alpha dog, and she would hate to square off against her.

"You must understand," Karim continued. "Today it's the

two of you who are asking for our help. But many times in the past, it has been Kurdistan asking the United States for help. And too often, we've been disappointed. Many Kurds—" and he hesitated, tilting his head toward the door, so that they could feel the director's absence "—spent their boyhoods listening to Voice of America broadcasts, worshipping President Nixon and Henry Kissinger, who they heard champion our resistance after the Ba'athist coup. They called us *freedom fighters*, but we were only a useful wedge in their ongoing proxy wars with the Soviets. Then Saddam and the Shah of Iran cut a deal, and we who had been loyal to the Shah were left out in the cold by his great friends. The back channels were closed. American aid was cut off. Saddam turned his guns on the Kurds, and many families fled to the mountains and to a useless life of exile in Iran."

That the Director of Diplomatic Affairs had not trusted them had been obvious. Juniper tried to picture the stout man with the salt-and-pepper mustache as a young boy in the mountains, earnest and scared.

"Many Americans don't know what a Kurd *is*. And why should they? From the very beginning, my people have been left off your maps, as if we never existed at all. I say the beginning, because World War I is when many in the West seem to think our history began—when you bother to think of us at all—but our history stretches back to the tenth century."

"You're right," April said, her tone a shade more conciliatory. "The Kurds have been good friends to the US, and we haven't always honored that relationship. During the First Gulf War, your people took our president at his word and drove Saddam's agents out of your cities. Then Bush got his cease-fire agreement, and you were left with Saddam and his army's guns pointed at you."

Karim nodded. "We were slaughtered. Again."

April didn't flinch. "Yes. The no-fly zone came too late."

Hundreds of thousands of Kurds fled Saddam's tanks and helicopters, some to Iran, others to the border of Turkey, where only a trickle were let through. The result was a refugee crisis so shameful that the international community demanded humanitarian intervention and the creation of a safe haven for Kurds. Juniper vaguely knew all this but she never could have articulated it, let alone to the KRG Representative himself. April knew what she knew and she said it. The names of people and places didn't jumble around in her head. She remembered exactly who had wronged whom and when.

"I'm not always proud of how my government operates, believe me," April said. She grabbed Juniper's hand. "We are coming to you not as citizens but as daughters."

Karim leaned back in his seat. He loosened his tie. His fingertips brushed lightly across the table. "We don't know where your father is. We don't know whether he was lucky enough to survive or unlucky, like Mahmoud Yassin."

"Unlucky?" April asked. Juniper's hand began to sweat, or maybe it was her sister's.

"Yes. His family recently recovered his remains."

April let go of Juniper and leaned forward in her chair. Juniper's heart started beating quickly. Until this moment, only the driver's whereabouts were known, and Frank, Tariq, and Yassin were all officially missing. Now they had confirmation that Yassin was dead. Juniper couldn't have spoken if she tried. She let her sister depose Karim for them both.

"How? Where did they find him?"

"It seems that Jabouri was helpful in that regard."

"His driver knew? Was he involved?"

"Apparently not. He had been Yassin's driver for many years. He loved the man. But there were some in Jabouri's family who could not understand how an Arab could deign to work for a Kurd. A wealthy Kurd at that."

"His family did this?"

"He suspected one of his nephews."

"But he never said."

"No. And as you know, he was questioned many, many times. He's a loyal man. Loyal to his family, loyal to Yassin. When he was released from prison, he wanted to make things right with Yassin's family. Our agents had him under surveillance. We told your government everything when we learned what he knew."

"When was this?"

"Eighteen months ago."

"Eighteen months! And nobody thought to tell us?"

Juniper felt as shocked as April, but was too angry to think straight. She'd assumed that most information in her dad's case would, eventually, trickle down to her. But her government apparently never intended to share this.

"Where is the nephew?" April asked, like a hunting dog who'd caught the scent of its prey. "Has he been questioned?"

Karim hesitated.

"He was killed."

"Killed? When?"

"Eighteen months ago."

Juniper could picture two likely scenarios after Jabouri led the Peshmerga to his nephew. Either the Peshmerga killed his nephew or US Special Forces had.

April leaned back—collapsed, really—into her chair, and Juniper knew what she was thinking. If they could just speak to the nephew...but whatever he knew died with him. Juniper thought she wanted closure—the truth, good or bad, about what happened to all four men in the SUV—but that word. *Remains.*

The air conditioner shut off again. The three of them sat in the quiet. Juniper reviewed what she knew about the status of the men. Jabouri was alive today. Yassin was not. Tariq and Frank both survived the initial abduction, and there was video proof they were alive in 2006. Tariq passed through Croatian customs last month and, if April's eyes could be trusted, Frank did, too.

Juniper realized that April had run out of questions for the representative. But she still had one.

"So Mahmoud Yassin was the kidnappers' target, not our father?" she asked.

"It appears so. And from what we understand, Yassin was killed during the initial abduction."

"Our father's blood was all over the car, too, but we know now that he and Tariq survived. What happened to the kidnappers' plan after their original target died?" If their plot was over, Frank should've turned up at that bus station after the ransom was paid.

Karim's face was full of pity, and she could see that he was a good man, that if this interview had been painful for them, it had been no less difficult for him.

"That is a very good question," he said. "I do, sincerely, hope you find the answer."

"I didn't know that's why you changed your name," April said as they buckled their seat belts. Neither had said a word as they'd been escorted out of the conference room, down the stairs, and to the building's front door. They'd been silent as they passed beneath the two flags, back onto the street. "I thought it was because it was too old-fashioned for you. Too femme."

Juniper shrugged. "That, too."

"You were smart. With a new name, you could be someone else. Go on like nothing had happened."

April words cut her, but it was a tiny slice on top of skin that was too badly scarred to bleed again after what May had said at the shower, that she'd moved on like fathers were optional.

For two whole years after their father went missing, Juniper had been going about her business, training herself to think of her team and of Hana, when she should have been fighting for his return. When they went to the College Cup her freshman season, he'd been alive. When they missed the NCAA tournament the next year after a loss to USC, and she cursed herself for letting everyone down—Hana, her team, Coach Mac, her father's sacrifice all for nothing—he'd been alive. In 2006, instead of crying over him, she was crying behind her sunglasses at Hana's graduation, because they wouldn't be teammates anymore and maybe without soccer to cement it, their love wouldn't last.

She had never meant to choose one love over the other. Couldn't. Wouldn't. It was just that finding Hana when she did had saved her. Hana always said the same was true for her. She said that her first two years at Princeton had been an experiment in trying not to show the strain of being the only one, the only Middle Eastern player on the team, the only Muslim. She said it was exhausting explaining how her family's beliefs or expectations for her were different than other families', not wildly so, but enough that there was always that hitch, that gap she had to close between herself and the white girls she dated. She said sometimes it didn't seem worth it to explain, and so she'd been holding herself apart, above, at a remove. The more that people misunderstood why she did this—they called her a heartbreaker, a power top, a stuck-up bitch—the more she pulled back. Meeting Juniper, she said, had taught her she was guarding too tightly what she was meant to give away. And she had! Of all the women she'd known, she'd given *Juniper* her heart.

The gratitude Juniper felt was encoded in the DNA of their relationship. Forget that soccer players falling for each other was as cliché as politicians lying or lesbians with undercuts. It had never happened to her before. Of course, she'd had her crushes over the years, but somehow none of the girls she'd played with had ever liked her back (or at least they wouldn't admit to it; her gaydar was still pinging on some of them). Not until Hana. It probably wasn't healthy to feel this lucky to be loved, but who would want to test out the alternative? Not Juniper. And, anyway, wasn't this what everyone wanted? To find The One (and Only)? So why did her life still feel so precarious all the time?

The therapist had told her years ago not to play the coulda-shoulda-woulda game with the kidnapping, and Juniper had done her best to train her thoughts, like a creeping vine, to go elsewhere. But the trick wasn't working anymore.

"You think the last ten years haven't been hell on me, too?"

"You told that guy you wanted to move on and find peace," April said, as if such a thought were sacrilege.

"I want peace for all of us. My God, don't you?" Juniper asked.

"I want to find Dad." April started the car. "I'll talk to Leyla again. She must have found out about Yassin when she started looking into the case again. So why didn't she tell me? There has to be more to it. Something they don't want us to find out."

"Mm-hmm," Juniper said, already tuning her sister out. She was exhausted and there was nothing more she could do today.

When the black SUV pulled up in front of Union Station, she waved goodbye without looking back. She went inside and glanced up at the clock above the café, backlit by the Main Hall's giant windows. She had just enough time.

Fifteen minutes later the train left the station. Juniper hunched against the window, raising the bottle to her lips, raising it high so there would be nothing, not even gravity, between her and this release.

16

July

July forgot it was Memorial Day so he'd forgotten about the damn parade, too. His internship in Baltimore started tomorrow, and he was back at his mom's house for the summer. He'd gone for an early run, hoping to sweat away some of the lingering shame of the kisstastrophe, as he'd begun to think of it. He'd jogged down Post Road, threading the corridor between the base and the train tracks, past his old elementary school and the Baptist church where the parade always kicked off. Then he rounded the corner into the Walgreens parking lot, his old shortcut from his days running track, and came face-to-face with a boy scout, knobby-kneed in shorts, cheeks already flushed in the burgeoning, wet heat. Over his brown shirt he wore a white harness that came to a V over his belly button, in the apex of which was planted a pole, and the pole was flying the POW flag.

He'd run right into an old humiliation. The first Memorial Day parade after the kidnapping had fallen just a few weeks shy of the one-year anniversary of Frank's disappearance. The whole family had marched at the front of the line and July, the "man" of the family, had been picked to carry the POW banner. He'd blubbered from start to finish, and wound up on the front page of the *Baltimore Sun* bawling like a little baby. For years if you googled *crying boy* and *POW*, his image was number one in the search results.

The kid was struggling. He hunched forward and arched back, looking for a way to balance a weight that was already too great, and he hadn't even started walking yet. The mournful silhouette on the flag seemed to watch on as he struggled. The whole thing felt hopeless to July. The kid was too young to be given such a burden. Sometimes it was the vets who led the parade, the oldest ones in wheelchairs, medals pinned to their blazer pockets, their old caps dusted off and placed atop their bald heads, the younger vets walking or wheeling alongside them with the flags held high. Sometimes it was the high school cadet corps, kids who were ROTC-bound for college. This year it was Troop 415. The troop master was helping a second boy fit the stars and stripes into his harness, and a third was smiling and ready to go, the droopy corner of the Maryland state flag tickling his shoulder.

The boy glanced over at his friends, who were in no danger of failing this test, and then down at the spot where the pole met the harness, and began to cry. Quickly he wiped his tears away. He shuffled over to the troop master, who whispered something and adjusted the harness. He patted the boy on his back. The boy nodded and stood still, determined and vigilant. Nobody else had seen his lapse in composure. July remembered the sensations of the harness cutting into his shoulder, the pole digging into his gut, ribbons of muscle in his back burning for days afterward. All these years he'd thought his only reasons for crying when it had been his turn to carry the flag had been grief and the terrifying prospect that he would have to be the man of the house now. There was some consolation in knowing the pain had been physical, too—some, but not much.

A familiar figure moved through the parking lot toward Starbucks. Nate Guillory. What was he doing here? July headed that way, tugged by his own curiosity.

From outside the glass doors he watched Nate give the barista his order and reach into his back pocket for his wallet. In profile his body was a capital *S*—strong shoulders, narrow hips, an ass July had failed to properly admire. After the kisstastrophe last week July had put Grindr and Scruff back on his phone. Over the years he'd downloaded and deleted the apps half a dozen times, but they never brought him closer to what he really wanted. All they ever seemed to do was confirm his loneliness. But he'd seen enough profile pics in the last few days—the sultry smiles, pecs framed in a bathroom mirror—to appreciate what he'd missed before. If he'd been pretty as a boy, Nate was handsome now.

July winced at his own reflection in the door of Starbucks. His face burned red whenever he did any cardio, and he was wearing a grungy T-shirt he'd designated for exercise after the armpits had yellowed. He looked like actual hell.

Too late to reverse course, July heaved open the door.

Nate noticed him. "Hey!" he said.

"Home for the long weekend?" July asked.

"Yeah. If only my folks would move to the city, I wouldn't have to keep dragging my ass out this way, but that ain't happening anytime soon."

"It's not all bad, is it?"

Nate ducked his chin and raised his eyebrows. "You defending this place?"

July laughed. "No. When do you leave for England?"

"A few weeks. What about you? What are you doing this summer?"

"I got an internship—"

"Ooh la la."

"Paid," July clarified. "At the Global Resource Society." He didn't want Nate to get the wrong idea, to think he would live off his mom like that.

"No kidding? I heard those GRS gigs are competitive."

July shook his head like he didn't know, didn't want to brag, but he *did* know, and he was glad Nate knew, too. It made up, slightly, for being caught looking like a lobster.

The barista called out, "Iced mocha for Nathan!"

"Hang on," Nate said, and he retrieved his drink. "Aren't you getting anything?"

July patted his thigh and remembered he had no pockets and no money—nothing to provide an excuse for following Nate in here. "Just came in to cool off for a bit," he said.

They walked out together. The boy scouts had taken the flags out of their harnesses and were sitting on the curb. A couple of trucks towing horse trailers had pulled into the parking lot and the drivers were guiding the horses down the ramps. July and Nate wandered over to get a closer look.

"I was in the parade once," Nate said. "Miss Deena's Dance School turned it *out* that year. My dad didn't wanna let me out of the house in those striped leggings, but my mom said he had to. I'd been practicing for weeks. I thought I was gonna get discovered, like Channing Tatum or some shit, out here in the Aberdeen Memorial Day Parade." Nate laughed at himself.

"What happened?" July asked.

"Heat stroke happened."

"Oh, no."

"Oh, yes. I passed out before we made it to the first turn. Got towed the rest of the way in a red wagon by a couple of librarians. Goodbye stardom."

"Hello, bookmobile," July said.

Nate laughed again, and July realized that Nate knew about the time July cried in the parade, and that this story was him saying it was okay.

A whistle blew and the paraders began to assemble on the

street. The boy scouts stood and hoisted their flags. The first boy exhaled hard to blow the hair off his forehead, but the weight he carried drew his head forward and a lock of hair fell in his eyes so that he looked just like the silhouette on the flag. *You are not forgotten.* Every time July saw those words, he fought tears.

"So you're saying I shouldn't be embarrassed that I was the softest gay that ever was?" July asked.

Nate nudged him with his shoulder. "I'm saying life goes on."

That was the truth. Eleven-year-old July never could've imagined that one day they'd be friends. He'd spent so many years jealous of Nate's self-possession and confidence. Then he went to Hopkins and forgot about him. But in a couple months they'd be in England together. It wouldn't be so bad, he thought, to have Nate in his corner.

A palomino took a gigantic shit in the road, cutting the moment short.

"And on that note…" July said.

"What are you doing today? Not hanging around here feeling mopey, I hope." He put his hands together, as if in prayer.

July lifted his shoulders and let them fall. He had no plans.

"Nope, not okay. You're coming with me."

After lunch, they met back up and caravanned to a house party in Annapolis, where Kiara's parents lived. Nate turned at the State House and July followed. As they skirted the Naval Academy and the harbor, July felt a familiar claustrophobia. After his internship last summer he knew Annapolis was not his town. It was too steeped in traditions he could never embody. He wondered if his father had secretly wanted to serve his country in the way these midshipmen would someday. Nancy said no, but July had a hard time believing her after he went to Iraq. Would Frank have preferred it if his only son were more like the just-arrived plebes, who trained in matching T-shirts and shorts every summer, their hair shorn and scalps pink, learning to patch boats and shoot guns? Would Frank have taught him to shoot someday the way he'd taught the girls, or would he have known not to bother with him?

They zigzagged through the neighborhood streets, tracing the creek's contours, then parked outside a house set into the heel of a cove. As July stepped onto the back porch and saw the plank path leading down to the dock, he felt the tightening in his chest release. He'd spent his life on this bay, and here was another finger of it.

The scene didn't scream art school, but when July looked closer, he saw clues. Tattooed sleeves, stretched ear lobes, beanies worn in summer.

"There you are!" Kiara said, coming up the lawn to give Nate a hug. She wore overall shorts over a bathing suit, and her long hair was tied up like some kind of origami crane, the bottom half of her head shaved bare.

"Hey," Nate said, squeezing her back. "I brought someone."

"I see that." She smiled at July.

"Thanks for having me," July said. "Happy Memorial Day!"

"Yeah, Happy Dead Soldier Day!" she replied.

July went with it. "Happy Hot Dogs and Parades Day. If only it were hot dogs *on* parade, though."

"Seriously," Nate agreed. "But wait—are we talking about dudes in hot dog suits with ketchup and mustard stripes, or wiener dogs?"

"He's talking about naked men, obviously," Kiara said.

"Obviously," July concurred, though he hadn't been.

She nodded, appraising him. She leaned into Nate. "Yep, I see what you mean."

"Pshhh." Nate shook his head and smiled.

July felt a twinge in his stomach. What did she see? What did Nate mean? On instinct July checked his shirt for toothpaste stains.

"It's not really a party yet, is it?" Kiara said, surveying the guests scattered in sleepy-looking pairs and threesomes. "Hazel'll take care of that. She's running late as usual. Hey, do you like to kayak?"

"Do I like to kayak?" July asked, momentarily thrown by the infinitive form of the verb. "Um, sure. I like to kayak."

"Take ours out, then. Please. Someone's got to be first."

Nate was waiting for a thumbs-up or down from him. July nodded as if to say, *Yeah, sure.*

They walked down to the dock together.

"I see what you mean?" July asked.

Nate's eyebrows lifted, as if caught on a hook. Too Cool for School Nathan Guillory was embarrassed, and July was enjoying it. They lowered themselves into a two-man sea kayak that bobbed in the greenish water. Nate and Kiara had talked about him, maybe even said nice things. Did Nate get crushes like every other mortal? Had he confessed one to Kiara? July smiled—unable to hide how happy the thought made him— and reached for the oars up on deck. He handed one to Nate and they pushed off together.

They got their strokes in sync, and within a couple minutes they'd left the party behind. Both facing forward, it was difficult to talk, which was fine with July. He liked being out on the water. After a while they held their oars up for a rest and the kayak slowed. Little ripples of brackish water plinked against the boat, rocking them gently. For the first time in days, July felt still and easy. He peered over the edge, looking for oyster beds.

July felt a tug on his shorts.

"What's this?" Nate asked.

July turned around and saw what Nate had found in his back pocket. "My passport."

"Yeah, I know. Why'd you bring it?"

"It came in the mail." He'd been carrying it with him everywhere, held it pressed against his stomach last night while he ate ice cream and gorged himself on *Downton Abbey.*

"I had to renew mine, too," Nate said.

"Have you been out of the country before?"

"We lived in Germany when I was a baby, when my dad was in the army. That's it."

"That's my first passport. Think of all the places it might go." Nate flipped to the photo page and whistled. "Cute pic."

"All right, all right," July said, taking the book back.

Up ahead a navy patrol boat shot along a busy channel that led toward the harbor. Soon they began to rock in its wake. They paddled in the other direction and stopped when they reached calmer waters.

July turned around again. "Did you ever think about joining the army like your dad?" He waved in the direction of the boat. "Or the navy or whatever?"

"Hell no. Did you?"

July shook his head. "Did your dad want you to?"

"No. Did yours?"

"I don't know. He wanted me to play baseball or soccer, but I wasn't really into team sports. Thank God for my sister."

Nate squinted into the sun. July took off his sunglasses and gave them to him.

"Thanks." Nate put them on.

"Wow, those look way better on you." How was a guy this handsome still single? But wait. Maybe he wasn't. Maybe there was no crush. Suddenly July felt a prick of jealousy.

Nate smiled. But even with the glasses on, there was something pinched about his face, something he was puzzling over.

"What?" July asked.

"My dad didn't join the army because he thought it would make him a man. He went because it was a job and free health care and money for college. And we weren't at war at the time, so."

"Right," July said, reminded that for all of its macho and patriotic overtones, the military was a practical choice, too.

"Are you asking if my dad's cool that I'm gay?"

July's stomach tightened. That was exactly what he wanted to know, but he hadn't realized it. "Yeah. Is that okay to ask?"

"Yeah."

Nate angled his face away from the sun. He rubbed the bridge of his nose, then pushed the sunglasses back into place. July watched with humble fascination. Here was that famous Guillory self-possession constructing itself right before his eyes. Nate turned back toward the sun, his cheekbones and forehead awash in light.

"So, he's not, like, thrilled about it. He's not running down the street hollering, *My son is gay! Meet my gay son!*" The way he said this was theatrical and overblown, like Oprah introducing Brad Pitt to a studio audience, and they both laughed. Then his expression became more serious. "But he's not asking me to prove I'm down, either. I think for him it's about toughness—mental toughness. It's always been important to him that I know my own worth. That, gay or straight, I never back down or let anyone think they're better than me. He taught me how to hold my head up."

"That's so great."

"Yeah. We'll see how he does if I ever bring someone home for Christmas. Your dad's really on your mind, huh? Ever figure out what went down in Croatia?"

July took a big breath. Now it was his turn to gather composure.

"Whoa. What happened?"

July told him everything, about the hit on Tariq's passport in Croatia and the video of his father alive in 2006, May's suggestion that their dad might've been staying away intentionally, mixed up in something he couldn't or wouldn't get out of. If he'd had a more adult relationship with his dad, July might've had his own hunches about why he'd been in Croatia or at that camp, but without one, he had to look to his sisters to fill in the gaps, and they all seemed to believe such different things. Was his dad a hostage or a terrorist? A well-meaning patsy or a willing collaborator? July took another deep breath and looked up to the sky, as if the answer might be written on one of those banners that were sometimes flown overhead, with ads for insurance and new tires.

"Wow," Nate said. "I don't know how you're doing it."

"What?"

"Breathing."

"I don't know, either. But this helps." He gripped the oar in his lap with both hands. "Thanks for getting me out of fucking Aberdeen."

"Man, thank you for spending the day with me. I'm honored."

July was shaking his head. He'd heard this before from other people, most recently Lucas. Look how that had turned out. "I don't want the tragedy points."

"No really, I am. I didn't mean it that way."

Nate looked earnest, and July blushed.

"Head back?" Nate asked.

"Yeah, sure."

July faced forward. He dipped his oar in the water and listened to Nate's break the surface behind him. Soon they had the kayak pointed back toward the inlet and were paddling together as one.

When they got to the dock, the party was in full swing. Someone had dragged speakers outdoors and Bob Marley was playing. July pushed out of the kayak first and gave a hand to Nate, who was still wearing his sunglasses. His glasses were touching Nate's skin, cradling his ears.

They were still holding hands as they walked up to the shore, even though they didn't have to anymore. July's stomach flipped.

At the coolers Nate let go and grabbed them a couple beers and they clinked bottles. They'd worked up a sweat and the beer went down easy.

July thought that the best thing he'd done for himself all week might have been following Nate into Starbucks this morning. He looked around at everyone assembled, the art kids and the weirdos like him, the gamers and the poets, the gays and the genderqueers, the lost and the found, and he noticed Hazel step out the sliding glass doors onto the deck. She was smiling and bouncing to the music already. The track changed and "Could You Be Loved" started. She was a little ball of light, and he went toward her. He reached out and touched Nate's hip. *Come,* he meant. He was giddy and free and it made his shock all the more violent when he saw Lucas appear next to her. Saw Hazel turn, press into his chest like that resting place had been hers forever, and lift her mouth up to his for a kiss.

Hours later July wondered when a memory would ever feel like just a memory and not a cruel joke. A perfect day ruined, not just by the kiss but by his reaction to it. It shouldn't have mattered to him—it was obvious that things had changed between him and Lucas. When he'd helped Lucas move out of their suite and into his off-campus apartment last week, he'd felt the chasm between them. It no longer made sense that he'd ever felt close enough to kiss him—not after Lucas pulled away and scrambled out of bed like July was some household pest. The kiss no longer seemed brave, just misguided. No chance of them being roommates again, next year when he was back. It had taken two awkward hours to do the move, and on the drive to Aberdeen afterward, July had rolled down the windows and screamed into the wind.

When he saw Lucas and Hazel together today, he'd been too stunned to play it cool, burning with shame. That Hazel was a new friend only made the betrayal sting more. How easily she had secured what July had been unable to. How quickly Lucas had jumped on the attraction. That's why he'd showed up at

Hazel's room that day, to find *her*, not him. Lucas had his arm wrapped around her today while they mingled, claiming her as confidently as if they'd been together for years, not days. *That* was what it looked like when he wanted someone, no mixed signals about it. July knew that the thing to do was to lean into whatever was brewing between him and Nate, to let it lift him up out of this embarrassment, his awareness of his own shortcomings, his sensitivity to every look and stroke of skin between Lucas and Hazel. He should've smiled when Hazel waxed on about how great it was that they were all neighbors now, Lucas in the same apartment complex as Hazel and Kiara, which was just down the street from the little green house on the corner where Nate lived under the back stairs. But he couldn't, and Nate knew it. Nate had been gentle with July at first, watching him tentatively when the happy couple approached, smiling at him during the uncomfortable pauses, laughing in the right places, doing his best to normalize relations for the four of them. But all July could do was reel, and eventually Nate drifted over to the bar and to Kiara.

July had blown it, in every way possible, and the only thing to do was leave. But with the way Nate said, "Uh, okay? Bye?" July understood that leaving had been the wrong thing, too.

When he got home, April's SUV was in the driveway. So was Tom's. He hadn't known his sister was coming over. Was it because of the parade? The holiday? Had Nancy guilted her into it? July parked on the street and walked through the garage into the kitchen.

The bizarre array of food laid out—a couple of fish sticks, a bowl of grapes, and some leftover pizza crusts—told him the visit hadn't been planned. April's kids were calling out to each other in the backyard, and the grown-ups were in the living room, their expressions grim. Could this day get worse? It could not. He wouldn't let it.

"More news!" Tom said as July entered, seemingly desperate for something to smile about, but April and Ross didn't look cheered.

For once his mother was without words. She made her living by her hands so she was careful with them, got regular manicures, sometimes slept in white cotton gloves when she did a deep-moisturizing treatment. But now she chewed her thumbnail, shook her head.

"Is it Dad?" July asked.

"No," Ross rushed to say. "We still don't know anything more about him. Go on and tell him, Ape."

Just once he'd like to look at his sister's face and see that there was nothing on her mind, no burden she was calibrating before she put it on him.

"Tell me."

"The State Department got confirmation that the person traveling on Tariq's passport in Croatia and Kosovo wasn't Tariq. They think it was his cousin, Hamza Fattahi."

"Was he traveling with Dad?"

"They still don't know."

"Oh," July said. He perched on the edge of the couch, next to his mom. "I don't get it. Tariq's cousin borrowed his passport. So? Big deal. Why do you all look like somebody died?"

Nancy took hold of his forearm. Her thumb was still a little wet and it cooled his skin where it rested.

"Right now our only link to Dad is Hamza Fattahi," April said. "And Hamza Fattahi is on a terrorist watch list."

"Oh," July said. Nancy smiled weakly. He wrapped his arm around her. "Oh, hell."

June 2014

17

April

April called Leyla Halabi first thing in the morning on the first Monday of June, the wedding only twelve days away. She'd called her over the weekend, too, after the president's televised address from the Rose Garden on Saturday, when he stood next to the freed soldier's parents and announced the transfer of five detainees from Guantanamo Bay to Qatar in a hostage exchange. Five years ago the soldier had been captured by the Taliban in Afghanistan. Now he was recovering in a hospital in Germany. When the president acknowledged all the other American citizens still unjustly detained abroad "who deserve to be reunited with their families," it was as if he was speaking directly to April. Finally, here was some political will! She called Leyla. Desperate, she even tried May, but she didn't leave a message. By lunchtime on Monday there'd been no return call from Leyla, who was clearly stonewalling, or from May, who hadn't cooled down from their fight a couple weeks ago. (Nancy said she hadn't been home much since the bridal shower, that she was out licking her wounds.) That's when April called Craig.

"Hey," he said, his tone a mixture of surprise and amusement. They rarely called each other, usually only texted. It had been a month since she'd last contacted him—not since the parking garage in Bethesda. It wasn't the longest they'd gone without meeting, but long enough to be meaningful. Every time she tried to cut him out of her life, something got in the way. Some urge or fear or doubt that sent her back to that shadow world where she could punch holes in her reflection and still, somehow, reemerge as April, Ape, Mom. This time was different. She wasn't looking for another tool to gouge herself with; she actually needed his help.

She still had no idea why her dad had been at that training camp in 2006; all that mattered when she watched the video was that he was alive, she hadn't hallucinated him. Tariq being in Dubrovnik the same day she saw Frank had only added weight to her belief. But now that she knew it was his cousin in Dubrovnik instead of Tariq, she had to consider the possibility that what May had said could be right. Was her dad consorting with terrorists? It wasn't a question she could just come out and ask a government official. If her dad had done something illegal, the last thing she wanted to do was incriminate him. But it could explain why he was in Croatia.

She needed to talk to someone else, a hostage expert who operated outside the government.

"What's up, Doc?" Craig said.

"Hi. I need to ask you for a favor."

"Go on."

The line crackled with expectation.

"No, a real one."

"Oh," he said, his voice gone limp.

"That friend of yours, the one who did a K&R table or something for your client—"

"Tabletop."

"Right. Do you think you could arrange a meeting?"

"I *probably* could, I guess."

"Today?"

"Really?"

April knew their relationship was mostly transactional. If there'd been a chance in the early days for something fuller and richer, she'd squashed it, always holding herself at a remove, keeping her feelings in check, never letting him know what was truly important to her. There'd been that one slipup six months ago, when she told him about her dad, but after that she'd gotten better at compartmentalizing. Now she was going to pay the price for it. She needed his help, but had nothing to offer in return.

"Please, Craig. I have to talk to him. I wouldn't ask if it weren't important."

The pause that followed was almost unbearable.

"I saw the news about that hostage," he said at last.

"Yes." She felt like a rope snapped tight and shaking. She'd barely slept. Her vulnerability—of a different kind altogether than the one Craig was used to seeing—was evident and unadorned.

He sighed.

"Okay, let me reach out."

They met at Risatti's after work, *after* being an approximation of the time most people went home to their families while April usually put in another two to three hours at the office or slipped away to meet Craig. A ribbon of guilt rippled through her when she spotted his car in the parking lot, even though what they were doing now was perfectly above board. There was no need to keep the meeting a secret, and yet she'd made up a work excuse for Ross.

Opening the door to the restaurant, she was nervous and strangely happy to see Craig. He hadn't needed to come too but there he was. He introduced her to two men: his buddy Neil, around her age and baby-faced compared to his colleague Joe, a former CIA agent who had about ten years on them and looked battle-hardened, solidly built, hair cropped short.

The hostess arrived with menus. Craig beckoned for April to go first and then followed. For months she'd been sorting Craig's and Ross's behavior into categories: dangerous/dirty/aggressive or loyal/supportive/safe. Her wires were getting scrambled because here she was feeling soothed by the way Craig tucked in her chair, the way they sat together on one side of the table, like a real couple.

April lined herself up opposite Joe. He would have the answers. She needed to focus on him, not Neil, and certainly not Craig.

Once they all put in their orders, April thanked the men for coming.

Joe nodded.

"Sure thing," Neil said. "Craig's a good friend, and I like to help my friends if I can. But to be honest, I was curious to meet Frank Barber's daughter."

April flinched. "I never expect anyone to remember him by now."

"In our business, we talk about that case a lot."

"How so?"

The two men shared a glance. Joe's hands were clasped on top of the table. He spun his wedding ring around his stubby finger, cleared his throat, and his eyes met hers. "Your dad's kidnapping is a case study in what *not* to do."

April's stomach twisted. What percentage of the last ten years had she spent stuck in a loop of second-guessing all the decisions they'd made? Should they have paid the $50K or the full ransom amount or nothing at all? Should they have gone to the FBI sooner, or should they have focused all their efforts on making sure the press never got a hold of the story? It was infinitely harder to negotiate for a famous hostage's release. Case in point, that soldier. April had never heard of him until two days ago. She closed her eyes, willing the tears that were forming to disappear. She blinked a few times.

"What should we have done?" she asked.

"Look," Neil said, "nobody expects to be kidnapped, or to be the loved one of someone who is. The average person just can't prepare for something like this. That's why companies with deep pockets come to us. Preparing for the worst is our job."

It was a sales pitch, and April didn't need it. She looked at Joe. "What did we do wrong?"

"The abduction caught CCA unprepared, which—given what was going on in Iraq at the time—it shouldn't have. He never should have been off-base without security. And the government's response was flat-footed and slow. The cards were stacked against you."

The saliva in her mouth began to sour, the first sign she might actually vomit. She took a drink of water.

"Agreeing to the ransom, even partially, was a good move," Joe said. April focused on his eyes. She nodded. "Nine times out of ten, when the family pays up, the hostage is returned. You got unlucky there, so I get why you went to the FBI next. Now, those guys, they're bound by certain laws. If you'd gone to them immediately, they would have advised you against paying the ransom—*it's against the policy of the United States government yadda yadda*—and that would have been a mistake. They would have intimidated you with the threat of imprisonment, when the reality is families are almost never charged for that sort of thing. After the FBI came on board, you lost contact with the kidnappers, did I hear that right?"

"Yes. The trail went cold."

"The email trail might have gone cold, but the money trail was still there to follow."

"They said they traced the wire transfer, but the account was opened with a false identity. The funds were withdrawn and the account was closed by the time the FBI got on the case."

Joe tilted his head side to side as if weighing two columns of facts against each other. "Not great news, but there are still ways to code a transfer like that and follow it as it changes hands. My guess is they did that, but didn't have enough intel on the guys it led them to. You can run into jurisdiction problems real fast on a case like this, and to break the logjam it helps to have industry cooperation. They didn't get that from CCA."

April smiled derisively.

"Not your favorite people, huh?" Neil asked.

"Hardly."

"I'm sure you know this," Joe said, "but it was hunting season in Iraq when your dad was taken. Kidnapping was the best business in town in 2004. Anyone who looked like he had two nickels to rub together was a target, even Iraqis, and not particularly wealthy ones, either. Middle class guys were getting snatched out of their cars on the ride home from work. And for companies like CCA, with a lot of foreigners on the payroll, that's a huge liability. So they lower their risk by putting their workers on limited-term contracts—not their responsibility now. But they also obfuscate and obstruct investigations. It says a lot about your dad that they even sent their guys to the bus station to look for him. He must have been well-liked, because the official protocol was undoubtedly Don't Get Involved."

April was touched, but she didn't want Joe to hold back. She needed to know what kept her dad stranded whereas others were saved. "What didn't we do that we should have?"

"If it had been me, my loved one who was missing, I would have gone to Iraq. That said, you don't have my training. You don't know how to get into a country we're at war with. Today it's simple. You can book a ticket direct to Erbil and you don't even need a visa. But ten years ago it was tough. Turkey had closed its borders; you'd have had to smuggle yourself across there. Syria used to be the back door into Iraq, until CNN fucked it all up for everyone, filming their reporters coming in just before the invasion. Damascus shut the route down after that. So that left Tehran, and to go that way you'd have had to get an Iranian visa. Not easy to come by."

While Joe was speaking, April heard a ringing in her ears. May had figured out all of this by herself.

"And then what?" she asked once he stopped.

"Then you get there and you knock on doors. You talk to CCA. You ask questions. What was Frank Barber doing in that SUV? What was he doing on that road, leaving Mosul? What business did he have with Mahmoud Yassin?"

"They said they didn't know. That whatever their meeting was about wasn't job-related. *Extracurricular*, CCA called it."

"Sure they did. But they knew what he was up to, mark my words."

"What do you think he was doing?"

"Up north? Well, that's a major smuggling route."

"Smuggling?" she said. "Smuggling what, people?"

"People, weapons, drugs, fuel, diapers. You name it. Yassin was in *import/export*—" he held up his fingers like air quotes "—from what I've heard, so I'd have a lot of questions about that. I'd start there, but I'd also talk to the locals."

"How? Which ones? That sounds like it could get dangerous."

"Right. And again, I'm not suggesting that you personally could have gone. An unaccompanied woman, a foreigner, and I'm guessing you don't speak Arabic?"

She shook her head. Again, there was that ringing. May had been all alone, a target—and still, she'd gone.

"For our clients, we have guys we can send, and fixers who can help us on the ground, make introductions. But the driver survived, right? So we'd have wanted to talk to him, talk to his family."

If there'd been a part of April that had been impressed by May's boldness that November, ten years ago, it had been small. It was five months after their father was taken—the Suits weren't talking anymore, and if they were, it was in platitudes and circles. The better part of April had thought May was stupid and impulsive, going to Iraq to search for Frank herself. *You could have been killed!* April had shouted afterward. And the trip had been an unqualified disaster.

"We recently found out that the driver's nephew—not the driver himself—was likely involved. An Arab with a grudge against rich Kurds. But the nephew's dead now," April said, throwing up her hands as if to say, *Of course.*

Joe's eyes narrowed. He shot a look at Neil.

"Who told you that?" Neil asked.

So Karim had given them information that wasn't common knowledge yet. "I'd rather not say."

"It was definitely a money job, then," Joe said. "At first."

"*At first*—why do you say that?"

"Keeping a hostage is expensive. If it's all about the money, they've got no motive to keep him after they're paid."

"Then what?"

"The simplest answer is they bungled the job. Something went wrong and they lost the hostage."

"Lost him?" she asked. You didn't just lose people, like they were a pair of winter gloves.

"Killed him."

She shuddered. The kidnappers *had* lost Yassin, but not her father. "There's new video footage—or not new, but newly identified—of my dad and his interpreter, Tariq Ibrahim, alive two years later."

"No way," Neil said.

April felt Craig's arm resting on the back of her chair. She'd forgotten he was there. Now that she was talking to Joe, she felt more sure of herself. There'd never been this much give-and-take with a Suit before.

"That would be interesting to see," Joe said. He didn't believe her.

"I've got it on my laptop. Right here." She reached for the briefcase at her feet.

"How'd you get a hold of that? Wait, not here." He pushed back his chair and stood up. She got up, too. Neil started to move, but Joe put out his hand to stop him. "We'll be back."

Craig raised his glass at her and took a drink, sidelined.

After she played the video for him three times, Joe closed the laptop. They were sitting in her SUV. In the rearview mirror, April caught a glimpse of a couple escorting an older woman slowly across the parking lot toward the restaurant's front doors. The sky was all pinks and purples, a beautiful sunset for someone else.

"My guess is they're in Syria," Joe said.

"Syria?"

"Yeah. Something about that topography. The way the topsoil was blowing around? 2006 was the start of a massive four-year drought in Syria, which devastated the country economically and was essentially the proximate cause of the civil war there today. If this video were from a year or two later, you wouldn't see that goat. He'd have been eaten by then."

"I don't know if the State Department knows where the video was shot or if they're just not telling me. My contact's not even returning my calls."

"I'm surprised they gave you the link to be honest. Your contact's gonna run out their string soon, if they keep helping you like this."

Joe fiddled with his wedding ring again.

"Do you have kids?" April asked.

He nodded.

"How old are they?"

"My daughter's eighteen. My boys are five and three."

She guessed he was on his second marriage. Probably hadn't worn the ring for the first one. Maybe it would've been a job hazard to wear it. Maybe he hadn't thought it necessary. Either way, she saw this tic of his in a new light. Spinning the wedding band around his finger wasn't just a way to keep his hands busy. It was a luxury—a treasure—to show that he loved and was loved.

"This work must get pretty dark," she said.

"Used to. I was away from my family a lot and didn't have the healthiest habits, shall we say, for processing what I was seeing. Now, it's different. This job's corporate so it's, you know—" she thought he was going to say *safe* but instead he said "—antiseptic. It's about insurance as much as anything."

"But you're home for your boys."

"That I am."

April knew she should let him go, return to the restaurant and get home, but she didn't want to. Here in the car with Joe, there was a logic to things; even the worst betrayals made sense. Out there, nothing did.

"My contact did tell me one other thing," she said. "Tariq has a cousin, Hamza Fattahi, who traveled on his passport to the Balkans a couple months ago. And he's on a terrorist watch list."

"They say who's he affiliated with?"

"No."

"Hezbollah? PKK? The Islamic State?"

"No, nothing."

July had been obsessing about Hamza being in Dubrovnik ever since they found out about him. He'd discovered online a conference held in Dubrovnik at the same time she was there that focused on the political situation in Kurdistan and seemed friendly toward the PKK, the Kurdistan Worker's Party in Turkey. What April knew about the PKK was what made the news—assassinations, kidnappings, suicide bombs—but they were also proponents of women's rights, environmentalism, and minority rights in a country with the largest Kurdish population in the world. Turkey had labeled the PKK terrorists and, as its ally, the US had followed suit.

April told Joe about the conference in Dubrovnik.

"I mean, you knew your father best. You tell me. You think he's the kind of guy to join up with an outfit like that?"

Maybe her father could've been theoretically sympathetic, especially if he'd formed a personal relationship with someone within the PKK, but actually becoming an adherent? She couldn't imagine it, even if May or July could. *Your first obligation is to your family*, he was always telling her. He would never turn his back on them.

"No," she admitted. "You said before, the simplest answer was the kidnappers bungled the job. What's the complicated answer?"

He rubbed his face, as if he'd been cramming for an impossible exam for hours. It was comforting to April that a professional could be as exhausted by all the angles as she was.

"That they traded your father. Either for more money, or to get in with a more powerful group."

"You think the government knows who to?"

"Unless they're total idiots, which…"

They shared a grim laugh.

"What do I do now? I thought maybe the State Department could get somebody, some government, to act as an intermediary between us and whoever took him. Like Qatar did with the Taliban for that soldier this weekend."

She didn't know what to think anymore. Was her father in Dubrovnik as someone's captive, or was he acting of his own volition, persuaded by some cause? The signs pointed in both directions. Either way, she wanted him back.

"April, I'm gonna be straight with you because…hell. Neil likes to sugarcoat things and our bosses like it when I talk in probabilities, but I think you've been living with this uncertainty for *way* too long. So here's the truth. The State Department ain't gonna get your dad back for you, if he's even alive. I know he was alive in 2006, but eight years is a long time for him not to pop up on anyone's radar. It probably wasn't him you saw."

April knew Joe could be right. It might not have been her dad in Dubrovnik, which made all the questions her family were asking themselves now irrelevant. If it wasn't him she saw, then he wasn't a terrorist. And if no one had seen him in eight years, that might be because he was already dead. She'd been waiting a decade for someone to tell it to her straight, but she couldn't help herself. She believed, maybe against all odds, that she would find her father if she just kept looking. She teared up again. This time she didn't try to hide it.

Joe turned his shoulder so that he was facing her head-on.

"Okay, look. My wife's a nurse. And she's always saying, if someone you love goes into the hospital, you go with them. You park yourself at their bedside and you ask every doctor and every nurse who comes into the room what they're doing and why. If you need to eat or rest, you have someone else take your place. And between the two of you, you pay attention. When something doesn't make sense or it feels like something important is getting overlooked, you speak up. You raise hell if you have to. Because no one cares more about that patient than you do.

"I'm impressed," he went on. "What you've been able to figure out on your own? Seriously, I'd hire you myself. Sounds like you've got some sources you haven't fully tapped yet. Talk to them. Stay on the trail. But don't wait for Big Daddy Government to swoop in and be a hero because it ain't gonna happen."

When they got back to the table, their plates had been delivered. Chicken marsala. What had she been thinking ordering something so cloyingly sweet? But it didn't matter. She'd lost her appetite. Joe flagged a waiter to bring the check. When it came, April started to reach for her wallet, but Craig put his hand on her arm and dropped his AMEX.

They said goodbye to Joe and Neil and then Craig walked her to her car. She leaned against it. "Thank you," she said. "I don't know how you knew to invite Joe, too, but he was a godsend."

"Good." Craig smiled. "I'm glad."

He touched her neck, and let his hand rest there. April leaned forward and kissed him in gratitude. What else was it that she wanted from him in this moment? She couldn't tell. Usually she came to their encounters for that feeling of abandon. You could get addicted to the way pleasure twinned with shame, both bottomless. She definitely had.

She stood back and he looked at her, puzzled. She was thinking about that woman in the video. What if there *had* been a romantic connection with her dad, some kind of entanglement? What if this pull she had toward Craig, toward other men, was in her blood? Like father, like daughter. Craig kissed her, deeply this time. Her body responded, but her thoughts were six thousand miles away. He pressed into her with his fingers, his tongue, his knee.

April wrenched away.

"What?" Craig asked.

He was frustrated. So was she.

"I can't right now," she said. She couldn't keep turning to Craig any time she felt lost.

"I thought this was what you needed."

"No. It's not. I need...space."

He laughed, obviously stung. "When have I ever not given you space?"

He was right. The problem was her, not him. She let herself into her car, backed up, and drove away.

Once again April was full of things to say with no one to say them to—except one person, who hated her guts right now. She called May anyway and got her voice mail.

"I wish you were here," she told the recording. "I don't know what to do."

She hung up.

She was expected home, but by whom? Not Ross. They'd been married so long they often fell into phases—they were in one now—where they exchanged the minimum amount of conversation and fellowship that marriage required. The children were fed and transported, the sex life was carried along, the work was done and the bills were paid, and the daily routines of family life were maintained, all without much need for a kindred spirit. The kids expected food in the fridge and clean underwear and money on demand, but except when they were sick, they didn't really look for her anymore. No, clearly, it was April who had expectations of herself, to be a beacon or sentry for her family. But who did that leave to watch over her?

She tried May another time as she turned into her subdivision. She slowed down. There were still a few kids out, circling on their bikes. The streetlights made little islands on the asphalt on which the bugs gathered. She heard the beep.

"I'm sorry I was so angry when you went to Iraq," April said. Something between them had snapped then and they'd never repaired it. "I was just so scared for you. And jealous, too, I think. I probably couldn't have gone anyway, with the baby. But you didn't even ask me to come."

April pulled into her driveway and killed the engine.

"It was brave of you to go." Not even when their dad was snatched had April felt this alone. At least then there'd been the baby growing inside her. "Anyway, I hope you're okay, wherever you are."

Inside the house was quieter than usual. The TV was off and Ross was sitting in the kitchen, drinking a beer and reading on his phone. She kissed him, then opened the refrigerator door, but her appetite hadn't returned.

"Where is everyone?" April asked.

"Coop's at Ethan's and Maddie's spending the night at Charlotte's house."

"Charlotte's?" April shut the refrigerator door.

"Yeah."

She wondered whether to tell Ross about Hudson the lothario. Had her conversation with Maddie been in confidence? It was just a crush. Nothing serious had happened. Their daughter would have lots of crushes—were they all supposed to be off the record?

"I think she's got a crush on Charlotte's brother, Hudson."

"Okay. Do we need to be worried?"

It was a good question. Maddie didn't seem sexually curious so much as self-conscious. If the boy made an actual pass at her, she would probably balk.

"No. I don't think so."

"Would you tell me if you were?"

There was that tone again. The last few days it seemed Ross bristled at anything April said.

"Of course, I would."

He was still in his work clothes. Usually he was in a rush to liberate himself from his corporate uniform when he got home. He changed into shorts and a T-shirt before he did anything else. But here he was with his shoes still laced, his tie still knotted. The way he looked at her now gave her a bad feeling.

"What?" she asked.

"Who's Craig?"

April frowned, like the name meant nothing to her, but her heart hammered in her chest.

"Ape, I found the messages on your phone. I wasn't snooping. I was holding your phone for you at the mall, after you got that call from Leyla. And a message came through, and I saw it."

She froze, her face still set against this bizarre mystery.

"I told myself I wasn't gonna say anything now when you've got so much else to deal with. But that's the problem, right? You always have so much to deal with."

She couldn't do this tonight. She didn't care if he was right. "He's just this guy I work with sometimes. He likes to flirt, and sometimes I flirt back."

"You're lying. I saw them, Ape. I read them all."

"Look, those texts, they look bad, I know they do. And I'm sorry. I'll delete him from my phone. I'll figure out a way not to work with him anymore."

"You're so calm when you're lying."

"Ross—"

"Did you sleep with him?"

It was like she was running on two tracks. Her stomach was churning and her head was shaking *no, no, of course not*, but her mind was racing ahead, calculating how much would be lost forever if she let this lie stand in their way. She stilled her moving parts. She'd once been certain she would never hurt him.

"Yes," she said.

His face didn't change but his neck clenched and then released, as if it were trying to absorb the shock for the rest of him. She was still in front of the refrigerator. He was still at the table. Time had stopped.

"I'm so sorry," April said.

"How long?"

"What?"

"How long," he snapped.

"I mean. You saw the texts."

His eyes widened. "That whole time?"

In April's more deluded moments, she'd felt Ross understood on some level how little control she had over her desires, that they were like dark matter in the universe, far-reaching and unpredictable, but also strangely binding, a skeleton upon which other parts of her hanged. But he didn't. Seeing his innocence, watching him realize now the full scale of her betrayal was breathtaking.

Ross stood. He walked toward the living room, then stopped. He took a few more steps, then stopped again. He turned around and came back to the edge of the kitchen.

"Was it better with him? Did you like fucking him more than me?"

"No," she said.

"Don't lie to me!"

"I'm not."

"Was it rougher?"

"Yes."

"You want it rough?" Ross shouted. He crossed the floor in an instant, pressed her up against the refrigerator, his hands on her shoulders, his face in her hair.

She wasn't afraid, but her stomach shook with small sobs.

"You broke my heart," he whispered.

Then he left. She looked at the spot on the counter by the door, where he always put his keys. Tonight they'd been in his pocket the whole time, that's how sure he was that he'd need to leave. She heard his car back away and the garage door close.

April was, finally, truly alone.

18

May

May knocked on Will's front door with the heel of her boot, holding two cups of coffee and a bag of pastries, Jack waiting patiently beside her. Four nights a week, Zoe stayed with Will, and the next four she stayed at her mom's house, and after two weeks of sneaking out before the girl woke up and then coming back as if she hadn't spent the night, the ruse was wearing thin. Not to mention she was going through a small fortune at the café around the corner.

"Doggy, doggy, doggy!" May heard Zoe bellow as she ran to the door. She opened it and hurled herself around Jack's neck. The first couple times he'd growled a little but now he bore her affection stoically.

"Good morning!" Will said, committing to the bit. "We were just about to have some breakfast, weren't we, Zozo? Come join us."

"You probably don't want this sprinkle cookie, then, do you?" May asked.

"Yes!" Zoe said, jumping up and down.

"Okay, okay. Lead the way then, kid," May said.

She trailed Zoe to the kitchen table and lifted her into her high chair. While Will circled the table with the skillet, dishing out a portion of scrambled eggs for each of them, she set the sprinkle cookie and a couple croissants on a plate. May sat and yawned, and Will squeezed her shoulder before taking the skillet back to the sink.

She was bone-tired in a way that had nothing to do with how early she had to rise to be out of the house before Zoe woke up or how much sex she and Will were having, which honestly wasn't that much, given how new they were and how good it still was. He still read her body better than any partner she'd ever had; he seemed to know when it was enough just to make out without the promise of anything more, when she wanted to be held, when she needed to rest. Since the bridal shower, she'd given up internet rabbit holes, and kidnapping school, and following wherever the next clue led. She'd seen the video— her dad was free to come and go. Let April solve the mystery of why Frank didn't want to come home. Instead May went to work, saw Will, and slept. Rinse and repeat.

"Are you excited about coming to the zoo today?" May asked, and Zoe nodded.

"Which animals do you want to see, Zozo?" Will gave her her sippy cup and then finally sat down himself.

"Ummm," she said, and then looked up at the ceiling. Her wheels were turning but nothing else came out of her mouth.

"How about a giraffe?" Will suggested.

"Ummm."

"A rhinoceros?" May offered.

"A unicorn," Zoe whispered with great reverence.

Will laughed in that way he must have developed since becoming a dad, noiselessly delighted.

"Oooh, me, too," May said. "I think the unicorn might be

on a trip today, but don't worry, there'll be lots of other animals we can say hi to."

Zoe picked the cookie crumbs out of her eggs and said, "Okay."

May took Will and Zoe on the all-access VIP tour normally reserved for donors and municipal bigwigs. They went to the children's farm and held the bunnies and chicks, they fed the giraffe apples, they went to the elephant barn and stroked Scout's ear through the vertical bars. Through it all May couldn't get past the feeling that none of them belonged there, not the animals and not her.

After Will and Zoe left and her shift concluded, May pulled up the voice mails from April. Her sister had left them two nights ago, and May had been doing her best to forget they were there. Time to get it over with. In the employee lot she sat in her car and listened.

The first one was short but left her feeling depleted. April was confused and overwhelmed. She needed someone to bounce her theories off of, but May couldn't be that person for her. The second message shocked her: an apology, of all things. April had called her brave, though May knew she wasn't. Going to Iraq had been a mistake. The problem was, no matter how many times she played what-if, and even knowing how badly it would end, she couldn't see any way that she *didn't* go to Iraq to try to save her dad.

She put the phone down and drove to Will's house. They had the place to themselves again, Zoe back at Kelly's for another four-day stretch, so May rallied and initiated, stripping her clothes off just inside the front door, Will doing the same and following her to the bedroom. They showed each other their true selves, their new bodies, all the scars, rolls, hair, freckles that time had added and taken away. They went slow, Will going down on her languorously, like he had all the time in the world.

"Don't wait for me," he lifted his head to say, and when he went back to it, she came in rolling waves.

She fell into a deep sleep and when she woke, it was dark out. She smelled garlic and onions and chicken browning. In the kitchen she poked her head over the stove to see what he was making—chicken soup.

"Sorry I fell asleep," she said.

"What sorry? I slept, too."

May sat at the counter where she could face him and watch him work. "Why don't you hate me?" she asked.

"What?"

"You're so good to me. You should be furious."

Will laughed to himself, an accidental blast twinged with pain. "Remember when I told you I didn't always like myself? I tried hating you. I sucked at it."

"I'm sorry. For the way I left things."

"But not for leaving me?"

It was terrible what she'd done, breaking up with him over email. She'd offered him no explanation, not because he didn't deserve one, but because she couldn't find the words. I'm a piece of shit, she wrote and deleted a dozen times, and ultimately changed it to I'm sorry, I can't, please don't call.

"I didn't know how else to be at the time."

He gave everything a stir. Then he put the lid on the pot and came around to the stool beside her. "I don't want to pry or nag. I promise I'll only ask you this once."

This was the moment she'd been waiting for, when Will would finally let loose the frustration he'd been carrying for ten years, that he'd been playing tricks with for the last month, like a magician hiding the queen.

"What happened over there?" he asked. "When all the fighting broke out in Mosul, I was scared out of my mind for you. I thought eventually you'd come back to me, but you never did."

She wanted him to understand that what happened in Iraq

had changed everything about the way she saw the world and her place in it. It was bigger than the two of them, too big, it had seemed for so long, to put into words. But she had to try.

"I know something bad went down. Please, talk to me."

He was right. It was time to tell him everything.

When they reached Mosul, it was night. They had the radio down and Adar drove hunched forward, scanning the side streets for danger but flying along so quickly May wasn't sure they could stop if they met it. They crossed a bridge whose metal walls zigzagged alongside the Toyota. May realized with a shock that they were over the Tigris. The river was shallow after the long summer, and the sound of the wheels echoed back at her. On the other side of the bridge, in west Mosul, the minaret at the Great Mosque of al-Nuri leaned like the Tower of Pisa. The streets narrowed as they headed into the Old City.

Adar turned off his headlights and at last they pulled up in front of an apartment building. May followed him inside and up a set of stairs.

His sister-in-law Mina opened the apartment door just as they reached it and shut it quickly behind them. Adar hugged her and they exchanged words. She was maybe in her mid-thirties, but it was difficult to gauge. Her hair was tucked under a white headscarf, showing off dark circles under her eyes, and her petite frame swam in a blue gown with pink flowers at the neckline. She glanced at May and then smiled, formally, while Adar spoke in Kurdish. Her husband, Adar's brother Saïd, was Peshmerga and his unit fought alongside US Special Forces; he'd died in the fighting in Halabja the year before. In another life, before the war took him, she must have sparkled.

"As-salum' alaykum," Mina said before disappearing down the hall.

In the living room two girls were reading on the rug and an

older boy sat at the window. The girls came and kissed their uncle's cheek. One of them accepted the pastries he'd brought and then left. Adar beckoned in a playful tone, and a pair of feet came scampering down the hall. He introduced the little boy, Beno, to May and they played peekaboo while dinner was prepared.

Beno's sister returned with an oilcloth that she spread out on the rug. Mina came behind her with a tray of food: the pastries and plates and bowls of vegetables, stewed beans, rice pilaf topped with chicken, and flatbread. She laid it all out on the blanket, and Beno scrambled down from Adar's lap.

"Chh," Mina said sharply, and Beno sat back on his heels and waited. She gestured at May to begin.

May reached for an olive. "Thank you," she said. "Shukran," she said again, in Arabic, wishing she'd learned a few words in Kurdish, too.

Another girl, the oldest, appeared with a tray of tea. That made five children altogether, three girls and two boys. Beno was the littlest.

They heard a volley of gunfire, off in the distance.

"Soran," Adar called.

His other nephew came away from the window and joined his family on the floor, but he obviously wasn't interested in the meal. He stared back at the window. Mina put a chicken leg on his plate and nudged him to eat.

May didn't have an appetite, either, but there was too much food to decline. She scooped a few spoonfuls of beans and rice on her plate and did her best.

The bus station wasn't far away; they'd driven near it on their way in. May hoped the skirmish would die down once the sun was up. Under ordinary circumstances, she could probably make it there on foot in about fifteen minutes, but she would need to see where things stood tomorrow.

Another blast of gunfire, this time much closer. Adar stood and flicked off the light. He and Mina herded everyone into an interior hallway. Mina pulled Beno onto her lap and drew one of the girls to her side. The fighting came toward them, gunshots growing louder, shouting becoming audible. May imagined a radar screen, with this apartment at the center and insurgents crossing imaginary bands of distance to reach them. Or maybe it was the Americans coming. She didn't know. Her mouth watered with a tinny taste she knew was fear.

She told herself there was no reason for anyone to single out this mother and her children. Surely the men with guns would pass them by. Adar was sitting closest to the door. She knew only what he'd told her about himself. She had to trust that he wasn't dangerous. As if sensing her thoughts, he eyed her back. She was a white woman, an American, in his family's home. If anyone had brought danger here, it was her, and still Mina had taken her in, shared her meal, served her first. May hoped none of the neighbors had seen her arrive.

They stayed in the hallway for hours, bursts of gunfire punctuating the long night. May didn't think she'd be able to sleep through the noise and the tension, but suddenly she understood that she was now awake, which meant she had slept, after all. She felt something in her lap and discovered Beno stretched out like a sling with his head on her leg and his feet on Mina's. May touched his hair, fine like a kitten's soft fur.

In the morning it was calm again. Adar spoke to Mina for a while, then he approached May. This neighborhood was majority Arab, he explained. A Kurdish family would make an easy target. And if they discovered the American hiding here, he said, but he let the thought go unfinished. On the other side of the river there was a large Kurdish population. Mina had friends there they could stay with. Adar had heard the Peshmerga was there, too. So they would all crowd into the Land Cruiser and drive to east Mosul.

But after Adar went out to have a look around, the plan

changed again. Two of his tires had been shot out. They would have to walk.

May watched as Mina packed a few things quickly and with purpose. Had she drawn up a list of necessities in the night, while her children dozed around her, or had she made her emergency plan long ago—after Saïd's death, perhaps, or the US invasion, or well before that? Mina brought out a small pile of black gowns from the bedroom. She handed one to May, gesturing at her to put it on, veil first, in one of the bedrooms. When May emerged, dressed in the abaya and veil, she saw how well she blended in with Mina, who'd changed out of her colorful gown into a black conservative one, and Yasemin, the oldest, who also wore the abaya over her jeans and sweatshirt. When everyone was ready, May followed Adar and the children out the door as Mina locked up the apartment behind her.

Adar led the way as they walked down the street. It would only have been a short distance to the nearest of the city's five bridges, but it was uncrossable; instead they had to chart a longer route toward the next bridge. Mina stayed a few steps behind Adar, Beno on her hip, her two younger daughters trailing her. May fell to the back, behind Yasemin and Soran, the two oldest children—all three of them assuming the natural responsibilities assigned to them by their families, to keep the younger ones safe.

It was quiet, sunny, a clear sky above them. To anyone regarding them, they probably looked like a pious family on their way to the market or Friday prayers. May began to doubt her memories of the gunfight. It had seemed so loud, so near, so intense, but before last night she'd never heard shots fired anywhere except the gun range. Maybe what had sounded like coordinated movements was isolated. Maybe they'd all overreacted.

They turned onto the avenue that led to the bridge. Traffic was light—too light?—only a couple cars going in either direction. In the distance was the leaning minaret they'd passed last night. Beno wiggled in Mina's arms and she set him down to let him walk along the road's dirt shoulder. They were the only pedestrians out. Up ahead a trio of elderly men sat at a table outside a tetería, a tea service spread before them. Beno jumped and fussed, but Mina held tightly to his hand.

"Chh," she said, ordering him to behave.

The road forked. Adar led them straight ahead, but down the road to May's right was the bus station. Once they crossed the bridge, they might not be allowed to return. This was her chance—maybe her only chance—to investigate. She slowed down, and the gap between her and Yasemin and Soran grew. If she ran, maybe she could get to the station and rejoin the family before they reached the bridge, but would running in an abaya draw attention? She had Mahmoud Yassin's address in the bag over her shoulder. His family was in east Mosul, too. Would they take her in if she got separated? She couldn't count on their compassion. They might blame Frank for the kidnapping; they might view May's presence in Iraq as a provocation. If May left Adar and Mina now, she had to assume she would be without protection until she reached Camp Freedom, at which point her ability to move freely in Iraq would be gone. She looked around to see whether anyone else but the old men might notice an un-chaperoned woman walking toward the bus station. They sipped their tea, their beards grown long and white.

May followed the road to the right. She moved slowly at first, and then quickly.

Just then Beno slipped free of Mina's grasp and ran after May. "Beno!" Mina yelled.

There was no telling what a boy that age had in mind, whether he was frightened of leaving behind the only home he'd known, or whether he ran simply because he could, because it was a beautiful day and he was free.

"No, no," May whispered, her plan to get away unseen crumbling to ashes.

Adar turned around and saw her, going her own way.

Outside the tetería the old man in the middle stood and May recognized that his beard was not white. He was tall and he gathered himself up easily, signaling across the wide avenue. On the other side of the road, a group of men appeared in the doorway of a building. They hadn't been there before. They came out and crouched behind a parked car, where they took turns poking their heads out and looking.

"May!" Beno shouted, his voice ringing like birdsong.

He ran toward her, his hand outstretched, and she squatted, ready to catch him up in her arms. His eyes were bright and he was laughing.

May glanced again at the men behind the car and at the old man who was not old. They all had guns.

Beno ran like a wild thing. May was wrong. He wasn't running to her, he was pointing beyond her, back down the road, where they'd just been. She looked over her shoulder. About a hundred yards away, a team of American soldiers in desert camouflage rushed forward, their bodies low, guns high. May leaned for Beno but he spun wide, his little body just brushing against her fingertips, breaking away.

Dammit! What was he thinking? But he was only a child. What had *she* been thinking? She'd come to Mosul on a rescue mission, but if anything happened to this boy, it would be her fault.

A bullet raced by, screaming in her ear like a mosquito. May dropped on instinct.

Then all was quiet, deadly quiet, until she heard Mina scream. *Fuck! Fuck! Fuck! Please let him be okay.* May lifted her head to see.

At the sound of his mother's voice, Beno had turned. He wasn't far from May, standing frozen in the street. A couple of steps and she could reach him.

Her heart pounded *get up, stay down, get up, stay down.* Then she said it aloud, "Get up!" commanding herself to rise.

Another bullet whistled toward her, pitched so high she

thought her eardrum might burst, and she dropped again. Each
time she took her eyes off him, she was afraid of what she might
see next. Beno stood there, terror written all over his face, his
arms limp as a sock puppet.

"Beno!" May said, clambering up again.

She crawled toward him. She didn't want to frighten him into
running. May grabbed his arm and pulled him to her, wrapping
herself around him like a robe.

"I got you," she said, but now what? They were in the middle
of the road, the no man's land between the men at the tetería
and the American soldiers. May heard Adar yelling. He had
the family pinned in a doorway on this side of the street, the
kids hunkered behind him, one of his arms preventing Mina
from running to her youngest. Her other son pounded on the
door, and Adar hollered at whoever was inside the building to
let them in.

Against her ribs the drumbeat continued. *Get up, stay down,
get up, stay down.* Her legs felt like noodles. Would they even
work if she stood up? She had to get Beno back to his family.

"May!" Adar shouted.

Go! She scooped the boy up and ran hunched forward to the
doorway. Her veil had fallen and a hank of hair fell across her
right eye.

It felt like running the wrong way on an escalator, the distance she had to cover seeming to hold steady the harder she la-
bored. Were the men still shooting? All she could hear was the
noise of her own blood hammering away inside her like water
against a sluice gate.

When she made it to the family, Mina snatched Beno from
her.

"He's okay!" May shouted, while mother inspected son for any
nicks or scrapes but found none. It was a miracle. "He's okay!"

I'm okay! she realized, too.

The door Soran had been pounding on opened slightly and the
children tumbled inside, accompanied by Mina and Beno, and

then Adar and May in a tangle. A man slammed the door shut behind them, then hurried Mina and the children to the back of the house, but when May tried to follow them, Adar stopped her.

"No. You cannot stay here," he said.

"But he's okay," May said. Couldn't Adar see that? She'd carried Beno out of harm's way. He didn't have a scratch on him.

"You'll get us all killed. I thought I could trust you, but you're only out for yourself."

The truth of it hit her like a slap to the face.

"I'm sorry."

"You Americans and your weak apologies. You bring so much damage, and yet you act as if it has no mother or father. It just happened, unavoidably."

She could've been honest with him this morning. She could've given him the choice whether to link his family's safety to her game plan to get to the bus station. But she hadn't.

"You're right. But where do you want me to go? It's not safe."

"Go to the bus station, if you want to see it so badly. But I won't let my family be a shield for you."

Then he opened the door and pushed her out into the street.

May crouched and covered her head with her hands, the way she used to when she lit a firework on the Fourth of July. She heard a pop, then another, then a hail of gunfire. The thud of bodies falling. Voices shouting.

A soldier grabbed her by the armpit and shouted, "Lady, move!"

She was up on her feet and being drag-pushed, past the bodies outside the tetería and the closed doors with families huddled inside, into the open door of a Humvee that sped down the road and across the bridge to safety.

May felt like a ghost in Will's kitchen. See-through. Trailing the past into uncomfortable enjambment with the present. How he must've lurched imagining Zoe in Beno's place, in May's hands.

The army convoy had whisked her away to Camp Freedom, but Adar and his family were left behind. *Wait, go back*, she'd shouted at the soldiers. Did Mina and her children make it across the river to safety? May never knew. She never made it to the bus station or talked to Mahmoud Yassin's wife. The entire journey to Iraq had been a pointless escapade at best, corrosive at worst. After she was interviewed at the base, the military attaché came and gave her a courtesy briefing about her father. The investigation was ongoing, they were doing all they could, but May being here only put others in jeopardy. A helicopter would transport her to İncirlik air base in Turkey. From there she'd board a military flight back to the States. The attaché asked if there was anyone she needed to call before they left. There was only one person May could bear knowing what a fuckup she was, because this person already knew, always had. This person hadn't been fooled for a minute.

"Yes," May had said. "My sister."

As the helicopter ascended, she was filled with the certainty that her father would never leave this place. The *ongoing* investigation had failed. She had failed. America had failed, which meant her father had failed in his work here. He was probably already dead.

The morning after she told Will, May woke to the sound of the coffee grinder. Jack looked at her with a pleading sympathy. He would wait as long as he could, but could she please get up now?

"Okay, buddy," she said, throwing her legs over the edge of the bed. "Let's go."

There'd been no Jack to urge her along when she came home from Iraq, no reason to get out of bed, to face the morning and give it a chance. Maybe adopting a dog then would've been one more thing to fuck up, or maybe it would've gotten her out of her own head. She could do things for Jack that she couldn't do for herself. Feed him. Love him, even if he shit the bed. She didn't always feel like it, but meeting his patient demands was good for her.

May led Jack to a patch of grass by the shed, where Zoe didn't play. He squatted gratefully, too old now to lift his leg.

May watched Will through the kitchen window. What must he be thinking, now that he knew the whole story? That she was a crisis averted in his orderly life? Was this thing between them going to be over as soon as it (re)started? Before she left for Iraq, she'd spent the night with him for what she'd assumed would be the last time. After months of despair she finally had a visa and a plan. She felt painfully alive. They made love over and over, sleep held at bay by hunger. He was scared for her, that was part of it. She felt him memorizing every inch of her. He'd wanted to go with her, but she'd said no, that it was a responsibility only she could carry. And she wasn't scared. If she died, let it be bearing the family's torch for her father. She was so sure she would find Frank.

When she brought Jack inside, Will was standing at the kitchen peninsula. He'd maybe been watching her through the window, puzzling her out, remembering, too.

"Coffee?" he asked, setting a mug before her.

"Yes, thank you." She pulled out a stool from under the counter.

He smiled, but there was a little hesitation in it, like he was waiting for something. She owed him the rest of the truth, if she could manage it, which is that she hadn't known what she'd had the first time they fell in love. She'd assumed they would break up eventually because that was what you did when you were just kids and one of you was joining the Peace Corps. She'd applied before they'd started dating, and it was only a matter of time before she got her assignment—she was hoping for the sustainable rural agriculture opening in Senegal or the well installation project in Malawi. Were they really going to last long-distance? Come on, was she even built for that? She wanted adventure and passion, not letters full of pining and a couple of much-anticipated (and therefore surely anticlimactic?) fucks a year.

When her dad disappeared, *eventually* came fast. Back then May wasn't thinking of Will as her endgame or herself as his. She didn't know how lucky she was to have someone who went toward pain instead of running from it, who'd bend toward her when she was distant and come looking when she'd been absent too long. But Will had wanted something she couldn't give, not while all her thoughts went toward her father. Better to just cut it off, she'd thought. Their last night together, before she left for Iraq, had been her goodbye, in her mind at least. And then, after, when nothing had gone as planned, she'd been scared shitless. The Peace Corps wanted *her* to promote a better understanding of Americans and other peoples? Were they kidding? What May understood is that she didn't understand a thing, that her country had meddled in Iraq and now so had she, that she was better off staying home, which was convenient because she couldn't get out of bed, anyway. She withdrew her application. She sent the email to Will, ending things for good.

For ten years May had kept to herself. She'd gone around in circles, knowing she had to do *something* with her life but not wanting to do any more harm. Now Will was standing before her, and she was old enough to know she had to jump at this chance, hold on tight this time. She wanted to. If only she didn't feel herself sinking again, into the spin cycle, into the gloom. She was fighting as hard as she could, but what if she sank right to the bottom and couldn't function again?

"Will," she said. "I'm sorry." She was sorry for abandoning him, sorry for having so little to offer him now. She was sorry for everything.

The doorbell rang, interrupting her.

"No, I'm sorry," Will said.

"Why?"

"Because that's your mom."

"What?"

His hands were in the air as he walked past her—held up in defense, then down in a shrug, then back up again—and his face said *don't hate me.*

"Hello, stranger!" Nancy boomed when he answered the door. Was that...were they...*hugging*?

"Hi, Mrs. Barber. Come on in. How are you?"

"Oh, fine. Just fine. What a beautiful home you have," she said with an enthusiasm that made May wilt. Had her mom been waiting all these years to visit her in a proper home with hardwoods and an open floor plan?

"Thank you," Will said. "I wish I could stay longer but I just remembered I have to take my car in for a smog check before the tags expire. But make yourself comfortable. There's fresh coffee in the pot." He pointed to his watch and mouthed *back soon* at May.

"Wow," May said, at the sound of the door closing. Will and her mom were in cahoots. And there would be coffee served at this ambush. She poured her mom a cup, handed it to her, and then sat on the sofa. It was a very nice sofa, you couldn't deny it.

"You didn't tell me where you were," Nancy said. "I know you're an adult and you don't owe me an explanation, but it's been two weeks. I was worried."

"I know."

"You missed the spa day."

"Shit." The hammam party for Juniper and Hana. "How was it?"

"It was lovely. Maryam's a very interesting woman. Did you know she started an adult literacy program at the library? In her second language! *And* she makes her own soaps. I felt positively lazy by comparison, and of course there I was, stark naked in a plunge pool. But I'll tell you what, if I'd done that before my own wedding, I would've been a much more relaxed bride."

"I'm sorry I missed it." In theory she was, at least.

"I didn't know Will was back in your life," Nancy said. "Is that recent?"

"Yeah. We ran into each other at work. It's still pretty...undefined."

"Look, the last thing I want to do is crash your romantic retreat, but I got the sense from Will that that's not what this is? He seemed worried about you when he called—"

"*Will* called *you?*"

Nancy joined her on the couch. "Yes. And by the way he beat it out of here, I have a feeling he thinks you need your mom. What's going on?"

Nancy ventured to put an arm around her. To her own surprise May leaned in, and Nancy put her other arm around her, too. May was so, so tired. Sometimes she missed her dad so acutely that she forgot to be grateful she still had a mom who was a little much sometimes, yes, but reliable as fuck.

"I'm sorry I ruined the bridal shower."

"This stuff with Dad is a lot to process," Nancy said. "It's taken a toll on all of us, in different ways, but with you..."

"I'm fine."

"That's what I always say, too, when anybody asks. *Who, me? Oh, I'm fine. I'm just worried about Frank.* Or *I'm just worried about my children. I'll bounce back.* But I didn't always bounce back. You know, everyone always says you're just like your father, and you are. But you and I are more alike than you think."

May snorted. *How?*

"Your father and I always wanted four kids, but after Junie was born we decided three was enough. It was just too tough on me. I loved being pregnant and I loved being a mom, but I had the baby blues after each one of you. That's what we called it back then. The baby blues."

"I didn't know."

"Your dad was supportive for the most part. With April, I

wouldn't let him help, but after you were born, he insisted. With Junie, we were both just so fried. When you have three kids under eight, patience is in short supply."

"Did Dad leave or something? I feel like I remember that. He was gone and you were crying and we ate at the Waffle House every night."

"No," Nancy said, as if it were the most ridiculous thing in the world, and May immediately felt better, safer. "He went out late sometimes to blow off some steam. And I just couldn't face cooking another damn meal every night. The waitress there was kind. She'd hold Junie and bounce her, and I'd order extra whipped cream on my pancakes. It felt like being taken care of.

"I'd switched gynecologists by the time I got pregnant with July—she was the one who talked to me about postpartum depression. She gave me a prescription, and I took it for a little while. It actually helped. Medication: what a concept! Right after your dad disappeared, I went back on it. I was having terrible thoughts. Dark thoughts."

She paused to see if May was following, if she needed her to spell it out.

May took her hand and nodded, *go on*. It felt as if her mom was telling her fortune.

"My doctor said I had to put the oxygen mask on myself first. Oh, honey, I should've seen sooner that you needed oxygen, too. You don't have to suffer the way you have. It seems obvious in retrospect, but at the time I thought, well…who *wouldn't* be having a hard time with everything we were going through? And then, when you changed your mind about the Peace Corps, I was relieved. I could keep an eye on you. Not everyone can have their life all mapped out for them like your sisters did, but I knew you'd figure yourself out eventually."

As May listened, the events of her life rearranged themselves into a new shape, a different narrative. She wasn't just sad and confused; she was depressed. It wasn't just the spin cycle; it was the cycles of being fine and not fine, telling herself each time that it was just another funk. Junior year of high school, when she had a falling out with her friends Maya and Margot, and instead of making more friends she just…didn't. Going to Iraq like that, alone, as if she were Jason Bourne and could count on dormant fighting skills materializing on demand; then coming home and slipping into the Big Sleep. Her mom making hearty soups loaded with superfoods and bringing them to her room when she didn't show up at the dinner table. Her brother walking Jack for her a few years ago, before he left for college, when she had that little rough patch over… She couldn't remember anymore what exactly had set it off, but come to think of it, she had a team of handlers, just like Scout did, picking her up whenever she fell. Their names were Nancy and July. After the last rough patch she'd had to push back the plan to move out. She'd found an apartment she could afford, nearby in Havre de Grace, but packing up her things, setting up the utilities, changing the address on all of her accounts, just to live in pokey little Havre de Grace? The thought of everything she would've had to do to make it happen had been too much.

"What, honey?" Nancy asked, seeing her face, the deepening shock at what she'd actually been contending with only now registering.

Depression wasn't something you could just leave behind, like a worn-out sofa deposited on the curb on moving day. It was a lifelong condition that May had been managing in the most improvised ways.

"I don't know if Will can handle it. I'm such a mess."

"You think he called me here because he's overwhelmed? May, he's in love with you. Just like before."

No, her mom had it all wrong. Will was kind, of course, and okay, fine, he definitely still wanted to fuck her, but there's no way he could love her. Not after everything he now knew.

"Your dad always said it wasn't a question of *if* with you two, but of *when*."

"You guys talked about Will?"

"Why do you think Dad monopolized him at graduation? He wanted to see for himself what was so great about this Will-person you wouldn't shut up about."

"Oh, my God."

It should've mortified her—the schoolgirl version of herself name-dropping Will like he was a pair of Jordans; her indifference to him a posture that fooled exactly one person, herself—but all she could feel was grateful. Her dad's words were a time capsule, a treasure from the past. Like the time she'd found an old birthday card he'd written her *(18! How can that be?)* or the Snaxco T-shirt she kept in a Ziploc bag in her dresser and was afraid to sleep in lest it start smelling like her instead of him. This was another piece of him to carry.

Her mom had given her a gift. April had, too, with the apology May still wasn't sure she deserved. Speaking of apologies, she owed Juniper one for blowing up at the bridal shower. She would talk to her, soon.

What the hell was going on with her family?

Were they actually getting along?

19

Juniper

"If you get the job, we should think about moving to Princeton," Hana said the morning of Juniper's interview, thoroughly jinxing her chances. "The schools, you know?"

"No pressure or anything!" Juniper answered from behind the refrigerator door.

Hana had her nose buried in her recipe binder, too harried to notice the bout of nerves her idle comment had provoked, or that the orange juice Juniper was drinking was actually a screwdriver. Juniper was already on edge. Ever since the meeting with Mustafa Karim, she'd been easily rattled, on eggshells anticipating the next clue about Frank. These days she needed something to calm down and get going every morning, something to remind her that there was more than just dread abiding in her future. A week from tomorrow she was getting married, but it felt like she was stranded at a depot waiting to see which train would arrive first, the one with bad news or the one with good.

Juniper downed the rest of her drink, then rinsed out the glass in the sink. Their kitchen was transforming into a veritable factory, right down to the rolling bakery racks, just delivered, that would soon be lined with tray after tray of sesame-pistachio cookies, shortbread cookies, and diamond-shaped, almond-topped slices of namoura cake for the henna party and the wedding. Juniper had been sent to four different Walmarts to buy as many boxes of shredded phyllo dough as she could get her hands on for the knafeh cake, the nest-like osmallieh, and the seemingly infinite varieties of baklava. She still got a stomach cramp recalling the politely devastating look Maryam had given the caterers at the cake tasting when they'd suggested they could provide their "world-famous" baklava as well for the reception. The wedding cake would feature five layers of flavor—whenever Juniper tried to list them, she invariably forgot one, like Santa's reindeers—but that was *all* the pastry chef would be making.

"Mama said she'd bring Salma, Bibi, and Jamila so we can work faster."

"Amazing. Thanks so much, babe," Juniper said.

Ever since the elopement spat, she'd been thanking Hana left and right, painfully aware how much more unified the Monsours were than the Barbers, who couldn't get through a single wedding event without someone having a meltdown. At the hammam party April had hardly said a word in the dry saunas, laughing too late at the aunties' stories. May hadn't even shown up, despite her RSVP, and July had left early, after the party moved from the coed saunas to the gender-separated bathhouse. Juniper hadn't been much of a host, either, dying for a drink while sweating out whatever was in her system, regretting that she had half the ingredients of a decent cocktail available to her with the cucumber slices and the lemon water, but nothing that would pack a punch. The Monsours weren't teetotalers by any means, but in deference to their guests, many of whom did abstain, they'd hadn't served alcohol at the hammam party and they wouldn't at the wedding, either.

"Do I look okay?" Juniper asked from the door. She'd put on the same outfit she'd worn to the engagement party.

Hana looked up from the recipe. "Perfect."

"Wish me luck?"

But Hana was already back in her binder, distracted by the task at hand, confident Juniper could handle this.

"Luck," she called out.

The sun glinted off the lake on her right as Juniper drove along Faculty Road, her old practice field on her left. It had been a quarry, practically, in her time; now it had a pristine turf and belonged to the field hockey team. The new soccer stadium had opened the fall after she graduated, and she felt fresh pangs of nostalgia for Lourie-Love Field, where she'd played all her games. Back then campus—especially this quarter of it—had been her sanctuary. Six weeks ago she'd been certain it was her destiny to come back, but now that seemed naive, and she felt shaky where she should have been sure-footed. This place had been a home when her own was crumbling. She needed to trust that it could be again. She slowed to turn into the parking lot outside Jadwin Gym, the nerve center of Princeton Athletics.

The email from Doug Tuttle had said she'd be expected to deliver a brief presentation on her coaching philosophy, as well as engage in a free-ranging discussion with the hiring committee. Juniper eyed her presentation notes, and immediately saw things she wished she could change. She'd been thinking like a D2 coach when she wrote it, those three winning seasons at Linden pumping her up, but why would a D1 program care about any of that? She closed her laptop and put it back in her messenger bag. She would have to improvise. Speaking from the heart would be better, anyway.

She could do this. She was nervous, but anybody would be. If she needed a friendly face, she would look at Mac. But would that be enough to hold herself together? She was on tenterhooks about everything—her dad, the wedding, the job. It was terrible being this anxious, this aware of herself all the time. In soccer you drilled and practiced until you developed muscle memory; skills became second nature. Each player had a unique part to play, but when everything was really clicking, you forgot yourself. You dissolved into the organism that was the team. Juniper wished so badly to dissolve, to forget. She reached into the center console for her flask and took a long pull, then another. Before she knew it, it was empty, but there was a bottle in her kit in the back seat. She put the flask between her legs and refilled it. A splash of vodka landed on her lap. *Shit.* She grabbed a jersey from her kit and dabbed at it. It would have to dry on the way. She got out of the car and hoisted her bag across her body, tucking the flask in the inner pocket and zipping it shut.

Andrea Landford was a Princeton legend—a champion in volleyball and softball in the '80s and, as of two years ago, the first female athletic director in the university's history. One day she'd probably have a fieldhouse named after her, so it was only fitting that she kept Juniper waiting twenty minutes for their meeting.

Juniper sat in the anteroom outside Andrea's office, flipping through a copy of *Princeton Alumni Weekly.* She skimmed the profiles of notable alumni who were performing cutting-edge medical research, writing award-winning novels, launching startups, and generally saving the world. She scanned the boldface names in the Alumni News section, looking for friends and classmates, finding the thinly told stories of new jobs and beautiful children and world travel, the CliffsNotes versions of people's lives, only the good parts, none of the mess.

Juniper had sent her own update to the magazine once, when she'd become head coach at Linden. She'd been proud of what little she had to report, pleased with the consistent narrative it would provide to anyone keeping tabs on her. In a couple months, maybe she'd write in again. *The Class of '08 is making strides in sports, too. Juniper Barber returned to campus this fall to helm the women's soccer team. She's the youngest head coach in the Ivies, but we're not surprised. Cheering her on from the stands of Roberts Stadium is her partner on and off the field and now her wife, Hana Monsour '06. Go Tigers!*

Or she would not send an update, because she would not get the job. They would hire someone older, a man, someone who'd played for the US national team. Maybe it was just a fluke that Juniper had made the shortlist, a courtesy.

Stop it, she told herself. *Think positively. Picture the outcome you desire and make it happen.*

Juniper went over her key talking points again. Her love of the game. Her respect for Mac—but she wouldn't be a toady about it; she'd let the committee know she had new ideas. Her debt to this school, which had nurtured and shaped her into the woman she was today. Her desire to repay that debt with the next generation of young women players.

Be yourself, Mac had told her. *Do the work and show up*. Juniper wouldn't let her down.

The waiting was the worst. Juniper's armpits were sticky, her palms damp. She wiped her hands on the seat. Between this and the Kurdish embassy, she'd had enough of anterooms and the nauseating air of suspense.

The latch turned and the heavy wooden doors opened. She was expecting Mac or maybe Doug, but there was Andrea Landford, in the flesh.

"Juniper!" Andrea said, taking her hand and pumping it, her smile a mile wide and her Texas twang still sharp despite half a life spent on the East Coast. "We've been looking forward to this. Thank you for coming in."

"I'm happy to be here." Juniper followed her into the office where Doug Tuttle and two other men sat in armchairs.

Andrea gestured at the empty couch. "Sit, sit."

Juniper put down her bag and shook the men's hands. Then she remembered the wet spot on her pants. Was it still there? If they hadn't noticed it, the last thing she wanted was to draw their attention to it. She sat and quickly crossed her legs.

She smiled at Doug and the other two men, who introduced themselves. One was a trustee and the other a booster. Mac wasn't here.

"Is this everyone?" Juniper asked.

"Ah, you're probably wondering where Mac is. She felt it best to recuse herself from this meeting, given your previous relationship, which we all thought was appropriate. You're the only former player we're considering, and she didn't think she could be impartial about your candidacy," Andrea said with a wink.

Juniper had been counting on Mac, not just to advocate for her during deliberations but to steady her. Why hadn't she said she was recusing herself? Was she really too biased to be fair, or did she question Juniper's fitness for the job?

Juniper forced herself to slap a smile over her doubts. "Makes sense," she said.

"Now, Juniper, I'm just going to go ahead and bring up the elephant in the room. You have less experience than any of the head coaches of the teams we play. Some might say it's not your time, that you need to mature in the profession. It's certainly a big responsibility, leading a team at this level. Why should we trust the job to you?"

"Well, I'm glad you asked that. And first, I want you to know how much I love this school."

Juniper was expecting nods and murmurs of agreement in return, but Andrea smiled at her blankly and the men sat motionless, their faces unreadable.

"It was such an honor to lead Princeton to the College Cup. I remember it like it was yesterday."

Andrea tilted her head, indulging her, like Juniper was a toddler telling a long-winded story about nothing. *An honor to lead?* She'd only been a freshman at the time, not the captain. And she shouldn't have put it that way, *like it was yesterday*. It only reinforced her youth.

"What I mean is, ever since I left this place, it's been my dream to come back."

She'd said this line out loud dozens of times in the last six weeks—in traffic, in the shower, in the middle of the night while she counted sheep—but today it tumbled out of her mouth like a stiff parking ticket.

"We all have happy memories of our time as student-athletes here. Some of us longer ago than others," Andrea said. "Jeff, let's hear from you. What are some of your concerns?"

The booster cleared his throat. "Hi, Juniper. I see Linden has had a good run these last few years."

"Yes! Yes, we have. It's really been awesome to help develop these players and watch them shine."

"Right, I'll bet. You've obviously got a great group of players right now. I'm wondering what you've been able to do with your budget resources to grow the program beyond this squad, beyond yourself even. How would Linden survive your defection?"

Juniper laughed. "Defection—that's putting it a little strongly."

"Maybe, maybe not. Emotions run high around sports." Jeff laughed, too, but she heard the tautness in his throat, the challenge behind the words.

"Right. True. I just meant that it's a college program. Players graduate. Coaches move on."

"But surely you feel some loyalty there? Or maybe not."

What was with this guy? She felt like an acrobat, and he kept flicking at the high wire, trying to make her fall.

"No, of course I do. I would never abandon them. If I left— if I were fortunate enough to get the position here—I would absolutely give my replacement at Linden a roadmap to follow. I always say I'm just a phone call away."

"So you would be working with Linden still, while you were coaching here?" the booster asked. "I'm not sure how that would work."

"No, Princeton would be my focus. My number one priority. My *only* priority."

"Well that's good," Jeff said, laughing uncomfortably.

The interview had just started. These questions were supposed to be softballs. She should have been answering them easily. How could anyone doubt her loyalty to Princeton?

"Bill," Andrea said to the trustee, "jump in here, please."

"I think Jeff is asking some really key questions about the budget at Linden, and I'm gonna want to come back to that in a minute."

Juniper's armpits began to drip. Sure, they could talk about the Linden budget. The budget was zero. Every year she was expected to do more with less. Last fall when her keeper lost her gloves, Juniper gave her Hana's old pair. The spreadsheet she submitted each spring to the administration was a joke. Was Jeff really asking a serious question about "resources"? Maybe other head coaches had more experience allocating funds than she did. If anyone wanted to hand her more money, she'd find ways to spend it, but what she knew how to do was save, skimp.

"But first," Bill went on, "I just want to ask about your father."

Juniper's stomach pitched. "Excuse me?"

"Of course, as a trustee and a fan, I remember what an incredible player you were, and I remember feeling just awful when I read about your dad in the *Daily Princetonian*. It brings the war that much closer when it touches one of our own."

Jeff and Doug shot confused looks at each other.

"Oh, my goodness," Andrea said. "Frank Barber. I didn't put it together. Frank Barber was your father?"

"Is," Juniper stammered. "Is my father."

"He was kidnapped in Iraq," Andrea explained to Jeff and Doug. "By al-Qaeda, was it?"

Juniper could only shake her head and lift her shoulders.

"Well some kind of insurgents. Just terrible."

"Wait, did you say *is* your father?" Bill asked. "He's alive?"

The four of them gawked at her like she was one of those grotesque creatures fishermen kept pulling out of the oceans with two heads and one tail, like something they couldn't believe they were witnessing up close.

"I don't know if he is or isn't."

"Oh, my," Andrea said.

There was a painful silence.

"That sounds awfully complicated," Bill said.

Doug and Jeff stared at their shoes, heads bent and lips pursed as if in prayer.

Did anyone want to ask her about soccer? Juniper had no idea how to get this interview back on track.

"I'm sorry," Juniper said. "Could I just... I just need a minute. Is there somewhere...?"

"Of course," Andrea said. "The ladies' room is outside, make a left, and it's down the hall on your right."

Juniper picked up her bag and walked out to the anteroom. Her stomach heaved. She hurried to the bathroom, but by the time she got there, she understood she wasn't actually going to be sick. Her hands were shaking with rage. What the fuck was wrong with these people? There were things you didn't pry into. Did you ask people with terminal cancer how long they had left to live? Did you ask sexual assault survivors the last time they'd seen their attackers?

And she'd let them rattle her! She was the young, disloyal, bad-with-money candidate who'd run out of the room. Whatever else happened, any answers she gave, her presentation to come, their deliberations, all of it would be viewed in the context of her inexperience and emotional fragility.

She reached into her bag and uncapped the flask, looking for a reason or a way to get back her confidence, or even get back into the room.

"Cheers to my successor!" Mac said at lunch later at Prospect House.

The walls of the Faculty Club were built entirely of windows that looked out onto a vale of trees and the garden where Mac would officiate the wedding next weekend. Afterward they'd retire to this very room to celebrate. But for now their waiter, a grad student as adept at balancing plates of food as a tray of petri dishes, had brought them each a glass of chardonnay.

"And to my mentor, who forgot to mention that she wasn't going to be there."

"You didn't need me," Mac said. She petted Juniper's arm affectionately.

"Why would I? It's only the most important moment of my career."

Mac flinched. "Come on, Barber. You need me to hold your hand in the bathroom, too?"

"I'm just saying, it was pretty intense in there. Would've been nice to see a friendly face."

"What happened?"

"Just…they grilled me pretty hard, okay? It got more… *personal* than I expected. And I didn't know I needed an MBA to coach soccer."

"Oh, that. They just like to impress people with the size of the endowment. Don't worry, they're looking for great teachers, not great business minds. What about your presentation? How'd that go?"

"There were some technical difficulties." She finished her glass and put up her hand to flag down the waiter.

"Show me someone who can get a projector working on the first try."

What Juniper didn't say is the room had felt funereal when she returned from the bathroom. They'd adjourned to the conference room for her presentation, where she'd hoped she'd get a reset, but then her laptop wouldn't recognize the projector and they had to wait for IT to come fix it. While they waited, Andrea said they might as well carry on with their earlier train of thought, and Juniper feared the trustee would ask about her dad again, but instead he pivoted back to the budget.

"Of course, we're fortunate to have such generous alums," Bill said, nodding at Jeff, "but in this economy we need to be smart about where we allocate our resources. Where would you recommend we spend the money?"

People with money—why did they always see poverty where there was plenty?

"Why not spend it on the students?" Juniper asked, afraid she'd offend them by stating the obvious.

"How so?" Andrea asked.

"Well, make tuition free, for one."

"But, Juniper, Princeton already has one of the most generous financial aid policies around. The average debt our students leave here with is… What is it, Bill?"

"About seven-thousand dollars. One of the lowest figures in the country."

"I know," Juniper began. "A lot of the Ivies are lowering tuition costs for lower-income families. I just wish this trend had started earlier. In 2004, my parents' two salaries still weren't enough. That's why my dad went to Iraq, to earn that extra hazard pay." Now she was the one steering the conversation back to her dad, but she couldn't help herself. Juniper swallowed painfully, remorse like a stone in her throat. "That his sacrifice would be unnecessary today is…" she wanted to say *infuriating, heartbreaking, personally destabilizing,* but settled on "…encouraging. But the real problem we need to deal with is the way that lower-income students are still disadvantaged in admissions. Great, costs are coming down, but only if those kids get in. And it's a lot harder to put your best foot forward in high school when you're working on top of studying, whether that's caring for your family or helping cover rent."

"I hear you," Doug said, "believe me, but does tuition really need to be free for the wealthiest students?"

"Forgive me if I get the math wrong on this, but Princeton has more than two-million dollars in endowment money for every student enrolled and gets a rate of return of about ten percent on that. So why are we charging tuition at all, for anyone?"

Doug nodded tersely, if reluctantly agreeing, but the other men checked out and Andrea tilted her head in that pitying way of hers again. They wanted a CEO or a pit bull or a cutthroat competitor, not a bleeding heart revolutionary. That they saw her as one when she was just stating facts made Juniper laugh out loud, and then IT arrived to restart the projector but it was too late to save her presentation or recover the room.

Juniper shuddered now, remembering it all. "Coulda, shoulda, woulda," she said, trying to place her regrets in the realm of the toss-off-able. "Just have to hope for the best. At least we'll have you beside us next weekend. You're our good luck charm, our fairy godmother. Thanks again, Mac. Really."

"I wouldn't be anywhere else," Mac said.

The wild part was she really seemed to mean it. Mac wasn't thinking about what time Varsity Liquors closed or how much simpler a wedding could be—just two lovers and a judge—or whether it was possible to fast-forward to the honeymoon, the one they hadn't planned yet because their planning brains were maxed the fuck out, but where, if it were tropical enough, a person might be able, at last, to sleep.

When she thought about Nancy walking her down the aisle, alone, Juniper in the cream-colored suit she'd paid too much for online and would never wear again, she got an ache in her throat that wouldn't go away. No one had said so out loud yet, not explicitly at least, but it felt wrong to be getting married without Frank.

Her dad would have been proud of her, though, if he'd known she had a meeting in the athletic director's office. He would've been waiting by the phone all day, crossing his fingers and toes.

The waiter returned.

"Can I get a Grey Goose martini?" Juniper asked. "The service is kind of slow here. Better make it a double."

★ ★ ★

"Juniper. Hey. *Junie.*"

Juniper was asleep, head down on her desk, and it was the rattling of keys in the lock on the ball cage that finally stirred her. Fariha had the cones and the ball bags out.

"Sorry, nodded off," she said and sat up. As she did, a knife stabbed at the back of her eyeball. She pressed it with her palm.

"What are you doing here?" Fariha asked, checking the air in the balls and sorting the duds into a pile.

Juniper unwrapped a fresh piece of gum. She nudged off her loafers and searched for her cleats. Then she recalled that, no, training wasn't starting, it was over. Fariha had led the weekly workout today so Juniper could focus on the interview. She was supposed to have gone straight home after lunch, but instead she'd come here, to Linden, on autopilot.

"I'm so tired lately," Juniper said, hoping to account in some way for how scattered she was.

"Guess you and Mac celebrated. Congrats, dude!"

Fariha inflated a ball. She jerked the pump quickly: whoosh, whoosh, whoosh.

"Thanks," Juniper said to the floor, her cheeks burning with humiliation.

"Not surprised you killed it. I knew they'd want you back. It's too perfect. Star player returns to take the reins from her former coach and leads a new generation of women to glory? I mean, the profile writes itself. Alums will eat it up, and Andrea Landford knows it. Puts a shine on her, too, for bringing you in. Win-win."

Juniper reached down to grab the next dud to inflate, but she lost her balance and tumbled out of her seat. "Whoops!"

"Whoa." Fariha dropped the pump and helped Juniper back into the chair. "Looks like someone was overserved."

Then, as if she'd just remembered the words to a long-forgotten lullaby, she stood tall, hands on her hips. "How did you get here? Did you drive?"

Juniper froze. She didn't know what to say. *Yes* felt both incredible and unnecessary. Fariha already knew the answer.

"Does my sister know you're here?"

Oh, god. Hana. She couldn't bother her with this. She'd be worried sick and pissed off, and she had enough on her plate already.

"I'll take you home," Fariha said, letting Juniper's silence speak for itself.

"I can't. Not yet." She needed more time to pull herself together.

Fariha touched her arm, and Juniper looked down at her friend's hand, shocked she could even feel it resting there. "The girls shouldn't see you like this. You're coming with me to the Abadis'." Mo and Nura were in town for another fundraiser, this one hosted by Nura's parents at their home, and Nura had promised to bring a pair of gold strappy heels that might work with Fariha's bridesmaid dress.

On the drive there Juniper shivered with shame and the sickening relief of a near miss. She could have killed someone. "Don't tell Hana," she said softly. "Please."

Fariha hesitated, then nodded. She steered them past the children's hospital, where Mr. and Mrs. Abadi both still worked, and into the leafy neighborhood where they lived. Juniper could tell they were close by the uptick of street-parked cars. Fariha pulled behind a Mercedes with diplomatic plates. Bigwigs. More money for Mo's campaign.

"I'll wait here," Juniper said.

"Come on," Fariha said, tugging her sleeves. "Don't be weird. There'll be snacks."

Reluctantly Juniper unbuckled her seat belt.

From the foyer Juniper took in the scene: the women in the library, gabbing; the men in the parlor crowded around the

World Cup on the TV—Brazil and Croatia, the match in its final minutes; between the two groups, a staircase leading up to the bedrooms. Juniper spotted the back of Mo's head high above the others, heard his booming laugh. He was so good at making an impression. Later he'd probably give a speech about the skills he could bring to Congress, but by then they would already be evident to everyone here.

"Let me find Nura," Fariha said, wading into the library.

As promised, there were snacks in the dining room. To drink, sparkling water and a pitcher of something with mint in it. Juniper poured a glass and tasted it, but it was only lemonade. She drifted toward the back of the house, where it was quieter. In the empty kitchen she checked the refrigerator and the cupboards. There was nothing, just a half-full bottle of vanilla extract. She tried it. It burned her tongue and she coughed. She left half an inch or so at the bottom and put the bottle back.

Off the kitchen was a sunporch. She wandered out there. Her grandmother had had a sunporch at her house on the Bird River. Juniper and her sisters had spent two weeks there every summer until she had the stroke. Each time it was the same. Juniper cried about being made to go to Grandma's, though she could have walked the distance back in an afternoon; then she cried again when the visit was over and she didn't want to leave. Frank would come for his girls and find them grown wild and natural, brave and tan. His mother could be quiet, even cold, but his daughters tasted freedoms at her house that they never knew at home.

"What's that?" Frank asked one summer, as he stood on Grandma's sunporch and pointed at the tent Juniper had pitched in the grass, about ten feet up from the waterline.

Juniper could see it now, not this manicured garden in suburban Philadelphia but the weeds grown up around her encampment, the river running out to the bay. April and May had done their own thing that summer. Junie was still a baby to them, too young to tag along on their canoe rides or join in games of pickle with the neighbor boys. Instead she'd set up right in the middle of the land, forcing them all to walk or run around her.

"That's my bedroom," she told her dad.

"Grandma let you sleep out there?"

"Mm-hmm."

"Every night? All by yourself?"

She must have been around seven or eight at the time, but she hadn't thought to be afraid.

"Want to see?"

She led him by the hand and showed him everything: the lawn chair she'd placed next to the tent flaps, where she could sit and read her *Choose Your Own Adventure* books; the foot locker that doubled as storage and a resting place for a cherry soda. They crawled inside the two-man pup tent and she gave him a tour of the bed she'd made out of a sleeping bag and Grandma's crocheted blanket, her stuffed animals lined up in the empty space alongside it. They stretched out together, his feet hanging just outside the flaps.

"What do you think?" she'd asked, furiously proud of the home she'd made but still, somehow, worried he wouldn't see how special it was.

"It's perfect." And with him lying there beside her, it finally was.

"It's a beautiful garden, isn't it?" someone behind her asked now, the voice familiar, bringing her back to the anxious present.

Juniper dabbed her eyes and turned around to find Mustafa Karim. What was the KRG Representative doing here? But, of course: the fundraiser. He couldn't donate as a foreign national, but he could network and influence. Perhaps he'd brought his wife along to catch up with Nura.

"Hello," Karim said.

"I'm sorry. I didn't think anyone else would be back here."

"I was just thinking that it's much too beautiful a day to stay indoors. Why don't we go outside?" he asked.

Karim made Juniper nervous. She might say the wrong thing. He might realize she'd been drinking, despite the fact that she was nowhere near as hammered as she wanted to be.

"They might be ready to start," she said. Just then the men roared in the parlor. Somebody had scored in stoppage time, Brazil probably.

"Doubtful." Karim held open the back door for her. "Shall we?"

She followed him. There was a table on the flagstone patio just beyond the French doors, but instead he roamed across the lawn, past the birdbath. When he reached the tree line, he stopped.

"You've been in my thoughts," he said.

"Thank you for meeting with my sister and me. I'm sorry if she was a bit abrupt."

"Understandable, given the circumstances. Have you learned more?"

"Not really. Well, yes, one thing. I guess Tariq, my father's interpreter, had a cousin who's been traveling on his passport. And this cousin is...on a terrorist watch list...or something. I don't know how valid those lists are. I'm sure there are plenty of people on them who are just regular people. Kurds and refugees and other people like that."

She was rambling. She backed away, fumbling for a reason to go inside. "Shouldn't you be in there?" she said, gesturing to the house. "You know, pressing the flesh?"

"Probably. But I told myself when I saw you standing in the driveway that it was a sign."

"A sign?" she asked after a little too long.

"My conscience, if you like. Telling me that I must speak to you. That I must tell you something important. To keep it from you would be deeply wrong."

Something important? Something about her dad. The hair on the back of Juniper's neck stood up.

Karim took her hands. He cleared his throat. She felt dizzy.

"Tariq Ibrahim. He is alive. He is alive and well and living in Mosul."

20

July

"I still don't like this," Nancy said. "I don't like it one bit. The wedding's only six days away. You've been trying to get Tariq on the phone in Mosul for two days now and haven't been able to. How do you know you'll find him over there? What if you don't make it back in time? What am I supposed to tell our guests? What do I do if something happens to you all?" She hovered in the doorway, watching July pack. He didn't need to look over his shoulder to know that she was pacing like a lioness, marking out a perimeter around him.

"Look at it this way," July said, tucking a pair of dress shoes into shoe bags. "If anything goes wrong, you'll know who to call this time. Har-har."

Would he need dress shoes over there? He had no idea what to expect, so he understood why his mom, who'd already lost a husband to the place, was going slightly out of her mind at the prospect of all four of her children leaving for Iraq. Tariq was alive! Word had spread like wildfire, from Juniper in Phil-

adelphia to April in Baltimore, May in College Park, and July
and Nancy in Aberdeen. With the information Karim provided, they'd been able to track Tariq down to the University of Mosul and, passing messages through a professor, he'd
agreed to talk to them. Maybe they'd finally get some answers
to all their questions. How had he and their father survived the
kidnapping? What were they doing at that training camp two
years later? And why did Frank go to Dubrovnik instead of returning home, like Tariq had? But news reports were swirling
about ISIS's push from Syria into Iraq. Militants had reached
the outskirts of Mosul, throwing everything there into chaos
and scrambling communication. If they waited for things to
stabilize, Tariq might disappear again. They couldn't let their
only connection to their dad slip through their fingers. July had
been saving up for a new laptop to take to Oxford, but now he
would use that money to pay April back for a plane ticket from
Washington Dulles to Erbil International Airport.

"You're losing all that space, packing those shoes like that.
You can stuff your underwear in there. Here, I'll show you."
His mother elbowed him out of the way, and before he knew
it, she'd removed the shoe from the cloth bag and slid a rolled-
up pair of boxer shorts into the toe box.

"Ew. No. Mom, I got this. Sit." He took her by the shoulders and guided her down onto his bed. He repacked his shoes
the right, hygienic way.

"I still don't understand," Nancy said. "Why can't the FBI
and the State Department handle this?"

"Good question. They've had plenty of time to—if we were
able to find him, they could've, too—but it doesn't seem to be a
priority for them. So we're going to talk to Tariq ourselves, face-
to-face. When we get to Erbil—"

"In Kurdistan?" she asked.

"Right. The capital of Iraqi Kurdistan. When we get there,

we'll wait for Tariq to make contact. He's making his way from Mosul."

"Which is not in Kurdistan?"

"No. It's in Iraq. But it's surrounded on three sides by Iraqi Kurdistan, and a lot of Kurds live there. And Arabs and Turkmen—it's an ethnically mixed city. So we'll meet up with him in Erbil, and then we'll get some answers."

"Did they say how long ago he was released? Or why? And why did Tariq turn up but not your father? Why didn't he reach out once he was free?"

His mom could work herself up over nothing, over him bringing home the wrong kind of milk from the store, so he had years of practice at staying Zen while she spun out. But this time was different. He was just as nervous and frustrated as she was.

"I don't know," he said.

"I should come with you, at least."

"And do what? Clean his teeth?"

"What if you don't find him? What if he won't talk to you?"

"Then we'll be no worse off than we are right now. We have his WhatsApp info, though."

"His what?"

For the thousandth time, July explained the internet to his mom. She nibbled her thumbnail and watched him pack.

An hour later Juniper and Hana arrived. In the driveway Nancy hugged all three of them fiercely. "Please be careful," she said. "Come back to me."

The car ride was quiet. Juniper looked out the window while Hana drove. July studied them both from the back seat. They didn't say much, just fragments of thoughts each seemed to understand: "Can you?" and "just a sec" and "no not like that" and "I told you," and then one of them would adjust the air-conditioning or check the traffic. He'd been amazed by their performance at the bridal shower, the way they finished each other's sentences, each question boomeranging back with the right answer. But things couldn't always be that perfect between them, could it? Was Hana pissed at Juniper for leaving so close to the wedding? Was she fed up with the Barbers and their baggage? She had to be, right?

His sister swiveled around and smiled at him. He could see pain behind it, but he smiled back before she turned forward again. Her hand was shaking. Hana reached for it and kissed her fingers, and their hands stayed entwined like that, atop the center console.

July crumpled inside. To have someone beside you when you shook with fear or ached with rage, someone who could find some measure of joy in your aptly worded resentments, who wasn't afraid of the chaos you tried to keep hidden… He thought of Nate, out on the kayak, the arms of July's sunglasses kissing the tops of his ears. The little tug on the back of his shorts when Nate found his passport. That way their hands gloved together on the dock. *Could he be loved?*

Devoting himself to Lucas had felt like belonging, but it had been an illusion, he knew now, and he'd messed everything up with Nate as a result. He'd let his attachment to a fantasy hold him back from gunning for the real thing.

If he *could* be loved, then it wasn't that complicated. July checked his watch. He still had time.

"Hey, guys," he said, "can we stop a minute?"

He left Hana and Juniper parked at the curb outside the little green house on the corner. As he walked the long driveway, he started to sweat. They hadn't spoken since Memorial Day. It would be dramatic enough, just showing up unannounced like this, but if he explained where he was going? Forget about it. Off the charts pathos. But if he chickened out, he'd have to explain it to his sister. If it were May in the car instead of Juniper, she would have sniffed out his desperation and lectured him about respecting himself. He would've been too embarrassed to come.

Halfway down the driveway he stopped. "Now what?" he said to the sky. What had he come here for? To say goodbye? To apologize? To make a fool of himself for the thousandth time?

The sky didn't answer back, unless the brightness of the blue, not a single cloud to trouble it, could be considered a form of speech.

He turned around, hands on his hips. There was the street, the car, the ride to the airport. Above him, the sky his plane would cut across. He checked his watch again. This was ridiculous. He headed back.

Wait. No. Maybe he didn't know what to say, or if he even wanted to say anything at all, but he still wanted to see Nate. He just wanted to see his face.

July went around to the back of the house. Nate's door was behind a set of stairs that slalomed up to the roof. July heard music from inside. He knocked, softly at first. Then pounded. The music stopped and suddenly there was Nate, filling the doorway. And there *it* was, the thunderbolt in July's chest, so strong he put his hand to his sternum. *Hey, you,* it seemed to say. *Pay attention.* He tried to, but where to begin?

"You're home," July said.

"Yeah, well, I live here, so." Nate smiled and something unfurled inside July, like a peony blooming in time lapse.

"Right. I was in the neighborhood, so."

Nate's smile dimmed. It was the wrong thing to say. "Ah," he said. "Lucas."

Shit. July could feel it coming on again, the emotional molasses he'd gotten trapped in at the picnic. "No. I mean. Can I come in?"

Nate considered the request. Then he stepped aside.

July entered the apartment. It wasn't at all what he'd expected,

not another version of the transient semi-independent living
quarters stacked one on top of another at Charles Commons.
Futons, plastic bins from The Container Store, design by Target. None of that. Here there was art hanging on the walls—real
art, not just prints. Maybe that wasn't surprising for an artist,
but in the kitchen there were boxes of spices and boxes of teas,
utensils hanging from hooks over the stove. The desk in the living room had accumulated a couple years' worth of habits and
order. The bookshelves were wood and custom.

"Is this yours?" July asked, moving closer to the canvas over
the sofa.

"Nah, a friend's. You want something to drink? Water, tea?"

"Sure, water. Thanks."

While Nate was in the kitchen, July wandered over to the
desk. Taped to the wall above it were dozens of sketches, studies, maybe, for a larger project. Two boys with their arms around
each other's shoulders; a father and son walking down the street,
boys playing basketball; a bike messenger listening to music
through his headphones; construction workers laughing, sandwiches and sodas in their hands. They were portraits of emotion in motion. July recognized Mr. Guillory and Nate's older
brother, Marcus, too. All these figures were people Nate recognized, even if he wasn't personally acquainted with them,
and July felt a twinge of something—regret?—not to be among
them. They'd moved through the same world most of their
lives. He'd had plenty of chances to become a part of Nate's vi-
sual vocabulary.

"Here you go," Nate said, and July's stomach jumped.

"Thanks. Is this for something you're working on?" he asked,
pointing at the sketches.

"Something I'm just playing around with. I've got a studio
on campus. I work in oils, so mostly I work there."

"Cool." He imagined a rainbow of tints fanned out across
a tabletop, running up the walls, over the canvas, and out the

window, where Nate stood in the morning light. What did he think about as he started to work? What did he feel?

"You want to sit down?"

"I can't stay," July said, sitting anyway.

"Okay," Nate said as he joined him on the sofa.

July parted his lips to speak but his throat felt dry as an empty riverbed. He swallowed a gulp of water. "I'm sorry," he finally managed to get out. "The picnic. I didn't handle that well."

Nate shrugged. The cords in his neck gently shook the collar of his T-shirt. Underneath, his shoulders pulsed and settled again. He had one foot up on the couch, knee bent, and was holding his ankle.

"I was having a really good time, out in the kayak, and then…"

"And then you weren't."

"Then I wasn't."

"Then Lucas showed up."

"No. It wasn't that. Or, okay, yes, that was part of it."

Nate hadn't taken his eyes off him since they'd sat down. It was disarming. July couldn't think of a single time in high school when they'd truly regarded each other. And with Lucas, they hardly ever made eye contact. So it was both wonderful and agonizing to watch Nate's feelings play out across his face. One minute he was open, the next he was guarded.

"You're in love with him, right?" Nate asked.

"Is it still love when somebody doesn't love you back?"

"Don't think it matters what you call it, if it's the way you feel."

"I do. Think it matters, I mean."

July stared up at the painting Nate's friend had done. He focused on the texture, the thick dabs of paint. He felt Nate's eyes still on him and put his hand to his lips. He wanted to get this right. "I was kidding myself for a while. A long time, I guess. And I'm not anymore. I wasn't that day, either. I just hadn't figured out yet how to…proceed…without the fantasy."

"The Lucas fantasy?" Nate asked.

July looked at him directly again. "No. The fantasy where nothing that had happened before I met him mattered."

"Ah." Nate chewed his bottom lip.

There it was again, the jolt, only now it was down in July's stomach. "Yeah," he said, trying to keep his voice steady.

Nate folded his bent leg down and swiveled to face him. "Well, sign me up for that fantasy. I mean, come on. No Macklemore? No Kardashians? No slavery?"

"That's right. No *Celebrity Apprentice*. No Ryan Seacrest. No AIDS."

By now July had tugged his own knee up on the couch and they were sitting there, knee to knee, almost touching.

"And no kidnapping," Nate said.

July nodded. He studied the contours of Nate's calf muscle. Was he a runner? Did he bike a lot? July's gaze wandered up to the bulge in Nate's shorts. Would his dad be appalled if he knew July was getting turned on right now, talking about him but wondering what Nate looked like naked?

"Really, though?" Nate asked, and July's eyes snapped up. "All that imagination wrapped up in some boring, repressed white guy? I mean, he's pretty but—"

"Wait, you think he's repressed?"

"Kinda?"

"Like has-sex-with-his-eyes-closed repressed?"

"Kinda. It's cool, though. If that's your type."

Could he be loved? Over and over Bob Marley's words rang in his head, telling him to go for it.

"Nah."

"Nah?"

July shook his head. Then before he could question it, he leaned in and kissed Nate.

Nate kissed him back.

"Oh, no," July said. *What* had he been waiting for? Why hadn't he kissed him sooner?

"What?" Nate asked, but July kissed him again.

Nothing in his life had prepared him for what a real kiss—a good proper kiss, with someone whose name you knew, someone you wanted even with their clothes on—would feel like. He didn't know whether to laugh or die. Nate took him by the neck, and July held onto Nate's forearms. Lips! Soon their tongues got acquainted, and their teeth, too. Actual fucking fireworks. Who knew? July slid his hand down Nate's wrist, over his watch, along his arm and down to his chest.

Wait. His watch. The time. July pulled back.

"Shit, I gotta go."

"Uh? Okay."

"I'm going out of town for a few days. But I'm going to call you when I get back."

"You don't have to if—"

"Yes, I do." July stood up. "I will."

"All right."

July smiled. *Goddamn.* "I'll see you soon," he said.

"See you soon," Nate said back.

"Jesus, July," Juniper said when he got back in the car, and Hana whipped the car back into traffic.

"Sorry, I had a thing to do."

"You better pray we don't miss this fucking flight. April's gonna kill us. And what happened to your lip?"

He touched his lip. There was a little spot of blood on his finger. He sucked it clean, soaring inside.

At the airport July watched Juniper say goodbye to Hana at the curb, a too-long hug that his sister was the last to pull away from. Juniper rubbed her eyes quickly and grabbed her bag and they headed into the terminal together.

"You better pray we're not late," he said, and then he hooked his arm around her shoulder so she'd know he was kidding.

April was waiting for them inside, guarding a check-in kiosk from the crowd behind her.

"What took you so long?"

Ignoring her, Juniper typed in her information. Ten feet away May hugged Will goodbye.

"Where's Ross?" July asked. April was the only sister whose partner hadn't come to see her off.

She squeezed her lips and raised her eyebrows like *who knows?*

"Everything okay?"

"I'm fine. Here, your turn."

After a moment he had his boarding pass, too, and the four Barbers climbed the escalator to security. They were the last to board the plane, and the flight attendant shut the door behind them, sealing them in. They formed a column down the aisle as they looked for their seats—April, May, June, July, four little ducks who'd scattered apart, now flying in formation.

21

April

They landed in Istanbul the following evening, at least according to the clock at the bottom of the departures board where April searched for their connecting flight to Erbil. Her internal clock was all screwed up. They'd left Dulles after night fell, all four of them littered about the cabin—May up at the front, April a row behind Juniper in the middle of the plane, both of them in middle seats, and July back by the bathrooms.

After takeoff, April heard Juniper order a cocktail—"To help me sleep," she'd said—which seemed like a good idea, so she did the same. Not long after that, they'd both drifted off. Or had they? Juniper was weaving on the concourse up ahead of her now, nearly bumping into a businessman and his rolling suit-case. She was drunk. April vaguely remembered the flight attendant stopping by once or twice when the cabin lights were off. When the blinds were up, she'd seen her sister upgrade her orange juice to a screwdriver. Had she slept at all? Or had she stayed awake expressly to drink in the privacy of a darkened cabin? Maybe she hadn't meant to get this messy. Maybe with the altitude the vodka went to her head. April herself felt a bit queasy and disoriented. It should have been morning, but instead it was almost dinnertime.

They were on their way to Mosul to see their last available connection to Frank. She couldn't shake the feeling that at any moment she would need to spring into action. This time she would be ready to run. This time she would catch him.

"April," July called out and then inclined his head toward the men's room and went in.

She scanned the concourse for May, who'd gotten off the plane way ahead of them. Back at Dulles she'd seemed more agitated than usual, saying little but snapping at them when she did, pacing by the window until their group number was announced.

April turned her phone back on to locate her sister, hoping Ross had called during the flight, knowing he probably hadn't. He hadn't come home the night of their fight. She'd waited up, trying to think of something to say that would make her betrayal less despicable. At two o'clock she gave up and cried herself to sleep. She cried through the hammam party the next day, too, the sweat and condensation in the baths disguising her tears. That night when the kids straggled home from their sleepovers, their summer break already in full swing, it was Maddie who'd told her where Ross was.

"Can we go to the movies tonight?" Maddie had asked. They'd made a movie out of her favorite book, the one where the sick girl and the dying boy fall in love. "We might as well see it while Dad's away."

"Away?" April asked.

"On his business trip."

"When did you talk to Dad?"

"He texted me this morning. You're being weird. What's going on?"

"Nothing. Here's my card. Go online and get us tickets."

While Maddie was buying the tickets, April started to text Ross, but the irony in trying to track him down via the same form of communication through which he'd discovered her affair was too much. She went up to her bedroom and called him instead. To her surprise he answered.

"You're on a business trip?"

"I told Maddie that so she wouldn't worry."

"You didn't care if I worried?"

Ross sighed. "Really? You're gonna do this?"

April paced the empty space between the foot of their bed and the dresser. The loose floorboard creaked when she stepped on it. She prodded it with her toe.

"Where are you?"

"At a hotel."

"For how long?"

"I don't know."

"Which hotel?"

"The Hilton."

They had points there. Even when Ross was disgusted with her, he was responsible.

"I gotta go," he said and hung up without saying goodbye.

The next few days April dove into work and when she was home, she cleaned out all the closets. It was a good project because it bored the kids, so they stayed out of her way. She was terrified they would ask her something she couldn't answer truthfully, like what city Ross was in or when he was coming home or whether they could go to Rehoboth again this summer. If she had to, she would make something up. She could lie easily, it seemed, even (or especially) to those she loved most. She hated that about herself.

On Friday night, while she was crouched inside the guest room closet, the phone rang.

"It's Aunt Juniper," Maddie yelled up the stairs.

After April heard the news about Tariq, alive and well in

Mosul according to Karim, she began to pack. Even before it became evident how difficult it would be to get any substantive messages through while Mosul was surrounded by ISIS, she'd decided. There was no question she was going to Iraq as soon as possible. Hadn't Joe told her she should? Forget the State Department, April would handle this mess herself.

"What's next?" July had asked when she called him and Nancy to pass on the news that Tariq had agreed to meet.

"Now I go to Erbil and get some answers."

"I'm coming, too."

"July," she'd said, "I've got this."

"If you tell me not to worry, I'm going to scream. And then I'm still going to come."

Half an hour later Juniper was on the phone. Nancy had called *her* in a frenzy, hoping she'd talk April and July out of going. Instead she'd decided to join them.

"Why not?" April had said. "It definitely won't be weird when all three of us show up. I'm sure that'll put him at ease and he'll just tell us everything he knows."

"Let's review. I'm the one who got Karim to talk to us at the embassy. I'm the one he chose to tell about Tariq. I'm coming. The end."

"Fine," April said. It was pointless to argue. "Has anyone talked to May? Never mind. I'll do it."

She'd ended up putting all four plane tickets on her card. It was amazing the bank didn't think it had been stolen.

Now, five-thousand miles later, her phone buzzed in her hand. Someone *was* trying to reach her but not Ross. It was May. She'd found a Starbucks at Gate 219.

A Starbucks, April thought, *even here in Istanbul. Ah, America.*

July emerged from the men's restroom, then Juniper from the

women's, her color edging back to normal, her upper lip dotted with sweat.

"Come on," July said, taking his sister's backpack and putting it on the front of his body, like a BabyBjörn.

They found May at a table outside Starbucks, head bent over her phone. Her forehead furrowed at the sight of them. "You guys. What the fuck? It's just jet lag."

"I'm too old to sleep sitting up," April said. "Aren't you?"

"Buck up. Mind over matter."

"I need coffee," Juniper said. She closed her eyes, as if visualizing the steps required to stand in line. Or else she was falling asleep on her feet.

"Jesus. Here." May gave up her chair.

Juniper shuffled toward it as July scrounged for others.

April followed May and they got in line. "So you and Will, huh?" April asked, remembering their goodbye kiss at the airport. "For real, this time?"

"Yeah. I mean, I think so."

"Wow, so domestic."

It was like they were switching places, May settling down just as her own life was unraveling. How would April recognize herself if she weren't the responsible big sister trying to tamp down her wild sister and her fevered plans? Their roles stretched all the way back to childhood. May always tested their boundaries: she'd been the first to jump overboard or walk to school alone, the first to fire the cap gun she "borrowed" from Grandma's neighbors and then, later, to play doctor with those boys out in the crawl space under the sunporch. May had worn these milestones easily, running straight into Frank's arms afterward, knees and elbows muddy but not a trace of shame on her skin, not a look to betray the lines they'd crossed when the adults weren't looking. The first to smoke pot, the first to fight with her fists (against a boy at school who'd called Junie a dyke, so legendary a showdown that even years later the town knew better than to fuck with July). The first to break curfew, to sneak out, to sneak back in. The first to go to Iraq. For so long April had resented these incursions into her territory as the first-born, the supposed trailblazer. She hadn't seen then what was obvious to her now—that May had always been willing to take on the risk and pain for herself.

They ordered four coffees and stepped down to the other end of the counter to wait.

"Ross took the kids," April said.

"Took them where?"

"Michigan."

"What for? What's in Michigan?"

"Not me, which is, I think, the main selling point."

His sister had a house on Lake Leelanau. April always had to remind him to call his sister on holidays or her birthday, so she knew what it meant that he'd reached out to her on his own.

"We need a break," he'd told April in the kitchen the night before she left, while the kids watched a movie. "When I get back next month, we'll talk."

"You sure this is what you want?" she asked.

"Yeah."

April didn't feel like she had a choice but to agree.

Now May gave her The Face. The hurry-up-and-tell-me-what-you-want-to-tell-me face that she'd been wielding since they were teenagers.

"I cheated on him." It was the first time she'd said it out loud.

"Wow," May said, her face registering genuine surprise.

"Yeah," April said.

There wasn't—as April had somehow known there wouldn't be—any judgment in May's expression. For the first time April thought she might be able to live with herself.

May said, "Yeah, well. I found this kidnapping school—"

"You what?"

"Where they teach you how to avoid capture and, if you can't, how to survive it. I wanted to go. I was going to pay them extra to waterboard me."

"What the fuck?" Maybe they weren't switching places, after all. Maybe that was impossible.

"Relax. I didn't have the money for any of it. But I thought it would help me understand what Dad went through, and then I'd know why he didn't come home."

"Oh. That's so—"

"I know, it's fucked up." May shoved her hands in her jeans pockets. "I'm seeing a therapist," she added, keeping the confessional streak going.

"No shit?"

"Maybe you should, too." There was a hint of a smile as she said it, but then she shrugged. She was teasing, yes, but not joking.

"I was going to say it's sweet, not fucked up. Sweet and sad," April said.

"That, too," May agreed.

The coffee arrived and they each grabbed two and added milk, no sugar, then carried them back to the table. July had his nose in a book. Juniper rested her head on her folded arms. They set the cups down, and Juniper reached for hers, but May slid it out of the way.

"Hey," Juniper complained.

"Okay, kids," May said. "Time for a geography lesson."

She placed two cups about six inches apart in the center of the table. She touched the one on the left. "This is Mosul." Then she touched one on the right. "This is Erbil."

She drew her hand through the space between them. "This is Iraq. Sometimes it's dangerous to go from here to here, even though they're so close."

She put a third cup to the south of Erbil. "This is Sulaymaniyah. All of this—" and now she drew a wide arc with her finger from Sulaymaniyah to Erbil to another cup she placed a couple inches north of the Mosul cup "—is Iraqi Kurdistan."

April understood that May was drawing a map of the route she'd followed ten years ago. It hadn't been safe to travel the highway between Erbil and Mosul and so she and her driver had taken the long way around, entering Mosul from the north. At the time April had been furious with the driver, too, thinking he was just some accessory to her sister's folly, but now she felt a deep well of gratitude to him. He'd escorted May into a war zone at great risk to himself, and he'd done what he could to minimize the danger along the way.

May tapped the fourth northernmost cup. "This is Duhok. Where Dad was headed when he was taken. Up here—" she put her palm on the table above Duhok "—is Turkey. Over here—" she moved her hand to the left of Mosul "—is Syria. And all of this—" she indicated everything to the right of Iraqi Kurdistan "—is Iran. I don't know what route Tariq's going to take to meet us."

May finished her demonstration and passed the cups out to her siblings. Juniper took a small sip of her coffee, then set it aside.

"We have to be careful. It's fun to play detective, but we're dealing with things we don't understand. And we're not going to suddenly become experts with a little online research. Trust me, I've tried. I know Dad liked Tariq, but we don't know him. We meet him in a public place. We do *not* get into a car with him. We keep our heads down and stay safe."

April had never seen May like this before. Her sister was... afraid. If May was scared, maybe she should be, too.

"I'm gonna charge my phone before we take off. I saw an outlet over there." July stood and walked over to an empty table with a charging station in the middle of it.

"I'll be back, too," Juniper said, heading for the restroom.

It was just April and May again.

"May? It wasn't your fault, what happened the last time."

May shook her head, unwilling to be forgiven. It didn't help that April had been so harsh with her in the aftermath. *What were you thinking? You're so selfish!* April had shouted when the military attaché at Camp Freedom put her on the phone.

"You wanted to help," April told her now. "You couldn't have known what you were walking into."

"Couldn't I?" May said, tears spilling over her cheeks. "And aren't we doing the exact same thing now?"

"No. We're not. We're…"

"Lost," May whispered, like it was a curse she'd been trying not to give power to.

But she was right. Something that for so long had seemed dense and crushing, sitting on April's chest, scrambled up and fluttered apart from her, like a butterfly. They *were* lost, weren't they? Wasn't it better to start from that premise than to pretend everything was okay, as they'd each been doing for the last ten years? They were all lost together.

Four hours later, after their next plane touched down on the outermost ring of a city that, from the sky, looked like an illuminated spiderweb, April and her siblings passed through the automatic doors of Erbil International Airport and into the black night of an unfamiliar country. She knew she should be scared, but it hadn't kicked in yet. Maybe it was hope she felt instead—a small glowing thing that filled her lungs—edging out the fear, or maybe it was that old confidence, bone-deep, that came from knowing that wherever May went, she would follow.

22

May

May lay next to April in their shared queen bed, April's bottle-blond hair crossing the invisible line dividing one sister's side from the other's. May rubbed a lock of it between her fingertips, trying to convince herself that this was all real. She wasn't dreaming. They were all really in Iraq.

April had just assumed May was coming when she called, and so she hadn't had to decide. She didn't know what she would've said if she'd been asked—*yes, I will come* or *no, I won't, I can't*—but now that she was here, she couldn't imagine letting her siblings go without her. She'd been carried along by their momentum, the weight and complexity of her feelings only becoming clear to her as she delivered her geography lesson, the same one Adar had given her in that café in Erbil over plates of lamb and bulgur and cups of strong black tea. There was so much she should've told them about her prior trip, and now there wasn't time. April knew only the broad strokes; Juniper, July, and their mom knew nothing at all.

She hadn't shared the whole story with her psychiatrist yet, either. Her first appointment with the psychiatrist Nancy's doctor recommended had been an intake meeting, straight down to business, no banter. He said her symptoms and history fit the pattern for unipolar depression. May was still getting used to the label, trying it on for size, wondering what she was supposed to do with it. He'd prescribed an SSRI and referred her to a social worker for talk therapy. *Shit*, she thought now, *what time is it?* She factored in the time change and realized she needed to take a pill. She swallowed it down with some of the water July had set on the nightstand for Junie.

In the other queen bed July yawned and Juniper rolled over. Her sister had spent the night back and forth between the bed and the cool tile floor of the bathroom, nursing a nasty hangover.

May turned on the TV, the volume down low. On the screen she recognized the images before she understood what she was seeing. The leaning minaret reaching up through a haze of smoke. A rusty bridge crowded with people in flight. The Islamic State was in Mosul. In the neighborhoods west of the Tigris, black flags were draped over police stations, banks, and other public buildings. According to reports, the Iraqi army had dropped their weapons and uniforms and melted into the tide of civilians. May hoped Tariq was safe in that tide and not one of the bodies littering the street. April had left him a WhatsApp message when they landed, with the name and number of the hotel, but he hadn't called back yet.

"Turn it up," April said, now awake.

On Al Jazeera, reporters were calling the Arab militants Daesh, but on CNN they called them ISIS. Whatever their name, they wanted to establish a caliphate in Iraq and Syria, the talking heads explained, and return the region to seventh-century religious laws. The group had formed under al-Qaeda's umbrella in 2004, but after a long power struggle they'd branched off, following a purer, more extreme vision of Sunni Islam and their leader, Abu Bakr al-Baghdadi. In the territories of the Levant

they'd already conquered—Raqqa in Syria, Fallujah in Iraq—
women were ordered to wear burkas or stay home. Stealing
was punishable by amputation. Music, alcohol, cigarettes, art,
photography—all were forbidden. They welcomed foreigners
to their jihad and yet they seemed to be against everyone: the
apostate Alawite regime in Syria, the idolatrous Shia majority in
Iraq, the secular West, infidels, unbelievers, kuffar. The camera
cut away to an angry mob in Fallujah, three months ago, ston-
ing a woman to death.

Juniper hurried to the toilet and retched. July went to check
on her.

"That poor woman," April said, her hand over her mouth.

May shut off the TV. In the bathroom she found July hovering
as Juniper leaned back against the tub, pressing her fingertips in
circles against her temples. Even assuming they made it home in
time, how could she get married in this state? She was a wreck.

"Sorry," May said to her sister. "That was awful."

She wasn't sure why she was apologizing. No one said this
would be easy, and throwing up seemed like an appropriate response to the realization that your life of relative safety was pur-
chased through violence. The US had brought two wars to Iraq,
which made the results, whether the average citizen was aware
of them or not, at least partially our responsibility, as far as May
was concerned. We sent our ambassadors and put boots on the
ground to advance our strategic interests, and most of the time it
was shockingly easy to forget—as we shopped online and gassed
up our tanks and watched *American Idol*—that it was not in our
strategic interest for Iraqis to be as safe in their homes as we were.

"But you were already sick," July said to Juniper. "Was it the
flight? Altitude sickness?"

"No," April said, standing behind May. "She's an alcoholic."

May flinched, but she knew immediately it was true. The way
her sister had had glass after glass of champagne at the bridal
salon, like a chain-smoker lighting the next cigarette off the one

before it, as if her survival depended on an uninterrupted ability to see things at a slant. It had been the same at the bridal shower.

July looked from April to Juniper and then up at the ceiling.

"Well, aren't you?" April said, pressing her way into the bathroom.

"I mean, that's a pretty strong word—" Juniper began.

"How many drinks did you have on the plane? I counted eight, and that was when I was awake."

"Eight!" July said.

"I don't know why it took me this long to see it," April said. "It's been going on since...college, right?"

"It has?" July asked, and May's heart beat for him. He was still young enough to be shocked by anyone unraveling. May was more shocked anyone ever kept it together.

"Hana covers for you," May said, thinking about the ways Nancy and July had picked up the slack for her over the years. "When you're late to work or can't make it in, she keeps you out of trouble."

A grim look passed over Juniper's face.

"What?" April asked.

"Nothing," Juniper said.

"Are you in trouble at work?"

"No."

"Yes, you are, Junie," May said. "It's written all over your face."

Juniper's eyes were dead with rage. "You think you know me? You don't know shit."

She was right. They'd barely spoken in years. After the kidnapping Juniper had moved on so cleanly, so brutally, or so it had always seemed.

July sat across from Juniper on the bathroom floor. He reached for her shoulder.

"Stop," Juniper said.

"Hey. It's just us homos."

"I can't remember what he was really like anymore." Juniper said these words so quietly that May had to lean forward to catch them, but she didn't need the words. May knew the feeling. April nodded as well.

"I feel like I never really knew him," July said.

"I'm so sorry," Juniper said, bursting into tears.

"Don't be sorry," he said.

"He wouldn't have been over here if it weren't for me. I had to play at Princeton. I could have gone to Middlebury. They would have given me a free ride. But no. I wanted to play D1."

"Oh, Junie." April took her hand. May lowered herself to the floor, too. They crossed their legs so they would all fit. "Dad would have taken that job, anyway. He never liked working at Snaxco. CCA was his big break. It was his chance to do something...meaningful."

"Killing people is meaningful?" July asked.

"July," April said.

"Is that such an unfair question? He worked with chemical weapons. Have you watched the videos from Damascus? Have you ever seen what happens when people are hit with sarin gas? Their bodies convulse. They foam at the mouth. They go blind."

He was talking about the attack in Syria last year. Assad had gassed his own people, then denied it. Obama had warned him not to cross that red line, but Assad had done it, unafraid. The international community was appalled for about a week, but quickly lost their stomach for bombing him. A diplomatic solution forced Assad to turn over his arsenal of chemical weapons, but wouldn't he just make more? Either way the civil war continued.

"Why would any scientist want to be involved in that?" July asked.

May was tired of debating Frank's motives, sifting through the evidence, trying to sort out if he was mostly good or mostly bad or if it was more complicated than that.

"To stop it from happening," April answered. "The US hasn't used chemical weapons in years."

July snorted. "We used white phosphorous in Fallujah during the war."

"What's that?" Juniper asked.

"It makes a big flash of light and a lot of smoke. It's good for flushing people out of their hiding places. Oh, and it also burns skin down to the bone."

"Dad wouldn't have done that," April said.

"Sure, yeah. No one sets out to hurt innocent people, but that's the downstream effect of our actions. What about bin Laden? That was a super idea we had, training him to fight the Russians in Afghanistan. He must have seemed like a real stable dude. Who could have predicted he'd turn around and fight us next?"

"Okay, okay," April said.

"You can't put the genie back in the bottle. You can kill him, but there's always gonna be someone to take his place. Next it's Zarqawi. Now it's Baghdadi—and as of today he's got control of the military base in Mosul. He's got American tanks and Humvees and guns. Look at what we enable. It's easy to say the problem is chemical weapons falling into the wrong hands, but whose are the right hands? Yassin's? Is that why Dad was meeting with him?"

The phone in April's hand rang, startling all of them. She turned it over and they all leaned in to look at the unknown number. "I think it's him," April said, and she pushed the button to answer.

May's heart thumped in her chest like a Labrador's tail against a screen door.

"Hello?"

April listened for a moment and then nodded at them. It *was* Tariq.

"Thank you so much for calling. Are you in Mosul? We've been watching on the news… Thank God." Then to them she whispered, "He's okay."

Tariq was safe, but so many others weren't. For the millionth time May wondered where Adar and his family were, if they made it across that bridge, if Mina and her children ever returned to their home in west Mosul, and if they did, was it still there waiting for them? Was it still standing today?

April listened again. "Okay. Yes. We'll meet you here in Erbil. The bazaar?"

May shook her head no. The bazaar was huge. They'd never find each other.

April wrinkled her face. "Uh-huh. The fountains?"

The fountains. Yes, May remembered them—next to the bazaar, beneath the citadel. They could find their way there. She nodded yes.

April's chin cocked to one side. "What?" she asked. "Yes, okay."

"What?" July whispered.

April put her thumb to her teeth. It was bad news; May could feel it. Then April closed her eyes, and May knew.

"How?" April asked, her voice small and vulnerable, reminding May of when they were girls. Finally she looked at them and shook her head.

May held her breath, the way she used to as a kid when they drove through the tunnel under the Baltimore harbor. The challenge then: to refuse to breathe until you came out on the other side. The challenge now: to refuse to breathe until she was alone with the news that her father was dead.

"Thank you for telling me. We'll see you later at the fountains. Six o'clock."

April hung up.

No one spoke. May didn't want anyone to. She didn't want to share this with her sisters and her brother. He was *her* father. She bolted out of the room.

May couldn't say exactly when she knew her father was dead, whether it was in the helicopter leaving Iraq the first time or sometime before or after. Every spin cycle she came back to this inescapable point: if he were alive, he would have returned to her. But believing he was dead was not the same thing as knowing he was, and neither verb precluded the kind of magical thinking that had allowed her to hope that one day he might hold her again.

Now he never would.

She walked the hotel halls in a daze. Outside the heat shocked her back into her body as she headed up the road to a lonely park where the grass was patchy and untended, the trees too thin to give shade, the stone paths crumbling. She collapsed onto a bench. An old man sat on another bench, too far away to see that she was crying. To be old! She resented everyone who'd ever had the privilege, even this man whose life had surely been no picnic. May knew it was cruel to think like this. Well, life was cruel, too.

Across a fallow garden she noticed a locked gate with plaster elephants on either side. The plaster was faded and cracked, and through the slats of the gate she saw a decrepit old zoo, the cages small like a pet store's. The animals were gone, but it crushed her that they'd ever, for a time, been kept here. Taken from their family, maybe traded illegally; it was no way to live. Sweat and tears came together like two tributaries, a river coursing down her cheeks. She lifted her face to the sun, its rays forcing catharsis, wringing her out.

When she could take it no more, she went back to the hotel.

In the room April and July dozed. May went to the bathroom and washed her face and neck. Then she looked at the beds again.

She shook April. "Where's June?"

"Huh?"

"Junie. Where'd she go?"

July sat up. "She was in the shower," he said.

"Not anymore. But I have an idea where she went," May said.

She hadn't been able to find her father, but she would find her sister.

She rode the elevator up to the rooftop terrace. It was mostly men up here, and expats. A pergola provided a bit of shade, and fans stirred the air. May walked to the edge and spun around, taking in the view—the wide plains, the citadel up on the tell, and the foothills beyond. At the bar, the bartender put four tumblers on a tray and filled them with Johnnie Walker Black Label.

"I'm looking for my sister," May said. "She's my height, looks kinda like me, longer hair."

"Yes, I know who you mean."

"She was here?"

He nodded.

"She left? Did she seem okay?" He was reluctant to answer. He was middle-aged, in his forties maybe. "Please."

"I told her I could not serve her anymore. She was not happy about that."

"Did she say where she was going?"

"No, but—"

"Somewhere she can keep drinking," she said, finishing the sentence so he wouldn't have to.

He lifted the tray, headed for a table of businessmen. He stopped. "For a woman, even an American, it is not seemly to drink this much. I told her this."

"Yeah, okay," May said, bristling at his paternalism even though she was mad at Juniper, too.

May rode the elevator downstairs and crossed the white marble lobby. Outside a row of cream-colored taxis was parked, their drivers standing under the portico, smoking.

"As-salamu alaykum," she said to them.

"Wa'alaykumu as-salam," the men said back.

"Do you speak English?"

There were half-nods of assent. "A little bit," one man said.

"Have you seen a woman who looks like me, this tall, with long hair? She might have been a little tipsy."

"Shouan took her. She wanted to go to Ainkawa."

"Ainkawa?" May asked.

"The Christian quarter." The man saw her confusion and added, "Where there are stores that sell alcohol."

May took a deep breath. "Okay, I appreciate your help. Shukran."

Back upstairs she found July in front of the television, watching live images of a city under siege. ISIS was threatening to destroy the al-Nuri Mosque, and there were reports that a group of civilians had formed a human chain of protection around it. CNN showed a picture of a ten-thousand dinar note, with the leaning minaret on the back. The reporter said some Iraqis believed the tower had acquired its signature tilt by bowing to the Prophet Mohammed when he ascended to heaven. Altogether it was a symbol of idolatry, and the militants wanted it destroyed. So far the civilians were holding them off.

The screen was filled with the figures of masked gunmen moving south on the main road from Mosul to Baghdad. The Islamic State was on the march.

The key card clicked in the lock and April entered from the hallway, looking like she'd seen a ghost.

"What is it?" July asked.

"I talked to Leyla. Come sit," April said, lowering herself onto their bed.

July sat next to her, but May didn't want to. "I'm tired of this. I'm tired of being jerked around by the fucking Suits. Dad's dead. I don't need to know anything else."

April patted the empty spot beside her. "Come. Grab that." She pointed at the laptop on the nightstand.

"Fine." She was tired of resisting, too.

April pulled up an email from Leyla and opened an attach-

ment. When the image loaded, May caught her breath. "He...
he looks so much like him."

"That's Tariq's cousin, Hamza," April said. "That's the man I
saw."

They were the photographs from the customs hall in Dubrovnik. In the first photograph, taken from somewhere up
high, they saw the man in full-length profile. He was tall, like
Frank, and he had the same slouch into his hips, the same wide
gap between his knees, the common lurch of the bowlegged that
May had, too. Hamza was wearing a dark baseball cap with a
P in the center. Her dad's hat. If it had been her in Dubrovnik,
she would have chased him, too. In the second picture Hamza
was staring straight-faced at the customs agent, and though it
was obvious he wasn't their father, he could have been a brother
or an uncle or a cousin. He looked like family.

"I'm sorry." May put her arm around her sister. "I know you
wanted to believe it was him."

"I dragged you guys halfway around the world and got your
hopes up again, for nothing."

"Not nothing," July said.

"At least we know the truth," May said. She didn't have the
whole story yet, but she knew for absolute certain that her father
wasn't coming home to her, and that was something.

"I guess this was our last wild goose chase," April said.

"Not yet," May said. "We have to get Junie."

They decided that July would stay behind, in case Juniper
came back. May and April would take a car to Ainkawa. If they
weren't back by 5:15, July would make his way to the fountains
next to the bazaar to meet Tariq. They still needed and wanted
to know what happened to their dad, right up to his last moment.

"Guys," he said, holding up Juniper's passport. "She forgot
it. Here."

May hugged him hard. "Keep your phone on. We'll catch up
as soon as we can."

Downstairs May asked the drivers, "Is Shouan back from Ainkawa?"

The men shook their heads no.

May had hoped her sister would have returned by now, brown bag in hand. She turned to the English-speaker. "Can you take us to Ainkawa?"

"Come." He waved them over to his taxi and opened the door.

"Shukran," May said, and April repeated it after her.

If Erbil was a clock with five concentric rings and the citadel at its center, the hotel was at six o'clock, on the first ring out, and Ainkawa was at twelve o'clock, on the outermost ring, just past the airport. On the inner ring road May could almost trick herself into believing she was in an American desert. The roads were well paved with sidewalks and curbs, though there were almost no pedestrians out in this weather. The median was dotted with trees and green grass that broke up the beige expanse. Heavy development was underway, a suburban sprawl of subdivisions, apartment buildings, and more hotels. But as they reached the road to Mosul, the illusion of calm evaporated like wet footprints on hot concrete. The Peshmerga manned a checkpoint, limiting access to the city. Stretching to the west as far as the eye could see, perhaps the entire fifty miles to Mosul, a flood of people lined up in cars, on bikes, and on foot. They looked exhausted, frightened, dehydrated. On the shoulder of the road, scores of cars sat empty, adding to the congestion. Who knew whether their owners would ever return.

The taxi passed through the checkpoint and drove on.

23

Juniper

Juniper had had two shots—hardly enough to feel, let alone get sloppy on—when the bartender cut her off. She looked around at the other guests, the German couple on the daybed and the table of businessmen, all day drinking on the hotel's terrace just like her, and wondered what the problem was.

"Is there some kind of limit in Kurdistan?" she asked the bartender. She wanted to be respectful. She was surprised (but grateful) they even had booze in Erbil—hence, the number of drinks she'd had on the plane. Had it really been eight like April said? That seemed extreme. The point being, she knew different norms applied here. She was a woman, an American, and depending on your view, young. The bartender was old enough to be somebody's father, just not hers. Hers was dead.

"When your husband joins you, I will be delighted to serve you another," the bartender said.

"But I don't have a husband," she said, and he bowed his head, as if in pity or prayer that this would be rectified.

"I'm getting married this weekend," Juniper added, and the bartender, still wiping the bar top, smiled, perhaps imagining something like the celebration that had gone on late into the night in the hotel's ballroom the day before. "But I just found out my father is dead."

He froze mid-wipe, mid-smile.

She'd left her brother and sister in the hotel room because for the last twenty-four hours she'd been sliding, as if down a chute through the rings of hell, from a terrible hangover to a well-monitored withdrawal (July hovering like a worried hummingbird, offering sips of water and a cool damp washcloth) to a sickening grief. Surely this entitled her to more than two measly shots of tequila, but she wouldn't find it here.

"Next time I come with my wife, we'll stop by."

She surprised herself with this dramatic flourish. This was assuming Hana would still have her, and there was no guarantee. The wedding was four days away. The henna party was in three. She was in Iraq.

I can't, she'd said, when she got home from the Abadis' with the bombshell about Tariq and Hana wanted to know if they should make three sheets of baklava for the henna party or four. *I need time*, she'd told Hana, as her family's travel plans came together, knowing she'd be skipping out on not just the party preparations but the emotional preparations. *I'll be back by Friday*, she'd promised, but would she? And then what? She'd stand in all the right places at the right times, like an understudy at her own wedding? Hana hadn't said *take all the time you need*, but she hadn't asked *can't this wait?*, either. Her lips had been a clothesline pulled tight—the timing, the extra work that would fall, once again, on her and her family—and Juniper had been relieved that Hana had held her peace. Because she couldn't not go.

Juniper wanted to see the bartender's face when he realized that in addition to being a Woman Who Drinks Too Much, she was a Woman Who Has Sex With Women, but she was also afraid of his disdain, and so she rushed to the elevator, her back to him like a coward.

While she'd had her two shots—it hadn't taken long; he'd been stingy with his pour—she'd flipped through a magazine written by and for expats in Iraqi Kurdistan, and that's how she'd known to ask the driver to take her to Ainkawa. She didn't know exactly where it was, whether it was part of Erbil proper or a suburb, but traffic was thick and slow. What were they waiting for? To pay a toll? For an accident to clear? Up ahead at the intersection she saw a bulldozer carrying a family in its scoop. She wondered if she was losing her mind.

She thought about that woman on TV, stoned by ISIS. A lesbian, the reporter had said. Juniper squeezed her eyes shut and opened them again, as if she were peering through a View-Master and could advance to the next image on the reel just by blinking.

"They'd stone us, too," she'd said to July when he'd found her on the bathroom floor.

"Us homos, you mean?"

"Yeah." But she knew it wasn't the two of them specifically who were at risk. It was people who looked, and loved, like Hana. Hana and Fariha and all the other Muslims who weren't the right sort of Muslims according to the Islamic State, not to mention Jews, Christians, Yazidis, and other religious minorities.

"Actually, I think they prefer throwing us off the rooftops," he'd said.

She'd leaned over the bowl and retched, but nothing came up. July had swept her ponytail behind her back.

They'd never really talked about it, the strange truth that both of them had turned out to be gay. When he was little, she hadn't wanted to burden him with her suspicions. He'd learn soon enough that Aberdeen was not an easy place to be different. When he was thirteen and he came out, he must have known she'd be useless because he'd never asked for her advice. All she'd ever known was how to stumble through, head down, praying no one would notice her. When Matt Larder called her a dyke in the seventh grade, she'd hoped everyone would just forget it—an impossible wish after May gave the kid a black eye. Juniper didn't want to be the cause of any more scenes after that. She just wanted to survive until she found a place where it was okay to be herself.

She'd thought that place was Princeton. But what was it Hana had said to her on the way to the airport, while they were waiting for July in the car? *Sometimes I think I'm talking to your clone, and the real you is hidden away somewhere.*

"You're shaking," Hana had said at the airport when they hugged goodbye.

"I'm scared," she'd said back. She knew that whatever happened when they met Tariq, whether they got their dad back or not, she wouldn't be the same person when she returned. Not that who she was now was so great. She was like the white space on a page, the absence that stared back at you after you took everything else away—first her dad, then the rest of her family, and finally the idea of herself as someone who was loyal and selfless. She was what was left.

In Erbil the car inched forward. The little girl in the bulldozer scoop squirmed, and the woman fanned the baby in her lap. Behind them Juniper saw an unbroken column of humans in flight. The Peshmerga were searching their back seats, in their trunks, under their axles. They checked papers. Their dogs sniffed luggage, the shirts on people's backs.

I'm scared. She'd foolishly said it aloud to Hana, and so on the plane she'd been trying to unsay it. Juniper hadn't only been uncertain whether Kurdistan sold alcohol. She'd been afraid. It had been a…what?…ten-hour flight to Istanbul? Eight drinks wasn't much, less than one an hour.

She was still trying to unsay it now. *I'm scared.* But she was scared of the bulldozer, the necessity of it.

Juniper closed her eyes. She put her head back against the seat. She didn't even like shots. Everyone knew that about her, but she'd seen the bottle of tequila already in the bartender's hand.

She felt weightless and insubstantial, like a cloud that was drifting away. After Tariq's call she'd felt an urge to get up and run, run so hard that her throat burned and her legs ached and her heart gave out. May did go, leaving the rest of them to acknowledge what they all knew to be true. Soon someone would say the words and Juniper didn't want to hear them spoken aloud. Then she realized that she could be the one to claim them. She opened her mouth and the words tumbled out.

"Dad's dead," she said.

"Yes," April answered, and two plump tears rolled down her cheeks.

Juniper's pulse was in her ears, throbbing so loud it drowned out the sound of anything else.

"How?" July asked. "When?"

"A heart attack. In 2006. Tariq said it's a long story and he'll tell us in person."

Juniper didn't want the long story or the short one. She wanted to go back in time, when the story had been that they were going to Iraq to find their dad. She wanted to go back to the moment when April's phone rang, when it had briefly seemed possible that she might see her dad's smile again—his real smile, not the grimace—and touch his cheeks and tell him how very sorry she was.

"He couldn't just tell you on the phone?" July said. "What an asshole."

"Actually, he sounded kind." April rested her head on Juniper's shoulder. "Do you remember the time Dad called the hospital?" she asked.

Juniper shook her head.

"Nope," July said.

"You were too little to remember. You'd just been born. I

was babysitting May and Junie. Dad came home to get us so we could meet our little brother."

"I burned my hand," Juniper remembered.

"I had my back turned, and you wanted to prove you were big enough to reach the stove. You reached it, all right."

"I don't remember burning it, just that you jammed my hand in a plastic cup, and I was afraid it was gonna get stuck."

"It was a cup of ice water. Dad comes in and you're crying, and May's yelling at you to stop, and I'm yelling at May to stop yelling at you. Then you start screaming, *you're killing me!* like it was *The Exorcist*."

"You're exaggerating."

"No, I'm not. So Dad calls the hospital. I think he was trying to get Mom on the phone to distract us. The nurse who answers is like, no, uh-uh. Your wife is *sleeping*. Dad was usually good at dealing with our bullshit, but he was off his game that day. Probably exhausted. So he says to the nurse, *Excuse me, ma'am. Do you have any miracle babies over there I could exchange for these three hellcats I've got here?* And you stopped crying *instantly*."

"You were trying to be good," July said to Juniper.

"Always," April agreed. "Then Dad takes one look at your face. Your big eyes and your quivering chin, and he laughs his big laugh and goes, *Get over here*. After that he's afraid for any of us to feel left out, so we all ride in the front seat to the hospital. You're on his lap, May and I are sharing a seat belt."

"Miracle baby?" July asked quietly.

"Yeah," April said. Through her shoulder, Juniper felt April's cheeks lift into a smile.

"I thought I was an accident."

"They were so happy they were having a boy. So happy about you."

Juniper remembered that day at the hospital, watching her sisters take turns holding their little brother. She wanted to hold him so badly, but she was afraid she would get it wrong, especially with her sore and bandaged hand. She wouldn't support his head right and it would snap off like a Barbie doll's. Her dad had helped her. He'd held the baby with one hand, crooked in his elbow like a football, and with his other hand he'd lifted Juniper onto his lap. Then he'd placed the baby in her arms and wrapped his arms around her, enfolding them both.

"What should we name him, June?" he'd said.

"Let's call him...July."

May had groaned, but her dad had said, "July. I like it."

For all Juniper knew, her parents were always going to name him July, or maybe they were going to name him Frank Jr., and changed their mind. Either way, the story stuck that she'd picked the name. She'd never felt so important or so connected to her father, who wanted just as deeply as she did to love and protect this little baby. Somehow she'd let go of that impulse, and now that little baby was a beautiful young gay man, and she'd done nothing to ease his way.

The driver lowered his window at the checkpoint. Off to the side were rows of cars, parked or abandoned. "As-salamu alaykum," he said.

Even on a day as hot as this one, the Peshmerga fighter was dressed in a short jacket and wide pants, a cummerbund wrapped around his middle. The soldier spoke to the driver, and the driver took something from his visor and showed it to him.

Then the soldier addressed Juniper. He said something she didn't understand. Then: "Passport?"

She reached for her back pocket, where her wallet was, with the dinars she'd withdrawn at the airport. But not her passport. She couldn't recall where it was. Had she given it to July?

"I'm sorry," she said.

The soldier tapped her window, and she felt around for the button to lower it. The driver put it down for her.

"I'm sorry," she said again, pantomiming the act of searching her pockets, finding them empty, a flourish in which the passport seemed to disappear midair like a magician's white dove.

The soldier opened her door and spoke sharply. The driver spoke back, his voice raised but his tone conciliatory.

The soldier beckoned at Juniper to get out of the car, and she stood up, swooning from the thick air on her face, hot like a furnace. She held onto the car's frame for ballast.

She didn't understand what he was saying to her. He banged on the driver's door and then walked around to the trunk, pounded on it. In a moment it popped open.

Now the driver was out of the car and hurried to the back. The soldier spoke. Juniper thought she heard the word *airport*. He seemed to think she was headed there. He tossed the trunk's contents around. The driver grew more distressed. He repeated the word *Ainkawa* several times, and at last the soldier paused to consider her.

She was wearing shorts and a polo shirt. Tevas. Her toenails were painted blue.

He waved her back inside.

"Shukran," the driver said, shutting the trunk and hurrying back to his seat. "As-salamu alaykum."

"Wa'alaykum as-salam," the soldier said, as the windows surged up.

The driver muttered under his breath. Juniper couldn't hear him, but she understood every word. They drove on.

She knew they were in Ainkawa when they passed a roundabout with a statue of Mary, in her blue robe with a crown on her head, looking down over the circling cars. The driver pulled up in front of a liquor store and turned in his seat, his palm outstretched for payment. They hadn't agreed on the fare in advance. She handed him a couple of ten-thousand dinar notes, and he took one. She tried to say *as-salamu alaykum*, but it came out wrong.

Inside she was surprised (and grateful) to see all the usual choices.

She's an alcoholic. Well, wasn't she?

Hana covers for you. Did she? Wasn't it what you did when you loved someone? Not *covering*, Juniper wouldn't have called it that and she didn't think Hana would have, either. But watching over her, putting up guardrails to keep her from spinning out, understanding when she sometimes did, anyway.

Her sisters thought they were helping, bringing up her problem, forcing her to talk about it. They were both so sure that once they named it, Juniper would know how to fix it, as if naming it were the problem. As if she hadn't spent her entire career in sports diagnosing weak spots and correcting them. As if she hadn't already tried to fix this and found herself utterly incapable.

She bought a bottle of Wild Turkey and left.

The taxi was gone.

Juniper walked, looking for a place to sit. Power lines crisscrossed the street, which was lined with parked cars. There were a lot of people about, mostly men, locals. Perhaps the foreigners would turn up once the sun set. She didn't know what time it was, but she no longer cared about the meeting with Tariq. There was no sense in going backward and reliving the pain.

The Princeton job had also been another way of going backward, she recognized. She was stalled. She was like a shark. People said sharks would die if they stopped swimming. Juniper read somewhere that this was a myth, instead they would sink to the bottom if they ever stopped moving. Juniper felt just like that, like a shark on the ocean floor, down where only the stingrays were supposed to be, burrowed in the sand.

She traced her steps back to the statue of the Virgin Mary and sat in the shade of its pedestal. The bourbon was dark and heavy going down. It tasted like lighter fluid. She wished she had Gatorade. On the field she reminded her players to hydrate, hydrate, hydrate. Heat stroke was their true opponent in preseason, and she'd quickly learn the topography of her players' faces in the summer, which ones burned up from the top of their heads and which ones in their cheeks. Which ones passed off the heat in rivers of sweat, their hair so drenched it was like they'd gone swimming, and which ones never sweat a drop. You had to keep an eye on those ones. Juniper was somewhere in the middle. She had to be careful, but as long as she was, she was usually all right. She took another drink and it curdled in her stomach. She bent forward and retched, the brown fluid splashing at her feet. It occurred to her that if she kept this up, drinking and retching in this heat, she might die. She asked herself if she could manage this life alone. It wasn't a question she could answer.

Not far away she saw the Classy Hotel. She needed air-conditioning.

At the front was a Greek restaurant, and beyond that a lobby with white leather sofas. She sat on one, ran her hand over the leather and then touched her thighs. She was burning up, but the room was cool. She lifted her shirt collar and mopped her face. Rested her head on the arm of the sofa and closed her eyes.

When she woke up, someone was nudging her. A woman smiled at her and offered her tea. She smiled and nodded. "Thank you, thank you," she said. She drank it quickly. The woman waited there patiently, so once she was finished, Juniper stood, waved goodbye, and left.

Outside the sky had changed. The sun was low, hiding behind the rooftops. The muezzin's call to prayer rang out in the distance. Juniper still had the brown bag with the Wild Turkey inside, but she was too ravenous. She stopped at a street vendor and ate a shawarma sandwich on the spot.

"Thank you," she said to the man, but without the right language it felt like her words were mist.

A few vendors had covered their wares with tarps to pray, and they returned now and resumed their business. Juniper noticed more families out than she'd seen earlier, some who knew where they were going and how to get there, and some who looked the way she felt, shell-shocked and confused. They followed the other families, and because she had nowhere to go, so did she.

They walked alongside a beige brick wall with crenellations at the top that teased and refused a view of what was on the other side. There was a feeling of suspense. Where were they going? What would come next? Juniper was supposed to be getting married next. She wondered what Hana would look like in her wedding outfit and whether she'd get the chance to find out. For that to happen she would have to make it home. Juniper saw a garbage bin and dropped the bottle, with the rest of the bourbon, into it. It wasn't helping anymore, if it ever had.

They came to a gate with crosses on the doors, and Juniper let herself be borne along with the tide. Inside was a church made of the same beige brick, the same crenellated walls. A cross was planted on top and in the tower there was a bell. The churchyard was packed with people—women with small children gripping their skirts, men carrying boxes stacked atop suitcases, teenagers darting away and hurrying back with news. There were far more people than the cathedral could hold.

Hoping to get out of the crowd, Juniper went around the corner. An arched portico ran along the left-hand side of the church, and there was a narrow path still clear to walk down, next to the families setting up camp under its cover. Through the arches, out in the yard, more families were setting up on the grass. It was the witching hour. Some children cried, tired and out of their element; others were wired and haunted. Juniper looked around her at Muslims and Christians, old and young, frightened and determined, all seeking refuge. How on earth would anyone manage sleep?

Behind the church it was more of the same. Men carried thin mattresses across the concrete yard. A young priest nested bottles of water in a kiddie pool filled with ice. A woman wailed, and he went to her and the girls gathered around her, maybe her daughters, who were hugging her and wiping her tears. Juniper thought of Maryam and Ahmed leaving Damascus, the family who'd followed them, the stubborn faith of those who'd stayed.

"Juniper! June! Junie!"

She turned toward the sound of her name, spoken at last in the language of her birth.

Her sisters rushed toward her, and she collapsed in their arms.

24

July

July tried to stay awake, but after April and May left to find Juniper, he fell into a deep sleep. When he woke up, it took a minute before he remembered: His dad was really dead and he was alone. There were no sisters fighting, no mother to console, no Suits to hide from. Just the truth, achingly simple.

But the time! The rendezvous with Tariq. Panicked, he checked his phone. Five o'clock. He hadn't overslept.

July studied the photograph April had given him so he'd be able to find Tariq at the fountains. He'd never seen it before today. In the picture Frank and Tariq stood with their arms around each other, grinning into the sun. Frank was tall and bulky and protective. Tariq was petite and genial. They'd only been working together two months at that point, but it was clear they had an ease and comfort with each other. July stared at Tariq: his dark eyes, the long eyelashes, like a fawn's. There was something about him that July couldn't look away from.

From his window on the tenth floor of the hotel, the tallest building for miles around, July stared out across the city. Who was out there on those streets? He wondered if there was a gay scene in Erbil—or whether *gay* was the right word here. It was Tuesday (at least he thought so). Even Grand Central back in Baltimore was sluggish on a Tuesday night. What did Tuesday nights mean in Erbil?

He took out his phone and got on Grindr. A stream of profile pics filled the screen, some with green dots indicating they were online, too, others with empty dots signaling their lapsed presence. He wasn't surprised, scrolling through the photos of bare headless chests, to see so many men in this very hotel looking for company. Here was the app's essential function in his life: to serve as a kind of gay census. Some of the guys were white expats and they showed their faces, the words *just visiting* or *looking* affixed to their photos, but as the search radius widened beyond the floors around him and out into the neighboring streets, July saw darker skin tones, display names in languages he didn't speak, no faces now, only bodies. Grindr had saved his life in high school. He'd never realized how many gays lived in Eastern Maryland—in Aberdeen itself—until Grindr. But the same thing happened whenever he left Hopkins to go home, and he could tell how close he was to Aberdeen by the sudden proliferation of torsos. The difference being that in the Middle East, the people who were like him—gay, men who had sex with men, whatever they called it—had much more to fear.

He looked again at the photograph April had given him. It was just a hunch, a sadness in Tariq's eyes that July thought he recognized. He searched for any identifying marks on Tariq's body to check against the men on his phone, but Tariq's chest and arms were covered in camouflage. July scrolled a bit more, but no one on the app resembled Tariq.

July called the hotel switchboard to see if anyone had left a message for him while he slept. No one had. Juniper wasn't back;

neither were April and May. He'd wanted to do this together, but it was 5:15. Time to go.

He walked up the main road linking the hotel and the citadel. On the news the roads were filled with the frantic energy of people fleeing violence and uncertainty, but here in downtown Erbil everything seemed normal. It was business as usual at the shopping mall he passed. He could have hailed one of the many taxis whipping along the boulevard, but he was close enough already. The citadel, which had been nothing more than a hue on the horizon when he started out, like smog, now hulked over its surroundings. It was one of the world's oldest continuously inhabited cities, resting atop a tell, a hundred feet high, layered with sediment and history.

When July arrived at the fountains in the plaza beneath the citadel, his shirt and briefs were both damp with sweat. He wanted to cool his feet in the pools, but he didn't dare. He'd worn crew-length socks with his sneakers because even baring his ankles had somehow seemed too gay. He sat on the stone rim around the largest fountain and dipped his fingers in the water instead.

A young boy selling lighters approached. He held one out and inclined his head. Did July want one?

"No, thank you," July said. "I'm waiting for a friend."

The boy moved on.

He didn't know why he'd called Tariq that. *A friend*.

July stood up to scan for a single man with a sweet face and a searching look in his eye. The sun was low in the sky, shining right in his face. He'd brought a baseball cap with him to Iraq, but he'd left it back at the hotel, worried that Tariq wouldn't spot him with it on. It would be hard enough for them to find each other without his sisters here, too. Tariq was expecting an American family, not a man alone.

As July circled the main fountain, the spray from its jets cooling him off, he felt queasy with anticipation. On either side of him was an arched colonnade with cafés tucked in the shade. On the left was the bazaar; on the right a minaret and a clock tower. It was six o'clock. A path led across a large pool, in which dozens more jets of water shot up, some high, some low.

Then July saw him walking across the path. Tariq was squinting. July knew it was him, but he wanted to see if Tariq would recognize him, too. Tariq's eyes scanned the square and…there… they caught on July.

He walked over to Tariq.

"July?"

"Tariq?"

"Yes, yes," they both said. Already a faint ping sounded on July's gaydar. He thanked Tariq for coming and apologized for his sisters' absence.

"Are you okay?" July asked. "Here, let's sit, out of the sun." They walked over to a café.

"You've come from Mosul," July said.

"Yes."

"How did you get out?"

"Daesh came from the west. I was in the east, across the river. I heard the mortar rounds and saw the black smoke in the sky. When I learned that the army had laid down their guns and disappeared, I decided it was hopeless to stay. This morning I walked to the highway and called your sister from a gas station. Eventually I found a ride to Erbil."

They passed rows of men sitting in front of the café, smoking from hookah pipes, and found a table for themselves behind them.

"I'll get us something to drink. Are you hungry?" July asked.

Tariq shrugged, which didn't seem like a yes or no, but something more awkward and complicated. The Kurds were famous for their hospitality; maybe that was part of it. If July had come a week ago, Tariq would have been hosting him.

July chose a couple bottles of Fanta and water from a cooler and then went up to the counter where he pointed at pictures on the menu. Hummus. Kebabs. He paid and then brought his number back to the table.

Tariq had removed his backpack, and large stripes of sweat ran down the front of his dark blue shirt where the straps had been. His hair was longer than it was in the photograph with Frank. He wiped his forehead, leaving damp curls pressed against his temples.

"My sisters and I are so glad you're safe. Is your family okay?"

"Some of them are still there. My parents and my brothers and their wives went to Duhok, but they'll be back."

"And you? How are you?"

"Me? I am the world's oldest college student." July smiled at the exaggeration. Tariq couldn't have been more than thirty. "I was a student when the war started, but I wanted to be of service, so I signed up to be a translator at CCA. Then…well, plans change. I finally enrolled again at the University of Mosul this spring, but yesterday they chained the doors. I want my degree. So. I will try again in Erbil."

A man delivered the food and July beckoned Tariq to serve himself first.

"Your sisters?" Tariq asked, spooning a couple dollops of hummus onto his plate. "They are well?"

"Yes," July said. How to explain their failure to appear? He was stuck with a choice, to lie or tell the truth about Juniper, either of which might alienate Tariq. "My sister is having a hard time. This has been hard on us all, in one way or another. She feels…responsible. We all wanted to meet you, but in the end, she couldn't. And my other two sisters are taking care of her."

Tariq nodded and slid the kebabs toward him.

July hadn't eaten all day. The rich smells of the grilled meat and the lemony chickpeas made his stomach growl. He filled his plate. They swallowed their first bites in silence.

Perhaps Tariq was also trying to steady himself. He took a

long sip of the soft drink and set the bottle down. He smiled. "So," he said. "Your father."

July nodded. This was the moment he'd been waiting for, and it felt like it was happening in slow motion.

"He was a good man," Tariq said.

So many people had told July that over the years that the words felt empty. What did they mean? That Frank paid his taxes and obeyed posted traffic signs? That he was a superhero, some kind of Captain America? He'd learned that most people simply meant Frank seemed friendly, like a nice guy with a family.

Tariq was looking at July, expecting him to say something.

"Sorry. I have so many questions for you that I don't even know where to start."

"How about at the beginning? Shall I tell you the first thing your father ever said to me?"

July smiled with gratitude. "Yes, please."

"He called me *a sight for sore eyes*. It was his second week at CCA. The first week nobody bothered to assign him a translator, because he was just supposed to meet the team and settle into his quarters. No one expected him to go off-base that soon and his meetings without an interpreter were…let's say, challenging. I was working with another team that never went outside the wire and I was very bored, so I looked forward to working with him, too. But *a sight for sore eyes*? I'd never heard that expression before. I thought he was telling me he had conjunctivitis. Later, when I thought back to how we met, I remembered what he said."

"It's a sweet thing to say, almost romantic."

Tariq blushed, and the sounding on July's gaydar grew louder. "Yes. He was always like that, wasn't he? Full of grand gestures. You always knew where you stood with him. He was a hard worker and could be very demanding, but if he liked you, he let you know it. If he was happy to see you, it was written all over his face."

July had a quick flash of running toward Frank one summer day, outside the community pool, knowing for certain that his dad was going to drop to one knee and stretch out his arms to receive him. There was a knot in the pit of his stomach. With every word Tariq spoke, the rope tightened in some places and loosened in others.

"You worked together every day?" July asked.

"Yes. Even when we were captives, they held us together. After we were rescued, too. We spent every day together for two years."

July tried to imagine it—spending two years with someone you hadn't chosen but whom fate had chosen for you. Tariq seemed like a pretty good companion. His eyes might have been fawn-like, but his energy wasn't skittish or juvenile. He looked like an old soul. Even the clothes he wore—a polo shirt with the collar buttoned up all the way, a black leather belt holding up his jeans—made him seem old-fashioned, centered, reliable.

They'd finished the meal, despite the hunger-killing heat. Tariq looked around and suddenly July was aware of how near the men smoking hookah were. He checked his phone, but there was nothing yet from his sisters. He thought he could trust Tariq. He would have to.

"Do you want to walk?" July asked.

"Sure," Tariq said, reaching for his backpack. "Where?"

"How about up there?" July pointed at the citadel's ochre walls. Sunset would be here soon. They'd have a good view of the city and some privacy.

Tariq led the way. They wound through the chairs of men with their hookahs and backgammon tiles, past the teenagers selling phone cards in the square. They crossed the pools where children stood on concrete pavilions stretching out their hands to catch the spray and passed the café at the foot of the citadel where old men lounged in front of prayer rugs, musical instruments, and woven purses they'd set out for sale. Along the cobblestone street they continued, where a truck driver unloaded tanks of propane for the shops in the bazaar. Beneath the south gate they mounted the steep ramp up to the citadel. July pushed with his thighs. He'd been running most of the spring, but only on flat ground. His calves began to tingle.

At the top they both caught their breath. It was quieter up here. Traffic murmured and a moped's horn was nothing more than a fly buzzing. July turned and looked up at the citadel's walls. Through a giant pointed arch he spied the ancient village within.

Down below the square began to thin out. The men smoking hookah stood and walked through the colonnade toward the mosque. Other men followed.

"Can I ask you..." July began, but it was hard to steer down the dark hole where this conversation was inevitably headed.

"Yes," Tariq said, "you can."

In the long pause the air around them seemed to whir. The sun hovered low over the foothills in the distance.

"What were you and my father doing the day you were kidnapped?"

Tariq took a deep breath. "Have you heard of the Anfal?"

"The Kurdish genocide? We studied it in my program at school."

"Really? That's good. Your father read about it, too, when he accepted his assignment in Mosul. He thought it was in the past, that it ended when Saddam was captured. He wasn't aware then of the scars the Anfal left behind."

"Scars?"

"Saddam had many methods for doing away with Kurds. Giving our lands to Arabs he felt would be loyal to him. Deportation. Imprisonment—thousands of men disappeared in his labor camps. These were some of the more subtle methods he employed. During the uprising in '91, he simply had his helicopter gunships mow us down. Before that, he gassed us."

"Chemical Ali," July said, referring to Saddam's cousin and Secretary General of the Ba'ath party. In the last throes of the Iran–Iraq War, he'd accepted his cousin's challenge to quash the Kurdish rebellion by any means necessary.

"What did you say you are studying?" Tariq asked.

"International relations."

Tariq smiled. "Ah."

"My dad was working on chemical weapons, right? They told us Mr. Yassin was a smuggler. Is that why they were meeting?"

Tariq's face darkened with confusion. "You think Frank was selling chemical weapons to Yassin?"

Now July blushed. "He wasn't?"

"No. Your father didn't want more war. I told you, the Anfal left scars. The mountains of Kurdistan were booby-trapped. Chemical weapons hiding in the ground, just waiting to be discovered by women, children, refugees. When Kurds are in danger, we go to the mountains, but the mountains weren't safe. Your father wanted to help."

"By defusing the bombs?"

"And teaching others how. Yassin was a businessman in Duhok—in places like that, on the road to Turkey, that means import-export. Smugglers bring their loads across the border on donkeys or their own backs, and people like Yassin provide the warehouses and trucks on this side. In heavy rains, unexploded ordnance is unearthed. So you can say that Yassin had a financial incentive to solve this problem. But he was also an important man in Duhok, respected. He wanted to help his people. When he and Frank met in Mosul, they saw these issues the same way. But CCA said their technology was proprietary and could not be shared, that their contracts were with the US government, no one else. Frank didn't agree with that."

July felt humbled, ashamed of the conclusions he'd jumped to. "Should we go in?"

"After you," Tariq said, pointing to the grand south gate they were standing before.

They walked through the arch into the citadel and along a paved road that led to an open square. There was restoration work underway, and here and there they saw ditches dug, metal poles propping up brick walls, parapets covered in tarp. They wandered along an alley and into an empty home with a large courtyard built around a tree. July had imagined that the citadel was surrounded by a great wall, but now he realized that the houses themselves were the wall.

They continued down the alley, which split off into more alleys, each smaller and narrower than the one before, like capillaries. As they worked their way around the ellipse of the citadel, the houses became more modest. Plaster was coming off the walls, and the beamed ceilings were braced with two-by-fours.

"People still live here?" July asked, not quite seeing how it was possible.

"They relocated everyone a few years ago to renovate. One family was famously left to occupy the place."

July entered a small abandoned house. He imagined what it would've been like to be a child here when it was still fully occupied, with his family and friends held close around him. The deeper he went, the more the sound of the streets below amplified. Suddenly there was a click and a hum in the air. The muezzin's chant rang out across the square.

"Do you need to...?" July asked.

Tariq shook his head no. July had figured he was Muslim, but maybe he wasn't. Maybe he was lapsed. Maybe it was nobody's business.

They went up a set of stairs. The rooftop was covered in dirt and grass and broken bricks. The light was golden, the sun molten on the horizon. They'd reached the highest point of the citadel. Only a tiled minaret and the KRG flag flew higher.

July sat cross-legged. Tariq joined him.

So his father had been trying to help Mr. Yassin. Maybe that was why he had stayed after the kidnapping.

"How were you rescued?" he asked.

"After the kidnappers killed Yassin, there was a lot of confusion. They hadn't meant to do it, and now their plan to ransom him was ruined. On top of that, they'd shot your father in the leg. They took off their masks and that's when Jabouri—Yassin's driver—saw that one of the thugs was his nephew. Jabouri was furious. I thought he might kill Ayan with his bare hands."

"Why was his nephew involved?"

"For the money, mainly. Yassin had it, and he didn't. The fact that Yassin was Kurdish was an added bonus. Ayan grew up in Kirkuk in a house that once belonged to a Kurdish family that was deported. They had built the house and, after some years, the Kurdish family returned to take it back. Yassin didn't have anything to do with that, of course, but he was a Kurd, too, and a convenient target for Ayan all the same. Jabouri was disgusted by this kind of tribalism. He'd been Yassin's driver for fifteen years and was devoted to him. He pummeled Ayan, until one of the other thugs—the one in charge—knocked him out. Ayan begged him not to kill his uncle, but the leader told the others to blindfold us, and then they put us in the back seat of their car and left Jabouri on the ground. They took Frank and me to an empty farmhouse on the edge of town."

His father had been shot. July rubbed his calf, trying and failing to imagine that kind of pain. "How badly was he hurt?"

"We weren't sure at first. There was a lot of blood and the bullet was stuck in his leg, but we tied a tourniquet over the wound. By the next day, the bleeding had stopped. The thugs couldn't agree on anything. One guy wanted to cut his losses and run. Ayan said why not collect the ransom anyway, and *then* run? The third guy said he didn't care what they did, he just wanted some tea—and anyway, how could they ransom a dead man and another man who couldn't walk? But the leader said he had a better idea. They had an American hostage now. Injured or not, he was worth something. Why not sell him?"

"Sell him? To who?" So the ex-CIA guy April had talked to was right. The kidnappers' Plan A was to ransom the hostages for money. After they bungled the job, they switched to Plan B, making a trade.

"We didn't know. He went outside to make a call. Then he left. He was gone all night, and the rest of them started to panic. I was scared they might kill us out of boredom, but Frank said they were too incompetent to kill us on purpose. It was only later that we realized the leader collected on the ransom. He got your family to pay, and Yassin's, and then he sold us anyway. We never saw him again, and no wonder he disappeared. Because the next day, just as it was getting dark, another car arrived. And out stepped Mergen Garayev."

"Who's that?"

"A gangster from Kirkuk. People say he had ties to the ITF." Tariq looked at him to see if he understood, but July made a question mark with his face. "The Iraqi Turkmen Front. Turkmen are an ethnic minority, much smaller in number than the Kurds. There are many still left in Kirkuk, fighting for their claim to the city. The kidnapper in charge knew Mergen from their childhood, so he went to him. We were blindfolded again and driven to another house near Tal Afar."

"Tal Afar," July said. "That's not far from Mosul." He'd seen it on the map. The town couldn't have been more than fifty miles west of Mosul.

"Yes, you might say we were hiding in plain sight. I don't think Mergen intended this to go on very long, certainly not the months that it did. He wanted to sell Frank to al-Qaeda and then ransom me back to my family. But Frank took a turn for the worse, and they couldn't make the trade with him in that state."

"His leg?"

Tariq nodded. "We knew the bullet was in there, but we were afraid to remove it. The wound was pretty deep. We didn't have any sedatives, and we didn't want to make it worse. They let me clean it and change the dressing every day. But after a few days in Tal Afar it was clear his leg wasn't healing. It was badly infected. Frank was burning up. He was delirious from the pain. I told them he was going to die if they did nothing, and then how would they make their money? They had to get him to a doctor."

"And did they?"

"No. Ayan said he would go for help. I think he felt guilty, in his pathetic way, because he was the one who'd shot him. Mergen said he could go, but only for medicine. Ayan brought back a couple months' worth of antibiotics, and eventually, little by little, Frank got better. One day he told me he could put weight on his leg again. I didn't want Mergen to know. I begged your father to play sick a little longer. As soon as they knew he was well, they would hand him over to people who would hurt him all over again."

Tariq had loved Frank. That much was clear. What July didn't know was what shape that love took—a romantic yearning or a brotherly love or the devotion of a son for a father?

The muezzin's song was over now.

"Thank you," July said. "You saved his life."

"He would have done the same for me." Tariq smiled wearily before continuing. "I was glad to have him thinking clearly again. It sounds crazy, but he kept me calm, not the other way around. He told me we had to keep our heads. That was all we had."

"Did you try to escape?"

"Yes. There was a window in the bathroom. We agreed that I should slip out and see how far I got. But Mergen paid a little kid across the street to keep a look out. The boy screamed when he saw me."

"Did they punish you?"

"Yes."

July watched Tariq's face for a signal. He would listen if Tariq wanted to tell him what they did to him. But Tariq looked away first.

"Mergen was around all the time after that. They watched us more carefully. They came into the bathroom with us and watched us shit and piss. Then one day Mergen left and when he came back, it was all arranged. Al-Qaeda would come for Frank the next night, and after my family paid five-million dinars, they would be given instructions for finding me."

"Five-million dinars? Is that as much as it sounds?"

"About five-thousand dollars US. But my family never intended to pay it. They just played along, and followed the trail of clues that led to Tal Afar."

"Your family? They were the ones who rescued you?"

"Yes. My father's cousin married a man my family never fully trusted. Everyone thought Zozan was trouble: reckless, undependable. He was gone a lot when I was a boy, and his son Hamza and I grew up together in Mosul. Everyone loved Hamza. He was fairer-skinned, too; people in our neighborhood called him The Golden Boy. But the summer before our first term at university started, Zozan reappeared. He had very strong views about Kurdish independence and he persuaded his wife and children to join him in Syria."

"To join the PKK?" July asked. He knew there was a large Kurdish population on either side of the border between Syria and Turkey—known to some as West Kurdistan and North Kurdistan.

Tariq scanned the rooftops to see if anyone was listening, but there was no need. There wasn't a soul in sight. He nodded.

"Hamza was conflicted. He wasn't wild like his father, but he also didn't follow the crowd; he was gentle but stubborn. Everything in the camp was decided by consensus, and he was too much of an individual for that. He liked some of their ideas, but not others. He believed in self-defense, but he felt the concept could be carried too far. He wasn't always comfortable being in a militia, until my father got word to them about my abduction."

"Where were the Peshmerga?"

"Who was I to them? Kurdish, maybe, but a nobody."

"You weren't a nobody to Hamza."

"No." Tariq's cheeks flushed.

Ahhh, July thought. Tariq had loved his dad, but he'd been *in love* with Hamza. As quickly as if he'd walked in on two lovers in an embrace, July backed away.

"So, what happened when help arrived?"

"Mergen was shrewd enough to know he was outmatched. He handed me over without question."

"And what about my dad?"

"I begged Zozan to take Frank, too. Frank told Zozan if they helped him, he would return the favor. He offered to teach the PKK what he'd been planning to teach Yassin's people. So they struck a deal: one year as their scientific advisor, and then Zozan would see to it that Frank made it safely home."

"And Mergen? Ayan and the others?"

"They ran. Went into hiding, I imagine, before al-Qaeda could kill them for botching the deal."

The sun had dipped so far that, even sitting up here on the rooftops, they could no longer see it. A breeze lifted the brown blades of grass, and July ran his fingers through them. He sighed.

"Are you okay?" Tariq asked. "It's a lot of information."

"I can understand my father feeling indebted to Zozan and wanting to contribute in some tangible way. Even feeling that he must honor Yassin maybe. But it was torture not knowing where he was." July winced at his choice of words. Not torture. Torture was, perhaps, what Mergen and his thugs had done to Tariq. He tried again. "It was very painful, living in that cloud of uncertainty. It broke my family in ways I'm still trying to understand. I wish he'd gotten word to us that he was alive. Even if it changed nothing that happened next."

Tariq sat up taller. "But he did! Frank wrote you many letters. I saw them myself."

"Letters?" Was this another secret his mother and his sisters had kept from July? No. It would have been too cruel. "We didn't get any letters. You gave them to Zozan to send?"

Tariq said, "Yes," but his eyes went glassy, as if he were recalling something opaque with new clarity.

"Maybe Zozan didn't send them. He might have worried we'd tell someone. And then you all would have been discovered by our government," July suggested, even as he felt himself falling, as if from a landing down a series of shallow steps he'd missed, caught off guard. His father had written to them. If only they could have known what his last thoughts were. What message might he have sent to July?

Tariq's face had gone pale. "I didn't give the letters to Zozan. I gave them to Hamza."

July sensed this was only the most recent in a string of disappointments where Hamza was concerned.

"But I didn't see him hand them over to my uncle. I didn't see it with my own eyes. My family didn't always trust Zozan, but he risked everything to save us. Your father used to wonder what might have happened if their roles were reversed, if Zozan had been born in Maryland and instead he was the one who'd come of age in Kurdistan, during such troubling times. I think he respected Zozan's choices, even if he couldn't be sure he would've made them himself. He used to play the I-wonder game a lot. *I wonder who won the Super Bowl this year, Tariq. I wonder how Juniper's playing this season. I wonder whether May's run off to join the circus yet.* It was more difficult for him when he thought about you. He knew the time he was away from you was time he wouldn't get back. *I wonder where July will go to school. I wonder what kind of man he'll be. I wonder if he'll ever be a father.* Even though there was no way, logically, that he could have known this, it was as if he knew he wouldn't get to see you grow up."

July had started to cry. He felt like a failure, a misfit, unknowable even to his father.

Tariq reached for his forearm and held it. "He always said you would help people. He said you have a big heart. He would have been proud of your studies. He would be so jealous of me for getting to talk to you right now."

"I never got the chance to come out to him. I always wondered whether he knew I'm gay."

The word lay there between them like a fish. July hadn't meant to just blurt it out, but he couldn't help it.

"But, July," Tariq said, "don't you see? A sight for sore eyes? It was you he saw when he looked at me."

July held his breath, listening to his heartbeat slow to a gentle patter. He imagined Tariq's pulse settling, too, their rhythms matching each other. Was it true that his dad saw their sameness? How had he known? What clues had he seen in his son and then found repeated in this young man?

"Your father and I talked about how difficult it would be for me. Hamza felt he had another choice he could make and left to live it. I did not. I can only be what I am. Of course, I can never tell my family, not directly. And if I stay in Iraq, I can never live openly. Your father was grateful that it wouldn't be this way for you."

July tried to receive this. He listened to the quiet and smelled the bitter scent of the crisp grass. He steeled himself for the end of the story. "How?" he stammered, his lungs caught in a vise grip. "How did he die?"

Tariq closed his eyes for a moment. Eyes open again, he began:

"When we got to camp, there was a medic who took care of everybody. He examined Frank and found that the bullet was the only thing keeping him alive. If we had removed it from his leg, he would have bled to death. Once Frank was strong enough, we started our task. We went to the mountains to make the borders safe. Widows and orphans comb the hills for shells, to sell for extra money, but always there are accidents. Tragedies. We needed a way to determine which shells were still active. There are machines that will do this, but they are huge and heavy and expensive. CCA had developed test strips, little pieces of paper no bigger than a bandage that change color on contact with a nerve agent. Frank took some to give to Yassin, but the thugs left them behind in the SUV. It took months to identify another source. Once we had a supply, we made up a grid for each hill and worked our way through it methodically, testing each shell. It takes some practice to learn to defuse a bomb. Your father was very good at it. Hamza also had steady hands. The rest of us were shaky.

"Time passed in this way, until one day, there were only two weeks left in Frank's arrangement with Zozan. Everyone had come to love Frank. Hamza's mother cooked a feast and we celebrated your father and the work we'd all done together. Frank stood to say a few words and I thought at first, when he grabbed his chest, that he was choking. He couldn't catch his breath and I reached my arms around him to help. But the medic came running. He knew, you see, that it wasn't a piece of chicken bone or an olive pit that was preventing him from breathing. It was the bullet. That old bullet that was keeping him alive all this time had traveled up the femoral vein to the pulmonary artery. And it stopped your father's heart. May he rest in peace."

July felt like his skin had turned inside out. Goose bumps broke out along his arms and legs, and he shivered.

"He went quickly," Tariq said. "I hope knowing that will give some comfort to you and to your mother and sisters."

July nodded. So there it was, the fact he had come here to collect. They could stand up now and leave the park.

But July didn't want to yet.

"What happened to Hamza?" he asked.

Tariq hugged his knees. "After your father died, Hamza carried on with the bomb-defusing work and weapons training with the militia. I worked in the garden and tended the goats. In the afternoons, Hamza would come back and help me bring in the herd. We used to wait until the light over the fields turned purple. After everything I'd done to get to university, my plans to be a doctor, suddenly I was a poor farmer! But I didn't want to leave Hamza. In spite of everything, I was happy.

"We formed an assembly in the camp to govern ourselves, and other villages around us began to form their own assemblies also. We cooperated and shared information, Kurds and Arabs and Turkmen and Yazidis, all organizing together. When Zozan's term on the assembly's authority ended, he wanted Hamza to take his place. Hamza didn't want the job, so he started a whisper campaign on behalf of his mom and she got the slot instead. I confess, I was glad. Sitting on the authority would have left him with no time for our walks together.

"Hamza began to grow more and more disillusioned with the militia. Sometimes they'd visit an Arab or Turkmen house and instead of defusing the bombs around it, they'd order the people to leave. *For your safety*, they'd say. Next thing we knew, these homes suddenly had Kurds living in them. When Hamza complained that this jeopardized the cooperative arrangement, he was told that the families who were sent away were connected to the rebel groups or to Daesh, but he didn't believe it.

"It felt like a noose tightening around us. I wanted to leave, but more than that, I feared for Hamza's safety if we stayed. When I was accepted into university, I begged Hamza to come with me, but he didn't want to go back to Iraq. He said he was done with all of these grand experiments, crumbling under the weight of other people's wars.

"So I gave him my passport. He couldn't use his own because of his activities in the militia. We left the camp at night, without saying goodbye to anyone. I drove him north to the border and we paid a smuggler to take him to Istanbul. Then I went home to Mosul. A month later, I got a postcard from him. Tariq Ibrahim, it seems, is alive and well in Stockholm, Sweden."

"Stockholm!"

Tariq nodded, the weary smile stretched between his cheeks wilting like a damp shirt on a clothesline.

So that was why Hamza had been passing through Dubrovnik—not to compare notes with other revolutionaries, but to journey toward a new life. He'd left the camp and renounced the PKK.

"Have you thought about going to Stockholm, too?" July asked. "You must miss him very much."

"More than anything. But…he made a choice, to be a different sort of person in Sweden, the Tariq it's not possible for me to be. He'll find a woman to marry, have a family, and live a happy life."

July's throat ached. "But you're his family, too. Can't he at least sponsor you?"

"Not with my passport, he can't. He's me now, you see."

A man appeared, waving his arms and shouting something in Kurdish.

"He says it's after closing," Tariq said. "We have to go."

"The hat," July said, as they retraced their steps to the giant arch. "My sister saw Hamza in a Princeton baseball cap."

"Ah, yes. Your father's. I kept it when he passed, to remember him by. And then when Hamza left, I gave it to him." Like his sunglasses, July thought; he'd been happier to see them on Nate's face than to wear them himself.

Outside the perimeter wall, they stood at the top of the ramp and looked out over Erbil. The sun had set, and as if to punctuate this fact, the muezzin's song rang out for the Isha prayer. Now the square was full. The fountains were lit up in shades of green and purple and pink. The skyline glowed with the neon signs of the hotels on the ring road and the lights in the high-rises beyond. The world's oldest city yielded to the new, but did either one have a place for someone like Tariq?

"So what will you do now?" July asked.

"I will get my degree, in Erbil if I have to," Tariq said, sweeping his hair across his forehead and adjusting the straps of his backpack. "That is first. It is something I have wanted for a very long time. In the meantime, I will try to sort out my papers, get my identity in order, if it can be managed without putting Hamza at risk. There are asylum programs for translators. Maybe one day I will leave, too."

July 2015

25

April
Morning

April parked next to the other cars lined up in front of her grandmother's house, which, according to the rental contract, belonged to the Barbers again for the week. Kingfishers rattled at their arrival and chickadees dee-dee'd like rusty swings. Maddie kicked off her shoes and tumbled on the lawn, her long legs pinwheeling at the sky, and Cooper stalked up the porch steps like a skeptical old man. Hands on hips, he surveyed this fragile kingdom. They had nine hours to whip it into shape for Juniper and Hana's wedding tonight, a year and one month after the first invitation promised.

"What do you think, Coop?" she asked her son. "Better later than never?"

His lips turned up at the corners, recognizing the game. "No pain, no gain?"

"She who laughs last, laughs best," April said.

"All's well that ends well!" Maddie bowed with a flourish. "William Shakespeare."

Her children had had to roll with the punches (another fine motto) a lot this year, shuttling between houses and parents, discovering that grown-ups were fallible, that they were capable at any age of screwing up as well as changing. They were learning to hold tight to their family, who were all coming together for a long-awaited celebration that had seemed inconceivable a year ago.

April had been afraid to let Junie out of her sight when they found her at the church in Ainkawa. After they met up with July, and got Tariq another room at the hotel, it became clear they had to get back to the States and get her real help. Nancy and the Monsours called all the guests to tell them the wedding was postponed. *A death in the family*, they'd said. *Unavoidable change of plans*, they'd said. *We'll be in touch.*

Back in the US, Hana met the siblings at the airport and drove Junie straight to the Ranch House.

"I hope she's okay," July said as they pulled away from the terminal's curb.

"I give her fifty-fifty odds of actually checking herself in," April said.

"I bet she does." Ever the optimist, her little brother.

"I bet she doesn't," May said.

Twenty-one days later April had driven them all to the Ranch House for Family Day.

Her mom was nervous going in. "They always blame the mother," she said several times.

"Then don't take it personally," May said when she'd finally had enough, "if it always happens."

The two were zinging each other a little extra, having finally realized how much they were going to miss each other. For three weeks May had been ferrying things to Will's house in College Park one laundry basket-full at a time, but they'd made the decision and told Zoe. May was moving in.

Meanwhile April's own marriage was on life support. There'd

hardly been a single fight in their sixteen years together in which Ross hadn't apologized first, even when she was the one in the wrong. This time—understandably—he wasn't making any effort to bridge the gap between them, and she didn't know what to say that wasn't a lie. She'd never meant to hurt him? What good were intentions—even if they were pure, which she doubted—when she'd wounded him this badly?

She couldn't pinpoint the moment it happened, but in the weeks and months after her dad was kidnapped, a small and sinful resentment had crept into her thoughts and taken root. Ross's sunny directness began to feel like an affront to her suffering. It was so easy for him to be happy and steady all the time, to laugh at some small thing and not feel it in his gut like a knife turned inward. His dad wasn't gone. April was grateful their kids had his constancy like a warm blanket over their childhoods, but she'd felt left out in the cold. Couldn't he dial his Ross-ness down, for her sake? Couldn't he see how much she was floundering? Probably he had, but she'd felt so alone anyway. It wasn't his fault he wasn't damaged, but she couldn't stop holding that against him. Over time she'd released herself from her promises to him the way a captured animal frees itself from a trap, with her own teeth.

On the outside the Ranch House looked like a boarding school for pampered adults. Hedgerows granted privacy around plush green lawns, and gently gurgling water features popped up practically every ten feet to encourage calm reflection. *You could get married here*, April thought nonsensically. It was that beautiful, that serene.

On the inside the place was careworn and institutional, and her panic about how Junie would pay for her stay downgraded somewhat from gravely concerned to merely worried.

Hana met them in the lobby and they hugged, but as the day went on her grudges became clear. The Barbers hadn't been much of a family for the last ten years. Where were they, Hana wanted to know, while Juniper was unraveling? April thought about her father's letters home, the ones they'd never received. She would've given anything—even if she couldn't be with him at the end—to have his counsel on this. But she knew what the letters would've said, some version of what he'd always wanted: for her to watch out for her little sisters and her brother, for them to take care of each other. She was trying to do a better job of it now.

It took a long time for Hana's anger to turn toward Junie, but with the help of the Ranch House counselor, eventually it did. "Why didn't you trust me with the truth? If you told me how responsible you felt for his death, I could've helped. I could've told you that you did nothing wrong," Hana said.

"Of course, you didn't, honey," Mom interjected to reassure Junie, and Hana shot her a look that said, in no uncertain terms, *Step off.*

"All this time," Hana went on, "I've felt like there were two of you, the one I fell in love with who was sweet and unguarded, and the other one who was just a little bit off. The one whose stories never added up, when you'd come home late or weren't where you were supposed to be. Then a new season would start and you'd clean up your act, you'd be there for your team, you'd be *you* again, and I would convince myself that I was crazy. I beat myself up for ever doubting you, and you let me. But all along I was right."

"But there was only ever one of me," Junie said. "The one you fell in love with was always a little bit off. And if we're being honest, wasn't that part of the attraction?"

The suggestion that Hana had somehow enjoyed enabling her was brutal, and in the long silence that followed, April tried to imagine being that honest with Ross. What if she'd come home from that business trip and told him about kissing a stranger? About the way she'd vibrated with excitement for hours after. What if she'd drawn out on butcher paper a *complete* map of her desire: over here on the frayed edge of the paper, the sanctity of their marriage; and this way, over roads Ross thought were closed, the routes to her thorniest fantasies; then, just when he thought the map had ended, she'd unfurl the roll to show him everything else she still wanted to explore. The wild places. Dark matter. Escape *from* herself (the most regimented parts) *to* herself, to all the versions of her that didn't exist yet but might.

In that suspended moment that seemed to last forever, Hana kept her eyes on Juniper, and April realized that she'd given up trying to communicate with Ross about this stuff long before her dad disappeared. The kidnapping—in her twisted logic, if nowhere else—had simply given her license to go off the map without her husband. She'd never fought for her marriage as hard as Junie was fighting for her sobriety. Now it was too late.

Finally Hana stood and left the room.

Oh, shit, April thought, and she could see May was thinking the same thing. Even the counselor looked worried. But it was Nancy who went after her. She wouldn't tell the others, when they asked later, what they'd talked about in the garden. Nancy said she just wanted to help; it was something she needed to do as a mother. Whatever it was that she said or did, it convinced Hana to come back inside.

Not long after Junie got out of rehab, she moved in with Nancy. Slowly the news trickled out. The wedding wasn't just postponed, it was off, which at that point seemed for the best.

There was a different summer wedding in the family, any-way. Last August they all met up at city hall to be witnesses for Nancy and Tom. It was time, and April was happy for them. Nancy invited Hana and she surprised everyone by actually coming, and they all pretended not to watch as she and Junie talked on the courthouse steps.

Nancy's wedding day was gorgeous and sunny, perfect for new beginnings, but it was hard for April to believe in the brightness of her own, after the separation. Ross had decamped to a rental

ALISON B. HART

house nearby, one with a pool and a slide that the kids couldn't stop screaming about, and as much as she was thankful for the care he was putting into this transition, sometimes it felt like her family was leaching out of "their" home and surging into his. She was going to have to be more present. Ross was right, she was running out of time with their kids—especially Maddie, now thirteen going on thirty, a fleet-footed chimera who only let her mother close when it suited her. April would have to be ready, patient, watchful but not too much.

That was a big part of why she decided to leave Sullivan, Hawthorne, and Pollard. Corporate law was all-consuming; plus, it was anchoring her to the worst versions of herself, competent without purpose, efficient but heartless. She wanted to set her own hours and choose her assignments. She'd been talking to people inside the State Department about Tariq's application for a special immigration visa, an exasperating process of documenting the self-evident. With no passport, did he even exist? And how could you take a reference from a dead man? The national security argument was even more frustrating. On the one hand Tariq had served the US faithfully in his time at Camp Mosul and saved the life of an American citizen at great harm to himself. On the other hand he was the family member of terrorists and at the time of his capture he'd been engaged in unauthorized (but humane!) activities. Without a legal advocate on his side, the facts threatened to cancel each other out. So she'd become that advocate. For the last year he'd been living in Erbil and studying at Salahaddin University, lucky to get one of the spots set aside for Mosuli refugees, but the glacial pace at which his asylum case here was being considered convinced April that she should devote her type-A, laser-focused, slightly addictive tendencies to immigration law instead.

About that: her new therapist wouldn't confirm she had an addictive personality; she was more interested in what those words signified for April. But wasn't she addicted to lust? How else to explain the number and frequency of the lies she'd told in pursuit of it? Ironically—or maybe this was just obvious—it had been easy to give up Craig (and for Craig to give up her) once her marriage was over. The affair had never been about him specifically. And once he was out of the picture, she realized she still wanted sex—God, did she!—but she wanted a different container for it than her affair with him or her marriage. She didn't know yet what the right container was. Tinder? Sex parties? Ethical non-monogamy? Who should she be? Whom should she be with? Honestly she was tired of all the should-ing—wasn't everyone? She was who she was, which was pretty spongy right now.

So it was fitting that they were back at her grandmother's house this morning, standing on the front porch with a long hot day stretching before them. The spongiest times of April's life had always been the summers she'd spent here, chasing after May, sprinting past Junie's tent and out to the put-in, waiting for boys, waiting for adventure.

"Ready?" she asked her children, and they nodded.

She knocked on the door and waited for her family to answer.

26

May
Noon

"Lunchtime!" Nancy called out, just before she and Tom burst through the door with a box of sub sandwiches.

Zoe came running, hyped about the near-certainty that there'd be a couple of sprinkle cookies in there, too. May's mom was an easy mark, and Zoe knew it. The kid didn't need more sugar, but who could deny her today? Maryam and her sisters had been in the kitchen all morning cranking out the sweets for tonight, and Zoe was quality control, tasting the baklava, leaving her honeyed fingerprints on every surface.

"I'll be back," May said to Will and slipped out the open door. Most of the front lawn was hidden under the dance floor now, dropped off this morning with chairs and tables they still needed to set up. But before they took that on, May wanted a moment alone. "You coming?" she asked Jack, who'd been snoozing on the porch unleashed, too old to bird-dog anymore. He considered her proposition, then pulled himself up. May carried him down the porch steps and set him down beside her. Then they headed for the gravel road that led to the put-in.

She'd come out to the Bird River a handful of times over the last year. Somehow it was less complicated to think about her dad here than in Aberdeen, where time needed to move on and finally had (her mom remarried, the unused bedrooms slowly transforming into an office/craft room and a guest room that was so pristine May was afraid to wrinkle the sheets by sleeping on them), or in College Park, where her life was too full and busy these days for much looking back.

May and Jack crested the rise. There was the river below, slowly coursing past the dock where Junie and Hana would say their vows tonight, the seagrass along the shore pruned back. An osprey circled high above, hoping she and the dog wouldn't disturb the fish. He had nothing to fear.

When she and Will were deflowering each other here for the second first time, she'd had no idea that this was the spot where they'd hold a memorial for her dad two months later. Nancy came with Tom, May brought Will and July brought Nate, April had Ross and the kids, and Junie came with Hana and Fariha. They all walked together down to the inlet, where the waves rolled in with a whisper, as if they knew the solemn work the people were here to do. There were no ashes to scatter or bones to bury. Frank's remains lay in Syria, where the fighting continued and every day families were torn apart. His children brought their memories, such as they were, and their stories. They dipped their hands in the water and each, in their turn and in their own way, said a new prayer to remember their dad and not the long grind of living without him.

Junie had been fresh out of rehab, and Fariha stood between her and Hana that day at the water's edge, linking them together like the human glue in a paper doll chain. To be honest May didn't think they'd make it. Yet here she was, six hours away from their wedding, in the same location.

"Your turn next!" their mom had cooed at May last night at the henna party.

Was there ever a time when those three words don't sound deranged, even when they were probabilistically accurate? She and Will weren't in a rush—living together, with a toddler part of the time, felt novel enough. And now that she was getting her degree in veterinary medicine, May had a full plate. She'd been in a pretty good place with her depression this year, but she worried what would happen the next time she had a low. What if she couldn't get out of bed again? That didn't really work when there was a four-year-old waiting for you to make chocolate-chip pancakes and take her to swim class. What if her mood dipped so low that it scared Zoe? Or Will? Or herself? What if she flunked out of vet school? Her therapist said these were all normal concerns and reminded her there were things they could do. They could talk through her feelings, they could try to identify any triggers; her doctor could adjust her medication. And May could make careful, considered decisions about the kind of environment that worked best for her, like she had in moving in with Will, and quitting the zoo last summer and getting a job as a vet tech until school started this January.

"Too sad," she'd told April when her sister asked why she'd left the zoo, and that was part of it. But May had also started to sense a theme in her preoccupations. Her whole life she'd sought out situations that would prove—to the world, herself, her dad?—that she was more than just the middle sister, that she was extraordinary. Signing up for the Peace Corps. Going to Iraq to find her father only to find the Battle of Mosul, and instead it was April who'd cracked the case in the end. On a goddamn cruise. Wasn't it time to acknowledge that May had been looking for distinction in all the wrong places?

"Isn't that what I've been doing at the zoo?" she'd asked Will not long after coming back from Iraq the second time. There was no denying that the lure of working with large animals was powerful. But the only thing more awesome than a three-ton African elephant in captivity, reclining on a pile of sand, was a whole herd of them plodding across the savannah, doing thirty miles a day. She used to tell herself she was at the zoo to make life better for the animals, but better was only relative. She was expanding her horizons by limiting theirs.

"Shouldn't I just climb down? Isn't it extraordinary enough caring for people's pets? Look at this face," she'd said, stroking Jack's neck while he licked her palm. He'd developed a cataract in his left eye but at his age, putting him under for surgery was risky. They were keeping him comfortable. They were enjoying the time they had.

"You will never be ordinary," Will had said, "no matter what you do."

"If it were up to him, I'd never leave his side for a minute. I think I'm done traveling."

"Sure you are," Will scoffed.

"I'm serious," she'd said, but of course she hadn't been. They started small, with camping trips at the Delaware Water Gap with Zoe and a long weekend in New York City, just the two of them.

She'd taken the train to Manhattan once before, a couple weeks after 9/11, when the smell of toxic dust and embers burning still laced the air. The trip had been on the books for a while. A friend who'd recently moved there had asked her to come help him get settled—after the tragedy he'd felt all the more unsettled—and she'd always been curious whether the city would feel like a good fit for her one day, after the Peace Corps or maybe instead of it. They'd spent most of their time in the theater district, where he worked the lights for near-empty houses, and in Harlem, where he lived. She hadn't wanted to gawk at a tragedy, and they weren't letting nonresidents below Canal Street anyway. It had been a sobering experience, of course, but she'd been sure she would return—New York would come back, would keep drawing people like (and unlike) her to its bustling streets—and her perspective on the city would eventually outlive its mournful beginning.

Thirteen years later she walked all over lower Manhattan with Will, the sights and smells at street level holding her rapt, piles of Napa cabbage and pomegranates, boxes of ginger and long beans, tacky T-shirts fluttering like prayer flags, soft pretzels announcing their overdone-ness in a big puff of yeast. But on her tongue was something inexplicable, like the second line of a poem she couldn't bring to mind, a rhyme she couldn't find. After dinner in Chinatown, they rode the ferry across the East River to Brooklyn. Two columns of light filled the night sky, and they and the other passengers hushed, speaking in whispers.

"The anniversary," Will said. It was still a few days away, but it wasn't a big anniversary with a round number. "They do it every year."

"It's incredible," May said, soothed by the giant loss made manifest. For so long she'd been carrying her grief privately, nibbling away at her own heart until it hardly functioned. The idea that she could share her agony ran counter to all her instincts for self-preservation, but she also thought it might save her.

Will squeezed her hand, and she knew that if she asked him to, he'd mount a searchlight on the roof of their house for Frank, too.

"Mayhem!" Zoe cried out, running down the road to the inlet with Will a few steps behind.

Yes, she'd picked up the nickname from her dad. No, she didn't have any real sense yet what it meant. But it had two *m*'s in it, like mom or mama—a perverse twist that made May laugh the first time she heard it, and after that it was easier to claim her place in the girl's life.

Will threw up his hands in defeat, a huge smile escaping. "Ready or not, here we come."

May wasn't hiding. Finally she was ready.

"Come back to the wedding!" Zoe said, reaching out her hand, but she was running too fast to stop herself so she crashed into May's legs like a football player into a practice dummy. This was her first wedding, and she couldn't wait for it to begin.

27

Juniper
Afternoon

At the witching hour Fariha blew her whistle from the porch steps. "Barbers! Monsours! Gather ye brides!"

This wedding was smaller than the first one they'd planned, but a hundred guests was still pretty big! All afternoon Juniper had been coordinating the preparations, a clipboard tucked under her arm that she didn't have to consult because these plays already lived in her brain. She looked at her team—her family and Hana's, putting the final touches on everything—and she was so happy she could cry. Tom and Will were testing out the sound system on the porch, while Zoe and Nancy turned pirouettes on the dance floor. Nate and July had dressed the tables and set up the buffet. Mo and Nura and their kids had festooned the dock with garlands from the florist, and April and May had gathered wildflowers that Hana and Fariha arranged into bud vases for the tables. Maddie and Cooper were in the kitchen with Maryam and the aunties, drizzling pastries with sugar syrup and dusting them with chopped pistachios, and Ahmed brandished a sword (sheathed, for now) that they'd cut the cake with later.

How did she get so lucky? To be here, to be alive, to be so loved. It didn't have to end like this.

It nearly didn't.

The conventional wisdom was that for sobriety to really stick, it had to be your choice. You had to hit rock bottom and surrender. And there was a moment, sitting between her sisters in the car that carried them from the church to the bazaar, speeding through the twilight to meet up with their brother and Tariq, when Juniper knew what she had to do. She wanted to be healthy enough to live a life of meaning. She wanted to be fully present at her own wedding and take her neck out of that noose of shame. She couldn't do it if she was drinking.

"I need help," she'd said.

But as soon as Tariq told them about the bullet in their dad's leg, she wanted a drink. No, she *needed* one. *I can't do this, I can't do this* went the drumbeat in her chest. By the time the bullet had traveled up Frank's body to his heart, she was shaking, the line between fear and withdrawal hopelessly blurred.

"Just one," she said to May once Tariq had gone to his own room.

"To shore me up," she said to April.

"Please," she said to July.

Of course, she was already lying again. One drink wouldn't help. It would need to be one continuous pour to get her from that hotel room in Iraq to the altar on the lawn at Princeton. Already she'd abandoned any notion of going to rehab. She was getting married that Saturday. The invitations said so. Hundreds of guests were planning on it. Hana was waiting for her. She couldn't let everyone down.

"She'll understand," July said.

"I'll talk to her," April said.

But it was May who got through. She told Juniper she'd seen

a doctor and was working with a therapist. She talked about the days, weeks, months when she'd felt nothing, less than alive. Juniper had had no idea.

"You don't have to suffer the way you have," May said.

Eventually April held up the phone and asked if she was ready.

"Okay," Juniper said. As promised, April did all the talking, first with their mother, then Hana, then Nancy again. She'd wanted to crawl out of her skin the whole time. She'd wanted to slink away into the muck and disappear forever.

And it wasn't even the hardest part about going to rehab. Learning to tell the truth was much more difficult. She knew it would need to be the cornerstone of her recovery. It had to become habit. But the positive feedback loop on truth-telling was so paltry and dry compared to the buzz you got from a bottle of vodka. There was no warm burn in your chest. Sometimes it even felt actively bad, like punching someone else's face but yours was the one that bruised. And you had to keep doing it. Your reward? Well, World War III didn't break out like you thought it would. You told the truth and survived. Hooray.

In rehab she began to realize she had to recover from people-pleasing as much as she had to recover from alcoholism. She'd never doubted their love for each other, but after a few weeks of one-on-one counseling and sitting in group and listening to the same stories come out of different mouths, it clicked that she and Hana were entrenched in some pretty unhealthy patterns. *Go along to get along*, that was Juniper's MO, and Hana worked overtime to always make things smooth for her. Too smooth. Take soccer out of the picture, and Juniper was a mess. She was the weak one and Hana was the strong one, and why did that work for them? What if Juniper wanted to be strong, too? What if Hana needed to be weak sometimes?

They needed to recalibrate.

After a few days at home from rehab she'd had to admit that nothing felt right anymore. If Hana mowed the lawn while Juniper worked out, was she over-functioning again? If Juniper did the meal planning for the week, was she just people-pleasing, pretending she had it all together? Was keeping track of how long it took Juniper to go to the grocery store and back a form of policing or just living in a time-bound universe? They were second-guessing all their routines to the point of irritation, like scratching a bug bite that would've healed quickly if they'd just left it alone, making it red, raw, and angry instead. After Frank's memorial, where things had felt so calcified between them that neither knew what to say anymore, Juniper had gone to stay with her mom. They didn't put labels on it. She had a month before Linden's preseason began, and Fariha offered to step in as head coach if Juniper needed more time. She didn't know if she'd ever come back, and that uncertainty crushed her.

Juniper slept—and slept—in her old room in Aberdeen, which was free now that May had moved in with Will. Nancy called it her home for wayward girls.

The Princeton job was long gone, filled by the former assistant coach of UCLA. Once Mac heard why she wouldn't be officiating the wedding after all, Juniper figured word would spread quickly to the hiring committee, so she withdrew her candidacy. Letting that dream go was painful at first, but eventually it felt like a blessing. She needed to find a new way forward, and Princeton was where all her bad habits had taken root.

Juniper navigated the long summer days one at a time, starting with morning meetings at St. Matthew's or First Presbyterian or Christ the King. She'd never been to church so much in her life nor drunk so much bad coffee. Sometimes she grabbed breakfast after with her sponsor, then worked out and wrote in her journal, a new thing she was trying, very self-consciously (she promised herself she would burn it one day). When Nancy and Tom got home, she made dinner, and Tom taught Juniper his secret rub for short ribs. At night they'd watch half of a movie and then turn in. The recurring nightmares were gone, thank God; she'd flushed them out of her system during detox.

One day Nancy came into Juniper's room and told her she and Tom wanted to get married. Just something small at city hall, she said, not a big production.

"But we won't do it now if you think it'll be too painful for you."

Juniper asked if she could take some time to think it over. She needed a minute in private to make sure she wasn't giving a knee-jerk response, part of her new stop-people-pleasing-so-much protocol. But hadn't they lived in limbo long enough? And all that time she'd been afraid to get to know Tom as anything more than her childhood dentist, repository of corny jokes and plaster molds of her teeth. She'd thought loving him would mean she was letting herself off the hook for what happened to her dad. But living in Aberdeen, hanging out with him and her mom, Juniper could see they were partners in every way that mattered. She wanted them to move forward. She wanted to forgive herself, too.

"Just one question," she said. "What are you wearing?"

"Oh, I don't think it really matters, does it?" Nancy asked.

"Sure it does."

And thus Juniper found herself at Talbots, dress-shopping again. It was so much easier, fun even, helping her mom look for the right bridal outfit than it had been looking for her own. It didn't take Nancy long to find what she wanted, a cream-colored sheath dress with a jacket to go over it that she just gravitated to like hands on a Ouija board.

"I know what I like. At my age, I better have figured that out, at least."

Something to aspire to, Juniper thought.

On the morning of the wedding Juniper woke up sad. Where was *her* wife? How had she let something so pure become contaminated by her shit? She did something she never would've done before. She shared at her meeting. She stood up and said exactly how she was feeling and a room full of strangers who were becoming more familiar to her *mmm*'ed with deep understanding—maybe they hadn't been through her exact situation, but they'd gambled with something or someone just as precious—and they told Juniper to keep coming back. When she got to the courthouse, it was good to see everyone. July was leaving soon to link up with Nate in Europe, effervescing with young love. She remembered the feeling, but she also knew that for a love like that to last, it would have to grow and be tested. Juniper gave him a kiss and hoped with all her heart that he'd found it.

She didn't expect Hana to show up, right as they were heading up the courthouse steps. She looked beautiful—a sight for sore eyes like Frank used to say—but hesitant. Hana had never needed to be nervous around her before, and Juniper hated that she was now.

"I don't want to intrude, but your mom invited me, and I thought it would be such a shame to miss it," she said.

And it was then Juniper just knew—they would be okay. They would figure out how to divvy up the load in their lives and carry it together, because they had the most important piece already covered. They both wanted to be there. Hana was right. It *would* have been a shame if she hadn't come, and when they all posed for the family photo afterward, Juniper was sodden with love (that deeper, tested, old love) and with the rightness of Hana being in the frame.

Nancy and Tom went on a little honeymoon—they drove up to Niagara Falls, because once the idea got into their heads, they couldn't stop giggling about it—and by the time they returned, Juniper was home again in Philadelphia.

Soon her players arrived on campus, classes started, the leaves turned red and golden, and the nights grew longer. Mo lost his race, but not because of her—the press had a fresh villain in ISIS and a horrible wave of kidnappings to cover; Frank was ancient history to them—and he wasn't afraid to run again. Worrying about everyone she'd let down—it wasn't in the past, but she tried very hard not to work it like a second shift. True, Hana's parents had been disappointed about the canceled wedding, but they loved Juniper like a daughter. They wanted her to be well. Hana promised her they'd take things day by day, and Juniper promised she'd always tell her the truth. Semesters passed and their love grew up.

Last month, just a couple weeks shy of getting her one-year chip, the Supreme Court ruled that same-sex marriage bans were unconstitutional under the fourteenth amendment, and marriage became legal for everyone, in every state. Talk about the universe giving them a sign. They almost tied the knot that day, but they both wanted their families around them.

And here they all were.

"See you soon," Hana said, kissing her softly at the bottom of the porch stairs. She traced the mehndi design on Juniper's palm—a dragonfly for rebirth—sending a shiver up her spine.

"Soon," Juniper whispered back.

Their mothers and sisters and nieces escorted them to separate bedrooms to get dressed.

"July! Get in here!" Juniper hollered, and he came, too.

"Someone has to make sure I do this right," April said. She'd found a hair-braiding tutorial on YouTube and had been practicing all week on Maddie. She had to be a pro by now, the humility just an act.

"Yeah, I'm not really That Kind of Gay, but I'm here for the moral support." July plopped cross-legged on the bed, out of the way, and alternately averted his eyes and nodded his approval as Juniper's look took shape.

"Perfect," he pronounced when she appeared to be done, but April wasn't finished until she'd tucked in a couple little sprigs of fleabane just so.

"Not too much," Juniper reminded her, as she had with the eyeshadow and the bronzer and the lip color. They were going for easy sun-kissed naturalism. They were going for Juniper but at a party.

"I know. I got it," April said.

"Now it's perfect," Maddie said, and in the mirror Juniper could see that it was.

It was time to get dressed and she unzipped the suit she'd had made by the bespoke tailor she'd started following on Instagram a few months ago. Scrolling through pictures of their clothes had helped her envision how she'd want to look and feel on a day like today. She'd donated the white suit she bought last year, never even tried it on again after the alterations had been made. It had felt like a costume or a compromise. This suit was a cheerful mid-tone blue—*azure* the tailor called it when they showed her fabric options—and it fit Juniper just right. It was too beautiful to wear only once. She was excited for all the awards dinners and friends' weddings and date nights where she could finally feel like herself, even when she was all dolled up.

Nancy smoothed down the lapels, eyelashes wet behind her glasses.

"Don't make me cry!" Juniper said, but it was too late.

She still struggled sometimes with feeling deserving of a second chance. But it wasn't just hers. This fresh start belonged to them all.

28

July
Twilight

July slipped out of the bedroom ahead of the others and found Nate sitting outside on the porch steps, one leg stretched out and one leg bent, fingers falling over his knee like berries from the vine, the sexiest motherfucker who ever was.

When Nate saw him, he stood. "All good?"

"They're almost ready. Mom's, like, Mrs. Bennet levels of delirious."

"Does that make Juniper Kitty or Elizabeth?" Nate asked.

"Jane, duh. *I'm* Elizabeth."

While the brides were primping, the others had tidied up the front yard, throwing away empty wrappers and shopping bags, taping down power cords, putting everything that wasn't beautiful out of site. It wasn't a neo-Gothic castle; it was better—intimate, homespun, shimmering, jubilant. Some of the family had put on their party duds there; others had gone to the hotel for a quick-change and were just returning. Hana's uncle Hassan stood apart from the others on the lawn, studying the notes inside his leather portfolio, more nervous than he needed to be. At the rehearsal yesterday he'd married them off just fine.

Nate was wearing July's old sunglasses—they belonged to him now—and a tan suit in honor of Obama. Lost in all the uproar over the president's supposed fashion gaffe last summer was the fact that he'd been talking about ISIS in Syria, while honoring the work of a Lebanese-American designer and looking fine as hell, too. "Fuck it, I'm reclaiming the tan suit," Nate had said when he tried it on for July last week.

"You really think marriage is regressive?" July had asked then. They'd been in England when the Supreme Court ruling came down, so they'd missed the chance to make out among the crowd on its steps and celebrate their right to be miserable-ever-after with the person of their choice. But the judgment had been a political win, and standing amid their boxes in Nate's apartment in Baltimore, reclaimed from the subletter and just days into the experiment of merging their things and braiding their lives, July's question was much more personal. As Nate knew.

He picked a path across the living room and circled his arms around July's waist. "Marriage, yes. Love, no."

July put his hands on the fake back pockets of Nate's pants and squeezed.

"And I damn sure want the option, anyway," Nate added, before July planted a big one on him.

"Come on, Mr. Darcy, let's go make the rounds," July said now, leading him down the porch steps. "Can I call you Darcy?"

Nate considered this, then shook his head. "Not with my clothes on."

"Cool. We'll try that tonight."

Will's daughter ran up and handed them each a ribbon stick from the basket she was carrying, for the processional. She waited for them to test the batons in front of her, and together they spun the fabric in dizzying circles and figure eights. Behind her May watched from a specific distance, a mystified smile on her face, tethered to the girl the way a middle finger is buoyantly leashed to a yo-yo.

April sauntered by them on her way to find Coop, who looked about as comfortable in a suit as July had been at his age. But she jutted out her elbow, and her son dropped his book and linked arms with her, and they skipped across the dance floor like Dorothy and the Scarecrow toward their Tin Man, Maddie. July laughed, surprised by how much ease his sister had found over the last year.

April had still been adjusting to her singledom—in a sort of shock, really—when she threw up the Bat Signal a few days after the memorial. The kids were with their dad in the new place he'd rented, and it was her first night alone in the house since they got back from Michigan. How that was any different than living solo while they were all at the lake, July couldn't say; regardless, April was panicked.

Nate hadn't left for Spain yet, and she'd wanted to get to know him better, so she'd ordered take-out Chinese and invited them over.

"This is what I wanted, right? Freedom," she'd said, as she plucked broccoli florets off her plate and into her maw with surprising speed. "I can have as much sex as I want. But I'm afraid I'll just end up replacing Ross with someone else. Sometimes I think I should have been in an open marriage. It's too much to put on one person, to ask them to love you *and* surprise you. Ross couldn't have handled the jealousy, but I think I could have. I think I could love two people at the same time."

"Ummmm," July mumbled through a mouthful of lo mein. Why was she telling *him* all this?

"What?" She looked at him like he was a worthless prude, and he got a terrifying glimpse then of what it must have been like to go to middle school with his sister. "You told me to start treating you like an adult."

"Yeah, okay, but—" he said.

"Shhhh. We are all ears," Nate said, refilling her Sancerre.

"On the other hand," she said quietly, "sometimes I don't ever want to be touched again."

It was the first time July ever considered that, maybe for this one reason only, he was lucky he'd been young when he lost his dad, because there was less of him to be fucked up by it. And he realized how fortunate he was to be cared for by someone who wasn't afraid to ask the nosy questions that had galled him in the beginning, who wouldn't let him split himself off into safe parts and messy ones.

When Nate left for Spain two days later, of course July had wanted to travel all August with him, but he had that internship already lined up, and going to Erbil had wiped out most of his savings. Plus, he wanted to stick around and help April with Tariq's visa application. The paperwork! The bureaucratic obfuscation and delay! It was maddening. Meanwhile there was no telling when Tariq could go home to Mosul. Days before the memorial, from the pulpit of the Great Mosque of al-Nuri, the one Mosulis had guarded with their bodies, Baghdadi declared himself caliph of the Islamic State, assuming religious and political authority over a territory that spanned large swaths of Iraq and Syria. July and April met with Leyla, who set them up to talk to the people in the special immigration visa program. His sister had a knack for advocacy, like a dog with a very tasty bone in her mouth. A year later, there still hadn't been a decision in Tariq's asylum case, but she was optimistic they'd win in the end.

July was afraid it would be awkward when he joined Nate in Madrid in September, and it was at first. Nate was relaxed and happy, living that afternoon siesta, late-night jamón y queso life, and July had spent the summer in a suit and tie, working so hard to impress people he nearly forgot who he was when nobody was looking. On his first full day in Spain, they walked through the Prado and July cursed himself for failing to take a single fuck-ing course in art history, trying to contribute something besides, *Oh, wow,* and, *Mmm,* and, *Is that Goya again?* Afterward they walked out into the plaza, where a little boy tripped, splat, down on his palms and knees. *I feel you, exactly, kid,* July wanted to say as the boy cried out for his mother. But then Nate took his hand, and suddenly July was one of those pencil sketches on the wall in his apartment, emotion in motion, zooming into life.

They traveled together for a month. By October they'd landed at Oxford for the start of the school year, staying in different colleges, their classes on different schedules. Whenever July started to wonder, *Really, how many days till this dude forgets about me?*, Hazel would rub her finger and thumb together like the world's tiniest violin *(at least you're not long distance!)* and beg July to cuddle with her. That would get him off his ass and out into the cold night to dance with his boyfriend at the extremely average gay bar in town for which they were nevertheless extremely grateful.

Huddled together on those cold English nights, he thought about Tariq. After he and Hamza brought in the herd, had they reached for each other in the dark like this? Had it felt like home? He hadn't understood that evening at the citadel what it had meant for Tariq to have given Hamza his passport, but waiting for the asylum case to be heard, he apprehended that sacrifice more keenly. Living without papers in Iraq was a crime. Tariq hadn't just handed over his identity; he'd put himself in jeopardy while offering up to Hamza his own chance at a new life. How dreadfully he must have loved him to help him go. Maybe he still did. July pictured Tariq studying in Erbil amid all those headless torsos, and he hoped he found some pleasure when he could.

At the same time the world watched in agonizing slow motion as ISIS pushed farther into the Levant, capturing oil and gas fields, kidnapping and beheading their enemies—journalists, Shiites, Jews, Christians, Yazidis, gays, the list went on and on—and inspiring terrorist acts worldwide. Hostages taken in a café in Sydney. Satirists murdered in Paris. Too many suicide attacks to count. In response, a US-led coalition launched air strikes in Mosul, Tikrit, and Ramadi in Iraq, and Aleppo, Kobani, and Raqqa in Syria. Tariq's family in Syria had joined in the fight against ISIS, too.

July tried to imagine the camp in Syria before, Zozan talking with his sons and daughters, the cows lowing in the field, his dad writing letters home by candlelight, hoping to impart to his children from a distance everything he believed and had stayed to fight for. As Nate's slumbering breath fluttered against July's neck, he knew his happiness was one of those things.

Finally the sun glittered low on the horizon. Nancy and Tom and Maryam and Ahmed walked with their daughters down to the inlet, family and friends following behind like a merry if messy band of pilgrims, bearing their love to the water, ribbons rippling in the air. Hana's niece imperfectly played "Ode to Joy" on the flute, and her uncle Hassan waited for the brides on the dock, his usual jocularity sidelined by the imperative to discharge this sacred responsibility.

Juniper and Hana faced each other, holding hands. What a leap of faith. To love in spite of loss, to begin again when you've already failed, to reach for joy knowing that it brings pain, too, that life is inseparable from damage.

Nate rubbed his thumb across July's knuckles, and July looked at him in the waning light. This bond between them, would it last? Was it wise, to care this much in this fucked up world? Love could go sideways in an instant or one terrible day at a time. But July knew himself too well to doubt that he'd keep on loving him anyway.

His grandmother had died when he was a baby, so he'd never played here on long summer days like his sisters had. He'd never caught frogs at night, like his dad had as a boy, closing his eyes along the water's edge and listening for their grumbly song. As the crow flies, they were only ten miles away from Aberdeen and its font of sad memories, but this was still the Chesapeake, the same watershed that sent each of them forth and called them home.

Wherever we go, may we all find each other again. This was the prayer he'd offered at the memorial last summer, and he delivered it now, too, to the universe and to Tariq and to his family all around him, glowing on the shore.

★ ★ ★ ★ ★

Acknowledgments

Profound thanks to Jenni Ferrari-Adler for being my staunchest advocate, and to Melanie Fried for seeing what this book could be and helping me bring that vision to life. For the second time, I couldn't be in better hands. I'm grateful to the entire team at Graydon House and HTP/HarperCollins, including Justine Sha, Diane Lavoie, Ambur Hostyn, Dana Francoeur, and everyone who has worked behind the scenes on the sales, marketing, publicity, and production teams. Thank you to Quinn Banting for the beautiful cover design. I'm also very lucky to have Jasmine Lake and Mirabel Michelson in my corner.

One of the reasons I wrote this book was to think more deeply about Iraq, a place that's been in the headlines throughout my life—and where even today the US maintains troops—but that I felt I understood only opaquely. In my research, I read a number of invaluable books of reportage, memoir, photography, and fiction that helped to fill in some of the gaps in my knowledge and that I recommend to readers who want to learn more, including: *A Stranger in Your Own City: Travels in the Middle East's Long War* by Ghaith Abdul-Ahad, *Invisible Nation: How the Kurds' Quest for Statehood Is Shaping Iraq and the Middle East* by Quil Lawrence, *Night Draws Near: Iraq's People in the Shadow of America's War* by Anthony Shadid, *My Father's Rifle: A Childhood in Kurdistan* by Hiner Saleem, *The Kurdish Spring: A New Map of the Middle East* by David L. Phillips, *Kurdistan: In the Shadow of History* by Susan Meiselas, *The Kurds of Iraq* by Michiel Hegener, *I'm in Seattle, Where Are You?* by Mortada Gzar, *The Dispersal* by Inaam Kachachi, *Guapa* by Saleem Haddad, and *The Corpse Exhibition: And Other Stories of Iraq* by Hassan Blasim.

April May June July is a labor of love that would not have been possible without my community who sustains me. For reading umpteen drafts and keeping the faith through life's highs and lows, abiding love and gratitude to Mira Jacob, Matthew Francis, Heather Abel, Luis Jaramillo, Matthew Brookshire, Francisco Guzman, Tamara Dunn, Amanda Lin, Aakiya Woods, Raphael Coffey, Julia Phillips, Sarah Bardin, and Deborah Shapiro. Thank you to Joanna Pearson, John Cahill, Scott Labby, Jennifer Lankford, Kerrie S. Allen, Shukri Sindi, Orly Stern, Antonio Massella, and Yara Cheikh for expert advice at the just-right moment. AYSO raised up this Title IX girl, and later Central Park Rangers FC was my home away from home in the city. My dad taught me everything I know about soccer, and I miss him every day.

Deep gratitude to all the authors who provided early support for this book, Mira, Julia, and Marisa (Mac) Crane. Thanks also to the booksellers, librarians, and other readers who have championed my work.

To my family—Bob, Pam, Steve, and Todd Hart—the fixed point in my universe, thank you for the longest relationships I'll ever have and for always keeping me straight on the military alphabet. And to Mike and Mia, my joy and my glue, for everything.